STA
WA

BY CAVAN SCOTT

Star Wars: The High Republic: Tempest Runner

Star Wars: The High Republic: The Rising Storm

Star Wars: The High Republic: The Great Jedi Rescue

Star Wars: Dooku: Jedi Lost

Star Wars: Life Day Treasury (with George Mann)

Star Wars: Adventures in Wild Space—The Escape

Star Wars: Adventures in Wild Space—The Snare

Star Wars: Adventures in Wild Space—The Heist

Star Wars: Adventures in Wild Space—The Cold

Star Wars: Choose Your Destiny—A Han & Chewie Adventure

Star Wars: Choose Your Destiny—A Luke & Leia Adventure

Star Wars: Choose Your Destiny—An Obi-Wan & Anakin Adventure

Star Wars: Choose Your Destiny—A Poe & Finn Adventure

STAR WARS

THE HIGH REPUBLIC

TEMPEST RUNNER

Cavan Scott

RANDOM HOUSE

WORLDS

NEW YORK

2023 Random House Worlds Trade Paperback Edition

Copyright © 2022 by Lucasfilm Ltd. & ® or ™
where indicated. All rights reserved.
Excerpt from *Star Wars: The High Republic:*
The Fallen Star by Claudia Gray copyright © 2022
by Lucasfilm Ltd. & ® or ™ where indicated. All rights reserved.

Published in the United States by Random House Worlds,
an imprint of Random House, a division of
Penguin Random House LLC, New York.

RANDOM HOUSE is a registered trademark, and
RANDOM HOUSE WORLDS and colophon are
trademarks of Penguin Random House LLC.

Originally published in hardcover in the United States
by Del Rey, an imprint of Random House,
a division of Penguin Random House LLC, in 2022.

ISBN 978-0-593-72215-2
Ebook ISBN 978-0-593-35900-6

Printed in the United States of America on acid-free paper

randomhousebooks.com

1st Printing

For all the fans who have taken
The High Republic to their hearts.
For light and life, my friends.

THE ⭐STAR WARS⭐ NOVELS TIMELINE

THE HIGH REPUBLIC

Convergence
The Battle of Jedha
Cataclysm

Light of the Jedi
The Rising Storm
Tempest Runner
The Fallen Star

Dooku: Jedi Lost
Master and Apprentice

I THE PHANTOM MENACE

II ATTACK OF THE CLONES

Brotherhood
The Thrawn Ascendancy Trilogy
Dark Disciple: A Clone Wars Novel

III REVENGE OF THE SITH

Inquisitor: Rise of the Red Blade
Catalyst: A Rogue One Novel
Lords of the Sith
Tarkin
Jedi: Battle Scars

SOLO

Thrawn
A New Dawn: A Rebels Novel
Thrawn: Alliances
Thrawn: Treason

ROGUE ONE

IV A NEW HOPE

Battlefront II: Inferno Squad
Heir to the Jedi
Doctor Aphra
Battlefront: Twilight Company

V THE EMPIRE STRIKES BACK

VI RETURN OF THE JEDI

The Princess and the Scoundrel
The Alphabet Squadron Trilogy
The Aftermath Trilogy
Last Shot

Shadow of the Sith
Bloodline
Phasma
Canto Bight

VII THE FORCE AWAKENS

VIII THE LAST JEDI

Resistance Reborn
Galaxy's Edge: Black Spire

IX THE RISE OF SKYWALKER

CAST LIST

ANDRIK KELLER: Er'Kit. Former Nihil, looking for help in all the wrong places.

ASGAR RO: Species unknown. Father of Marchion Ro and uniter of the Nihil.

AVAR KRISS: Human. Jedi marshal of Starlight Beacon. Quickly becoming a legend in her own lifetime.

BALA: Twi'lek. Lourna Dee's teenage lover and a bad egg if ever there was one.

BURRYAGA: Wookiee. Empathetic Padawan.

CAPTAIN REESE: Human. Instructor at Carida Military Academy.

CAPTAIN SECARIA: Twi'lek. Captain of the palace guard on Aaloth.

CHIEF TARPFEN: Mon Calamari. Head of Republic security on Starlight Beacon.

DAL AZIM: Human. Fifteen-year-old Padawan of Oppo Rancisis.

DELLEX: Cyborg. One of Kassav Milliko's Storms. Has a mechanical effect on her voice to illustrate her cybernetic nature.

ESTALA MARU: Kessurian. Master and head of operations on Starlight Beacon. Likes order and mei-mei tea.

FRY: Human. Unsympathetic guard on the *Restitution*. Bully.

H7-09: Droid. Male programming, mechanical-type voice. Formally of Pan Eyta's Tempest.

HALEENA: Twi'lek. Lourna Dee's older sister.

INUN: Twi'lek. Lourna Dee's younger brother.

JANO: Barolian. Excitable Skyhawk pilot.

JINNIX: Colicoid. Insectoid Storm in Pan Eyta's Tempest.

KASSAV MILLIKO: Weequay. Party-loving Tempest Runner. Now dead. Smelled just as bad when he was alive.

KEEVE TRENNIS: Human. Recently minted Jedi Knight. More capable than she believes.

LALUTIN: Selkath. Senior cadet at Carida Military Academy.

LOURNA DEE: Twi'lek. Tempest Runner.

MACKEN: Snivvian. Controller on Relay Post Epsilon One.

MARCHION RO: Species unknown. The Eye of the Nihil. Not to be trusted. By anyone.

MUGLAN: Gloovan. Prisoner on the *Restitution.* Speaks like she's gargling sewage.

NIB ASSEK: Human. Jedi Master of Burryaga.

NOORANBAKARAKANA: Frozian. Jedi Knight. Pilots the *Ataraxia* in the Battle of Relay Post.

OLA HEST: Ottegan. Prisoner on the *Restitution.* Intimidates everyone and for good reason.

OPPO RANCISIS: Thisspiasian. Jedi Council member. Half snake/half hair!

PAN EYTA: Dowutin. Former Tempest Runner. Betrayed by Lourna Dee.

PARR: Aqualish. Prisoner on the *Restitution.* Speaks in Aqualish.

QUIN: Bivall. Prisoner on the *Restitution.* Former Cloud in Lourna Dee's Tempest.

RALEIGH: Human. Technician on Relay Post Epsilon One.

RL-18: Pilot droid. Male programming, voice similar to RX-24.

SESTIN BLIN: Twi'lek. Prisoner on the *Restitution.* Approaching the end of her sentence.

SSKEER: Trandoshan. Jedi Master. Sskeer has had a troubled few months. As well as losing an arm, he has been losing his connection to the Force. His fellow Jedi know about this, but not the extent of it, other than his former Padawan Keeve Trennis.

TASIA: Cathar. A Storm in Lourna Dee's Tempest. Catlike humanoid species.

TEFF: Barolian. Skyhawk pilot.

TRILOK: Gormak. Pan Eyta's new lieutenant.

VARDEM KROLEYIC: Zygerrian. Slave trader.

VELKO JAHEN: Soikan. Senior administrator on Starlight Beacon.

WET BUB: Gungan. Storm in Kassav Milliko's Tempest.

WILSON: Human. Senior cadet at Carida Military Academy.

WITTICK: Human. Senior guard on the *Restitution.*

XANAVEN: Frong. Tempest Runner.

YUDIAH DEE: Twi'lek. Lourna Dee's father. The Keeper of
Aaloth.

TEMPEST RUNNER

ANNOUNCER:
A long time ago in a galaxy far, far away. . . .

CUE THEME

ANNOUNCER:
Star Wars: The High Republic

Tempest Runner

By Cavan Scott

ANNOUNCER:
The galaxy mourns.

The villainous Nihil have struck, killing thousands at the Republic Fair on Valo and unleashing the monstrous Drengir on the galaxy. In the wake of the atrocity, Chancellor Lina Soh has tasked the Jedi with leading the response against the Nihil.

With the Drengir destroyed, Nihil leader Marchion Ro orders his forces to scatter among the stars, safe in the knowledge that the Jedi don't even know he exists. Instead the Jedi believe that Twi'lek Tempest Runner Lourna Dee is the malevolent Eye of the Nihil.

Now the hunter has become the hunted, with Dee on the run from both Jedi and Republic forces.

She will not go down without a fight . . .

PART ONE

RETREAT

SCENE 1. INT. CANTINA. SRAN—NIGHT.

A cantina on a blasted rock of a planet in the area of galaxy known as the Ash Worlds. The place is empty, save for the serving droid and a hulking figure, who is sitting at the bar. We can hear the hiss and wheeze of the ventilator strapped to his massive body, and when he speaks, his voice has a slight electronic distortion from the mask he wears.

Some kind of cantina-type music plays in the background, tinny as if through slightly broken speakers. Cutting back to this will be a good indicator that we've switched scenes or times.

FX: Doors slide open. Wind rushes in from outside, bringing dirt and grit with it. There's a storm outside. Footsteps as an Er'Kit stumbles in—Andrik. The door shuts with a hiss.

ANDRIK:
Woo-ee! That's quite a storm you have blowing up out there. Dust gets everywhere, eh?

SERVING DROID:
Welcome to Sran, buddy. They don't call them the Ash Worlds for nothing. What can I get you?

ANDRIK:
Got any Tovash?

SERVING DROID:
No.

ANDRIK:
Juma juice?

SERVING DROID:
No.

ANDRIK:
What *have* you got?

HULKING FIGURE: (MASKED)
Nothing good.

ANDRIK:
I hear you, pal.

SERVING DROID:
Enough of that talk, or I'll cut you off.

HULKING FIGURE: (MASKED)
Promises. Promises.

SERVING DROID:
How about a glass of utoz or vematoid.

ANDRIK:
Which is better?

HULKING FIGURE: (MASKED)
Neither.

ANDRIK:
I'll go for the vematoid. Neat.

HULKING FIGURE: (MASKED)
You'll regret it.

ANDRIK:
I'll take my chances.

FX: A drink is poured and placed in front of Andrik, clunking on the bar.

SERVING DROID:
Enjoy.

ANDRIK:
Thanks.

FX: Scrape as Andrik picks up the glass and takes a drink.

ANDRIK: (CONT)
(RECOILS) Ugh! What in void's name?

HULKING FIGURE: (MASKED)
Told ya.

ANDRIK:
(COUGHING) It's disgusting. Pure gutrot.

SERVING DROID:
Another?

ANDRIK:
You bet.

HULKING FIGURE: (MASKED)
(LAUGHS) I like you.

ANDRIK:
Good to know. And a . . . a welcome change. The name's Andrik.

HULKING FIGURE: (MASKED)
You're an Er'Kit.

ANDRIK:
Yeah.

HULKING FIGURE: (MASKED)
Don't see many of you around here.

ANDRIK:
I can believe it.

SERVING DROID:
Here you go.

FX: Another glass is slammed down in front of Andrik.

ANDRIK:
Thanks.

HULKING FIGURE: (MASKED)
You running from trouble?

ANDRIK:
No.

HULKING FIGURE: (MASKED)
Then you must be looking to cause it. Those are the only reasons anyone comes to Sran.

ANDRIK:
What about you?

HULKING FIGURE: (MASKED)
I'm still working that out.

FX: Andrik's stool scrapes as he looks around at the empty bar.

ANDRIK:
Pretty dead in here. Pity.

HULKING FIGURE: (MASKED)
If you're looking to party, you've come to the wrong place, friend.

ANDRIK:
I'm not looking for a party, but you might be able to help me.

HULKING FIGURE: (MASKED)
How so?

ANDRIK:
(LEANS IN, CONSPIRATORIALLY) I'm looking for . . . muscle.

HULKING FIGURE: (MASKED)
(LAUGHS) Are you now?

ANDRIK:
Mercs. Bounty hunters, even.

HULKING FIGURE: (MASKED)
Must be desperate. You got credits?

ANDRIK:
Sure.

HULKING FIGURE: (MASKED)
Don't look like you got credits.

ANDRIK:
Appearances can be deceptive.

HULKING FIGURE: (MASKED)
You're telling me.

ANDRIK:
Okay, okay. I admit it. I'm not exactly . . . flush right now.

HULKING FIGURE: (MASKED)
(NOT SURPRISED) Is that right?

ANDRIK:
But there's this job . . . a good job . . .

HULKING FIGURE: (MASKED)
With riches beyond my wildest dreams, I'll be bound.

ANDRIK:
Not just riches. *Power.* Real power.

HULKING FIGURE: (MASKED)
You don't say.

ANDRIK:
So what d'ya think?

HULKING FIGURE: (MASKED)
I'm not interested.

ANDRIK:
Oh. I didn't mean you. I mean . . . you're a big guy, but no offense or anything, you . . . you don't sound like you're in the
best shape.

HULKING FIGURE: (MASKED)
There's a reason for that.

ANDRIK:
I bet. All I need is pointing in the right direction.

HULKING FIGURE: (MASKED)
To the muscle.

ANDRIK:
It'll be worth their while.

HULKING FIGURE: (MASKED)
What've you got in mind? A hit job? Protection?

ANDRIK:
A rescue. Well, more of a breakout, I guess. It's not gonna be easy.

HULKING FIGURE: (MASKED)
Things never are. And who *exactly* are you breaking out?

ANDRIK:
(BEAT, AND THEN LOWERS VOICE AS IF THERE WERE SOMEONE ELSE IN THE BAR WHO COULD HEAR)

Have you ever heard of a woman called Lourna Dee?

SCENE 2. INT. STARLIGHT BEACON. BRIEFING ROOM—DAY.

Atmos: A large room on the Republic's gleaming space station. There is an excited buzz in the room, pilots and Jedi alike talking, waiting for the briefing. Let's give Starlight a trademark hum that we play in the background of every scene set on the station, a distinctive ambience that will subconsciously help listeners start to orient themselves.

FX: Footsteps as Jano hurries over.

JANO: (COMING UP ON MIC)
(CALLING OUT) Teff? Teff, is that you?

TEFF:
Jano? What are you doing here?

JANO:
Same as you, buddy. Fighting the good fight.

FX: They embrace, slapping each other's backs.

JANO: (CONT)
It's been too long, man. Too long.

TEFF:
You still flying that old crate of yours?

JANO:
No way. Check out the badge.

TEFF:
A Skyhawk. You and me both. What squadron?

JANO:
Firebird, flying out of the Aurora IX.

TEFF:
You're kidding me.

JANO:
Just transferred.

TEFF:
Me too. Shipped in a week ago from the Kolaador system.

JANO:
(LAUGHS) It's fate, that's what it is.

FX: Footsteps as they start walking to their places.

TEFF:
Don't let the Jedi hear you say that. That Maru guy . . . the Kessurian in the white robes?

JANO:
Haven't met him.

TEFF:
Oh, you will. He gave the entire squadron a lecture yesterday on how the Force had brought us here.

JANO:
And there I was thinking it was the Republic Defense Coalition. Can you believe this place, though? I mean, I'd heard it was—

TEFF:
Impressive?

JANO:
Jaw-dropping, but I wasn't prepared for this. Just the scale of it, man. It's . . . it's . . .

TEFF:
(AS IF THE NAME SAYS IT ALL) Starlight Beacon.

JANO:
Even the name gives me chills. I mean, we're here, Teff. Actually here.

TEFF:
A long way from Baroli, huh?

JANO:
And then some.

FX: A door slides open on the other side of the room.

TEFF:
Looks like it's starting.

FX: Footsteps. Avar Kriss walks in, followed by a group of Jedi. The noise in the room quiets slightly.

JANO:
(WITH AWE) That's her. It *is* her, isn't it?

TEFF:
Avar Kriss.

JANO:
(IMPRESSED WITH HER PRESENCE, NOT HER LOOKS) Wow. She's . . . she's something else.

TEFF:
Are you going to be like this all the time?

JANO:
Like what?

TEFF:
Like an overexcited whifflemonk.

JANO:
Can you blame me? A Skyhawk waiting for me in the hangar . . .

FX: He punches Teff in the arm.

JANO: (CONT)
My best buddy at my side. This is a good day, Teff. A good day.

VELKO JAHEN: (OFF MIC)
Members of the Republic Defense Coalition. Assembled Jedi. If I could have your attention.

TEFF:
(SOTTO) Try not to self-combust.

JANO:
(SOTTO) Can't promise anything. I'm a whifflemonk, remember?

FX: They sit. The crowd falls silent, save for the odd sound of rustling clothes and maybe coughs to remind the listener that there's an audience.

VELKO JAHEN:
Thank you for joining us. My name is Velko Jahen and I am the senior administrator here on the Beacon.

For those who have recently arrived, welcome to Starlight. I only wish that you were joining us in happier times.

This will be a general briefing to bring you up to date on Operation Counterstrike. I am aware that many of you will be familiar with our current situation, but I want to make sure that we are all on the same flight path. With that in mind, I will hand you over to Marshal Avar Kriss of the Jedi Order.

JANO:
(SOTTO) Hero of Hetzal herself.

TEFF:
(SOTTO) Seriously, you're enjoying this far too much.

AVAR KRISS:
Thank you, administrator. It has now been three months since both the defeat of the Drengir and the devastation on Valo.

As you know, the Jedi Order has been charged with coordinating the response to both disasters, a response which has been, to date, incredibly successful. In the last weeks alone, the defense coalition has engaged the Nihil on Carlac, Magaveene, and in the Dreighton Nebula.

It is the belief of both the Jedi Council and the Republic that the Nihil are scattering, what little remains of their chain of command on the point of collapse.

However, their leader—the so-called Eye of the Nihil—has so far eluded us, the Twi'lek known as—

CUT IMMEDIATELY TO:

SCENE 3. INT. CANTINA. SRAN.

Atmos: As before.

HULKING FIGURE: (MASKED)
Lourna Dee? Can't say I've heard of her.

ANDRIK:
You'd recognize her if she crossed your path. (BEAT) Can I trust you?

HULKING FIGURE: (MASKED)
'Course you can. Another vem?

ANDRIK:
Don't mind if I do.

HULKING FIGURE: (MASKED)
Droid.

SERVING DROID:
Coming right up.

ANDRIK:
She's Nihil.

HULKING FIGURE: (MASKED)
Hmm. Those pirates.

ANDRIK:
We're more than that.

HULKING FIGURE: (MASKED)
"We." You're Nihil, too?

ANDRIK:
I was. I mean I am.

HULKING FIGURE: (MASKED)
Sounds to me like you can't make up your mind.

SERVING DROID:
Here is your drink.

FX: A glass is put in front of Andrik.

ANDRIK:
Thanks.

HULKING FIGURE: (MASKED)
Put it on my tab.

ANDRIK:
(TAKES A SIP) It's been bad out there. When I joined the Nihil, it was . . . well, it was different. You asked if I was look-ing for a party? That's what it was back then, for all of us. We went where we wanted. Did what we wanted.

HULKING FIGURE: (MASKED)
Took what you wanted?

ANDRIK:
You got a problem with that?

HULKING FIGURE: (MASKED)
No. My attitude's always been that if you don't take, you don't get.

ANDRIK:
Ha! I knew we'd get along. Cheers.

HULKING FIGURE: (MASKED)
Cheers.

FX: They clink, but the hulking figure doesn't drink.

ANDRIK:
(GULPS HIS DRINK DOWN) Then it all changed. The Eye . . .

HULKING FIGURE: (MASKED)
Who?

ANDRIK:
Marchion Ro. The Eye of the Nihil. Our leader, kinda. He told us to hit the Republic Fair.

HULKING FIGURE: (MASKED)
I saw the holos.

ANDRIK:
It was . . . it was a bloodbath. Just like they said it would be.

HULKING FIGURE: (MASKED)
Ro.

ANDRIK:
And the Tempest Runners.

HULKING FIGURE: (MASKED)
Who?

CUT TO:

SCENE 4. INT. STARLIGHT BEACON. BRIEFING ROOM.

Atmos: As before.

AVAR KRISS:
We have learned from prisoners taken at Carlac that the Nihil are divided into three main warbands, known internally as the Tempests and led by Tempest Runners, individuals who wield a great deal of autonomy within the organization.

JANO:
(SOTTO, DISMISSIVE) "Organization." Makes them sound like a guild.

TEFF:
(SOTTO) Quiet.

JANO:
(SOTTO) They're nothing more than animals, Teff. I had friends on Valo. They got out, but the things they saw, that those monsters did . . .

AVAR KRISS:
Yet we are unsure what relationship the Tempest Runners hold with the Eye, although it's believed that she is above them in the overall hierarchy.

CUT TO:

SCENE 5. INT. CANTINA. SRAN.

Atmos: As before.

ANDRIK:
Heh. Pan would've had a fit if he found out that the Republic think that Lourna's in charge.

HULKING FIGURE: (MASKED)
Pan? Another Tempest Runner?

ANDRIK:
Never met him myself, but heard enough.

SERVING DROID:
Another drink?

HULKING FIGURE: (MASKED)
(TO THE DROID) Why not? (TO ANDRIK) I take it you're not a fan . . . of this Pan.

ANDRIK:
He had ideas above his station, that one. I mean, he was a Tempest Runner. It comes with the territory.

HULKING FIGURE: (MASKED)
"Was"?

ANDRIK:
He's dead now. Thanks to Lourna.

CUT TO:

SCENE 6. INT. STARLIGHT BEACON. BRIEFING ROOM.

Atmos: As before.

AVAR KRISS:
The only Tempest Runner we know by name is Pan Eyta, captured on security footage a year ago on the planet Rion. One of his own warband identified him after their capture at the Battle of Cyclor.

FX: A holodisplay activates.

TEFF:
(SOTTO) A Dowutin. They're tough. Real tough.

JANO:
(SOTTO) Nah. You could take him with one hand behind your back.

TEFF:
(LAUGHS) Somehow, I doubt that.

AVAR KRISS:
Eyta is believed to have gone down with his ship, the *Elegencia,* which was destroyed during a failed raid on the Cyclorrian shipyards just after the Valo atrocity . . .

CUT TO:

SCENE 7. INT. CANTINA. SRAN.

Atmos: As before.

HULKING FIGURE: (MASKED)
And this Lourna was responsible for Pan's death.

ANDRIK:
(LAUGHS) She stitched him up like a Vorusku kipper. (TAKES ANOTHER DRINK)

FX: He slams his glass down, starting to get tipsy.

ANDRIK: (CONT)
He thought he had the measure of her. The Republic thinks so, too.

HULKING FIGURE: (MASKED)
But he was wrong.

ANDRIK:
He's dead now, isn't he? Flew straight into a trap, thinking Lourna's Tempest would have his back.

HULKING FIGURE: (MASKED)
You sound quite enamored with her.

ANDRIK:
Damn right. She's my Tempest Runner. And unlike Pan, she looks after her own.

CUT TO:

SCENE 8. INT. THE *LOURNA DEE.* FLIGHT DECK.

A busy bridge. Computers bleeping. Nihil at their stations. The ship is traveling through hyperspace. The engines rumble in the background, the ship creaking in a way Republic ships don't. It's a similar effect to being on a submarine, a slight reverb to everyone's voices, which will provide a contrast with the Republic ships; these should have a crisper sound.

Also, let's find a pulse to indicate we're on a Nihil ship to help the listener.

TASIA:
Report.

ANDRIK:
We're approaching the target, my Storm.

TASIA:
Excellent.

FX: Double doors open. Footsteps as Lourna Dee slinks in, all happening beneath Andrik's next line.

ANDRIK:
Should we inform the Tempest Runner?

LOURNA:
No need. I'm already here.

TASIA:
(SUDDENLY MORE ALERT) Runner. I was about to—[hail you.]

LOURNA:
I know exactly what you were about to do, Tasia. Any word from the other Storms?

TASIA:
Only Drohon.

LOURNA:
I was asking Aychseven.

TASIA:
The droid?

H7-09:
No other reports, Tempest Runner.

LOURNA:
Damn.

TASIA:
Should we be worried?

FX: Lourna grabs Tasia's head.

LOURNA:
What did you say?

TASIA:
(GASPING WITH PAIN) I only asked . . . if we have lost contact with the rest of the Temp—

FX: Lourna shuts Tasia up by headbutting her hard, the Cathar's nose crunching.

TASIA: (CONT)
(A CATLIKE SCREECH)

FX: Tasia goes down.

LOURNA:
I ask you again, Tasia. What did you say?

TASIA:
(SNIFFING) Nothing, Lourna.

LOURNA:
What's that?

TASIA:
Nothing . . . my *Runner.*

LOURNA:
I'm glad to hear it. Now stop bleeding all over my flight deck.

TASIA:
Yes, Runner. (SNIFFS)

LOURNA:
(TO THE ENTIRE FLIGHT DECK) I won't have that kind of talk on board the *Lourna Dee.* Do you hear me? What are we?

COLLECTED NIHIL:
(A LITTLE TIMID) We are Nihil.

LOURNA:
I said, what *are* we?

COLLECTED NIHIL:
(WITH MORE PASSION) We are Nihil!

LOURNA:
We do not worry. We do not fret. We take. We plunder. We ride the storm. Are you with me?

COLLECTED NIHIL:
Aye!

LOURNA:
Are you with me?

COLLECTED NIHIL:
(STRONGER) Aye!

LOURNA:
Excellent. Let's remind the Republic what happens when they reap a whirlwind.

CUT TO:

SCENE 9. INT. RELAY POST EPSILON ONE—DAY.

A space station in deep space. Slight hum of computers. A steady beep of a comm signal in the background.

RALEIGH:
(SLIGHTLY BORED) Starlight Beacon. This is Relay Post Epsilon One. Reporting in. Signal strong. No degradation.

FX: Door opens. Footsteps as controller Macken enters.

MACKEN:
You could sound a little happier about it.

RALEIGH:
Like they care. As long as the comm network is running, they don't need a song-and-dance number.

FX: Beeps as Macken checks a computer.

MACKEN:
Raleigh. What's happened to the Targes scanner?

RALEIGH:
Nothing.

MACKEN:
Then why isn't it operating?

RALEIGH:
(REALIZING THEY'VE GAFFED) Because I forgot to activate it?

FX: More beeps. Controller Macken starts activating controls.

MACKEN:
Stars' end, Raleigh. What's the point of having these new giz-mos if you don't turn them on?

RALEIGH:
So we turn it on now. It's no great shakes.

MACKEN:
No great shakes? You heard what Starlight said. It's supposed to warn us if anything is coming out of hyperspace.

FX: At the press of one last button, the Targes device activates with an electronic whoosh.

RALEIGH:
Yeah. I'll believe that when I see it.

FX: The Targes device starts beeping urgently.

RALEIGH: (CONT)
See. It's malfunctioning already.

FX: The beeps get faster.

MACKEN:
That's not a malfunction. Get Starlight on the comm. Tell them we have incoming.

RALEIGH:
Are you serious?

FX: We hear the thud of the Lourna Dee *jumping in. An automatic klaxon sounds.*

MACKEN:
What do you think?

RALEIGH:
Look at the size of that thing.

MACKEN:
Raleigh! Make the call!

CUT TO:

SCENE 10. INT. THE *LOURNA DEE.* FLIGHT DECK.

Atmos: As before.

ANDRIK:
Relay Post Epsilon One, Tempest Runner.

LOURNA:
Excellent. What's your name, Strike?

ANDRIK:
Andrik. Andrik Keller.

LOURNA:
Then take a shot, Andrik, Andrik Keller. Tell them we're here.

CUT TO:

SCENE 11. INT. RELAY POST EPSILON ONE.

FX: A large impact as the relay post is fired upon. The klaxon is still wailing.

MACKEN:
(CRYING OUT WITH THE IMPACT) This is why you activate the scanners!

RALEIGH:
The defense grid is holding.

MACKEN:
But for how long?

FX: She opens a comm.

MACKEN: (CONT)
This is controller Macken of Relay Post Epsilon One. We are under attack. I repeat: We are under attack.

FX: There's another hit.

RALEIGH:
(CRIES OUT)

MACKEN:
(TO COMM) It is the Nihil.

CUT TO:

SCENE 12. INT. THE *LOURNA DEE.* FLIGHT DECK.

Atmos: As before.

FX: Tasia checks controls.

TASIA:
They have shielding.

LOURNA:
Not for long. Prepare gas torpedoes.

FX: Another beep.

ANDRIK:
Target locked and ready to fire, Runner.

LOURNA:
Let them have it. War-cloud away.

FX: We hear the torpedoes launch.

CUT TO:

SCENE 13. INT. RELAY POST EPSILON ONE.

FX: There are more hits. Explosions elsewhere in the relay post. The entire place shakes.

RALEIGH:
Direct hit.

MACKEN:
All hands report in.

FX: A comm opens.

RELAY POST CREWMEMBER: (COMMS)
Hull breach on level three.

MACKEN:
Any casualties, Darvel?

RELAY POST CREWMEMBER: (COMMS)
That's a negative, Control.

FX: Over the comm, we hear the hiss of gas. The Nihil are deploying their war-cloud.

MACKEN:
What's that?

RELAY POST CREWMEMBER: (COMMS)
Gas. (COUGHS) Spreading fast.

MACKEN:
Get out of there, Darvel, and seal the deck.

RELAY POST CREWMEMBER: (COMMS)
(COUGHING) Ma'am.

FX: She flicks a switch.

MACKEN:
Starlight. I really hope you can hear me. The Nihil are preparing to board. Starlight? Are you there?

ESTALA MARU: (COMMS)
Relay Post Epsilon One. This is Jedi Master Estala Maru. We hear you . . . and we are on our way.

CUT TO:

SCENE 14. INT. STARLIGHT BEACON. BRIEFING ROOM.

Atmos: As before.

VELKO JAHEN:
Before we hear from Council member Gios on Coruscant, our chief of security has an update on current Nihil tactics. Chief Tarpfen, if you would li—

ESTALA MARU: (COMMS)
Hub to briefing room. Come in please.

TEFF:
(SOTTO) That's him. The Kessurian.

AVAR KRISS:
Apologies, administrator. Maru, this is Kriss.

ESTALA MARU: (COMMS)
Marshal, we have received a distress call from Relay Post Epsilon One in the Galov system. They are under attack from a Nihil ship that matches the transponder signature provided by the Graf family.

AVAR KRISS:
It's the *Lourna Dee*?

ESTALA MARU: (COMMS)
It appears so, yes.

TEFF:
(SOTTO) The *Lourna Dee*? She named her ship after herself. Talk about ego.

JANO:
(SOTTO) This is happening, isn't it? This is it.

AVAR KRISS:
Administrator Jahen, we need to postpone the rest of the briefing.

JANO:
(SOTTO) What did I tell you!

VELKO JAHEN:
Understood. Skyhawk squadrons, prepare to deploy.

FX: Pilots start to scramble.

AVAR KRISS:
Jedi, to your Vectors.

CUT TO:

SCENE 15. INT. THE *LOURNA DEE.* FLIGHT DECK.

Atmos: Everything is heightened. The Nihil are ready to attack.

ANDRIK:
The war-cloud is spreading, Tempest Runner.

LOURNA:
Prepare the boarding parties.

TASIA:
They're standing by.

H7-09:
Tempest Runner, we have an incoming communication.

LOURNA:
They can wait.

TASIA:
It's from the *Gaze Electric.* It's the Eye.

LOURNA:
Dammit. Why now. Put him through.

H7-09:
Connecting.

FX: She presses a switch and a holo of Marchion Ro appears. The holo crackles throughout the sequence, the Nihil's communication network on its last legs.

LOURNA:
Ro.

MARCHION RO: (HOLO)
Lourna. What is your status?

LOURNA:
Busy. What's yours?

MARCHION RO: (HOLO)
(WORDS LOST IN STATIC)

H7-09:
We are losing the signal.

LOURNA:
Shame.

MARCHION RO: (HOLO)
(COMING OUT OF STATIC) Lourna, respond. Do you read?
What is your status?

LOURNA:
(SIGHS, ANNOYED) We are about to board the relay station.

MARCHION RO: (HOLO)
Have they signaled for help?

TASIA:
The scrambler is running, my Eye.

MARCHION RO: (HOLO)
That *doesn't* answer my question.

LOURNA:
If they have, we can simply issue a retraction as soon as we take
the station. Claim that it was a false alarm.

MARCHION RO: (HOLO, DISTORTED)
We need that relay post, Lourna. Communications—

LOURNA:
(INTERRUPTING) Communications are a top priority, I
know, you said. Perhaps if you'll let us do our job . . .

TASIA:
Boarding parties are standing ready.

MARCHION RO: (HOLO)
Then send them in.

ANDRIK:
Runner?

LOURNA:
(THROUGH GRITTED TEETH) Do as he says.

FX: The bleep of a comm.

TASIA:
All parties. Ride the storm. Go!

MARCHION RO: (HOLO)
Ride the storm indeed. For all our sakes . . .

CUT TO:

SCENE 16. INT. AURORA IX. HANGAR BAY.

Atmos: Starfighter engines are coming online. Pilots running. Astro-mechs bleeping. General buzz and excitement.

FX: Footsteps as Teff and Jano come running.

ANNOUNCER:
All pilots, board your Skyhawks. Support crew to positions. Prepare for preflight checks.

JANO:
Look at them, Teff. All lined up and ready to go.

TEFF:
Just try not to get yourself blown up, yeah?

JANO:
Not a chance. Those gasheads won't know what's hit 'em.

FX: Jano runs straight into a Wookiee running the other way, his footsteps thundering. It's everyone's favorite High Republic fuzzball—Burryaga!

BURRYAGA:
(ROARS IN SHYRIIWOOK)

JANO:
Whoa! Sorry, pal.

FX: Footsteps as Jedi Nib Assek runs ahead of them.

NIB ASSEK:
(CALLING BACK) Burryaga. Stop playing with the pilot and get to your ship.

BURRYAGA:
[SHYRIIWOOK—Yes, Master.]

FX: Footsteps as Burryaga runs off.

BURRYAGA: (CONT)
(CALLING BACK) [SHYRIIWOOK—I hope you're not hurt.]

JANO:
A Wookiee Jedi. Now I've seen everything.

FX: Nearby, boots against metal as Teff clambers up the ladder to his Skyhawk.

TEFF:
Just watch you don't barge into him when we're out there, okay.

JANO:
(SARCASTIC) Ha-ha.

TEFF:
See you on the other side.

FX: Nearby, a mechanical whine as Teff pulls down his canopy. At the same time, we hear Jano clamber up into his own cockpit, the soft whump of him swinging into the seat.

JANO:
(EFFORT TO MATCH ACTION) Roger that.

FX: A whine as he pulls down the canopy and it seals.

CUT TO:

SCENE 17. INT. JANO'S COCKPIT—CONTINUOUS.

Atmos: Continuing from the previous scene, the atmosphere changes as the cockpit is sealed. We're closer to Jano, hearing him breathe, his adrenaline running.

FX: Beeps as Jano accesses his controls, the engine whirring on. We hear him continuing his flight preparations under the following exchange.

FIREBIRD LEADER: (COMMS)
Firebird Squadron, this is Firebird Leader. Commence flight prep and report in.

TEFF: (COMMS)
Firebird Two, ready to fly.

FIREBIRD THREE: (COMMS)
Firebird Three, ready to fly.

JANO:
Firebird Four, ready to fly!

FIREBIRD LEADER: (COMMS)
We launch as soon as the Aurora arrives at the target location. Confirm.

JANO:
Roger that, Firebird Leader.

AVAR KRISS: (COMMS)
Ataraxia to Longbeams, prepare for the jump to hyperspace. May the Force be with us.

JANO:
Damn right it will be. Wee-hoo!

CUT TO:

SCENE 18. EXT. SPACE.

FX: Two large ships blast into hyperspace, the Ataraxia *and two Long-beams, including the* Aurora IX.

CUT TO:

SCENE 19. INT. RELAY POST EPSILON ONE.

As before, klaxon wailing.

Both the technician and the controller are choking on the Nihil's war-cloud.

MACKEN:
(COUGHING) Seal the door, Raleigh.

RALEIGH:
(COUGHING) Can't even see where it is. Damn gas. (COUGH) Burns.

MACKEN:
It's right there.

FX: She hits a control. The door slides shut.

MACKEN: (CONT)
Run ventilation.

FX: Raleigh hits controls frantically.

RALEIGH:
It's not working. *Nothing* is working.

FX: The comm activates.

RELAY POST CREWMEMBER: (COMMS)
(URGENT) Controller Macken. The Nihil have boarded. We can't—

FX: Over the comm, we hear the percussive beat of rotary blasters.

RELAY POST CREWMEMBER: (CONT, COMMS)
(SCREAMS)

MACKEN:
Wilkes? Wilkes, are you there?

FX: There's a thud on the door.

NIHIL: (MUFFLED THROUGH DOOR)
Open up.

RALEIGH:
(PANICKED) Oh, kriff!

MACKEN:
The door will hold.

FX: Another even louder thump.

RALEIGH:
I don't know, Mack.

MACKEN:
You heard what the Jedi said. They're coming.

RALEIGH:
They should already be here!

FX: A burning torch starts burning through the door, continuing until the end of the scene.

RALEIGH: (CONT)
Do you hear that? They're cutting their way in.

MACKEN:
You just need to have faith, technician. The Jedi will be here in time.

FX: The cutting continues.

MACKEN: (CONT)
(SOTTO) Please be here in time.

CUT TO:

SCENE 20. INT. THE *LOURNA DEE.* FLIGHT DECK.

Atmos: As before.

TASIA: (HOLO)
The boarding party has reached the operations center, Runner.

MARCHION RO: (HOLO)
They should have taken it by now.

LOURNA:
They will. We just need to give them time.

MARCHION RO: (HOLO)
They shouldn't need more time. Pan's Tempest wouldn't need more time.

LOURNA:
(QUIETER, ONLY TO RO) Seriously. You're going to pull that one? After the way you betrayed him.

MARCHION RO: (HOLO)
(QUIETER, ONLY TO LOURNA) After we *both* betrayed him, Lourna. You had your own fun with Pan, if I recall.

FX: A siren goes off. There is a thud of ships arriving from hyperspace outside.

LOURNA:
What now?

ANDRIK:
Ships coming out of hyperspace.

H7-09:
Confirmed. Jedi cruiser and two Longbeams.

LOURNA:
No.

MARCHION RO: (HOLO)
Ready your weapons.

LOURNA:
(ANNOYED) I know what to do.

CUT TO:

SCENE 21. INT. JANO'S COCKPIT.

Atmos: As before.

AVAR KRISS: (COMMS)
All wings. Target confirmed. It is the *Lourna Dee.*

FIREBIRD LEADER: (COMMS)
You heard the marshal. Firebird Squadron, prepare to launch.

JANO:
Roger that.

AVAR KRISS: (COMMS)
Aurora IX, deploy your Skyhawks.

FIREBIRD LEADER: (COMMS)
All hawks: Go, go, go.

FX: Jano fires his engines, the Skyhawks streaking out of the hangar.

JANO:
(WHOOPS)

FIREBIRD LEADER: (COMMS)
Steady, Firebird Four. Keep your eyes on the target.

FX: The soundscape changes subtly as the Skyhawks are now in space. We hear the swoop of their engines as they come about.

JANO:
The target is kinda hard to miss, Leader.

TEFF: (COMMS)
How come our regular sensors couldn't find that thing? It's large enough.

FIREBIRD LEADER: (COMMS)
Techs say it's rigged for silent running. Sealed engines. Energy recycling . . .

JANO:
Shame we've got to frag it.

FIREBIRD LEADER: (COMMS)
Remember: We're supposed to disable, not destroy.

FIREBIRD THREE: (COMMS)
It's only what they deserve.

JANO:
Now you're talking, Firebird Three.

FIREBIRD LEADER: (COMMS)
Target the propulsion systems. Nothing else. Coalition Command wants prisoners.

JANO:
Yeah, yeah. We're only messing with you, Leader. We know the drill.

FIREBIRD LEADER: (COMMS)
Then show me what you've got.

FX: The scream of Nihil fighter engines outside.

TEFF: (COMMS)
Incoming fighters.

FIREBIRD LEADER: (COMMS)
I see them, Firebird Two. All wings, prepare to engage.

FX: Outside, lasers as the Nihil fighters open fire.

CUT TO:

SCENE 22. INT. THE *LOURNA DEE.* FLIGHT DECK.

Atmos: The ship is shaken by explosions as it's attacked.

TASIA:
Strike fighters are away.

FX: Another explosion rocks the flight deck.

LOURNA:
(GRUNTS AS SHE'S ALMOST THROWN FROM HER FEET)

H7-09:
Shields are holding.

ANDRIK:
Just.

LOURNA:
Ro. We need reinforcements.

MARCHION RO: (HOLO)
Impossible.

LOURNA:
What?

MARCHION RO: (HOLO)
Zeetar's Tempest will never make it in time.

LOURNA:
Then what about the *Gaze*?

FX: Another explosion.

LOURNA: (CONT)
Ro!

MARCHION RO: (HOLO)
Ride the storm, Tempest Runner.

FX: The holo fizzes off.

LOURNA:
RO!

TASIA:
Is that it?

LOURNA:
(IGNORING THE QUESTION) What news from the relay station?

TASIA:
He's just abandoning us?

LOURNA:
(STERN) What news?

TASIA:
(SULLEN) Nothing.

FX: More explosions rock the ship.

LOURNA:
Prepare scav droids.

H7-09:
Swarm standing by.

ANDRIK:
What about the Republic?

LOURNA:
Target the nearest Longbeam.

TASIA:
Laser turrets locked.

LOURNA:
Fire!

FX: Turbolasers fire.

CUT TO:

SCENE 23. INT. JANO'S COCKPIT.

FX: A massive explosion nearby.

JANO:
Did you see that?

FIREBIRD LEADER: (COMMS)
We saw it, Jano. All wings: The *Karvoss Dawn* is hit. Take evasive action.

FX: The Longbeam explodes.

JANO:
Holy kriff! (STUNNED, UNBELIEVING) It's . . . it's gone.

FIREBIRD THREE: (COMMS)
Gasheads got lucky. Must've hit a fuel line.

JANO:
How many people were on that ship?

TEFF: (COMMS)
Too many. (SUDDEN, URGENT) Jano, watch your tail.

FX: There are lasers from behind, rocking Jano's Skyhawk.

JANO:
(PANICKED) I've picked up a marauder.

FX: More shots, sounding even nearer.

JANO: (CONT)
Can't shake them!

TEFF: (COMMS)
Hold on, Jano. I'm coming about.

JANO:
It's no good!

FX: More shots. They hit the Skyhawk.

JANO: (CONT)
(CRIES OUT) He's clipped my wing!

TEFF: (COMMS)
I can't see you.

JANO:
Stick's not responding. I—

FX: An explosion from behind.

TEFF: (COMMS)
Jano!

JANO:
(BREATHLESS) I'm all right. I'm all right. He's vapor. Was that you?

TEFF: (COMMS)
No. I still can't find you.

JANO:
Then who—?

BURRYAGA: (COMMS)
[SHYRIIWOOK—The Force is with you.]

JANO:
(LAUGHS IN RELIEF) Thank you, my Wookiee friend. You showed them.

NIB ASSEK: (COMMS)
Firebird Four, do you require more assistance?

JANO:
Who's this?

NIB ASSEK: (COMMS)
Jedi Nib Assek. My Padawan just saved your life.

JANO:
And I'm very grateful to him.

FX: The roar of Jano's engines as he brings the Skyhawk up.

JANO: (CONT)
It's all good. The yoke's responding.

BURRYAGA: (COMMS)
[SHYRIIWOOK—Your starboard wing is hit.]

JANO:
Sorry, pal. I don't speak Wookiee.

NIB ASSEK: (COMMS)
He says your starboard wing has taken damage.

JANO:
They haven't got rid of me yet. I can still fly.

AVAR KRISS: (COMMS)
All wings, this is the *Ataraxia.* Concentrate on the *Lourna Dee.*
We mustn't let them escape.

CUT TO:

SCENE 24. INT. THE *ATARAXIA*. FLIGHT DECK—
CONTINUOUS.

Atmos: Less of an engine rumble than Lourna's ship, the power core more stable, slightly higher-pitched as if it's better tuned. We can hear beeps and trills of the computer systems, but everything sounds more advanced. The Jedi flagship's flight deck is calmer overall, although there is still an urgency to Avar Kriss's words as we cut to her mid-communication.

AVAR KRISS: (CONT)
Not this time.

NIB ASSEK: (COMMS)
What about the relay station, Marshal? Have we made contact with the crew?

AVAR KRISS:
Not yet, Nib, but I can still hear their song. Their fear is palpable, the poor people.

BURRYAGA: (COMMS)
[SHYRIIWOOK—Shall we attempt to get on board?]

AVAR KRISS:
No, Burryaga. We need you in your Vector. The crew will be saved, I have no doubt of that.

CUT TO:

SCENE 25. INT. RELAY POST EPSILON ONE.

FX: The cutting equipment continues to slice through the door, nearly completing its work. It continues throughout the scene.

RALEIGH:
They're almost through!

FX: A locker opens and a couple of blasters are removed.

MACKEN:
Here, take this.

RALEIGH:
A blaster? But I thought regulations state—

MACKEN:
You want to fight the Nihil with regulations, technician?

RALEIGH:
No, I do not.

FX: A clunk to indicate a blaster being primed.

NIHIL: (MUFFLED THROUGH DOOR)
We're gonna skin you alive when we get in there. Should've opened the door when you had the chance.

RALEIGH:
Yeah. (COUGHS) 'Cause you just wanted to chat, I'm sure.

MACKEN:
It's been an honor to serve with you, Raleigh.

RALEIGH:
You too, Skip. We are all the Republic.

MACKEN:
That we are.

FX: A lightsaber ignites on the other side of the door.

RALEIGH:
What in stars' name?

FX: Again through the door, we hear not one but two lightsabers wielded. The cutting stops abruptly.

NIHIL: (MUFFLED)
(SCREAMS)

MACKEN:
Do you hear that, Raleigh?

FX: A blaster fires on the other side of the door, only to be blocked by a lightsaber. Another strike of the blade.

MACKEN: (CONT)
They kept their word.

FX: The door crashes down in front of them.

SSKEER:
Of course we did. A Jedi'sss word is their bond.

KEEVE TRENNIS:
You can put those blasters down now. You're safe.

RALEIGH:
What? (REALIZING HE'S AIMING AT THEM) Oh, sorry.

FX: The Jedi deactivate their lightsabers, entering the room.

KEEVE TRENNIS:
My name's Keeve Trennis and the lug with one arm is Sskeer.

SSKEER:
(GROWLS AT HER IMPERTINENCE)

KEEVE TRENNIS:
Are you hurt?

MACKEN:
Just finding it hard to breathe.

SSKEER:
Jedi . . .

KEEVE TRENNIS:
The Force is with us.

SSKEER & KEEVE TRENNIS TOGETHER:
The Force is strong.

FX: The low bass effect of the Force in use plus a whoosh as the air is cleared.

SSKEER:
Isss that better?

MACKEN:
(COUGHING) How did—? Actually, it doesn't matter. Thank you.

KEEVE TRENNIS:
We have medics on the *Ataraxia.* They'll be able to help.

RALEIGH:
We have a medic of our own. (REALIZING) Oh. We don't, do we? That's what you're saying.

KEEVE TRENNIS:
(SINCERE) I'm so sorry.

SSKEER:
May I?

MACKEN:
Hmm?

SSKEER:
The comm.

MACKEN:
Oh. Yes, of course.

FX: *Heavy footsteps. Sskeer stomps over and activates the comm.*

SSKEER:
Sskeer to *Ataraxia*. The relay post is sssecure, Marshal.

AVAR KRISS: (COMMS)
Force be praised. What of casualties?

SSKEER:
Nihil or Republic?

AVAR KRISS: (COMMS)
Both, Master Sskeer.

SSKEER:
The Nihil didn't go quietly . . .

KEEVE TRENNIS:
(SOTTO) For kriff's sake, Sskeer. (TO KRISS) We did take a number of prisoners, Marshal. Ceret and Terec are restraining them as we speak.

AVAR KRISS: (COMMS)
And the relay staff?

KEEVE TRENNIS:
We are with the controller and chief technician.

SSKEER:
They are the sssole sssurvivors.

AVAR KRISS: (COMMS)
(QUIET, SORROWFUL) Saber's Grace.

FX: *We hear an alarm sounding over the comm.*

KEEVE TRENNIS:
That doesn't sound good.

SSKEER:
Ataraxia. What's happening?

AVAR KRISS: (COMMS)
Stand by, relay station.

MACKEN:
What are they saying?

SSKEER:
That'sss what I am trying to hear.

AVAR KRISS: (COMMS)
Sskeer, Keeve—a wave of scav droids has launched from the Nihil ship.

KEEVE TRENNIS:
Heading?

AVAR KRISS: (COMMS)
Toward you.

MACKEN:
Scavenger droids? Why?

KEEVE TRENNIS:
To dismantle the station bit by bit.

SSKEER:
The Force will protect us.

KEEVE TRENNIS:
And we'll protect the survivors.

AVAR KRISS: (COMMS)
I have no doubt, Keeve. All wings. Those droids must not be allowed to reach the relay station.

FIREBIRD LEADER: (COMMS)
Understood, Marshal. Firebird Squadron. Target those scavvers.

FX: We hear the starfighters open fire over the comm.

CUT TO:

SCENE 26. INT. CANTINA. SRAN.

Atmos: As before.

ANDRIK:
The scav droids didn't stand a chance. There were just so many of them. We launched wave after wave of fighters and the Republic . . . (TAKES A DRINK) . . . I've never seen anything like it.

HULKING FIGURE: (MASKED)
And your leader?

ANDRIK:
What about her?

HULKING FIGURE: (MASKED)
What did she do?

ANDRIK:
What could she do? We were outnumbered . . . outgunned . . . there was only one option left.

CUT TO:

SCENE 27. INT. THE *LOURNA DEE.* FLIGHT DECK.

Atmos: As before, but even more highly charged, rocked with explosions.

TASIA:
It's a massacre out there.

LOURNA:
And the scav droids? Did any get through?

TASIA:
Not enough.

ANDRIK:
Should we send more Strikes? Another boarding company?

LOURNA:
The Tempest must survive. There's no way we can take the station, not now. But if we can't have it . . . Tasia, get the boarding parties off that thing. Aychseven, target the station.

H7-09:
Gladly.

FX: Bleeps as a missile comes in.

ANDRIK:
Incoming!

FX: There's another hit, an explosion on the flight deck.

H7-09:
(GIVES AN ELECTRONIC SCREAM)

LOURNA:
Aychseven.

H7-09:
(BURBLING) I have en . . . en . . . endured damage.

TASIA:
That's an understatement.

LOURNA:
Transfer targeting controls to my station.

FX: Andrik's console bloops unhelpfully.

LOURNA: (CONT)
Well?

ANDRIK:
I can't. The . . . the system isn't responding.

LOURNA:
Void's teeth. Doesn't anything work around here?

FX: Hurried footsteps as she moves to H7's position.

LOURNA: (CONT)
Out of the way, Aychseven.

H7-09:
Attempting to com-com-comply.

LOURNA:
Let me help you.

FX: She pulls him aside, his metal body crashing to the floor.

H7-09:
(ELECTRONIC CRY)

FX: Lourna sits in his seat.

H7-09: (CONT)
Commencing self-rep-repair.

LOURNA:
Then you better make it quick!

Pulling the corpse aside.

LOURNA: (CONT)
(GRUNTING WITH THE EFFORT)

FX: Nearby, Tasia opens a comm channel.

TASIA:
All Nihil. Get the hell out of there. Do you hear? Get off the relay post.

FX: Uncooperative bleeps as Lourna tries to get the targeting computer to respond.

LOURNA:
The targeting rig's fried.

H7-09:
Suggest switching to man-man-manual.

LOURNA:
Yes. Thank you for the advice.

FX: She flicks a control.

TASIA:
Boarding parties. Please tell me you're running.

LOURNA:
If they're not, it's too late.

CUT TO:

SCENE 28. INT. CANTINA. SRAN.

Atmos: As before.

Andrik is now well and truly oiled.

SERVING DROID:
She opened fire on her own people?

ANDRIK:
She gave them ample time to get away. Had Tasia warn them.

HULKING FIGURE: (MASKED)
I bet they thanked her for it as their atoms were scattered.

SERVING DROID:
What about the droids?

ANDRIK:
The scavvers? What about them?

SERVING DROID:
She sent them into that place.

ANDRIK:
Scav droids exist to tear things apart. That's all. They don't care if they live or die. It's not like you things are alive in the first place, are you?

SERVING DROID:
Us . . . "things"?

HULKING FIGURE: (MASKED)
I'm sure it's nothing personal.

ANDRIK:
Look, neither of you understand. How could you?

HULKING FIGURE: (MASKED)
So why don't you tell us?

ANDRIK:
We know what we're getting into when we become Nihil, okay.
We take what we want—

HULKING FIGURE: (MASKED)
And burn what we can't.

ANDRIK:
Hmm?

HULKING FIGURE: (MASKED)
That's the way it goes, isn't it? Your code. Take and burn. Take
and burn . . . And stars help anyone who's caught in between.

CUT TO:

SCENE 29. INT. RELAY POST EPSILON ONE. CORRIDOR.

Atmos: The sounds of battle reverberate through the relay post as Sskeer and Keeve lead controller Macken and technician Raleigh down the corridor. There are lightsabers versus blasters in the distance and the whir and screech of cutting tools and saws against metal.

MACKEN: (RESPIRATOR)
(CHOKES)

KEEVE TRENNIS: (RESPIRATOR)
Controller Macken?

MACKEN: (RESPIRATOR)
My rebreather isn't working.

FX: Keeve pulls off her rebreather.

KEEVE TRENNIS:
Here. Take mine.

MACKEN: (RESPIRATOR)
Don't you need it?

KEEVE TRENNIS:
The Force will protect me.

FX: Blaster bolts whistle from down the corridor.

RALEIGH: (RESPIRATOR)
It's going to have to.

FX: The Jedi ignite their lightsabers.

SSKEER: (RESPIRATOR)
Get behind usss.

MACKEN: (RESPIRATOR)
No, we can help.

KEEVE TRENNIS:
You just concentrate on staying alive.

FX: More blaster bolts, plus the skittering of crablike droids heading toward them. These are scav droids, each roughly the size of a large dog with multiple manipulator arms/legs—tipped with a sharp point— that clatter as they scuttle. Other limbs have cutting torches and saws that whir menacingly. There should also be some kind of electronic chatter among them as they communicate, a bit like the buzz droids of the prequels.

FX: The Jedi block the bolts with their lightsabers.

RALEIGH: (RESPIRATOR)
What are those things?

SSKEER: (RESPIRATOR)
Those are your ssscav droids. They can ssstrip a sssstarfighter of its hull in ssseconds.

KEEVE TRENNIS:
(COUGHING SLIGHTLY) Although some genius has given these ones blasters.

FX: The lightsabers continue to bat the bolts away.

TASIA: (COMMS, DISTANT, ALREADY RECORDED FOR SCENE 27)
All Nihil. Get the hell out of there. Do you hear? Get off the relay post.

MACKEN: (RESPIRATOR)
Did you hear that? They're giving up.

KEEVE TRENNIS:
I don't know. Something's wrong.

RALEIGH: (RESPIRATOR)
You think?

KEEVE TRENNIS:
(URGENT) Sskeer. Brace yourself.

FX: The relay post is hit by a sudden turbolaser attack, an explosion blossoming in front of them.

CUT TO:

SCENE 30. INT. THE *ATARAXIA*. FLIGHT DECK.

Atmos: As before. Lots of energy in the delivery of the lines.

NOORANBAKARAKANA:
(URGENT) Marshal, they're targeting the relay post.

AVAR KRISS:
They're trying to destroy it.

FX: The beep of a comlink being opened.

AVAR KRISS: (CONT)
Nib. Burryaga. Take out that turbolaser.

NIB ASSEK: (COMMS)
Roger that, Marshal. Burry, at my wing.

BURRYAGA: (COMMS)
[SHYRIIWOOK—I'm with you, Master.]

FX: We hear lasers over the comm.

AVAR KRISS:
Anything from the relay station?

NOORANBAKARAKANA:
Nothing, Marshal.

FX: Beeps as Avar switches channels.

AVAR KRISS:
Sskeer?

CUT TO:

SCENE 31. INT. RELAY POST EPSILON ONE. CORRIDOR—CONTINUOUS.

Atmos: Air is whistling from the breach in the corridor ahead.

AVAR KRISS: (CONT, COMMS)
Sskeer, please respond.

SSKEER: (REBREATHER)
(WITH EFFORT) We're a little busy . . . trying not to get sssucked out of a hull breach.

MACKEN: (REBREATHER)
Raleigh! Hang on!

RALEIGH: (REBREATHER)
I can't! (SCREAMS AS HE LETS GO)

KEEVE TRENNIS:
Technician! (GRUNTS WITH EFFORT)

FX: Low bass of Force effect.

RALEIGH: (REBREATHER)
(CRIES OUT) What the—

KEEVE TRENNIS:
(WITH EFFORT) I have you . . . in the Force. Try not to panic.

RALEIGH: (REBREATHER)
Try not to panic? I'm about to be sucked into space!

KEEVE TRENNIS:
(EFFORT) No, you're not. Sskeer?

SSKEER: (REBREATHER)
We need to plug the breach.

KEEVE TRENNIS:
The hull plate across from the breach. Can you rip it free?

SSKEER: (REBREATHER)
I will try. (WITH MUCH EFFORT) The Force is with me. I am one with the Force.

FX: The hull plate buckles slightly.

MACKEN: (REBREATHER)
It's no good. You'll never be able to do it.

SSKEER: (REBREATHER)
Not if you keep distracting me, no I won't. (GRUNTS)

FX: The metal creaks again.

KEEVE TRENNIS:
(EFFORT) I can't hold him much longer.

RALEIGH: (REBREATHER)
(DEFINITELY PANICKING) Please try!

KEEVE TRENNIS:
Sskeer!

SSKEER: (REBREATHER)
The Force is with me. I am one with the Force. (REPEATS OVER AND OVER UNDER THE FOLLOWING)

RALEIGH: (REBREATHER)
AAH!

MACKEN: (REBREATHER)
(OVER SSKEER) He's moving!

KEEVE TRENNIS:
(EFFORT) I won't let him go.

SSKEER: (REBREATHER)
The Force is with me. I. Am. One. With. The. *Force!*

FX: On the last word, the deck plate rips from one wall, clanging into place over the breach. The depressurization drops . . . as does technician Raleigh.

RALEIGH: (REBREATHER)
(GRUNTS AS HE HITS THE FLOOR)

KEEVE TRENNIS:
(PANTING FROM THE EXERTION) I'm sorry. I couldn't hold you up any longer.

RALEIGH: (REBREATHER)
(CATCHING HIS OWN BREATH) You're sorry? You saved my life. Thank you.

FX: The relay post shakes again under more hits from the Lourna Dee.

SSKEER: (REBREATHER)
(EXHAUSTED) We're not sssafe yet. Not while they're ssstill out there.

KEEVE TRENNIS:
(CONCERNED) Sskeer, are you—?

SSKEER: (REBREATHER)
The Force heard me. That's all that matters, my former Padawan. Let's get these people to our Vectors . . .

KEEVE TRENNIS:
If our Vectors are still in one piece.

FX: They start running.

SSKEER: (REBREATHER)
There's only one way to find out.

CUT TO:

SCENE 32. INT. THE *LOURNA DEE*. FLIGHT DECK.

FX: Lourna is still firing the turbolasers. Avar's voice crackles over the speakers.

AVAR KRISS: (COMMS)
Nihil craft. This is Avar Kriss of the Jedi. Cease firing and surrender.

LOURNA:
Never!

ANDRIK:
Runner. Two Jedi Vectors are coming in. Targeting the turbolaser!

FX: A massive explosion as the Jedi destroy the weapon. The flight deck shakes.

ALL:
(REACT)

TASIA:
They did more than target it.

LOURNA:
Fire concussive missiles.

ANDRIK:
How many?

LOURNA:
All of them!

FX: A beep from the computer.

TASIA:
It's no good.

ANDRIK:
The launch tubes are blocked.

LOURNA:
What about fusion rockets?

TASIA:
Not responding.

LOURNA:
Flak guns?

TASIA:
Lourna, the entire grid is offline. Nothing's responding.

LOURNA:
Then tell me we still have thrusters.

ANDRIK:
(NOT QUITE BELIEVING WHAT HE'S HEARING)
Runner?

AVAR KRISS: (COMMS)
Nihil craft. Your weapons have been destroyed. Prepare to be boarded.

LOURNA:
Not a chance, lady. (TO HER CREW) Bring us about. Prepare to make the jump.

CUT TO:

SCENE 33. INT. THE *ATARAXIA*. FLIGHT DECK.

Atmos: As before.

FX: An alarm sounds.

NOORANBAKARAKANA:
Their Path drive is activating, Marshal.

AVAR KRISS:
They're going to run.

NOORANBAKARAKANA:
That's not all. Sensors are picking up explosions on the relay station.

AVAR KRISS:
The scav droids?

NOORANBAKARAKANA:
More likely a chain reaction from the attack. We didn't stop it in time.

FX: The relay station explodes.

AVAR KRISS:
No.

NOORANBAKARAKANA:
It's gone, Marshal.

FX: Avar opens a comm.

AVAR KRISS:
Sskeer? Keeve? Come in.

NOORANBAKARAKANA:
Enemy Path drive ready to deploy.

AVAR KRISS:
Please respond. (NO ANSWER) They can't be dead. I didn't feel them pass.

SSKEER: (COMMS)
And for good reason.

AVAR KRISS:
(OVERJOYED) Sskeer! You made it. What of the others?

KEEVE TRENNIS: (COMMS)
Bringing in survivors, Marshal. Permission to dock.

AVAR KRISS:
As if you even have to ask.

NOORANBAKARAKANA:
Marshal, the Nihil cruiser.

AVAR KRISS:
I see them, Nooran.

FX: A beep of the comm control.

AVAR KRISS: (CONT)
All wings. Target the Nihil's engines. They cannot escape.

CUT TO:

SCENE 34. INT. THE *LOURNA DEE.* FLIGHT DECK.

FX: The whine of the Path engine building in the background.

LOURNA:
Tasia. Why are we still here?

TASIA:
The Path drive has sustained damage. It's still calibrating.

LOURNA:
Any word from the Eye?

H7-09:
N-nothing.

LOURNA:
Then damn him to the Nightlands.

FX: The whine reaches its crescendo.

TASIA:
Path plotted.

LOURNA:
Finally!

TASIA:
Engines ready.

LOURNA:
Deploy! Deploy!

FX: A barrage of lasers hit the Lourna Dee, *resulting in a series of explosions. The whine of the Path drive cuts out as sparks rain down on the flight deck and Tasia's console explodes.*

ALL:
(REACT TO THE EXPLOSION)

TASIA:
(SCREAMS)

LOURNA:
Tasia?

TASIA:
(THROUGH CLENCHED TEETH) It's nothing . . . just a burn.

ANDRIK:
The same can't be said for the ship. Propulsion systems are shot.

LOURNA:
The drive?

H7-09:
Not re-responding.

TASIA:
Nothing's responding.

AVAR KRISS: (COMMS)
Nihil vessel. Prepare to be boarded. Lay down your weapons and you will not be harmed.

LOURNA:
(BUILDING TO A SHOUT OF FRUSTRATION) Doesn't that woman ever shut up?

FX: Beeps as Lourna starts operating controls.

TASIA:
What are you doing?

LOURNA:
Not all our weapons are offline.

FX: A flurry of beeps. Clicks as text scrolls across a screen.

TASIA:
(UNBELIEVING) Nova charges?

LOURNA:
Courtesy of Krupx Munitions. At least one of our raids went to plan.

FX: She continues working.

LOURNA: (CONT)
The Jedi are in for a shock if they think they're taking my ship.

FX: The computer bleeps.

LOURNA: (CONT)
No.

FX: And it bleeps again.

LOURNA: (CONT)
NO!

TASIA:
What is it?

LOURNA:
The timer's wrecked. They'll have to be detonated manually.

ANDRIK:
I'll do it.

TASIA:
Sounds good to me. Lourna, let's go.

LOURNA:
(RESOLUTE) No.

TASIA:
What?

LOURNA:
Where is my mask?

ANDRIK:
Here, Runner.

LOURNA:
Bring it to me.

ANDRIK:
Runner.

FX: Scrape of metal as he retrieves it.

TASIA:
Why are we still here, Lourna?

LOURNA:
Clear the flight deck. Make for your fighters.

TASIA:
What about you?

LOURNA:
Where's that mask, Andrik?

ANDRIK:
Here.

FX: She takes it.

LOURNA:
You're a good man, Andrik. A loyal Nihil. A loyal *Storm.*

ANDRIK:
Are you serious?

TASIA:
My thoughts precisely. This is hardly the time to be handing out promotions.

LOURNA:
It's the perfect time.

FX: She puts on her mask. When she speaks next, her voice is electronically distorted, so it doesn't even sound like her.

LOURNA: (CONT, MASKED)
And I'll bust you down to Strike if you don't move, Tasia.

ANDRIK:
You're not coming with us?

LOURNA: (MASKED)
A Tempest Runner goes down with her ship . . . and takes out as many stinking Jedi with her as she can.

TASIA:
What about the droid? Aychseven can barely move. Let him do it.

H7-09:
My repairs are ne-ner-nearly complete.

LOURNA: (MASKED)
Listen to me. All of you. Tell them how Lourna Dee met her death, riding the storm one last time.

TASIA:
You can't be serious?

LOURNA: (MASKED)
Just go!

CUT TO:

SCENE 35. INT. THE *ATARAXIA*. FLIGHT DECK.

Atmos: As before.

NIB ASSEK: (COMMS)
Nib Assek to *Ataraxia*. We have boarded the *Lourna Dee*.

AVAR KRISS:
Who do you have with you?

NIB ASSEK: (COMMS)
Most of Firebird Squadron.

BURRYAGA: (COMMS)
(MAKES HIS PRESENCE KNOWN IN SHYRIIWOOK)

NIB ASSEK: (COMMS)
Yes, and you too, young one.

AVAR KRISS:
(TO THE COMM) I'm coming over.

NOORANBAKARAKANA:
Do you think that's wise, Marshal?

AVAR KRISS:
We have no idea if Lourna Dee herself is still at large. We need as many Jedi as possible in the search. And that goes for you too, Nooran. The support crew can look after the *Ataraxia*.

FX: Footsteps approach, one set significantly heavier than the other.

KEEVE TRENNIS: (COMING UP ON MIC)
Room for two more?

AVAR KRISS:
The two of you look like you've been through enough.

SSKEER:
The Force will sssustain.

AVAR KRISS:
Then I can't think of anyone else I would rather have at my side. For light and life, my friends. For light and life.

CUT TO:

SCENE 36. INT. THE *LOURNA DEE.* NEAR HANGAR BAY.

FX: Blasters fire. We're with Tasia and Andrik as they cover themselves from attack. In the background we can hear lightsabers being wielded.

TASIA:
This is hopeless. We'll never make it to the hangar bay.

ANDRIK:
Remember what happened last time you spoke like that, Tas. Lourna won't like it.

TASIA:
Lourna isn't here.

FX: She fires off some shots.

REPUBLIC PILOT:
(SCREAMS)

ANDRIK:
Good shot.

TASIA:
Lucky shot. Andrik—behind you!

FX: He whirls and fires. A body crashes down.

ANDRIK:
Thanks.

FX: More shots blast near them.

TASIA:
There's too many of them! (WINCES)

ANDRIK:
Your hand. Did you get hit?

TASIA:
It's fine.

ANDRIK:
Doesn't look like it.

FX: A clank of canisters in his hand.

ANDRIK: (CONT)
Will these help?

TASIA:
Battle stimulants? You might've said you had them.

ANDRIK:
(TAKING THEM BACK) If you don't want any . . .

TASIA:
I didn't say that.

FX: She snatches one of the stim canisters.

ANDRIK:
Might join you myself.

FX: A hiss as they shoot the stims into their arms.

TASIA:
(GASPS AS THE STIMS HIT HER SYSTEM)

ANDRIK:
(WIRED) Better?

TASIA:
Much. Let's go!

FX: They run, firing all the time.

CUT TO:

SCENE 37. INT. THE *LOURNA DEE.* CORRIDOR.

Atmos: Another battle raging. Lightsabers swing, deflecting bolts.

Nib's and Burry's lightsabers are on throughout this scene.

AVAR KRISS: (COMMS)
Jedi Assek. What is your position?

NIB ASSEK:
We are closing in on the bridge.

JANO:
At least we think we are.

TEFF:
Jano!

AVAR KRISS: (COMMS)
I'm sorry?

FIREBIRD LEADER:
Forgive Firebird Four, Marshal. His mouth has a habit of running away with itself.

JANO:
I can't help it if this ship makes no sense. Nothing is where it's supposed to be.

BURRYAGA:
[SHYRIIWOOK—Look out!]

FX: Sudden flare of a flamethrower, which continues blazing beneath the following exchange. Firebird Leader is immolated in an instant.

FIREBIRD LEADER:
(CRIES OUT)

AVAR KRISS: (COMMS)
Nib?

NIB ASSEK:
(PITCHING UP TO BE HEARD OVER THE FLAMERS)
We've lost Firebird Leader.

JANO:
No!

NIB ASSEK:
Flame cannons.

TEFF:
I can't get a shot.

NIB ASSEK:
Burry. Are you with me?

BURRYAGA:
[SHYRIIWOOK—Always.]

JANO:
What are you going to do?

NIB ASSEK:
Push back the flame, Padawan. The Force will protect us.

BURRYAGA:
[SHYRIIWOOK—The Force is strong.]

FX: Low bass of Force use. The flames are pushed back.

TEFF:
I don't believe it.

JANO:
Like it's hitting an energy field.

BURRYAGA:
(GROANS WITH THE EFFORT)

NIB ASSEK:
Careful, apprentice. Focus.

FX: A sudden explosion down the corridor followed by a wall of flame.

TEFF:
Back!

FX: The flames rush past.

JANO:
What in varp's name was that?

NIB ASSEK:
The pressure must have burst the flamer's fuel canister.

TEFF:
Talk about fighting fire with fire.

JANO:
The Nihil? Are they?

TEFF:
Toast.

BURRYAGA:
(MOANS IN DISTRESS)

JANO:
Cheer up, big guy. You did good.

NIB ASSEK:
Taking life is never good.

TEFF:
At least the corridor is clear.

BURRYAGA:
(WHIMPERS)

NIB ASSEK:
(WITH GENUINE EMPATHY) We will meditate on this later, apprentice.

BURRYAGA:
(MEWS)

NIB ASSEK:
I know, Burry. I know.

JANO:
So? Are we doing this?

TEFF:
Jano. You need to calm down.

JANO:
Calm down? Errington's dead, Teff. That could've been us. We need to finish these scumslugs once and for all.

TEFF:
And we will, for Errington. For everyone who died out there. But only if we listen to the Jedi.

NIB ASSEK:
The Force will guide us, pilot.

BURRYAGA:
[SHYRIIWOOK—But only if we listen. Master, I sense—]

NIB ASSEK:
Yes, I sense them, too, Padawan.

TEFF:
Sense what?

NIB ASSEK:
More Nihil, converging on this position.

FX: Opens comm.

NIB ASSEK: (CONT)
Assek to Kriss. We are proceeding to the flight deck.

AVAR KRISS: (COMMS)
Understood, Jedi. Please be careful—

CUT TO:

SCENE 38. INT. JEDI SHUTTLE—CONTINUOUS.

FX: The whine of the shuttle's engine as it comes in to land in the Lourna Dee hangar bay.

AVAR KRISS: (CONT)
—Force only knows what surprises the Eye has left us.

SSKEER:
If that's truly who she is.

NIB ASSEK: (COMMS)
Hopefully we'll have answers soon enough, Sskeer.

AVAR KRISS:
And we'll be with you. Keeve is just bringing the shuttle in to dock.

BURRYAGA: (COMMS)
[SHYRIIWOOK—May the Force be with you.]

AVAR KRISS:
And you, Padawan. Kriss out.

FX: The comlink bleeps off. Outside we hear the whir of the shuttle's landing gear.

KEEVE TRENNIS:
Landing gear deployed . . .

FX: And the clunk of the shuttle landing.

KEEVE TRENNIS: (CONT)
. . . and down.

SSKEER:
Couldn't have done better myself.

KEEVE TRENNIS:
I've seen you fly, remember. Even walked away from some of the landings.

SSKEER:
(GOOD HUMOR) I don't remember you being this funny when I was training you.

KEEVE TRENNIS:
Then maybe you should've paid more attention.

AVAR KRISS:
Are you ready?

KEEVE TRENNIS:
(HURRIED, EMBARRASSED) Yes. Sorry. For light and life.

FX: Footsteps as Avar strides off, leaving the other Jedi behind.

KEEVE TRENNIS: (CONT)
Why is it *always* more impressive when she says it?

SSKEER:
Do you really want me to answer that?

FX: They follow after her.

CUT TO:

SCENE 39. INT. THE *LOURNA DEE*. HANGAR BAY.

Atmos: Largely empty, although the Jedi shuttle's engines are still cycling down.

FX: Footsteps as Tasia and Andrik run up.

TASIA:
Finally. We'll take that Strikeship.

ANDRIK:
We'll never both fit in there.

TASIA:
I could always leave you behind.

ANDRIK:
What if we take *that*?

TASIA:
A Jedi shuttle?

ANDRIK:
If we're going to turn tail and run, we might as well do it in style.

FX: There is a hiss and the ramp starts to lower.

TASIA:
(HISSED) Get down. They're still on board.

FX: Three sets of footsteps as Avar, Sskeer, and Keeve stride purposely from the shuttle.

AVAR KRISS: (OFF MIC)
Wait.

FX: The Jedi stop.

SSKEER: (OFF MIC)
What is it?

AVAR KRISS: (OFF MIC)
I sense—

KEEVE TRENNIS: (OFF MIC)
Danger.

ANDRIK:
(WHISPERED) What are they *doing*?

AVAR KRISS: (OFF MIC)
(CALLING OUT) We know you're here. It's no good hiding.

TASIA:
(WHISPERED) We need to go back.

ANDRIK:
(WHISPERED) Where? Have you seen how fast they can move?

CUT TO:

SCENE 40. INT. CANTINA. SRAN.

Atmos: As before.

PAN: (MASKED)
You've been up against Jedi before, then?

ANDRIK:
Let me see. Two arms, two legs. Do I look like I've been up against Jedi?

PAN: (MASKED)
I only asked.

ANDRIK:
I was scared witless, I don't mind saying. It was *her.*

SERVING DROID:
Her?

ANDRIK:
You know . . . Avar Kriss.

PAN: (MASKED)
The Hero of Hetzal.

ANDRIK:
Flowing robes. All the . . . hair.

PAN: (MASKED)
Hair, you say. She sounds terrifying.

ANDRIK:
You weren't there. And she had this Trandoshan with her, built like a battle cruiser.

PAN: (MASKED)
So what did you do?

ANDRIK:
Only thing I could.

CUT TO:

SCENE 41. INT. THE *LOURNA DEE*. HANGAR BAY.

Atmos: As before.

AVAR KRISS: (OFF MIC)
(CALLING OUT) This is your last warning.

FX: Sskeer ignites his lightsaber.

KEEVE TRENNIS: (OFF MIC)
Sskeer.

SSKEER: (OFF MIC)
I sssee no problem in underlining the threat.

ANDRIK:
(WHISPERED) That does it.

TASIA:
(WHISPERED) What does?

FX: A hiss as Andrik unloads a stim-shot into his leg.

TASIA:
(WHISPERED) You had another stim?

KEEVE TRENNIS: (OFF MIC)
Over there.

TASIA:
(WHISPERED) You *idiot*!

ANDRIK:
(JACKED UP) I'd like to see them catch me now. (SHOUT-
ING OUT) Ride the storm!

FX: He breaks cover, firing wildly.

TASIA:
Andrik, no! For void's sake . . .

FX: She joins the firefight, lightsabers blazing in response.

CUT TO:

SCENE 42. INT. CANTINA. SRAN.

Atmos: As before.

PAN: (MASKED)
Didn't realize I was talking to a ghost.

ANDRIK:
It's all a blur to be honest.

PAN: (MASKED)
That'll be the stims.

SERVING DROID:
(TO HIMSELF) And the vematoids.

ANDRIK:
What's that?

SERVING DROID:
Another, sir?

ANDRIK:
Sure. Why not?

PAN: (MASKED)
So, how come you're still here?

ANDRIK:
Because of Lourna.

PAN: (MASKED)
I thought you left her on the flight deck.

ANDRIK:
Yeah. Yeah, we did.

CUT TO:

SCENE 43. INT. THE *LOURNA DEE*. APPROACHING FLIGHT DECK.

Atmos: Battles in the distance. Nib, Burryaga, Jano, and Teff come running, the Jedi's lightsabers humming.

BURRYAGA:
[SHYRIIWOOK—There. Straight ahead.]

NIB ASSEK:
I see it, Padawan.

JANO:
That's the flight deck.

TEFF:
Looks like it.

FX: The doors start closing.

JANO:
They're trying to lock us out.

FX: Bolts fly toward them, shot by a repeating blaster.

NIB ASSEK:
Burryaga! Protect the pilots.

FX: Burry deflects the bolts with his lightsaber.

JANO:
You'll have to show me how to do that one day.

BURRYAGA:
[SHYRIIWOOK—A lightsaber isn't a toy.]

FX: The door closes.

TEFF:
Too late. It's closed.

FX: The beeps of Nib checking the locks.

NIB ASSEK:
And locked.

JANO:
You saw who it was in there, didn't you?

TEFF:
I saw the mask.

JANO:
The woman from the briefing. The Eye.

TEFF:
How are we going to get in?

BURRYAGA:
[SHYRIIWOOK—Stand back.]

FX: Burryaga plunges his lightsaber into the metal door and starts cutting, the Wookiee continuing to carve a perfect hole beneath the following exchange.

TEFF:
Like a blade through butter.

JANO:
Is there anything those things can't do?

NIB ASSEK:
Assek to Kriss. We've found her. We've found Lourna Dee.

FX: The comlink opens and we hear the sound of a blaster and lightsaber battle going on in the hangar bay.

AVAR KRISS: (COMMS)
Excellent work, Nib. Can you handle things until we're finished here?

NIB ASSEK:
Having fun?

AVAR KRISS: (COMMS)
(EFFORT) Not in the slightest.

NIB ASSEK:
We'll keep Dee busy. Assek out.

FX: The comlink beeps off.

NIB ASSEK: (CONT)
(TO BURRY) Nearly through, Burry?

BURRYAGA:
[SHYRIIWOOK—Almost.]

NIB ASSEK:
Okay, you two. Stand back.

JANO:
Why? What's he going to do? Use the Force?

NIB ASSEK:
You don't always need the Force when you're a Wookiee.

BURRYAGA:
(CRY OF EFFORT IN SHYRIIWOOK)

FX: Burryaga pushes the metal circle he's cut into the flight deck.

NIB ASSEK:
In!

FX: More bolts from the repeating blaster.

JANO:
How? That's a mighty big blaster she's got.

NIB ASSEK:
We'll deflect the blasterfire. You follow us.

TEFF:
Got it.

NIB ASSEK:
Burry . . . now!

FX: Their lightsabers bat away the bolts.

NIB ASSEK: (CONT)
(SHOUTING OVER THE BLASTS) Put down your weapon.
You don't want to do this.

LOURNA: (MASKED, AS BEFORE)
And you do not want to try your mind tricks on me, Jedi.
They will not work.

JANO:
Yeah? Then what about this?

FX: He fires a blaster shot, which strikes Lourna in the helmet.

LOURNA: (MASKED)
(A SHORT SHARP GRUNT)

JANO:
Right between the eyes!

TEFF:
Jano!

FX: Her body drops, the blaster firing wildly.

TEFF: (CONT)
Look out!

FX: She clatters to the deck, the blaster cutting off finally.

JANO:
Did you see that? What a shot, huh? Right between the eyes.

NIB ASSEK:
We wanted her alive!

JANO:
And I wanted her to stop shooting at us.

FX: Teff runs over to her.

TEFF:
There's no pulse.

JANO:
How can you tell under all that armor?

BURRYAGA:
[SHYRIIWOOK—She's gone.]

JANO:
What?

NIB ASSEK:
He says she's gone. We can't sense her.

TEFF:
At least we can get this helmet off.

FX: We hear a click as he tries to remove it.

TEFF: (CONT)
Hmm. Won't budge. Ah. There's a catch here.

BURRYAGA:
[SHYRIIWOOK—Look out.]

TEFF:
Hmm?

FX: There's a sudden rapid series of escalating beeps.

JANO:
Booby trap!

NIB ASSEK:
Burry! Throw them clear!

JANO:
Wait? *What?*

FX: The booby trap explodes.

CUT TO:

SCENE 44. INT. CANTINA. SRAN.

Atmos: As before.

HULKING FIGURE: (MASKED)
And that's how she died. The great Lourna Dee. Shot by a lousy
Skyhawk pilot.

ANDRIK:
Nah.

HULKING FIGURE: (MASKED)
What do you mean?

ANDRIK:
(DRAINS HIS GLASS WITH RELISH)

FX: The glass comes down on the bar.

ANDRIK: (CONT)
She wasn't finished yet.

CUT TO:

SCENE 45. INT. THE *LOURNA DEE*. HANGAR BAY. ANDRIK'S POV.

Atmos: The battle is still raging, both Nihil firing on the Jedi, who are batting the beams away.

ANDRIK:
Seriously. Why won't they die?

TASIA:
Because they're Jedi, you idiot! You'll get us both killed.

FX: We focus on the firefight before switching POVs.

CUT TO:

SCENE 46. INT. THE *LOURNA DEE.* HANGAR BAY. AVAR'S POV—CONTINUOUS.

SSKEER: (BETWEEN BATTING AWAY BOLTS—IMPACTS MARKED AS [HIT])
I [HIT] have had [HIT] enough of thisss.

KEEVE TRENNIS:
They're not going to give up.

AVAR KRISS:
Then we will have to advance.

SSKEER:
Or remove their cover.

KEEVE TRENNIS:
What do you mean?

SSKEER:
Thisss!

FX: Sskeer grunts with effort as he uses the Force, focusing on the ship that Tasia is hiding behind. Importantly for this character, the bass thrum of the Force isn't as strong.

CUT TO:

SCENE 47. INT. CANTINA. SRAN.

ANDRIK:
You should have seen it, man. I mean, I've heard about the Jedi and what they can do. We all have, but seeing it in action . . . that was something else.

The shuttle that Tasia was hiding behind . . . it just moved!

CUT TO:

SCENE 48. INT. THE *LOURNA DEE.* HANGAR BAY. ANDRIK'S POV.

SSKEER:
YAAAAARGH!

FX: An earsplitting screech of metal as the shuttle in front of Tasia slides to the left.

TASIA:
What the hell?

ANDRIK:
Tasia!

KEEVE TRENNIS:
There she is.

AVAR KRISS:
I have her.

TASIA:
I can't move. Andrik, I can't move.

ANDRIK:
Stinking Jedi.

FX: Andrik fires over and over under the next bit of narration.

ANDRIK: (V.O.)
I saw red. I don't mind saying. I just fired and fired, but the leader, the Kriss woman, she didn't even flinch. She just swept up that damn saber and swatted my blaster bolt away like she was batting for the Hadros Vipers . . . straight into Tasia's leg!

TASIA:
(SCREAMS)

ANDRIK:
(YELLING) Tasia!

KEEVE TRENNIS: (OFF MIC)
We don't want to hurt you. Just stop firing.

TASIA:
(PAINED) Andrik. Do as they say.

PAN: (MASKED, V.O.)
And did you?

ANDRIK: (V.O.)
Did I, hell!

FX: Andrik runs. We stay with him, hearing his fear through his ragged breathing.

ANDRIK:
Need to get away. Need to get away!

AVAR KRISS: (OFF MIC)
He's running.

ANDRIK:
I'll do more than that.

FX: He squeezes off another couple of shots as he runs. Again we go with him.

SSKEER: (OFF MIC)
I'll get him.

KEEVE TRENNIS: (OFF MIC)
Not on your own, you won't.

SSKEER:
No. You deal with the Cathar under the shuttle. The marshal needs to get to the flight deck. The Er'Kit is mine.

ANDRIK: (V.O.)
I've seen a Trandoshan on the hunt. There used to be one in Pan's Tempest. Sslanno, they called him. Lost his scales in a plasma blast and they never grew back. I once saw him pull out a Whiphid's spine with his bare hands. You should have heard that Whiph squeal. I vowed I'd never be in a situation where I'd be the Whiph, and yet there I was . . .

CUT TO:

SCENE 49. INT. THE *LOURNA DEE*. CORRIDOR—CONTINUOUS.

FX: Andrik runs down a corridor, panting.

ANDRIK: (CONT, V.O.)
Yeah, so he was a Jedi. And yeah, I know they *say* they don't kill unless they really need to. But you can't fight your own nature, you know. There was something about this one, something in his eyes. Behind all those robes I knew he was no better than Sslano. No better than an *animal*.

FX: Andrik's boots scrape as he hides for a moment, breathing heavily.

In the distance we hear Sskeer's lightsaber. He's tracking Andrik slowly, purposefully, more in control than we saw in issue two of the Marvel series, but still fighting his instincts.

This is Sskeer at his most dangerous.

SSKEER: (OFF MIC)
(CALLING OUT) You don't have to do this, Nihil. You could ssstop running. You could sssurrender.

ANDRIK:
(TO HIMSELF, STILL WIRED) Yeah, you'd like that, wouldn't you? None of your pals around to see you tear me in two.

SSKEER: (OFF MIC)
There is no essscape.

ANDRIK:
Yeah. Yeah, there is.

FX: He fires off a couple of shots, the lightsaber flaring on the other end of the corridor as Sskeer blocks the bolts.

Andrik runs.

ANDRIK: (CONT)
(RUNNING) Escape pod. There's an escape pod down here. I know it.

ANDRIK: (V.O.)
And I was right, there was . . . but it wasn't that simple.

PAN: (MASKED, V.O.)
Nothing ever is.

FX: Scuff of boots as Andrik goes around the corner and comes to a sudden halt.

ANDRIK:
Oh no. No, no, no, no.

ANDRIK: (V.O.)
The corridor had collapsed ahead of me, crushing four, maybe five Strikes as they'd tried to escape. There was a gap, but I had no idea if it was big enough. Whether I could get through. (BEAT) But I had no place else to go.

FX: Andrik starts pushing himself through the gap, metal creaking as he tries to shove the wreckage back. All the time, Sskeer's footsteps are approaching, his lightsaber blazing.

ANDRIK:
I'm gonna die. I'm gonna die, I'm gonna die, I'm gonna die.

FX: Fabric snags.

ANDRIK: (CONT)
Aah! No. Stupid thing. Why have you got to snag?

FX: Sskeer comes around the corner and comes to a stop, more menacing than we expect a Jedi to be, partly because this is Sskeer, partly because we're seeing this through Andrik's terrified, jacked-up mind.

SSKEER:
I told you not to run.

ANDRIK:
(TERRIFIED) Oh stars. Oh stars!

SSKEER:
Do not sssstruggle. The more you twist, the more you will become ensssnared in the metal.

ANDRIK:
Don't tell me what to do.

FX: Andrik fires his blaster at point-blank range. Sskeer bats the bolts away.

SSKEER:
(GRUNTS WITH FRUSTRATION) I'll have that.

ANDRIK: (V.O.)
My blaster . . . he just pulled it out of my hand . . . without even moving.

ANDRIK:
No!

SSKEER:
You won't be needing it anymore.

FX: The blaster clatters to the floor.

SSKEER: (CONT)
Now do as I say. Ssstop. Sssstruggling.

ANDRIK: (V.O.)
There was something about the way he said it . . . or maybe it was his eyes . . . those yellow eyes . . . staring at me like a snake . . . I just listened . . . just did what he said.

SSKEER:
You are calm. You are in control.

FX: Sskeer brings his lightsaber up.

SSKEER: (CONT)
I'm going to cut you free and then you will sssurrender.

STAR WARS: TEMPEST RUNNER   119

ANDRIK:
(ENTRANCED) And then I will surrender.

SSKEER:
That's right. Sssoon you will be free.

FX: Sskeer raises his lightsaber and . . .

Lourna comes running at him swinging a vibro-ax, its blade humming.

LOURNA:
(BATTLE CRY)

ANDRIK: (V.O.)
It was her. Lourna.

FX: The vibro-ax buries itself into Sskeer's shoulder.

LOURNA:
(GRUNT OF VICTORY)

SSKEER:
(ROARS IN PAIN)

ANDRIK: (V.O.)
You've never seen anything like it. No mask. No armor. Just her . . . and a vibro-ax on maximum power. (BEAT) But he still had fight in him.

SSKEER:
(SNARLS)

FX: Lourna is thrown back and connects with the bulkhead.

LOURNA:
(CRIES OUT)

ANDRIK: (V.O.)
He didn't even touch her but she flew back—bang—straight into the wall. That lightsaber of his? (MAKES THE SOUND OF IT FLYING THROUGH THE AIR UNDER THE FOLLOWING SOUND EFFECT)

FX: A whoosh of the lightsaber zooming up from the floor, slapping into his palm, and igniting.

SSKEER:
That was a missstake.

LOURNA:
(PANTING) Yeah? Well, here's another one.

FX: She throws a grenade down. It bounces as Andrik narrates.

ANDRIK: (V.O.)
I realized what she had thrown right before it went off. A flash grenade. BOOM!

FX: The sudden whoomp of the flash-bang going off under Andrik's voice-over.

ANDRIK: (CONT, V.O.)
I didn't wait around. I pushed against the metal. Still got the scar where it caught my arm, see?

ANDRIK:
(CRIES OUT IN PAIN)

ANDRIK: (V.O.)
And then she was there, Lourna, encouraging me on. At least, I think that's what happened? It's all a bit of a blur.

LOURNA:
Just move! Out of the way!

FX: She shoves him and he hits the deck on the other side.

ANDRIK:
(GRUNTING WITH PAIN) Thanks.

LOURNA:
Don't just lie there. Get to the escape pod. Get it primed.

ANDRIK:
(BREATHLESS) Yes . . . yes, my Runner.

FX: He scrambles up and runs.

LOURNA: (OFF MIC)
Is it working?

FX: Beeps as Andrik operates the controls.

ANDRIK:
Yes.

FX: The door grinds open.

ANDRIK: (CONT)
I've done it!

LOURNA: (OFF MIC)
Don't you dare leave without me.

SSKEER: (OFF MIC)
You're going nowhere.

ANDRIK: (V.O.)
It was the Trandoshan. He . . . he pulled her back . . . back through the wreckage.

LOURNA: (OFF MIC)
(CRIES OUT).

ANDRIK: (V.O.)
I don't know what happened, I just heard a crunch . . .

FX: We hear the thump of Lourna striking the wall.

ANDRIK: (CONT, V.O.)
And then that damn sword.

FX: Off mic, Sskeer's lightsaber flares on.

SSKEER: (OFF MIC)
(STRUGGLING TO KEEP CONTROL) Ssstay down. Sstay down.

FX: Footsteps as Keeve runs up off mic.

KEEVE TRENNIS: (OFF MIC)
Master!

SSKEER: (OFF MIC)
Keeve, I . . . I . . .

KEEVE TRENNIS: (OFF MIC)
You're bleeding.

SSKEER: (OFF MIC)
The Force . . . for a second I . . .

KEEVE TRENNIS: (OFF MIC)
The Force is with you. Do you hear me? The Force is with you.

SSKEER: (OFF MIC)
(GAINING CONFIDENCE) The Force . . . is with me . . .

KEEVE TRENNIS: (OFF MIC)
Is this who did this to you?

SSKEER: (OFF MIC)
Twi'lek . . . came out of nowhere . . .

FX: Keeve crouches down beside Lourna.

KEEVE TRENNIS: (OFF MIC)
She's alive . . . just. How hard did you throw her?

SSKEER: (OFF MIC)
I tried to keep control.

KEEVE TRENNIS: (OFF MIC)
And you did. You remembered yourself. Where is the other one?

SSKEER: (OFF MIC)
Pushed through that wreckage . . . Can't have gone far . . .

FX: Keeve ignites her lightsaber.

KEEVE TRENNIS: (OFF MIC)
Leave him to me. Just breathe, okay? We'll get you patched up as soon as we can.

FX: She slices through the wreckage.

CUT TO:

SCENE 50. INT. CANTINA. SRAN.

HULKING FIGURE: (MASKED)
And that's when you left her. Your precious Tempest Runner.

ANDRIK:
What was I supposed to do? I had no weapon. I was bleeding.

HULKING FIGURE: (MASKED)
Not to mention coming down from the stim.

ANDRIK:
Whatever you think of me, I'm no fool. Two Jedi? Even one cut to the bone? I'd never make it past them.

HULKING FIGURE: (MASKED)
So you ran.

CUT TO:

SCENE 51. INT. THE *LOURNA DEE*. ESCAPE POD.

FX: The metal falls away under Keeve's blade.

ANDRIK:
(CALLING OUT) I'm sorry, Runner. I'll come back for you. I promise. I'll find you.

FX: Keeve runs toward him.

KEEVE TRENNIS: (OFF MIC)
Stop!

ANDRIK:
No fear.

FX: He slams a button. Inner doors slide shut and—whoosh—the pod jettisons.

We stay in the escape pod for a few beats, calm after the storm, hearing him catching his breath, exhausted.

ANDRIK: (CONT)
(QUIETLY) I'll find you. I promise.

CUT TO:

SCENE 52. INT. CANTINA. SRAN.

FX: Andrik picks up his glass, has a drink.

HULKING FIGURE: (MASKED)
So that's why you're here? Lourna Dee is here?

ANDRIK:
(SNORTS, NOW REALLY SLURRING HIS WORDS) In this dump? Not likely. They took her, didn't they? The Jedi. Took everyone. Tasia. Lourna. Took the entire bloody ship.

HULKING FIGURE: (MASKED)
Took her where?

ANDRIK:
(NOT LISTENING) I was lucky, I guess. The pod drifted away with debris from the fight. Wasn't the only one. I caught up with another survivor on Cerea, a Frizznoth who abandoned ship when the Jedi first arrived. He'd heard things. About what happened. Where they took them.

HULKING FIGURE: (MASKED)
(TRYING TO KEEP HIS TEMPER) And . . . ?

ANDRIK:
And what?

HULKING FIGURE: (MASKED)
Where was it?

ANDRIK:
(A BEAT AND THEN WITH REAL VENOM) Starlight.

CUT TO:

SCENE 53. INT. STARLIGHT BEACON. MEDCENTER.

Atmos: Starlight's medcenter. The bleeps of computers. Ventilators hissing. The bubble of a bacta tank. We hear the same hum of Starlight below everything.

MEDCENTER ANNOUNCEMENT: (LOUDSPEAKER)
Nurse Okana, please report to the trauma center. Nurse Okana to the trauma center.

FX: Footsteps approach.

NIB ASSEK:
Keeve?

FX: The rustle of Keeve's leathers as she turns.

KEEVE TRENNIS:
Master Assek.

NIB ASSEK:
Nib. Please.

KEEVE TRENNIS:
Sorry. Nib.

NIB ASSEK:
How is he doing?

KEEVE TRENNIS:
Sskeer? He didn't like going into the bacta, but Dr. Gino'le insisted.

NIB ASSEK:
As did the marshal, no doubt.

KEEVE TRENNIS:
(SMILING) She was a little more persuasive.

NIB ASSEK:
You're worried about him.

KEEVE TRENNIS:
He's survived worse . . .

NIB ASSEK:
It's more than that. I know about his . . . condition.

KEEVE TRENNIS:
(UNCERTAIN WHETHER SHE SHOULD SHARE) He says he's losing his connection to the Force.

NIB ASSEK:
That is impossible.

KEEVE TRENNIS:
Until it becomes a self-fulfilling prophecy. And then what will we do?

NIB ASSEK:
You will help him. We will all help him.

KEEVE TRENNIS:
I'm sorry . . . I didn't ask . . . Are you hurt? I heard there was an explosion . . . Lourna Dee . . .

NIB ASSEK:
Lourna Dee is dead. One of the Skyhawk pilots killed her . . . but she had her revenge . . . a thermal detonator in her armor, rigged to go off when her mask was removed. We tried to save them . . .

KEEVE TRENNIS:
The pilots.

NIB ASSEK:
I pushed the body away, tried to contain the blast, while Burryaga—

FX: *Burryaga runs up, agitated.*

BURRYAGA:
[SHYRIIWOOK—Master!]

NIB ASSEK:
Burry?

BURRYAGA:
(BABBLES IN SHYRIIWOOK)

NIB ASSEK:
Whoa, whoa. Slow down. I can't understand you.

BURRYAGA:
[SHYRIIWOOK—He's gone. The pilot.]

NIB ASSEK:
Who's gone?

KEEVE TRENNIS:
What's he saying?

BURRYAGA:
[SHYRIIWOOK—We need to find him.]

NIB ASSEK:
Burry tried to get the pilots clear of the blast, but only man-
aged to save one . . . Jano Brayson. The other . . . the other
didn't make it.

BURRYAGA:
(MOURNFUL) [SHYRIIWOOK—Please—they don't know
where he is.]

NIB ASSEK:
Jano's gone missing. He's not on his ward.

BURRYAGA:
[SHYRIIWOOK—We need to find him.]

NIB ASSEK:
We will find him, Burry. I promise.

KEEVE TRENNIS:
I'll help.

BURRYAGA:
[SHYRIIWOOK—I think I know where he is.]

NIB ASSEK:
What do you mean?

FX: Burryaga rushes off, calling over his shoulder.

NIB ASSEK: (CONT)
(CALLING AFTER HIM) How do you know where he is?

BURRYAGA:
[SHYRIIWOOK—I have a bad feeling . . .]

CUT TO:

SCENE 54. INT. STARLIGHT BEACON. MEDCENTER. NIHIL WARD.

Atmos: Similar to other ward, the hiss of a ventilator nearby.

TASIA:
(WINCES) Nurse. Nurse, I need more painkillers. (BEAT) Nurse!

FX: Footsteps approach slowly.

TASIA: (CONT)
It's about time. Didn't you hear me calling?

JANO:
(SOFTLY, SINISTER) I heard you.

TASIA:
(ALARMED) You're not a nurse.

JANO:
No. I'm a pilot. A good one. But not as good as my friend. You would've liked him. Everyone did.

TASIA:
Do I look like I care? I'm in pain here. Nurse!

JANO:
Good.

TASIA:
What?

JANO:
Look at you all. In your nice comfortable beds. On your ventilators.

FX: More footsteps as he walks toward another of the beds.

JANO: (CONT)
What about this one? Healing nicely are you, poor little head-tails?

TASIA:
Stay away from her. (SHOUTING) Hey! Can we get some help here?

JANO:
No one's coming. I've locked the door. No one can get in. It's just you and me.

TASIA:
(STILL TRYING TO GET HELP) Hey!

JANO:
It was a Twi'lek who killed him, with a bomb. How cowardly is that? I shot her myself. You should have seen it. Bam. She's gone, but the Jedi, they didn't care. They looked at me like *I* was the bad guy? I was on their side.

But that's when I saw it. Saw them for what they are. For all their powers, they're just like her. They're cowards. All of them. What's the point of them if they can't finish the job?

FX: Nearby, Burryaga bangs on the ward doors.

BURRYAGA: (MUFFLED THROUGH GLASS)
[SHYRIIWOOK—Jano! Stop!]

TASIA:
Hey! Wookiee! You need to get in here. He's out of his mind.

JANO:
No. They can't finish the job . . . but I can.

TASIA:
What do you mean?

JANO:
Who should I start with? You or the . . .

Music: Sudden sting as he grabs the patient's throat.

JANO: (CONT)
Or the Twi'lek.

TASIA:
Leave her alone.

JANO:
Why should I? It's only fair. One of you killed my friend. You should watch as I kill one of yours. Throttle the life out of her and there's nothing you can do about it.

FX: More banging from the door.

NIB ASSEK: (MUFFLED THROUGH GLASS)
Pilot Brayson! Don't do this!

TASIA:
Did you hear what I said? Stop it.

JANO:
I heard, but I'm not going to listen. Don't worry, I'll get around to you soon enough.

NIB ASSEK: (MUFFLED)
Jano!

TASIA:
I said . . . stop it!

FX: Tasia flies forward, despite her injuries, attacking him.

JANO:
(CRIES OUT) Get off me.

TASIA:
Attack one Nihil and you attack us all.

JANO:
Sounds good to me.

FX: He brings his head back, headbutting her, knocking her back.

TASIA:
(CRIES OUT)

FX: She hits the floor. And then he's on top of her.

JANO:
Sorry. Did that hurt? Does this?

TASIA:
(SCREAMS OUT IN PAIN)

JANO:
You all deserve to die. For what you've done. To the galaxy.

TASIA:
(GAGGING AS HE THROTTLES HER)

NIB ASSEK: (MUFFLED)
Stand back.

JANO:
For Teff!

FX: The glass smashes.

JANO: (CONT)
(GASPS)

FX: Glass tinkles down all around.

NIB ASSEK:
Release her, Jano.

JANO:
I'll kill them all. You can't stop me.

LOURNA:
No, but I can.

FX: A thunk as Lourna hits him with a ventilator unit.

TASIA:
(PAINED, BARELY AUDIBLE) Lourna?

LOURNA:
(HISSING) Don't say my name.

NIB ASSEK:
Drop the ventilator. No one will hurt you if you cooperate.

LOURNA:
I'm cooperating. I'm cooperating.

FX: She throws the ventilator aside.

KEEVE TRENNIS:
She's the one who attacked Sskeer.

LOURNA:
He was in my way.

NIB ASSEK:
That's not a justification.

LOURNA:
I just wanted to get to the escape hatch. But I'm not attacking anyone now . . .

KEEVE TRENNIS:
Tell that to Jano.

LOURNA:
He was *trying* to kill her.

NIB ASSEK:
And we would have stopped him.

LOURNA:
Attack one of us and you attack us all.

NIB ASSEK:
That's a cycle that we need to break. In you. In him.

LOURNA:
Good luck . . . (SUDDENLY WOOZY) with that. (GROANS)

FX: She crumples.

NIB ASSEK:
Careful!

FX: Burryaga catches her.

BURRYAGA:
[SHYRIIWOOK—I've got her.]

LOURNA:
Thanks. You move quickly . . . for a big fella.

NIB ASSEK:
Get her back on the bed, Burryaga.

LOURNA:
I can manage.

NIB ASSEK:
Doesn't look like it.

BURRYAGA:
[SHYRIIWOOK—Let me help.]

LOURNA:
Your friend the Trandoshan did a number on me.

TASIA:
He's not the only one.

KEEVE TRENNIS:
Let me help.

TASIA:
I don't need your help. I can manage.

LOURNA:
I think we *all* need their help. There's been enough fighting.

NIB ASSEK:
Now, that I can agree with. Jedi Trennis, fetch the doctor.

KEEVE TRENNIS:
Are you sure?

NIB ASSEK:
Burry and I can handle things here.

BURRYAGA:
(AGREES IN SHYRIIWOOK)

KEEVE TRENNIS:
I'll be right back.

FX: She rushes off.

NIB ASSEK:
My name is Nib Assek. What is yours, friend?

LOURNA:
Friend?

NIB ASSEK:
No more fighting, remember?

LOURNA:
No more fighting. (BEAT) My name . . . my name is Sal. Sal Krost.

CUT TO:

SCENE 55. INT. CANTINA. SRAN.

Atmos: As before.

HULKING FIGURE: (MASKED)
The Jedi don't know who they've got.

ANDRIK:
(REALLY QUITE DRUNK NOW) That's what the Frizznoth said. They think she died, on the flight deck, when the thermal charge went off . . .

HULKING FIGURE: (MASKED)
And why didn't she?

ANDRIK:
My best guess, it was Aychseven.

HULKING FIGURE: (MASKED)
Who?

ANDRIK:
This old droid. Been with her Tempest since the beginning. Wearing full . . . full body armor. Maybe even fake lekku. I don't know.

HULKING FIGURE: (MASKED)
A decoy. The oldest trick in the book. And the Jedi fell for it.

ANDRIK:
But I can get her out.

FX: Andrik pulls out a data card. He fumbles it drunkenly, and it clatters on the bar.

ANDRIK: (CONT)
Whoops. Silly me.

FX: He picks it up.

ANDRIK: (CONT)
See this locator? That's how I'm going to find her. The Frizznoth showed me how.

HULKING FIGURE: (MASKED)
And where is this Frizznoth now?

ANDRIK:
He sold me out. We got into trouble on Fimster. Left me for dead. But I don't need him. I'm going to get myself an army. Whatever it takes.

HULKING FIGURE: (MASKED)
And then you're going to rescue Lourna Dee.

ANDRIK:
Like she rescued me.

HULKING FIGURE: (MASKED)
(LAUGHS HEARTILY, ONLY FOR HIS LAUGHTER TO DESCEND INTO A WHEEZING COUGH)

ANDRIK:
What's so funny?

HULKING FIGURE: (MASKED)
She didn't rescue you. She was trying to get to the escape hatch herself.

ANDRIK:
You're wrong.

HULKING FIGURE: (MASKED)
Whatever she calls herself, whatever lies she tells the Jedi, she only ever thinks about herself, only *cares* about herself.

ANDRIK:
You don't know what you're talking about. You don't know her.

HULKING FIGURE: (MASKED)
Oh, I do. I've known her a long time . . . And unlike certain people, I know when I've had enough to drink.

ANDRIK:
What?

HULKING FIGURE: (MASKED)
Time to pay the tab.

FX: He blasts Andrik, who crashes to the ground.

SERVING DROID:
You shot him.

HULKING FIGURE: (MASKED)
Yeah, I did.

FX: He blasts the serving droid, metal parts hitting the floor.

HULKING FIGURE: (CONT, MASKED)
And now I've shot you.

ANDRIK:
(WEAK, DYING) Why?

HULKING FIGURE: (MASKED)
You're not the only one looking for her.

FX: The hulking figure stamps on Andrik's head, killing him.

ANDRIK:
(GRUNT AS HE DIES)

HULKING FIGURE: (MASKED)
Rest in peace.

FX: The hulking figure—in reality Pan Eyta, full of venom in every sense of the word—activates a comlink.

PAN: (CONT, MASKED)
Pan Eyta to Trilok. Prepare the ship. I know where she is.

FX: A beat of him breathing in anticipation.

PAN: (CONT, MASKED)
I know where to find Lourna Dee.

END OF PART ONE

PART TWO

REMEMBRANCE

SCENE 56. INT. STARLIGHT BEACON. CELL—DAY.

Atmos: A small cell in Starlight's security wing. The buzz of multiple energy fields.

FX: Lourna wakes with a start, sitting up from her back.

LOURNA:
(GASPS, THEN STRUGGLES TO CATCH HER BREATH)
Where?

TASIA: (IN NEXT CELL)
Where do you think you are? Where we've been for days. Starlight Beacon. Aren't the cells pretty?

LOURNA:
Tasia?

TASIA:
That's my name. Remind me . . . what's yours?

LOURNA:
Shut up.

TASIA:
(LOWERING HER VOICE, OOZING WITH MENACE)
Why should I? Why shouldn't I tell everyone who you really are?

LOURNA:
Because I'll get us both out of here if you keep quiet.

TASIA:
Is that right? Like you were going to go down with the ship? I almost bought that. Should've known you just wanted us out of the way so you could scurry off to your own private escape pod. Same old Lourna.

LOURNA:
(LIKE TALKING TO A CHILD) Lourna Dee is dead. She died in an explosion on the flight deck of her ship.

TASIA:
Yeah. 'Course she did. Wasn't a *droid* at all.

LOURNA:
You need to keep your voice down.

TASIA:
Why? Because it's embarrassing. Because the *old* Lourna Dee would have had a dozen volunteers lining up to sacrifice themselves in her name. But not now. Now she had to use something she could program.

LOURNA:
(SIGHS, THINKING IT'S NOT WORTH IT)

TASIA:
Who's Bala?

LOURNA:
(SURPRISED, ON THE WRONG FOOT) What?

TASIA:
You were moaning his name in your sleep? (MOCKING) Bala. Ba-la.

LOURNA:
He's not important.

FX: A door opens across the room. A guard enters.

GUARD 1: (OFF MIC)
I'm here for Prisoner Thirty-Eight. Sont Eval.

GUARD 2: (OFF MIC)
Cell seven.

FX: Footsteps as the guard marches toward cell 7.

LOURNA:
What's happening?

TASIA:
They're taking us for questioning, one at a time.

GUARD 1: (OFF MIC)
Stand back from the energy field.

FX: Beeps as the guard presses controls and the energy field shimmers off.

EVAL:
(GIVES A BATTLE CRY AS HE ATTACKS THE GUARD)

GUARD 1: (OFF MIC)
No, you don't.

FX: The sudden buzz of a stun baton.

EVAL:
(SCREAMS)

LOURNA:
Stun batons.

TASIA:
And they say *we're* the monsters.

GUARD 1:
I don't want to have to do that again. Are you going to come quietly?

EVAL:
(COWED) Yes.

GUARD 1:
Yes?

EVAL: (OFF MIC)
Yes, sir.

FX: Footsteps as Eval is led off.

TASIA:

I wonder if he's going to be the one who gives you away. He never liked you.

LOURNA:

No one is going to give me away.

TASIA:

Is that right?

LOURNA:

Because no one except my flight crew has ever seen my face.

TASIA:

We both know that's not true.

LOURNA:

You sure about that? Most of those who've seen my face are dead thanks to the Republic. And as for those who have . . .

TASIA:

Is that a threat?

LOURNA:

I don't want it to be. I saved your life.

TASIA:

(IRONIC LAUGH) When?

LOURNA:

In the medcenter. That pilot was going to kill you.

TASIA:

He wishes. And so do you.

FX: Footsteps as Lourna moves nearer the energy field that separates them.

LOURNA:

(KEEPING HER VOICE DOWN) Tas, listen. If we stick together we might just survive all this.

TASIA:

Might survive it more if I give you up. Who knows where they're going to throw us? The Pinnacle? Jubilar? Whatever pit they find, they're not going to let us forget what we've done. That pilot? He was just the beginning. How many people died on Valo, eh? In the Emergences? Life is going to be hard wherever we end up, but perhaps it'll be a bit easier for me if I let them know exactly who they have in you.

LOURNA:
You need to think smarter, Tasia.

TASIA:
Oh, I'm thinking smart all right. And I'm remembering when Lourna Dee headbutted me for asking a question on her flight deck. Do you remember that, Sal?

LOURNA:
You're right. They're not going to forget, for all their platitudes. And no one's coming to rescue us, either. You heard Ro. He doesn't care what happened to us. He only cares about himself.

TASIA:
Sounds like he's got his head screwed on.

LOURNA:
You don't mean that.

TASIA:
Don't I?

LOURNA:
I saved you in the medcenter, but you saved me first.

TASIA:
Only because I didn't realize it was you in that bed!

FX: The door opens again. Another guard enters.

GUARD 3:
Prisoner Forty-Two. Sal Krost.

GUARD 2:
Cell three.

FX: The guard walks toward Lourna's cell.

LOURNA:
Just think about it. Please.

GUARD 3:
Stand back from the field.

FX: Scrape of Lourna's boots as she does as she's told. The door control beeps. The energy field drops.

GUARD 3: (CONT)
Are you going to be trouble?

LOURNA:
No.

GUARD 3:
Good. Come with me.

FX: Lourna follows the guard.

TASIA:
Bye, "Sal." Catch you later.

CUT TO:

SCENE 57. INT. STARLIGHT BEACON. INTERVIEW ROOM—MOMENTS LATER.

Atmos: A small featureless room with little in the way of background noise, except for the background buzz of Starlight Beacon.

FX: A door chime sounds.

CHIEF TARPFEN:
Enter.

FX: The door opens. Footsteps as the guard leads Lourna in.

GUARD 3:
Prisoner Forty-Two.

CHIEF TARPFEN:
Thank you. Take a seat, please.

LOURNA:
Me or her.

CHIEF TARPFEN:
That's how it's going to be, is it?

LOURNA:
(SIGHS) No.

CHIEF TARPFEN:
Then we're going to get on just fine. Take a seat.

LOURNA:
(BREATHES OUT, TRYING TO KEEP HER TEMPER)

FX: Footsteps as Lourna moves to the table. The metal legs of the chair scrape across the floor as Lourna pulls the chair out.

CHIEF TARPFEN:
(TO THE GUARD) Thank you. That will be all.

GUARD 3:
Chief.

FX: The guard leaves, the door sliding shut behind her.

LOURNA:
Do you think that's wise? Sending them away?

CHIEF TARPFEN:
Is that a threat?

LOURNA:
I'm just surprised, that's all.

CHIEF TARPFEN:
I can handle myself.

LOURNA:
I'm sure you can. Mon Cala Royal Guard?

CHIEF TARPFEN:
I'm sorry.

LOURNA:
The way you're sitting. It's either that or the Dac Ballet . . . and you don't look like a ballet dancer.

CHIEF TARPFEN:
(NOT RISING TO IT) I'm going to record this interview. Do you have a problem with that?

LOURNA:
Would it change things if I did?

CHIEF TARPFEN:
I would register your protest.

STAR WARS: TEMPEST RUNNER   151

LOURNA:
No need. Do what you want.

CHIEF TARPFEN:
Thank you. Recorder on.

FX: There is a beep and then a tone beneath the scenes from this point, a reminder that the conversation is being recorded.

CHIEF TARPFEN: (CONT)
Okay, then. My name is Ghal Tarpfen. I am the head of Republic security on Starlight Beacon.

LOURNA:
Congratulations.

CHIEF TARPFEN:
Thank you. And you are Sal Krost.

LOURNA:
I am.

CHIEF TARPFEN:
A member of Lourna Dee's warband.

LOURNA:
We prefer Tempest.

CHIEF TARPFEN:
Understood. When you were brought in you had no markings.

LOURNA:
Markings?

CHIEF TARPFEN:
On your face. One bolt for a Strike, two for a Cloud . . .

LOURNA:
Three for a Storm.

CHIEF TARPFEN:
So what are you?

LOURNA:
None of the above. (BEAT) Not anymore.

CHIEF TARPFEN:
Is that so.

LOURNA:
I washed them off. When the ship was attacked.

CHIEF TARPFEN:
Is it that easy? To walk away from the Nihil?

LOURNA:
Not usually, but the Nihil aren't what they were.

CHIEF TARPFEN:
And so who are you now?

LOURNA:
Me? (SHRUGGING) I'm a prisoner. Your prisoner.

CHIEF TARPFEN:
A prisoner of the Republic.

LOURNA:
Same thing.

CHIEF TARPFEN:
Because of the crimes you have committed.

LOURNA:
I was following orders.

CHIEF TARPFEN:
The orders of Lourna Dee.

LOURNA:
Yes.

CHIEF TARPFEN:
The Eye of the Nihil.

LOURNA:
(SLIGHT HESITATION) Yes.

CHIEF TARPFEN:
You hesitated.

LOURNA:
She's dead.

CHIEF TARPFEN:
So it appears. She was a Twi'lek, too. Like you.

LOURNA:
There are lots of Twi'leks in the galaxy.

CHIEF TARPFEN:
Did you know her?

LOURNA:
No. No one really did.

CHIEF TARPFEN:
Did she come from Ryloth?

LOURNA:
I don't know.

CHIEF TARPFEN:
Do *you* come from Ryloth? Originally I mean.

LOURNA:
(ANOTHER HESITATION) No.

CHIEF TARPFEN:
You interest me, Sal Krost.

LOURNA:
Thank you.

CHIEF TARPFEN:
Your teeth. They're sharpened.

LOURNA:
They are.

CHIEF TARPFEN:
Did you do that?

LOURNA:
Yes.

CHIEF TARPFEN:
That's unusual, isn't it? For a Twi'lek woman. I thought only the men sharpened their teeth.

LOURNA:
I didn't always look like this. Didn't even sound like this. None of us did.

CHIEF TARPFEN:
And what did you look like, Sal? Before you joined the Nihil? Who were you?

CUT TO:

SCENE 58. EXT. THE PLAINS OF AALOTH—LONG AGO.

Atmos: A sunny spring day. Wind is blowing through fields of long grass, exotic birds singing in the air. On the surface, Aaloth appears to be a paradise. It is not.

FX: Two mounts are lolloping toward us. Blurrg exported from Ryloth. On their backs are a teenage Lourna and her younger brother Inun. Lourna is ahead, her blurrg panting heavily.

INUN:
(CALLING FORWARD) Lourna. Slow down.

LOURNA (TEENAGE):
(CALLING BACK) Why?

INUN:
(CALLING FORWARD) You're running your blurrg too hard. You're going to wear it out.

LOURNA:
(CALLING BACK) More like you can't keep up. (KICKS HER MOUNT) Raa! Raa!

FX: The blurrg complains but speeds up, leaving Inun behind.

INUN:
(CALLING FORWARD) Lourna!

LOURNA:
(LAUGHS)

FX: The blurrg stumbles and wails, falling, crashing to the ground.

LOURNA: (CONT)
(CRIES OUT)

INUN:
Lourna! What did I tell you?

FX: His blurrg comes to a halt. Inun jumps down.

LOURNA:
(IN PAIN) Get it off me. Get it off me, Inun.

FX: The blurrg cries out.

INUN:
(EFFORT AS HE TRIES TO PUSH IT) I can't. It's too heavy.

LOURNA:
It's crushing me!

INUN:
I knew this would happen. I just knew it.

FX: The blurrg cries again.

LOURNA:
Do something!

FX: Inun opens a comlink.

INUN:
Hello. Can anyone hear me? It's an emergency. Hello?

HALEENA: (COMMS)
Inun?

INUN:
Haleena. Thank Zariin. It's Lourna. She's hurt.

HALEENA: (COMMS)
Hurt? How?

INUN:
She's trapped beneath a blurrg.

HALEENA: (COMMS)
She's *what*?

LOURNA:
Just send help, sister. Our brother is useless . . . as usual.

HALEENA: (COMMS)
Where are you?

INUN:
On the Sal Plains.

HALEENA: (COMMS)
What in Zariin's name are you doing out there? Especially now. Father won't be happy.

LOURNA:
I'm not happy! Send a skimmer! Send anything! Just get here!

CUT TO:

SCENE 59. INT. STARLIGHT BEACON. INTERVIEW ROOM.

Atmos: As before, the recording buzz continuing.

CHIEF TARPFEN:
You had a family.

LOURNA:
No.

CHIEF TARPFEN:
No?

LOURNA:
I know what you're doing.

CHIEF TARPFEN:
You do?

LOURNA:
Repeating my words. Echoing what I say. Classic interrogation tactics. Make it sound like you're interested, that you're curious. That you understand.

CHIEF TARPFEN:
I *am* curious.

LOURNA:
Why? What does it matter? What does any of this matter? You're going to lock me up anyway.

CHIEF TARPFEN:
Lock you up?

LOURNA:
Now you're just mocking me. Tell me what you want me to say, and I'll say it.

CHIEF TARPFEN:
I want you to tell the truth.

LOURNA:
Truth is relative.

CHIEF TARPFEN:
I want to understand what makes someone join the Nihil, to turn their back on the galaxy.

LOURNA:
I never turned my back on it. I *love* the galaxy. The galaxy is full. The galaxy is rich. The galaxy gives me what I want . . . or it did.

CHIEF TARPFEN:
That's what this is all about? Riches? Money?

LOURNA:
Isn't it always?

CUT TO:

SCENE 60. EXT. AALOTH PALACE GATES.

Atmos: A crowded town square. A demonstration is under way. Lots of angry voices in the throng.

FX: The whine of a landspeeder. It can't get through the crowd.

TWI'LEK GUARD 1:
(CALLING OUT) Stand aside! Coming through.

LOURNA (TEENAGE):
(IN PAIN) I need painkillers.

INUN:
(KEEPING HIS VOICE DOWN. NERVOUS) You need to be quiet!

TWI'LEK GUARD 1:
Get back.

TWI'LEK PROTESTOR 1:
Why should we?

TWI'LEK PROTESTOR 2:
Hey. Is that a member of the first family? It is! It's Lourna'dee!

TWI'LEK PROTESTOR 1:
And her runt of a brother.

TWI'LEK PROTESTOR 3:
She looks hurt.

LOURNA:
I *am* hurt. Idiot.

INUN:
(SCARED) Lourna! Don't antagonize them.

LOURNA:
It's too late for that. (SHOUTING) Let us through!

TWI'LEK PROTESTOR 2:
Aww. Is the little princess hurt?

TWI'LEK PROTESTOR 3:
Leave her alone. She needs help.

TWI'LEK PROTESTOR 1:
We need help. Not them. They need to *do* something.

TWI'LEK PROTESTOR 2:
Let's help them out of there.

FX: They start pushing the landspeeder, trying to turn it over.

TWI'LEK GUARD 1:
Stop that! Step back from the speeder!

TWI'LEK PROTESTOR 1:
Why should we?

INUN:
They're going to tip us over!

FX: More jeers from the crowd as they rock the speeder.

LOURNA:
Do something, you fool!

FX: The guard activates a comlink.

TWI'LEK GUARD 1:
Control. Require immediate assistance. The first family are in danger.

TWI'LEK PROTESTOR 1:
I've got the kid.

INUN:
Let go of me! Let go!

FX: Blasterfire rings out across the crowd.

CAPTAIN SECARIA:
Everyone down! Get back from the speeder!

TWI'LEK PROTESTOR 3:
It's the palace guard.

TWI'LEK PROTESTOR 1:
Forget the kids. Get them!

FX: The mob turns on the guards. It's a full riot.

CAPTAIN SECARIA:
Get the children inside! Drive!

FX: The speeder pushes forward, through the fight. More cries. More violence. More blasters.

CUT TO:

SCENE 61. INT. STARLIGHT BEACON. INTERVIEW ROOM.

Atmos: As before, the recorder buzzing.

CHIEF TARPFEN:
So, if you aren't from Ryloth . . .

LOURNA:
(SIGHS) I was from a colony.

CHIEF TARPFEN:
Which one?

LOURNA:
One that didn't matter.

CHIEF TARPFEN:
What kind of family did you come from? You did have a family, didn't you?

LOURNA:
Yes. Yes, I did. (BEAT) The usual kind.

CHIEF TARPFEN:
Rich? Poor? Powerful?

LOURNA:
(LAUGHS)

CHIEF TARPFEN:
What's funny?

LOURNA:
My family was pathetic. Every single one of them.

CUT TO:

SCENE 62. INT. AALOTH PALACE COURTYARD.

Atmos: An echoey internal courtyard. We can hear the fight going on outside.

FX: The speeder comes in. Haleena hurries up.

HALEENA:
(CALLING OUT, COMMANDING) Get those gates shut!

INUN:
Haleena!

HALEENA:
Zariin's breath. Look at the state of you both.

FX: The gates clang shut. The noise of the riot is now muffled outside.

HALEENA: (CONT)
Where are the blurrgs?

LOURNA (TEENAGE):
Is that *really* what you're worried about, sister?

INUN:
We left them in the fields.

HALEENA:
Which means now we'll have to recover them. Wonderful.

LOURNA:
Unless the workers get them first.

HALEENA:
Which is more than likely.

LOURNA:
Hope they choke on them.

INUN:
Wait? Are you saying they'll eat the blurrgs?

HALEENA:
They'll eat anything these days.

LOURNA:
Should've let them have you, Inun. (WINCES)

HALEENA:
Let's get you to the infirmary. Father is going to be furious.

LOURNA:
Doubt it. That would mean he cares.

CUT TO:

SCENE 63. INT. STARLIGHT BEACON. INTERVIEW ROOM.

Atmos: As before.

CHIEF TARPFEN:
So you didn't get along with them? Your family.

LOURNA:
Did you get along with yours?

CHIEF TARPFEN:
What?

LOURNA:
Your family? Are they proud of you? Head of security on Starlight Beacon. They must be, right?

CHIEF TARPFEN:
We're not talking about me.

LOURNA:
I wish we were. At least that would be interesting. My family? They were nothing. Nobodies.

CUT TO:

SCENE 64. INT. AALOTH PALACE. INFIRMARY.

Atmos: A calm medcenter within the building. Slight echo from the high ceilings.

YUDIAH DEE:
Lourna, you can't keep doing this.

HALEENA:
I've told her. I told her what you'd say.

YUDIAH DEE:
Let her speak, daughter.

LOURNA:
Father, I'm tired. I need to sleep.

HALEENA:
You're lucky to be alive.

LOURNA:
Don't exaggerate. My leg was crushed. It's no big deal.

YUDIAH DEE:
Your sister wasn't talking about the accident and you know it. Out there. In the demonstration.

LOURNA:
(LAUGHS) That's what we're calling it now, are we?

YUDIAH DEE:
And what would you have it called?

LOURNA:
What it was . . . a riot. Those people, they need to be controlled.

YUDIAH DEE:
Controlled? Lourna. They are hungry.

LOURNA:
Then feed them. You're the Keeper of Aaloth, aren't you? We're the first family.

HALEENA:
And what exactly would you feed them, Lourna? Where is all this food coming from? The harvests? There hasn't been a good harvest in three seasons. Not that you'd know.

YUDIAH DEE:
Haleena.

HALEENA:
No, Father. She needs to hear this. It's fine for her, chasing over the plains or holed up here in the palace. She has no idea what it's really like out there, for the people.

LOURNA:
Because you never talk to me about it.

HALEENA:
Because you never listen. (GROWLS IN FRUSTRATION) I can't talk to you when you're like this. Father, we need to go. The assessor is due any moment.

LOURNA:
The leech, you mean.

YUDIAH DEE:
Lourna, please. You don't understand.

LOURNA:
I understand that those people out there will have our gates down sooner or later. And some days I can't blame them.

HALEENA:

How can you say that? After everything Father has done.

LOURNA:

And what *is* that, Hal? Tell me . . . either of you. What have you done, Father? Fawn over the assessor? Pay our dues with credits we don't have? Let Ryloth bleed us dry?

HALEENA:

This is pointless. She's acting like a child.

LOURNA:

Only because you treat me like one.

FX: Haleena marches off.

HALEENA:

I'll meet with the assessor, Father. Tell him you're on the way.

LOURNA:

Yes, off you go. (SHOUTING AFTER HER) Running away as usual.

FX: Haleena closes the door behind her.

YUDIAH DEE:

Lourna . . . why does it always have to be this way?

LOURNA:

Because whatever she says, you're the one that doesn't listen. Neither of you ever listen.

YUDIAH DEE:

And what would you do . . . if you were me?

LOURNA:

You know what I'd do, Father.

YUDIAH DEE:

(SIGH) Which is why we can't have this conversation.

FX: He, too, starts to walk away.

LOURNA:

(CALLING AFTER HIM) I'd do what every other Twi'lek colony does. What Ralchon and Malus do. What Ryloth *itself* does, for Zar's sake.

FX: Yudiah Dee stops at the doorway.

YUDIAH DEE:
We are not mining on Aaloth.

LOURNA:
Why *not*? I've already done the work. Haleena claims that I don't do anything, but I've been out. I've surveyed the plains. If we mine the Krost Mountains . . .

YUDIAH DEE:
(INTERRUPTING) No.

LOURNA:
There's ryll down there. I know there is.

YUDIAH DEE:
We do not deal in spice! We are an *agricultural* colony!

LOURNA:
We are nothing! Nothing! And that will never change, not until you grow a backbone.

YUDIAH DEE:
(SIGHS) Try to get some rest.

LOURNA:
No. Don't just leave. Father.

FX: He shuts the door.

LOURNA: (CONT)
Don't just leave!

CUT TO:

SCENE 65. INT. STARLIGHT BEACON. INTERVIEW ROOM.

Atmos: As before.

CHIEF TARPFEN:
You had no one to support you growing up?

LOURNA:
I'm sorry. I'm confused here. Are you a security chief or a social worker?

CHIEF TARPFEN:
I'm a security officer who is required to fill out an assessment on each and every prisoner in the cells.

LOURNA:
Bet you didn't think it would be like this when you left the royal guard, did you? What was it? Did you get bored, hanging around palaces? Bored of bowing and scraping every time the king passed?

CHIEF TARPFEN:
Sounds to me like it was the other way around. What aren't you telling me, Sal Krost?

CUT TO:

SCENE 66. INT. AALOTH PALACE. INFIRMARY.

Atmos: As before.

FX: The creak of the bed as Lourna tries to stand.

LOURNA (TEENAGE):
(SUCKS IN AIR IN PAIN)

BALA:
Shouldn't you be lying down?

FX: Footsteps approaching.

LOURNA:
(DELIGHTED) Bala!

BALA:
What *have* you been up to?

LOURNA:
What are *you* doing *here*?

BALA:
I came in on the assessor's yacht. Thought I'd see the old place.

LOURNA:
Is that all?

BALA:
What do you think?

FX: He gathers her into a passionate embrace and they kiss, until he pulls away.

LOURNA:
Mmmm. That's the best kind of medicine.

BALA:
How long have you got to keep it on?

LOURNA:
What?

BALA:
The magna-cast.

LOURNA:
I don't know. Three, four days.

BALA:
What if you took a dip in a rejuv bath?

LOURNA:
We don't have any rejuv.

BALA:
No, but the assessor has, on his ship.

LOURNA:
Can you sneak me on board?

BALA:
We used to sneak everywhere.

FX: She slaps his chest.

LOURNA:
Before you left.

BALA:
You still upset about that?

LOURNA:
No. (BEAT) Maybe a little.

BALA:
You could've come with me.

LOURNA:
You never gave me a chance, Mr. Spicerunner.

BALA:
Mr. *Merchant.* It's a legitimate business.

LOURNA:
(SIGHS) For everyone else.

BALA:
You've been arguing with old Yudiah again.

LOURNA:
(TEASING) That's Keeper Dee to you.

BALA:
(BOWING) My lady.

LOURNA:
(ANNOYED SIGH) It's just the same as always, though. He still won't listen.

BALA:
He has principles.

LOURNA:
And where is that going to get Aaloth? Where is it going to get me? Every other Twi'lek colony is dealing in spice. *Ryloth* is dealing with spice.

BALA:
They're dealing with a lot more than that. You'll never guess who I saw in the assembly building the other day.

LOURNA:
What were *you* doing in the building? You were in Lessu?

BALA:
That doesn't matter. Guess.

LOURNA:
I don't know. The Clan Father. The Keeper of the Gifts.

BALA:
A contingent from the Zygerrian Alliance.

LOURNA:
Slavers?

BALA:
Former slavers. Officially at least.

LOURNA:
Ryloth is dealing in slavery?

BALA:
It wouldn't be the first time.

LOURNA:
The Republic would never allow it.

BALA:
The Republic doesn't know. From what I've heard, the Zygerrians are setting up camps on Malus.

LOURNA:
This was what I was trying to tell Father. What good are principles when our neighbors don't have any.

BALA:
That may be a little strong.

LOURNA:
Is it? We're getting left behind, Bala. All I need is to open one mine. Find one seam of ryll. But no. "Our colony was founded on hard work, Lourna. On doing the right thing." Haleena's the same.

BALA:
From what I've seen, working a spice mine isn't exactly a picnic.

LOURNA:
At this rate I'll never know.

BALA:
(SPOTTING SOMETHING) Maybe. Or maybe it won't have to come to that.

LOURNA:
What do you mean?

BALA:
Stay still.

LOURNA:
What is it?

BALA:
Don't move.

LOURNA:
Bala!

FX: He grabs something from her shoulder.

BALA:
Got it.

LOURNA:
Got what?

BALA:
Look.

LOURNA:
(NOT IMPRESSED) A spider. Great.

BALA:
Not just any spider. Do you see the markings on its legs?

LOURNA:
(NOT REALLY CARING) Yeah.

BALA:
It's a spice spider.

LOURNA:
Spice?

BALA:
They're incredibly rare. Found only in the deepest mines. At least, that's what I thought.

LOURNA:
And we're excited about this, because . . . ?

BALA:
Because their webs are pure glitterstim. It packs twice the punch of ryll. Could they be here? In the palace?

LOURNA:
Or out on the Sal Plains.

BALA:
Is that where you were? When you had your accident?

LOURNA:
Yeah. I was racing with Inun.

BALA:
Can you show me?

MUSICAL SEGUE:

SCENE 67. INT. AALOTH PALACE—LATER.

VARDEM: (COMMS)
Are you sure, Bala?

BALA:
Yes. I've seen it with my own eyes, Vardem. The fields are lousy with the things, nests everywhere. And if they're above the ground . . .

VARDEM: (COMMS)
There must be plenty of spice below. Has the assessor got wind of any of this?

BALA:
No. We haven't told him.

LOURNA (TEENAGE):
We haven't told anyone yet.

VARDEM: (COMMS)
I'm sorry. I'm still not sure who you are.

BALA:
This is Lourna. Daughter of Yudiah Dee.

VARDEM: (COMMS)
The Keeper? I thought his daughter was Haleena.

LOURNA:
(PUT OUT) That's my sister.

VARDEM: (COMMS)
And what does Keeper Dee say about your discovery?

FX: Yudiah and Haleena enter the chamber.

YUDIAH DEE: (COMING UP ON MIC)
What discovery would that be?

LOURNA:
Father!

BALA:
(TO THE SCREEN) Just give us a minute, Vardem.

HALEENA:
Bala. What are you doing back on Aaloth?

BALA:
Just visiting. Haleena, you are looking as lovely as ever.

LOURNA:
(HMPH!)

HALEENA:
And you're looking just as shifty.

YUDIAH DEE:
And who is this?

VARDEM: (COMMS)
I am Vardem Kroleyic.

BALA:
Of the Zygerrian Alliance.

YUDIAH DEE:
So I see.

VARDEM: (COMMS)
We are interested in opening trade agreements with Aaloth, Keeper.

YUDIAH DEE:
Trade? I wasn't aware the Zygerrians kept blurrgs.

VARDEM: (COMMS)
We don't.

BALA:
Let me handle this, Vardem.

HALEENA:
Handle what?

LOURNA:
(BLURTING OUT) We've found spice.

BALA:
(WARNING) Lourna . . .

YUDIAH DEE:
You've found *what*?

LOURNA:
And not even underground. There are these spiders, out on the plains, and . . .

HALEENA:
Spiders?

LOURNA:
They spin glitterstim.

YUDIAH DEE:
Which plains?

LOURNA:
Sal. Near the mountains.

YUDIAH DEE:
Where you had your accident?

LOURNA:
Yes.

YUDIAH DEE:
Haleena. Have the palace guard travel out to the plains. Burn the grasses. All of them.

LOURNA:
What?

BALA:
Keeper, we should take a moment to discuss. Haleena, surely you can see the opportunity here?

VARDEM: (COMMS)
Let's not be hasty, Keeper.

YUDIAH DEE:
Close that channel.

LOURNA:
Father.

YUDIAH DEE:
Close it!

BALA:
Yes. Yes, of course.

VARDEM: (COMMS)
Bala—

FX: The channel is closed.

BALA:
There.

YUDIAH DEE:
Excellent. Thank you. Now you may leave, Bala.

LOURNA:
Leave?

YUDIAH DEE:
Get off my colony. And never come back.

LOURNA:
Father, you don't mean that.

BALA:
Keeper Dee.

FX: Yudiah Dee grabs him and pulls him physically away from the console.

YUDIAH DEE:
(LOSING HIS TEMPER) I said go! You're not welcome here. Not in the palace. Not on this planet.

LOURNA:
(STRUGGLING WITH HIM) Father. You can't do this. Let him go.

YUDIAH DEE:
(CALLING OUT) Captain of the Guard!

BALA:
No. It's fine. I'll go. But you're making a huge mistake, Keeper.

YUDIAH DEE:
The only mistake I made was welcoming you into our lives. Get out!

FX: Multiple footsteps as the guard run in.

CAPTAIN SECARIA:
Keeper?

YUDIAH DEE:
Escort this reprobate to the spaceport, will you, Captain? He's just leaving.

CAPTAIN SECARIA:
At once.

FX: She marches forward.

BALA:
Don't trouble yourself, Kalla. I'm going.

FX: He storms out.

CAPTAIN SECARIA:
Sir, I—

YUDIAH DEE:
(SUDDENLY TIRED) Just make sure he gets where he's supposed to go, Captain Secaria. You too, Haleena. And then see to the plains.

HALEENA:
Of course, Father.

LOURNA:
You . . . you idiot. You narrow-minded, shortsighted—

YUDIAH DEE:
(INTERRUPTING, TIRED) Lourna, please.

LOURNA:
Can't you see what you're throwing away?

YUDIAH DEE:
Throwing away? Lourna. What's happened to you?

LOURNA:
What's happened? Nothing's happened. Nothing ever happens. Because of *you*. Because you can't see what's happening in front of your own stupid face. This will be the end of us, Father. The end.

MUSICAL SEGUE:

SCENE 68. INT. AALOTH PALACE. LOURNA'S ROOM.

FX: The sound of furniture being thrown around. Lourna is having a tantrum.

LOURNA:
(SHOUTING IN FRUSTRATION)

FX: A door creaks open.

INUN:
Lourna?

LOURNA:
(BREATHING HEAVILY) Not now, Inun.

FX: Hesitant footsteps as he enters.

INUN:
Are you okay?

LOURNA:
(FRUSTRATED) Do I look . . . (CATCHING HERSELF) I'm fine. Really. Go back to your room. I'm sorry I disturbed you.

INUN:
I heard you quarreled with Father.

LOURNA:
You could say that.

INUN:
Haleena says he's banned you from even having a comlink.

LOURNA:
It'll pass. One way or another. He's . . . he's being so stubborn.

FX: He takes a couple of steps toward her.

INUN:
Here. Take this.

LOURNA:
A comm. Even after what Haleena said.

INUN:
They asked me to give it to you.

FX: The sound of him passing it to her.

LOURNA:
Who did?

FX: The comlink activates.

BALA: (COMMS)
Lourna?

LOURNA:
(HAPPY) Bala!

BALA: (COMMS)
Your brother's a good kid, you know? Thanks, Inun.

INUN:
Just don't get me in trouble, okay?

BALA: (COMMS)
We won't. I promise.

LOURNA:
(TEASING) Now get the hell out, you little wimp.

INUN:
Hey!

LOURNA:
Don't make me kick you in the ass.

INUN:
Couldn't even if you tried. Not with that leg. (LAUGHS)

LOURNA:
(MOCK ANGER) Out!

FX: Footsteps as Inun runs out.

LOURNA: (CONT)
(CALLING AFTER HIM) And shut the door!

FX: He does as he's told, the door shutting.

BALA: (COMMS)
How was it? After I'd gone.

LOURNA:
After you'd been kicked out, you mean. Oh, Bala. It was bad. Really bad. Father's just so pigheaded, Bala. He won't see sense.

BALA: (COMMS)
He'll have to soon enough.

LOURNA:
Why? They've burned the fields. The spiders will be gone. Roasted in their oh-so-valuable webs.

BALA: (COMMS)
No one has burned anything. Listen to me, Lourna. Kalla is with us.

LOURNA:
Kalla? Kalla Secaria?

BALA: (COMMS)
And the rest of the guard, too. I've talked to my family. They're out in the streets now, stirring up the people.

LOURNA:
To do what?

BALA: (COMMS)
To storm the palace. To put you in charge.

LOURNA:
Me?

BALA: (COMMS)
You said it yourself. Your father will never see sense, and Haleena's no different. But *you,* you've got your head on straight. When the people come—and they're coming tonight, Lourna—the guards are going to open the gates.

LOURNA:
Are you serious?

BALA: (COMMS)
Protocols are the same on every colony. In instances of insurrection, the first families are taken to the safe rooms. Locked in.

LOURNA:
Yes, I know.

BALA: (COMMS)
Go with them. Go with your brother, your sister. Go with your father. Act as if you know nothing. And then once the people are in . . . unlock the doors.

LOURNA:
Unlock them? Why?

BALA: (COMMS)
So we can arrest your father and install you as Keeper.

LOURNA:
I'm too young. I'm not sure I can . . .

BALA: (COMMS)
I'll be with you, Lourna. Every step of the way. By your side . . . if you want me to be.

LOURNA:
Of course I do. But they can't be hurt, Bala. I may not agree with them half the time . . . one hundred percent of the time . . . but I don't want them hurt.

BALA: (COMMS)
They won't be. Not if you command it. You'll be in charge, Lourna. Everyone will have to listen to you. Finally.

FX: There's a boom elsewhere in the castle, followed by distant blasterfire.

LOURNA:
(SHOCKED) What's that?

BALA: (COMMS)
It must be starting.

LOURNA:
Already? Bala . . . I'm not sure . . .

BALA: (COMMS)
You can do this, Lourna. You *need* to do it. For Aaloth. For us.

LOURNA:
(BREATHLESS) Yes. Yes, okay. I love you, Bala.

BALA: (COMMS)
I love you, too.

FX: The door is flung open. Lourna shuts off the comlink.

HALEENA:
Lourna. We need to get to the safe room, now. Can you walk?

FX: Lourna starts to hobble over.

LOURNA:
Yes.

HALEENA:
Let me help.

LOURNA:
There's no need. I can manage.

CUT TO:

SCENE 69. INT. AALOTH PALACE. CORRIDOR.

Atmos: In the background we can hear the sounds of scuffles. Blasterfire. Shouts. It's terrifying, continuing beneath the following.

INUN: (OFF MIC)
They're coming. They're coming.

YUDIAH DEE: (OFF MIC)
Oh, thank Zariin. Hurry now. Hurry.

FX: Two sets of footsteps, Lourna's limping, punctuated by a crutch.

HALEENA:
Why won't you let me help you?

LOURNA (TEENAGE):
I don't need any help.

INUN:
Where are the guards?

YUDIAH DEE:
Protecting the palace.

HALEENA:
The mob had blasters.

LOURNA:
(HONESTLY SURPRISED) They did?

HALEENA:
Can't you hear?

YUDIAH DEE:
Never mind that now. In. In.

HALEENA:
I'll close the door.

LOURNA:
No, let me.

YUDIAH DEE:
Can you manage?

LOURNA:
Will everyone stop asking me that!

FX: The sound of the mob gets closer.

INUN:
They're getting closer!

LOURNA:
I'm on it.

FX: She presses buttons and the door swings shut. Heavy locks clang— one, two, three. The sound from outside is muffled.

INUN:
(SCARED) I don't like it.

LOURNA:
It's all right, Inun. Everything is going to be all right, do you hear?

HALEENA:
What I don't understand is how they got in. What was Kalla thinking?

YUDIAH DEE:
Recriminations can wait. Here. Help me with the weapons.

INUN:
Weapons?

YUDIAH DEE:
There should be a cache of blasters. Maybe even a lyaer'tsa.

INUN:
I don't know how to use a lyaer'tsa.

HALEENA:
Then it's high time you learned.

FX: Yudiah Dee pulls out a crate, pressing a combination lock before opening it.

YUDIAH DEE:
No. No!

HALEENA:
Father?

YUDIAH DEE:
It's empty.

HALEENA:
It can't be.

YUDIAH DEE:
See for yourself.

INUN:
Why is it empty?

LOURNA:
(TO HERSELF) Just like they planned.

HALEENA:
What?

FX: There's a bang at the door behind Lourna.

EVERYONE:
(JUMPS)

TWI'LEK PROTESTOR 1: (MUFFLED THROUGH DOOR)
Open up!

YUDIAH DEE:
Everyone. Get back from the door.

TWI'LEK PROTESTOR 1: (MUFFLED)
We know you're in there.

YUDIAH DEE:
We're safe as long as we're in here.

INUN:
What if they blast through the door?

YUDIAH DEE:
Inun, it's solid vintrium. They won't be able to, I promise.

HALEENA:
Lourna. Get over here.

LOURNA:
I'm sorry.

HALEENA:
Sorry?

FX: Lourna presses the door control. Beep. Beep. Beep.

YUDIAH DEE:
Lourna!

FX: Footsteps as Inun runs over and struggles with her.

INUN:
Lourna, don't. You'll let them in!

LOURNA:
(STRUGGLING WITH HIM) Get off me, Inun. It's going to be all right. Everything's going to be all right.

HALEENA:
What in Zariin's name are you doing?

LOURNA:
You had your chance, Haleena.

FX: Lourna presses the last button. Beep. The door is shoved back. Footsteps as Captain Secaria steps in.

CAPTAIN SECARIA:
All of you. Back against the wall. Move.

YUDIAH DEE:
Captain?

CAPTAIN SECARIA:
Did you hear what I said?

HALEENA:
Inun. Come here.

INUN:
(SOBS)

YUDIAH DEE:
What about Lourna? Doesn't she need to join us?

FX: Bala pushes through the crowd. Footsteps as he enters.

BALA: (COMING UP ON MIC)
Lourna?

LOURNA:
Bala? You're already here?

BALA:
I never left. You were wonderful. Absolutely wonderful.

YUDIAH DEE:
What have you done, daughter?

BALA:
She's given Aaloth a chance of life, old man.

YUDIAH DEE:
The people won't stand for this.

CAPTAIN SECARIA:
The people are standing behind us, Keeper. They've gone hungry long enough. We *all* have.

YUDIAH DEE:
And this chance of life you speak of. It all centers on the Sal fields, does it?

HALEENA:
Or what lies beneath them.

BALA:
You should have listened to Lourna. She got it. Even here, inside this palace, the people's palace, she understood.

CAPTAIN SECARIA:
Aaloth is being left behind.

YUDIAH DEE:
The Republic—

BALA:
This is not the Republic! This is Ryloth!

YUDIAH DEE:
But the Clan Assembly signed the articles of membership.

BALA:
And as long as Coruscant gets its dues they will leave us alone. That's how it works. Aaloth pays taxes to Ryloth and Ryloth pays taxes to the Core. That won't change, but our fortunes will. How we live our lives will.

HALEENA:
You don't live here anymore, Bala.

BALA:
I've come home.

LOURNA:
To govern by my side.

YUDIAH DEE:
What?

BALA:
Lourna . . .

LOURNA:
You won't be harmed. Any of you. I'll see to that.

HALEENA:
(SKEPTICAL) You will.

LOURNA:
Maybe we'll send you to the estate on Sirna?

YUDIAH DEE:
You're exiling us to the moon?

INUN:
(STARTING TO SOB) I don't want to live on the moon. I want to live here.

LOURNA:
Then maybe you can stay, Inun. Just you. Maybe you can help.

HALEENA:
(DISGUSTED) How could you? How could you do this to your own family?

BALA:
Lourna. We should go. There are matters to attend to.

LOURNA:
But the others . . .

BALA:
They'll be comfortable. We'll see to that.

LOURNA:
But what about Inun?

BALA:
He'll be fine. Trust me.

LOURNA:
Yes. Yes, of course. (TO HER FAMILY) I'll see you soon. I meant what I said. Everything is going to be all right. You'll see.

YUDIAH DEE:
Don't do this. Lourna. Please don't do this.

BALA:
Let's go.

INUN:
Lourna!

LOURNA:
I'll be back soon, Inun. I promise.

FX: The door shuts behind them.

BALA:
And it's done.

LOURNA:
Wait. Why are the guards still in there with them?

BALA:
(IGNORING HER AND TURNING HIS ATTENTION TO
THE CROWD) All of you. You know what to do.

LOURNA:
Bala.

BALA:
(STILL TO THE CROWD) Find anyone who is loyal to the
family.

TWI'LEK PROTESTOR 2:
Yes, Keeper.

LOURNA:
No. If they're loyal to the family, they'll be loyal to me.

BALA:
Let's get you back to your chambers.

LOURNA:
I'm not going to my chambers. We need . . . to plan. To talk
with Vardem . . .

BALA:
(STERNER) Lourna. I'm not going to argue.

LOURNA:
(REALIZING) They called you Keeper. Why would they call
you Keeper?

FX: Blaster shots fire from inside the safe room.

LOURNA: (CONT)
No!

FX: Bala grabs her.

BALA:
(STRUGGLING WITH HER) Lourna. Don't go in there. Don't go in.

The blasts have stopped. The door opens. The guards exit the room.

CAPTAIN SECARIA:
It is done.

LOURNA:
I . . . I don't understand . . .

BALA:
You should have waited until I got her away.

FX: Lourna moves to reenter the room, Bala stopping her.

LOURNA:
(CRYING OUT, STRUGGLING WITH HIM) Inun! Father! Haleena!

BALA:
Lourna, stop it. We need you to sign the declaration.

LOURNA:
The what?

CAPTAIN SECARIA:
Abdicating your right as Keeper and transferring power to Bala.

LOURNA:
No. I won't. You said we'd govern together, Bala. You said you'd be by my side.

BALA:
Maybe not such a wise head after all.

FX: A hiss of an injector against her neck.

LOURNA:
(GASPS) What are you—(GROANS)

FX: She sags in his arms.

BALA:
That's it, that's it. (HIS VOICE BECOMES ECHOEY AS THE DRUG TAKES HOLD) Nice and easy.

LOURNA:
(CLOSE TO MIC, SLURRED) What did you give me? Bala . . .

The entire soundscape becomes echoey and dreamlike as Lourna falls prey to the drug.

CAPTAIN SECARIA: (ECHOING)
She's never going to do it. You know that, don't you?

BALA: (ECHOING)
She will if she wants to live.

CAPTAIN SECARIA: (ECHOING)
What did you give her anyway?

BALA: (GETTING MORE AND MORE ECHOING)
What do you think? The finest web in all Ryloth.

LOURNA:
(SLIPPING AWAY, CLOSER EVER TO THE MIC) Kill . . . kill you . . .

CUT TO:

SCENE 70. INT. STARLIGHT BEACON. INTERVIEW ROOM.

Atmos: As before.

CHIEF TARPFEN:
Sal? (BEAT, THEN MORE FORCIBLY) Sal.

LOURNA:
Hmm? (GENUINE) I'm . . . sorry.

CHIEF TARPFEN:
Sounds to me that's a word you're not used to saying very often.

LOURNA:
No. No, it's not.

CHIEF TARPFEN:
(SOFTER. THERE'S A CONNECTION FORMING HERE)
Look. We haven't much time.

LOURNA:
More of my kin to process . . .

CHIEF TARPFEN:
Is that who they are to you? Family?

LOURNA:
The Nihil? No. I'm not sure I know what family means anymore. Do you?

CHIEF TARPFEN:
(MORE GUARDED) I've told you. This isn't about me.

LOURNA:
No. But you get it, don't you? I can see it in your eyes. You know the pain of looking back, because that's what it is . . . pain . . . it hurts, because once you start looking . . .

CHIEF TARPFEN:
You can't stop. And then you remember. Remember what was done to you.

LOURNA:
And what you did right back.

CHIEF TARPFEN:
What did you do, Sal?

LOURNA:
What I've been doing ever since . . . I ran.

CUT TO:

SCENE 71. EXT. AALOTH LANDING PAD.

Atmos: In the distance we can hear the echoey sound of a ship preparing to take off. Lourna is dreaming again, the following voices distorted.

INUN: (DISTORTED)
(SHOUTING) Lourna! Lourna, come back!

LOURNA (TEENAGE):
(CLOSE TO MIC, GRUNTS IN HER SLEEP REACTING TO HER BROTHER'S CRY)

INUN: (DISTORTED)
Lourna! Don't leave me.

LOURNA: (CLOSE TO MIC)
(IN SLEEP, WORRIED) Inun.

INUN: (DISTORTED)
No! No—

FX: Distorted blaster shots in dream.

INUN: (CONT, DISTORTED)
(SCREAMS)

Lourna wakes up, bringing the real soundscape into sharp relief.

LOURNA:
(WAKES WITH A CRY, THEN PANTING)

MEDICAL DROID:
You are awake.

LOURNA:
What?

MEDICAL DROID:
Prepare to be scanned.

FX: A clank of shackles.

LOURNA:
What is this? Where . . . where am I?

MEDICAL DROID:
Remain still.

FX: Scan commences. Shackles clatter as Lourna tries to escape.

LOURNA:
Let me out of all this.

MEDICAL DROID:
Do not move.

LOURNA:
Stop telling me what to do!

FX: Footsteps as Vardem approaches.

VARDEM:
Well, well. Look who's awake.

LOURNA:
Vardem?

FX: Scan stops.

MEDICAL DROID:
Scan complete.

VARDEM:
Results?

MEDICAL DROID:
There are traces of glitterstim in the unit's system.

VARDEM:
Hardly surprising.

LOURNA:
Glitterstim?

VARDEM:
How would you grade her?

MEDICAL DROID:
The unit is strong. Or it will be once its leg has been set.

VARDEM:
A grade two?

MEDICAL DROID:
Maybe even grade one.

VARDEM:
Excellent. Tag for the Hutt Cartel then.

MEDICAL DROID:
Understood.

LOURNA:
Tag?

FX: Lourna struggles against her chains again.

LOURNA: (CONT)
Vardem. Where's Bala?

VARDEM:
Busy. As am I.

FX: Vardem starts walking away.

LOURNA:
No, wait. My family—?

VARDEM:
(OVER SHOULDER) Don't know. Don't care.

LOURNA:
What are you going to do with me?

FX: Vardem stops. Turns.

VARDEM:
Come now. You're not *that* dim-witted, are you? I'd hate to have to downgrade you. You're surprisingly good stock, for a pampered princess.

LOURNA:
I'm not a princess.

VARDEM:
Not now you're not.

FX: Twi'leks approach.

TWI'LEK PROTESTOR 1:
The first batch is prepared, superintendent.

VARDEM:
Excellent. Get a collar on this one.

TWI'LEK PROTESTOR 1:
Yes, superintendent.

FX: Twi'leks approach Lourna. We hear a slave collar being opened.

LOURNA:
No, you're not putting that on me. I am Lourna'dee, rightful Keeper of Aaloth.

TWI'LEK PROTESTOR 1:
(SNORT) Don't think so.

MEDICAL DROID:
You are Unit 4978/7179. Do not comply and you will be sedated.

LOURNA:
No . . . No, I've had enough of that.

MEDICAL DROID:
You will comply.

LOURNA:
(QUIET) Yes.

MEDICAL DROID:
Proceed with the application of the collar.

TWI'LEK PROTESTOR 1:
Don't worry. It'll be over soon enough.

LOURNA:
For you . . . anyway.

FX: Lourna lashes out, kicking him.

LOURNA: (CONT)
(EFFORT WITH KICK)

TWI'LEK PROTESTOR 1:
(GRUNT)

TWI'LEK PROTESTOR 3:
You okay?

TWI'LEK PROTESTOR 1:
'Course I'm not. Little rycrit kicked me right in the . . .

TWI'LEK PROTESTOR 3:
All right, all right. I don't need to think about that, thank you.

LOURNA:
I'll do more than kick you . . .

TWI'LEK PROTESTOR 3:
Hold her down.

FX: Lourna struggles as she's pinned down.

LOURNA:
Get off me!

TWI'LEK PROTESTOR 1:
Nearly got. Can't . . . quite . . .

FX: The collar snaps shut followed by an electronic beep.

LOURNA:
(SCREAMING) No. No!

MEDICAL DROID:
Collar attached.

TWI'LEK PROTESTOR 1:
Let's see you get out of that. (SPITS ON HER)

LOURNA:
(REACTS)

MEDICAL DROID:
The unit must not be damaged.

LOURNA:
(SOBBING TO THE END OF THE SCENE)

TWI'LEK PROTESTOR 1:
Little spit won't hurt her.

TWI'LEK PROTESTOR 3:
Only what she deserves.

CUT TO:

SCENE 72. INT. STARLIGHT BEACON. INTERVIEW ROOM.

Atmos: As before.

FX: A comm chimes.

VELKO JAHEN: (COMMS)
Chief Tarpfen. You're needed in the Hub.

CHIEF TARPFEN:
Understood. I'll be right there, Administrator Jahen.

FX: An electronic beep as Tarpfen turns off the recording.

LOURNA:
I guess we're done.

FX: Door opens.

CHIEF TARPFEN:
Take the prisoner back to her cell.

GUARD 3:
Chief.

LOURNA:
So what's the verdict? Am I a threat to society?

CHIEF TARPFEN:
That depends on you.

FX: An electronic beep as Tarpfen adds a note to the record.

CHIEF TARPFEN: (CONT)
I've just assigned you to the *Restitution*.

LOURNA:
A prison ship?

CHIEF TARPFEN:
A correctional vessel.

LOURNA:
For how long?

CHIEF TARPFEN:
Ten years.

LOURNA:
Ten? I thought it would be longer.

CHIEF TARPFEN:
I know this might not seem like it, but this is an opportunity to turn things around.

LOURNA:
That's easy to say from your side of the desk.

CHIEF TARPFEN:
Maybe. But on the *Restitution,* you'll receive training, be taught new skills. You can start again. Rebuild your life.

LOURNA:
Why?

CHIEF TARPFEN:
You don't want to?

LOURNA:
No, I mean, why do all that? Why not just throw me in a pit and leave me to rot?

CHIEF TARPFEN:
Because that's not how the Republic works. Because everyone deserves a second chance. If they want one.

LOURNA:
And you think I deserve that?

CHIEF TARPFEN:
I don't know. But sometimes you have to take a leap of faith. And that's what you are, Sal Krost. You're my leap of faith.

MUSICAL SEGUE:

SCENE 73. INT. STARLIGHT BEACON. DETENTION BLOCK.

Atmos: As before.

FX: Door opens. Guard 3 enters with Lourna. They walk back to the cell.

TASIA:
Huh. Wasn't expecting to see you again.

LOURNA:
Been pining for me?

TASIA:
Barely able to console myself.

GUARD 3:
Enter the cell.

LOURNA:
I know the drill.

GUARD 3:
Stand back.

LOURNA:
Yes. Yes.

FX: The cell energy field activates.

LOURNA: (CONT)
There we are. All tucked up.

GUARD 3:
Funny.

FX: The guard leaves.

TASIA:
What did you tell them?

LOURNA:
Enough.

TASIA:
Enough for what.

LOURNA:
To survive.

TASIA:
(BITTER LAUGH) They're bigger fools than I thought.

LOURNA:
Don't worry. You won't have to look at me for much longer. I'm being sent to a prison ship.

TASIA:
The *Restitution*?

LOURNA:
How did you know?

TASIA:
Take a guess.

LOURNA:
You've been assigned there, too.

TASIA:
Didn't I mention it? We might even be cellmates. Imagine that. Just like the old days.

LOURNA:
Yeah. Wouldn't that be great.

TASIA:

It won't be exactly the same, of course, you and me. You're going to need someone around to look out for you. To help keep your secret. I mean, it would be terrible if someone let slip who you *really* are . . . Sal.

END OF PART TWO

PART THREE

RESTITUTION

SCENE 74. INT. SHUTTLE.

FX: The sound of a shuttle coming in to land from inside the craft. Landing gear deploying.

PILOT: (COMMS)
All prisoners, we are arriving on the *Restitution.* Prepare for landing.

TASIA:
And here we are. Our new home.

LOURNA:
Give it a rest, Tasia.

TASIA:
Why, *Sal*? Nervous?

LOURNA:
I just want to get this over with.

QUIN:
Don't we all.

TASIA:
You. Bivall. I know you, don't I?

QUIN:
I don't think so.

LOURNA:
Leave her alone.

TASIA:
(LEANING IN CONSPIRATORIALLY) You're Nihil, aren't you? You were part of our Tempest.

QUIN:
Yeah.

TASIA:
Did you hear that, Sal? This one was part of Lourna's Tempest. How about that?

FX: A thump as the shuttle lands.

PILOT: (COMMS)
And we're down. Prepare to move the prisoners.

TASIA:
(TO QUIN) What's your name?

QUIN:
Quin.

TASIA:
I'm Tas. Did you ever meet her?

QUIN:
Who?

TASIA:
Lourna.

QUIN:
No. I saw her. Twice.

TASIA:
You did?

QUIN:
Once seen . . .

TASIA:
Never forgotten.

QUIN:
That mask.

TASIA:
Terrifying.

FX: They share a laugh.

LOURNA:
The security droids are looking.

TASIA:
So? We're not doing anything wrong.

QUIN:
What's her problem?

TASIA:
Sal? She's just worried about her medical. She was injured. On
the *Dee.* Not up to scratch just yet, are you, Sal?

LOURNA:
I'm strong enough.

TASIA:
We'll see.

*FX: The hatch at the back of the shuttle opens, lowering to become a
ramp that clangs to the deck.*

SECURITY DROID:
Prisoners will stand.

LOURNA:
(SIGHS)

FX: The twenty prisoners on the shuttle stand.

SECURITY DROID:
Prisoners will disembark.

TASIA:
After you.

LOURNA:
So kind.

CUT TO:

SCENE 75. INT. THE *RESTITUTION*. HANGAR BAY—CONTINUOUS.

Atmos: The sound of the shuttle cooling, bursts of steam. The bay is large, cavernous. Echo on FX and voices. Again, the Restitution *has its own particular ambience, a specific hum that will help identify the location.*

FX: The prisoners stomp down the ramp.

FRY: (OFF MIC)
That's it. That's it. Keep moving. We haven't got all day.

TASIA:
Looks to me that we have all the time in the worlds.

WITTICK:
Enough of that. Get in line.

LOURNA:
Don't provoke them, Tasia. You don't want to draw attention to yourself.

TASIA:
And you don't get to tell me what to do anymore.

LOURNA:
I'm just looking out for you.

TASIA:
Don't make me laugh.

LOURNA:
I mean it. This is going to be harder than you think.

QUIN:
Why? You been locked up before?

LOURNA:
You could say that. A long time ago . . .

FADE INTO:

SCENE 76. EXT. SLAVE PENS. ZYGERRIA. NIGHT— LONG AGO.

Atmos: Cages in the open air. It is night, cricket-type insects chirping in the background, the odd trill of a distinctive lizard, hoot of birds. Wind blows constantly so we have a noticeable difference from the prison ship.

The pen is crowded, full of beings of all different species. We hear snoring, whistling of noses, the odd cough as most people sleep.

GAMORREAN:
(WHEEZING HEAVILY THROUGHOUT THE SCENE)

LOURNA (TEENAGE):
Hey. Gamorrean. How about you get that snout out of my face? I'm trying to sleep.

GAMORREAN:
(COUGHS WETLY)

LOURNA:
For Zar's sake.

SLAVE:
Just ignore it.

LOURNA:
Ignore it? The disgusting sow is wheezing all over me.

SLAVE:
Are you surprised, the way we're packed in here? It's a slave pen, honey, not a luxury hotel.

LOURNA:
But she stinks!

SLAVE:
You don't smell so sweet yourself. Don't worry. They'll give us a good clean when the buyers arrive. Now keep quiet.

GAMORREAN:
(COUGHS WORSE THAN BEFORE)

LOURNA:
That does it. (CALLING OUT) Hey! Zygerrian! Zygerrian, get over here.

SLAVE:
What are you doing?

FX: Footsteps as a Zygerrian guard approaches on the other side of the bars.

ZYGERRIAN:
Quiet.

LOURNA:
I don't think so.

ZYGERRIAN:
The merchandise will be quiet.

LOURNA:
I'm not merchandise.

SLAVE:
This isn't wise.

LOURNA:
I'm Lourna'dee of the—

FX: A few rapid beeps similar to the moment when Lourna's slave collar closed, leading to it crackling with energy like a Taser.

LOURNA: (CONT)
(CRIES OUT WITH PAIN)

ZYGERRIAN:
Do I have to repeat myself?

SLAVE:
(HISSED) Answer them. For your own sake.

ZYGERRIAN:
Well?

LOURNA:
(PAINED) No!

ZYGERRIAN:
Good.

FX: The energy cuts off.

LOURNA:
(GASPS, CATCHES BREATH)

ZYGERRIAN:
Better.

FX: The Zygerrian goes to walk away.

SLAVE:
That's it. Keep your head down. Don't make a fuss, ever.

LOURNA:
(CALLING OUT, STILL OUT OF BREATH) It's just that this Gamorrean . . .

FX: The Zygerrian stops.

SLAVE:
Are you *insane*?

LOURNA:
(IGNORING HER) She's sick. I mean, I think she's *really* sick.

FX: The Zygerrian walks back . . . slowly. Ominously.

ZYGERRIAN:
Is that right?

LOURNA:
(GETTING BOLDER) Something should be done about it.

ZYGERRIAN:
It will be.

FX: Beep, beep, beep and then the collar activates again, continuing to the end of the scene.

LOURNA:
(CRIES OUT)

ZYGERRIAN:
When I say be quiet, I mean be quiet. Understand?

LOURNA:
(PAINED) Yes.

FX: Zygerrian walks away.

LOURNA: (CONT)
(PAINED, CALLING OUT) I said yes. Did you hear? I said yes!

SLAVE:
They heard. And they aren't coming back. Not for a long time. Maybe next time you'll listen.

LOURNA:
(WHIMPERS)

STAY ON LOURNA FOR A MOMENT BEFORE CUTTING TO:

SCENE 77. INT. THE *RESTITUTION*. HANGAR BAY.

Atmos: As before.

There is a certain weariness to Wittick when he speaks—the sense that he's done this many, many times.

WITTICK:
Prisoners, my name is Counselor Wittick, and this is Counselor Fry.

TASIA:
(SOTTO) "Counselor." Who are they trying to kid? I know a guard when I see one.

LOURNA:
(SOTTO) Will you shut up.

TASIA:
(SOTTO) What's the matter? Don't you like a man in uniform?

QUIN:
(SOTTO) I know I do. Especially if it'll help me get by.

TASIA:
(SOTTO) I like the way you think, Quin.

WITTICK:
Settle down. Settle down! (BEAT) Okay. Welcome to the *Restitution.* You are here to make amends. To serve the good people of the Republic. Good people you have wronged.

TASIA:
(SOTTO) How many times do you think he's given this speech?

QUIN:
(SOTTO) Too many.

WITTICK:
The *Restitution* is on a never-ending journey, traveling from planet to planet, from system to system. As we travel, you will be taught new skills. Construction, engineering, agriculture, and medicine. Skills that will be put to good use wherever the Republic sends us. You will form work parties that will be sent down to the planets we visit to rebuild settlements that have been destroyed by local conflicts and external forces. You will fix equipment. You will offer aid. The work will be hard, but it will be rewarding.

TASIA:
(SOTTO) Sounds it.

WITTICK:
Prisoners will each have an account, in which three credits will be deposited every day.

QUIN:
(DERISIVE) Three credits.

WITTICK:
These credits will pay for your food in the commissary as well as other refreshments, contacting family members through the appropriate channels, and certain leisure facilities that will be made available to you.

TASIA:
(SOTTO) How much did we earn for a day in the storm? Three hundred? Three *thousand*?

LOURNA:
(SOTTO) Be quiet.

TASIA:
(SOTTO) Seriously?

LOURNA:
(SOTTO) I want to listen.

WITTICK:
There will be rules, which will be made clear to you. There will be expectations, challenges, and if you are disruptive, there will be consequences.

TASIA:
(SOTTO) I bet there will be.

FRY:
I'm sorry. Have you something to say?

TASIA:
Um. Nope. Not me. We understand perfectly, Counselor Fry. Don't we, Sal?

LOURNA:
(HISSING) Leave me out of it.

WITTICK:
I hope you do, all of you. Because until your release, this is your world now. How that will be depends on you. The system will treat you with respect if you respect the system. Yes?

FRY:
He asked a question.

ALL:
Yes, Counselor Wittick.

WITTICK:
(A HINT OF DISAPPROVAL) Yes, thank you, Fry. The droids will take you for processing, where you will be provided with your number, block, and uniform.

FRY:
Okay. Let's move.

SECURITY DROID:
Prisoners will follow.

FX: The whir of the droids' repulsors as they lead the group on. We go with the prisoners, hearing the tramp of their feet.

QUIN:
I can't do this. I won't do this.

FX: Footsteps as Quin breaks from the line and runs.

LOURNA:
Quin. Don't.

FRY:
Stop her!

SECURITY DROID:
Prisoners will remain in line. Return to the line.

QUIN:
Not likely.

FX: The hum of the security droids whirring as they surround her.

TASIA:
Will you look at that?

SECURITY DROIDS:
You are surrounded. Please remain calm. You are surrounded. Please remain calm.

QUIN:
(FRUSTRATED) Let me out.

FX: Footsteps as Wittick walks up as calmly as possible.

WITTICK:
What's your name?

QUIN:
Quin.

WITTICK:
There's nowhere to go, Quin.

QUIN:
So why don't you stun me and be done with it. That's what the stun batons are for, aren't they?

WITTICK:
They're a deterrent, but one we do not like to use.

TASIA:
(SOTTO) Fry looks like she wants to use it all right.

WITTICK:
(RAISING HIS VOICE POINTEDLY) None of us want to use it. Isn't that right, Counselor Fry?

FRY:
(NOT QUITE BELIEVABLE) That's right.

WITTICK:
(KEEPING HIS VOICE CALM) Physical punishment is always a last resort. Do you understand?

ALL PRISONERS:
Yes, Counselor Wittick.

WITTICK:
And what about you, Quin? Are you ready to rejoin the group?

QUIN:
(RELUCTANTLY) Yes.

WITTICK:
Excellent. Droids?

FX: The droids move apart so she can move.

QUIN:
(NOT FEELING IT) Thanks.

FRY:
That's it. Droids, take them on.

FX: The hum of the droids, footsteps as the group continues.

TASIA:
Are you good?

QUIN:
Yeah. Never been so humiliated.

TASIA:
I think I'd rather face a shock baton.

LOURNA:
You really wouldn't.

TASIA:
And there she goes again, the voice of experience. What's the matter, Sal? That prison you were in not a five-star establishment like this place?

LOURNA:
I never said it was a prison. (BEAT) It was far worse than that . . .

CUT TO:

SCENE 78. EXT. ZYGERRIA. SLAVE PENS—NIGHT.

Atmos: As before, the same lizard trilling to help the transistion.

GAMORREAN:
(WHEEZING MORE THAN EVER BEFORE)

LOURNA (TEENAGE):
(QUIET) I can't take much more of this.

SLAVE:
There's nothing you can do. The sooner you accept that, the better. For all of us.

LOURNA:
(CALLING OUT, BUT NOT SO FORCIBLY) Hello? Is someone there?

SLAVE:
You're going to get us *all* punished.

FX: The Zygerrian walks up.

ZYGERRIAN:
I thought I'd made myself clear.

LOURNA:
(QUICKLY) You did. And I will be quiet, I promise, but . . . if there is something wrong with this Gamorrean, if she's ill . . .

well, what if it spreads to the rest of us? We won't be worth as much if we're sick.

SLAVE:
(SOTTO) Getting sick is the least of your worries.

A tense beat as the Zygerrian considers this, the Gamorrean wheezing all the time.

ZYGERRIAN:
Hmm.

FX: A comlink is activated.

ZYGERRIAN: (CONT)
I require assistance in holding pen three. A sick Gamorrean needs to be removed.

FX: Deactivates comlink.

ZYGERRIAN: (CONT)
(TO SLAVES) Everyone move back. Do you hear?

LOURNA:
We hear you.

SLAVE:
Maybe you're not as thick as you look.

LOURNA:
I'm learning.

GAMORREAN:
(SPLUTTERS)

SLAVE:
Poor sow is probably going to be fed to a brezak.

LOURNA:
As long as it's not us. That's all that matters.

MUSICAL SEGUE:

SCENE 79. INT. THE *RESTITUTION*. K BLOCK. COMMON AREA.

Atmos: The general hubbub of a general living area in the prison ship. A door opens.

FX: Multiple footsteps as Wittick, Fry, Lourna, Tasia, and Quin enter.

WITTICK:
Welcome to K Block, your new home on the *Restitution*.

TASIA:
Delightful.

FRY:
Prisoner One-Three-Six: Quin—with me.

QUIN:
Yes, Counselor Fry.

FX: Two sets of footsteps as they move off.

WITTICK:
One-Three-Four: Krost. One-Three-Five: Tasia—this way.

LOURNA & TASIA:
Yes, Counselor Wittick.

FX: Three sets of footsteps as they walk through the common area.

WITTICK:
This is your common area where you'll spend the majority of your time when you're not working or exercising.

TASIA:
(SOTTO) Quite a few familiar faces, eh, "Sal"?

LOURNA:
(SOTTO) Tasia. I'm really tired. I don't want to—

FX: Another prisoner barges into her, an Aqualish by the name of Parr.

LOURNA: (CONT)
(OOF!)

PARR:
(GRUNTS AGGRESSIVELY IN AQUALISH)

WITTICK:
That's enough of that, Parr. Move along.

PARR:
[AQUALISH—Yes, Counselor Wittick.]

FX: Footsteps as Parr continues on her way.

FX: There's a bong that will denote an announcement throughout.

PRISON ANNOUNCEMENT: (LOUDSPEAKER)
Two minutes to lockdown. Two minutes to lockdown.

FRY: (OFF MIC)
Prisoners will return to their cells.

WITTICK:
Let's keep going.

TASIA:
She was pleasant.

WITTICK:
Hmm?

TASIA:
The Aqualish.

LOURNA:
Who's that she's talking to? The Ottegan with the beard.

WITTICK:
Ola Hest. She's been here a long time.

TASIA:
And rules the roost by the look of things.

WITTICK:
I didn't say that.

TASIA:
You didn't have to. She's got her own gravitational pull, that one, although that could be the lump of meat beside her. What *is* that?

LOURNA:
A Gloovan.

TASIA:
Are they all that slimy?

FX: Wittick stops walking.

WITTICK:
Here's your cell. Twenty-two. In you go.

FX: Another bong.

PRISON ANNOUNCEMENT: (LOUDSPEAKER)
One minute to lockdown.

CUT TO:

SCENE 80. INT. THE *RESTITUTION*. LOURNA'S CELL—CONTINUOUS.

Atmos: A much smaller room; the sound of the common room slightly muffled.

FX: Two sets of footsteps as they enter.

TASIA:
Just in time to be locked up nice and safe.

WITTICK: (FROM DOOR)
You should have everything you need for the night. Water. Bunks.

TASIA:
And a vac tube. You are spoiling us, Counselor.

WITTICK:
More furniture will be available to purchase once you've started to earn.

TASIA:
Because there's so much room.

LOURNA:
Tasia.

TASIA:
I'm just trying to keep our spirits up. That's important, isn't it, Counselor?

WITTICK:
Do you really want my advice?

TASIA:
We're hanging on your every word.

WITTICK:
You're nervous. I get that. So you're running your mouth. We see that a lot. And that's fine, as long as you keep out of trouble.

LOURNA:
Trouble like Ola Hest.

WITTICK:
You're a quick learner. Good. That's good.

FX: An alarm sounds signaling that the doors are about to close.

WITTICK: (CONT)
That's lockdown for the night. Try to get some rest. Orientation will continue tomorrow morning.

LOURNA:
Can't wait.

COMPUTER:
Cell doors: Closing.

FX: The cell door closes, shutting them in, changing the acoustics of the room, deadening the space, muffling the sound from outside.

Wild track: Prisoners shouting in their cells.

FX: The clunk of the lock.

COMPUTER: (CONT)
Cell doors: Locked.

TASIA:
Will you listen to that, Sal? Even the computer sounds happy we're here.

LOURNA:
Do you want top or bottom?

TASIA:
Hmm?

LOURNA:
The bunks.

TASIA:
Oh. Bottom.

LOURNA:
(NOT HAPPY WITH THAT BUT GOING WITH IT) Fine.

FX: She throws her clothes on the top bunk.

TASIA:
Cheer up. This isn't what you're used to, I know, but it's not all bad.

FX: The creak of the ladder as Lourna starts to climb.

LOURNA:
You've no idea what I'm used to.

TASIA:
Wittick's right, though. We'll need to watch ourselves. Especially from Hest and her two heavies. I really don't like the look of that Gloovan. Of course, when I say "we" . . .

FX: A clank as Tasia pushes Lourna against the ladder.

TASIA: (CONT)
I mean you.

LOURNA:
(GASPS) Tasia. What are you doing? Let me get onto the bed.

TASIA:
You're going nowhere until we set a few ground rules. You're gonna be the one who watches out for me, do you hear?

LOURNA:
(EFFORT) And why would I do that?

TASIA:
Because otherwise I'll let everyone out there know exactly who you are. The great Lourna Dee.

LOURNA:
(PAINED) They won't care.

TASIA:
You sure? You should have looked harder. I saw at least two of Pan Eyta's Tempest when Wittick gave us the guided tour. There might be others on other blocks. I bet they'd love to know what really happened to their Tempest Runner. How he was *betrayed*. Cast *aside*.

Saying that, I don't know of any former Nihil, from any Tempest, who wouldn't want to kill the great Lourna Dee. Imagine the bragging rights. The *prestige*.

FX: Tasia lets her go.

LOURNA:
(GASPS AND THEN CATCHES BREATH)

TASIA:
I've half a mind to do it myself.

LOURNA:
And what makes you think I won't kill you first?

TASIA:
When I'm asleep?

LOURNA:
Maybe.

TASIA:
Quin.

LOURNA:
You've told her.

TASIA:
Yeah, while we were waiting to be given our nice new uniforms. If something happens to me . . .

LOURNA:
She goes to the others.

TASIA:
And vice versa. Of course, it's not just the other prisoners. There's the Republic, too. The Jedi. Just imagine what they'll do if they find out that Lourna Dee was under their hand and they didn't realize.

LOURNA:
I get it.

TASIA:
You'll watch our backs.

LOURNA:
Yes.

TASIA:
Make sure we're safe. Especially from Hest.

LOURNA:
Yes!

TASIA:
(SMUG, IN CONTROL) I'm glad we understand each other. Now out of my way. I want to try that bunk out for size.

FX: The squeak of springs as Tasia flops into her bunk.

LOURNA:
(SOTTO) I understand you all right, Tasia. Don't you worry about that.

CUT TO:

SCENE 81. EXT. ZYGERRIA. SLAVE PENS—DAY.

Atmos: As before, but now it's day. The planet is still buzzing with life, the atmosphere hot and humid so lots of buzzing flies.

The young Lourna is being corralled with the other slaves, the pens now open.

FX: A crack of a laser whip.

ZYGERRIAN:
Get in line, slaves. Move.

SLAVE:
(WHEEZING)

LOURNA (TEENAGE):
Are you all right?

SLAVE:
Don't make a fuss. (TRIES TO HIDE A COUGH)

LOURNA:
It's what that Gamorrean had, isn't it?

SLAVE:
(WHEEZING) No. I'm fine.

ZYGERRIAN:
Faster!

FX: Another crack of the whip.

SLAVE:
(WHIMPERS)

LOURNA:
You can barely stand.

SLAVE:
I can stand just fine. You're not getting *me* fed to a brezak.

LOURNA:
You think that's what I want?

SLAVE:
As long as you survive, isn't that how it goes?

FX: Footsteps. Vardem approaches.

VARDEM:
Is the merchandise ready?

ZYGERRIAN:
Yes, Lady Kroleyic.

VARDEM:
Doesn't look like it to me. Look at the state of them. I want them ready to show as soon as we make planetfall.

ZYGERRIAN:
Yes, my lady. It will be done.

SLAVE:
(RAGGED, LABORED BREATH, CONTINUED THROUGH-OUT)

VARDEM:
What's that?

ZYGERRIAN:
My lady?

VARDEM:
Can't you hear that?

SLAVE:
(DESPERATELY TRYING NOT TO COUGH)

VARDEM:
Who is it?

SLAVE:
(WHISPERED) Please . . . don't say anything. They'll kill me.

VARDEM:
There. That woman there. The human. She looks like death.

SLAVE:
(DESPAIRING) No.

VARDEM:
What were you thinking? She could have infected the entire batch.

ZYGERRIAN:
I am sorry, my lady.

FX: The click of a blaster being raised.

VARDEM:
All of you. Step back from the human.

No one moves.

VARDEM: (CONT)
I said, step back.

FX: The throng starts to move.

SLAVE:
No. Please.

FX: She grabs Lourna's arm.

LOURNA:
Let go of my arm!

SLAVE:
Help me! You're strong. You can stand up to them.

VARDEM:
Twi'lek. You're standing in my line of sight. I don't want to have to shoot you as well.

SLAVE:
Don't leave me.

LOURNA:
I don't want to die.

FX: She pulls her arm free.

LOURNA: (CONT)
I'm sorry.

FX: Suddenly there are explosions nearby.

VARDEM:
What is that?

ZYGERRIAN:
The camp is under attack, my lady.

VARDEM:
I can tell that!

FX: Lasers fire. More explosions.

A comlink crackles on.

ZYGERRIAN 2: (COMMS)
Lady Vardem. It is the Republic!

VARDEM:
What?

ZYGERRIAN 2: (COMMS)
Multiple Jedi.

LOURNA:
This is it.

SLAVE:
What is?

LOURNA:
Our moment.

SLAVE:
What do you mean?

LOURNA:
(CALLING OUT) Everyone! Run! There are more of us than
them! They can't stop us all.

FX: Another explosion.

LOURNA: (CONT)
Especially with all this going on.

VARDEM:
Wrong on every count, Princess.

FX: Vardem fires her blaster.

CUT TO:

SCENE 82. INT. THE *RESTITUTION*. COMMISSARY.

Atmos: A mess hall. Prisoners eating. General babble of voices. Scrape of cutlery on plates. The same low hum of the ship's engines in the background.

FX: Something horrible is slopped onto a plate. Quin is working in the kitchens.

LOURNA:
(DISGUSTED) What is that?

QUIN:
Protein mash. Enjoy your meal.

LOURNA:
I'll try. Thanks, Quin.

FX: She carries on walking.

QUIN:
(CALLING AFTER HER) Don't forget to scan your credits, Sal.

LOURNA:
Of course. Thank you. (TO HERSELF) My hard-earned cash.

FX: The beep of a reader.

FX: Behind her, more protein mash is slopped onto another plate.

FX: Footsteps as she walks to a table.

LOURNA: (CONT)
Is this seat taken?

ALIEN PRISONER:
Bolla Ka Dokuna! [Go screw yourself!]

LOURNA:
I'll take that as a yes.

SESTIN: (OFF MIC)
(SPEAKING WITH MOUTH FULL) You can sit here.

LOURNA:
Thanks.

SESTIN:
Don't mention it and don't make a fuss.

FX: Lourna sits. Sestin continues to eat noisily.

LOURNA:
Friendly bunch.

SESTIN:
Not that you'd notice.

Sestin shovels more in her mouth.

LOURNA:
Are you actually enjoying that?

SESTIN:
No. But you need to keep your strength up. I'll have yours if you're not eating it.

LOURNA:
No. I'm good.

FX: Scrape of the food as she takes a bite.

LOURNA: (CONT)
(GAGGING) Ugh. No, I'm not.

SESTIN:
Disgusting, isn't it?

LOURNA:
I'd like to say I've tasted worse, but . . .

SESTIN:
No one has. (BEAT) She a friend of yours?

LOURNA:
Who?

SESTIN:
The Bivall working in the galley.

LOURNA:
Quin. Not exactly.

FX: She takes another mouthful.

LOURNA: (CONT)
I'm Sal.

SESTIN:
Sestin. Good to see another Twi'lek on the block. Where are you from?

LOURNA:
Lots of places.

SESTIN:
I get it. Ask no questions, get told no lies. (TAKES ANOTHER MOUTHFUL) You are one of them, though, aren't you? The Nee-heel?

LOURNA:
The Nihil. And yeah, I was.

SESTIN:
"Was"?

LOURNA:
I don't think they exist anymore.

SESTIN:
Probably for the best, from what I heard.

LOURNA:
You don't mind eating with me, though.

SESTIN:
Why should I? Besides, I'm a sucker for a hopeless case.

LOURNA:
And that's what I am?

SESTIN:
I mean no offense. Just like to chat. Passes the time.

LOURNA:
How long have you been here?

SESTIN:
On the *Restitution*? Three years, two months, and six days.

LOURNA:
(GOOD-HUMORED) How many hours?

SESTIN:
(LAUGHS) Before that, ten more years moving around from facility to facility.

LOURNA:
Who did you kill to get that long?

SESTIN:
Who said I did?

LOURNA:
Point taken.

FX: Sestin scrapes her plate clean.

SESTIN:
I used to work for the Guild of Compassionate Merchants on Wroona. Can you believe they actually called themselves that? Turns out they weren't so compassionate when they discovered I'd been siphoning away funds for years.

LOURNA:
Over a decade for embezzling?

SESTIN:
No. Your first instincts were right. Got caught, went on the run. The guild sent an enforcer after me and there was a blaster fight.

LOURNA:
Ah.

SESTIN:
Yeah. Turns out I'm better with a blaster than numbers. But it was only that once. That I can promise you.

LOURNA:
Why did you need the money . . . ?

SESTIN:
Gambling habit. My own fault. Needed to pay off my debts. And here I am, still doing it all those years later.

LOURNA:
But you'll be out soon enough?

SESTIN:
Counting the days, my friend. Counting the days. The thing is, I'm proof that this isn't the end of the galaxy. It's not a bad place, all things considered. I've sure as hell been in places that are worse.

LOURNA:
You and me both.

SESTIN:
You just need to keep your head down and your nose clean.

LOURNA:
Stay out of trouble.

SESTIN:
Got it in one, missy.

LOURNA:
(SLIGHT LAUGH) You remind me of someone.

SESTIN:
Who?

LOURNA:
Someone I knew a long time ago, in a place . . . well, in a place that makes the *Restitution* look like a pleasure cruiser. Food was just as bad, though.

SESTIN:
Heh.

LOURNA:
A Zygerrian slave pen.

SESTIN:
Oh. That's . . . that's tough. How did you get out?

LOURNA:
The Jedi.

SESTIN:
Glad to hear they're as good as everyone says.

LOURNA:
There was this woman, a fellow captive. I don't even know her name. We were about to be unloaded and the Jedi attacked. We took advantage. Rioted. Took the fight to the slavers.

SESTIN:
Good for you.

LOURNA:
Trouble was, the superintendent, she pegged me as the ring-leader and . . . (MAKES A BLASTER SOUND)

SESTIN:
She shot ya?

LOURNA:
She tried. But this woman . . . this other prisoner . . . she saved my life. I still remember it now. Like slow motion . . .

CUT TO:

SCENE 83. EXT. ZYGERRIA. SLAVE PENS—DAY.

Atmos: As before, but the slaves are rioting. General chaos. Shouts. Cries. Energy whips. Explosions in the background.

VARDEM: (AS BEFORE)
Wrong on every count, Princess.

FX: The blaster fires.

LOURNA (OLDER): (V.O.)
She didn't even hesitate.

SLAVE:
What are you doing? Let go of me!

LOURNA (TEENAGE):
I'm sorry.

LOURNA: (V.O.)
Just threw herself in front of me.

SLAVE:
Don't!

FX: The sound of a scuffle as Lourna pulls the slave around to block the bolt.

LOURNA: (V.O.)
Took the shot.

FX: The blaster hits the slave.

SLAVE:
(CRIES OUT)

VARDEM:
Some hero. Using one of your own as a shield.

LOURNA (TEENAGE):
She's nothing to do with me. (SCREAMS A BATTLE CRY)

LOURNA: (V.O.)
I ran at the Zygerrian, well, hobbled really. I'd broken my leg, but it was healing. I was just so angry. It was all such a waste.

FX: Sound effects to match the description below.

LOURNA: (CONT, V.O.)
I knocked the blaster out of her hand. But she was too quick for me.

FX: Vardem gets the upper hand in the fight, beating the teenage Lourna.

VARDEM:
Did you really think you could beat me, you worthless piece of—

Suddenly everything else goes quiet so one commanding voice can be heard.

OPPO RANCISIS:
Stop.

LOURNA: (V.O.)
That's when they appeared. The Jedi.

The noise of the scene resumes. The fight continuing. Laser whips. Lightsabers, Oppo Rancisis's lightsaber in particular burning nearby.

VARDEM:
No!

FX: The deep bass of the Force and the whoosh of Vardem being pulled into the air.

LOURNA: (V.O.)
The Zygerrian was pulled off me. Just flew into the air.

VARDEM:
Ah!

FX: Whump as her body hits the dirt.

VARDEM: (CONT)
(GRUNTS)

FX: Oppo Rancisis's lightsaber hums.

OPPO RANCISIS:
I suggest you stay where you are, slaver.

LOURNA (TEENAGE):
(GROANS)

FX: Footsteps run up to teenage Lourna.

DAL AZIM:
Can you stand?

LOURNA:
I . . . Yes.

DAL AZIM:
My name is Dal. That's my Master, Oppo Rancisis. We're here to help.

LOURNA: (V.O.)
All I could think about was the woman who had saved me.

LOURNA (TEENAGE):
The slaver . . . she shot my friend. Shot her dead.

DAL AZIM:
I'm so sorry. But it's going to be all right now. You're safe.

CUT TO:

SCENE 84. INT. THE *RESTITUTION.* COMMISSARY.

Atmos: As before.

SESTIN:
Sounds to me like you had a lucky escape.

LOURNA:
I vowed I'd never be locked up again.

SESTIN:
How's that going?

LOURNA:
Badly. Same as always . . .

CUT TO:

SCENE 85. EXT. ZYGERRIA. OUTSIDE THE SLAVE PENS—DAY.

Atmos: As before, but the battle has stopped.

FX: Dal and Oppo approach, the sound of the Thisspiasian slithering across the dusty ground toward the young Lourna.

DAL AZIM: (COMING UP ON MIC)
This way, Master. Here she is.

OPPO RANCISIS:
Hello there.

LOURNA (TEENAGE):
(UNSURE) Hi.

OPPO RANCISIS:
I hear that you led the revolt.

LOURNA:
I . . . I'm not sure you could call it that.

OPPO RANCISIS:
It was very brave of you, but I sense much conflict in you.

LOURNA:
My friend . . . died. My family . . .

OPPO RANCISIS:
Where are you from?

LOURNA:
Nowhere.

DAL AZIM:
Everyone is from somewhere.

OPPO RANCISIS:
Indeed they are, my Padawan. And as for you, my young friend, you're a Twi'lek. We could return you to Ryloth.

LOURNA:
No. I told you. I have nowhere to go. Nowhere at all.

OPPO RANCISIS:
You are angry.

LOURNA:
Of course I'm angry. They herded us together like rycrits. They— (HER VOICE CRACKS)

OPPO RANCISIS:
Well, perhaps we can start with that collar. It will be an interesting task for you, Dal. Can you remove it?

LOURNA:
No. It can't be removed without a key. It will shock me.

OPPO RANCISIS:
The Force is the only key a Jedi needs. Padawan?

FX: A swelling of the atmosphere, everything becoming more heightened as Dal uses the Force.

DAL:
The Force is with us.

FX: An electronic beep as the collar deactivates before it clicks open. The heightened atmosphere fades away.

DAL:
(RELIEVED) Always.

LOURNA:
Thanks.

DAL:
You're welcome. Here, let me.

FX: Slight clank as he removes it from her neck.

OPPO RANCISIS:
And now we must decide how best to help you. If Ryloth is out of the question . . .

LOURNA:
It is.

OPPO RANCISIS:
Then we must place you on a different path. Let's start with something simple. What is your name?

LOURNA:
Unit 4978/7179.

OPPO RANCISIS:
Your *real* name.

LOURNA:
It doesn't matter anymore. It's not like I can go back.

OPPO RANCISIS:
In that case, we should go *forward* . . .

CUT TO:

SCENE 86. INT. THE *RESTITUTION.* COMMISSARY.

Atmos: As before.

SESTIN:
Doesn't sound so bad to me. Sounds like he was trying to help.

LOURNA:
Doesn't mean I made it easy.

SESTIN:
You're not the first and you definitely won't be the last.

FX: There is a commotion from across the mess hall.

MUGLAN: (OFF MIC)
Where is it, newbie?

SESTIN:
Especially in here.

MUGLAN: (OFF MIC)
Where is it?

LOURNA:
What's happening?

SESTIN:
Remember what I said. Keep your head down. That's Muglan.
She's—

LOURNA:
Loyal to Ola Hest.

TASIA: (OFF MIC)
I didn't do anything.

LOURNA:
(NOT HAPPY) And unfortunately I'm loyal to Tasia, for the time being at least.

SESTIN:
What do you mean?

FX: The sound of Tasia being pushed onto a table on the other side of the room.

TASIA: (OFF MIC)
AAH! Get off me.

LOURNA:
Where are the guards?

SESTIN:
She must have got rid of them.

LOURNA:
Who? Hest?

SESTIN:
Just keep your voice down.

FX: The sound of Tasia getting punched.

TASIA: (OFF MIC)
(GRUNTS WITH THE PUNCH)

LOURNA:
(THROUGH CLENCHED TEETH) I don't believe this.

FX: Quin rushes up.

QUIN:
What are you waiting for? Do something.

SESTIN:
She can't. It isn't worth it.

QUIN:
Stay out of this, old-timer.

LOURNA:
(SIGHS)

FX: Lourna stands.

SESTIN:
Where are you going? Sit down.

LOURNA:
I can't.

CUT TO:

SCENE 87. INT. THE *RESTITUTION*. COMMISSARY. TASIA'S POV—CONTINUOUS.

FX: Muglan grabs Tasia. Slamming her against the table. Gloovans are covered in a sticky mucus so whenever Muglan moves there's a gloopy, slimy sound.

TASIA:
(CRIES OUT) Let me go!

MUGLAN:
Not until you tell me where it is.

TASIA:
Have you got sludge in your ears? (SPELLING IT OUT) I-don't-know-what-you're-talking-about.

MUGLAN:
I'll rip your head off.

OLA HEST:
Muglan, Muglan, Muglan. We need to give the poor shaakling a moment to think about the situation she finds herself in. (TO TASIA) We haven't been properly introduced yet, honey. My name is Ola Hest.

TASIA:
I know who you are.

OLA HEST:
And you . . . you don't want to get on the wrong side of Muglan. She has a habit of making good on her promises, and the last thing any of us wants to see is that beautiful fur of yours all messed up.

PARR:
(GRUNTS)

OLA HEST:
Parr, you are positively wicked.

TASIA:
What did she say?

OLA HEST:
She said at least it's already red. Your fur, I mean.

MUGLAN:
Won't show the blood.

OLA HEST:
But there's no need for any of this unpleasantness. Just tell us what you did with it, and we'll be on our way.

FX: Lourna approaches.

LOURNA:
What did she do with what, Ola?

PARR:
[AQUALISH—**** off.]

LOURNA:
I only asked a question.

OLA HEST:
And Parr told you . . . well, we all heard what Parr told you. Enough to make a spacer blush, but the meaning was clear. I'd run along to your seat if I were you.

LOURNA:
And what if I don't?

OLA HEST:
(COLDER) Then you would be making a mistake.

FX: Sestin appears behind Lourna.

SESTIN:
(HISSED IN LOURNA'S EAR) Sal. Don't do this. Walk away.

OLA HEST:
Will you look at that? The little wormheads sticking together. Isn't it adorable?

LOURNA:
What did you call us?

SESTIN:
I'm putting my neck out for you here, Sal. Listen to Hest and come back to your seat.

TASIA:
(CHOKING) They say I took their comlink, Sal.

OLA HEST:
A comlink? Who said anything about a comlink? Did Muglan mention a comlink? Did Parr? We just said that someone had been in my cell.

MUGLAN:
Someone who doesn't know how things work.

FX: Muglan puts more pressure on Tasia.

TASIA:
(CRIES OUT) You're crushing me!

OLA HEST:
That's kind of the point, honey.

LOURNA:
Let her go.

SESTIN:
(HISSED) Sal, don't.

LOURNA:
It was me.

OLA HEST:
What was?

LOURNA:
I took your comlink. And destroyed it.

OLA HEST:
And why exactly would you do that?

LOURNA:
Because you shouldn't have it. If it was discovered . . .

OLA HEST:
(HONESTLY INTRIGUED) What? What would happen then? We'd all get more counseling? Who's going to punish me, little wormhead?

FX: Lourna takes a step forward.

LOURNA:
I will unless you let her go.

OLA HEST:
Is that right? Muglan. You heard the lady. Are you going to let her go?

FX: Muglan punches Tasia.

TASIA:
(REACTS)

OLA HEST:
I guess not.

FX: Another punch.

LOURNA:
Stop it.

FX: Another punch.

TASIA:
(CRIES OUT)

LOURNA:
(IRRITATED SIGH) Fine.

FX: Lourna lunges at Muglan with a shout. They clash.

SESTIN:
For void's sake. Sound the alarm. Sound the alarm. Someone's going to get hurt.

LOURNA:
(FIGHTING) That's (PUNCH!) the general (PUNCH!) idea!

PRISONERS: (CHANT, CONTINUING BENEATH EVERY-THING)
Fight! Fight! Fight! Fight!

FX: All hell breaks loose. The sounds of the scrap. Punches. Kicks. An alarm finally sounds.

FX: Footsteps as Fry comes running.

FRY:
Hey. Hey, what's going on.

SESTIN:
Finally!

FRY:
Break it up. Break it up.

MUGLAN:
Gladly.

FX: Muglan piles in all the harder. The sounds of the fight, the cheering of the prisoners, everything intensifying.

END OF PART THREE

PART FOUR

RECRIMINATION

SCENE 88. INT. THE *RESTITUTION*. MEDBAY.

Atmos: The rhythmic beep of medical equipment above the usual hum of the engine.

FX: Footsteps approach.

WITTICK:
Krost.

LOURNA:
Counselor Wittick.

WITTICK:
This isn't the best start, is it?

LOURNA:
The fact that I got into a fight, or that I lost?

WITTICK:
The former. And that you're in sick bay as a result.

FX: The beep of a datapad.

WITTICK: (CONT)
Three fractured ribs. A broken radius. Internal bleeding. Swelling at the bottom of your spine.

LOURNA:
You should see the other gal. Oh, you can't, can you? She's back on the block, as if nothing happened.

WITTICK:
That's not true.

LOURNA:
She's been put into isolation?

WITTICK:
No. She's been reprimanded. A permanent mark on her record.

LOURNA:
Reprimanded? What next? Anger management lessons?

WITTICK:
Yes.

LOURNA:
(LAUGHS)

WITTICK:
Are you going to be trouble, Krost?

LOURNA:
Not while I'm in a medbed.

WITTICK:
Look. There's going to be an inquiry. We're going to find out exactly why no security droids were in the commissary at the time of the attack. How things escalated that quickly.

LOURNA:
Are you really telling me you don't know? All of you, so proud of your prison. Sorry. Of your "correctional vessel," with its programs and its rehabilitation. You actually believe it, don't you? All the lies about this ship. About the Republic. That it's somehow better than everywhere else. It's all a veneer, Wittick. You see that, don't you? You see that it's just fresh paint on rotten wood? Ola Hest runs this place. She has guards in her pocket and spies on every block.

WITTICK:
Spies.

LOURNA:
Tell me you're not that blind.

WITTICK:
(SINCERE) We will get to the bottom of it all.

FX: The creak of her bed as she leans back.

LOURNA:
(GIVING UP) Yes. Of course you will.

WITTICK:
I'm not here to argue, Sal. Or to reprimand, or whatever you think this is. I saw the cam footage. Saw what you did. How you stepped in when others were standing by and letting it happen. I also saw how you fought back. Muglan's a tough customer. She's strong. To come that close to taking her down.

LOURNA:
Do I get a medal?

WITTICK:
You really aren't what I expected.

LOURNA:
Sorry?

WITTICK:
For a Nihil.

LOURNA:
And what did you expect?

WITTICK:
Not someone who stands like a soldier. Who fights like a soldier.

LOURNA:
You've been watching me?

WITTICK:
You stand out. Especially when you're trying so hard to blend in.

LOURNA:
Story of my life . . .

CUT TO:

SCENE 89. EXT. CARIDA MILITARY ACADEMY— THE PAST.

Atmos: A reptavian calls out in the sky above, a wind blowing across the rocky terrain.

FX: We hear Oppo slithering across the rocks, the young Lourna walking beside him.

OPPO RANCISIS:
Well? What do you think, my young friend?

LOURNA (TEENAGE):
A military academy, Master Rancisis? That's where you've brought me?

OPPO RANCISIS:
Carida Military Academy. The finest in the Republic.

LOURNA:
You're *enrolling* me?

OPPO RANCISIS:
No. That you must do for yourself.

LOURNA:
Forgive me, Master Rancisis, but handing me over to the military doesn't seem very . . .

OPPO RANCISIS:
Jedi?

LOURNA:
Not in the slightest.

OPPO RANCISIS:
I can't see you thriving in a Temple Outpost, and while there are numerous foster systems throughout the Republic—

LOURNA:
(INTERRUPTING) I don't want another family. I can't . . .

OPPO RANCISIS:
And there it is. You don't have to be a Jedi to sense the anger in you. The frustration. And not just because of what happened with the Zygerrians. It goes deeper, far deeper, but of course you won't share what it is.

LOURNA:
There's very little to tell.

OPPO RANCISIS:
Carida is more than a military academy. Those who graduate from here do great things.

LOURNA:
In the Republic.

OPPO RANCISIS:
And beyond.

LOURNA:
By becoming a warrior?

OPPO RANCISIS:
By becoming a *peacekeeper*. A guardian. In the same way you stood up for your late friend on the Zygerrian cruiser.

The discipline you will learn here will help focus that passion that burns within you. It will help you find direction. Find purpose.

LOURNA:
But will it be the right direction?

OPPO RANCISIS:
Trust in the Force, my child. Trust in yourself.

FX: Footsteps approach, clipped and military, along the path.

CAPTAIN REESE: (COMING UP ON MIC)
Master Rancisis.

OPPO RANCISIS:
Captain Reese. It is good to see you again.

CAPTAIN REESE:
And this is our new recruit?

OPPO RANCISIS:
If she so chooses . . .

CAPTAIN REESE:
And does she have a name?

OPPO RANCISIS:
I don't know.

CAPTAIN REESE:
I'm sorry?

OPPO RANCISIS:
That she has chosen to keep to herself.

LOURNA:
She is standing right here.

CAPTAIN REESE:
Well, I'm afraid we're going to have to know what to put on the enrollment forms . . .

OPPO RANCISIS:
Yes, that is a dilemma. What to do? What to do?

LOURNA:
Inun.

OPPO RANCISIS:
What's that?

LOURNA:
It's what you can call me. My name is Inun.

MUSICAL SEGUE:

SCENE 90. EXT. CARIDA MILITARY ACADEMY. EXERCISE FIELD—A FEW DAYS LATER.

Atmos: Open air. Birds singing. Slight wind blowing.

FX: The tramp of feet. A group of cadets running up a hill. An instructor hovers after them, staying with Lourna.

Wild track: The cadets running, panting. Continues throughout.

INSTRUCTOR DROID:
Faster. Faster. What are you waiting for?

LOURNA (TEENAGE):
(RUNNING) What am I waiting for? To kick you right up the recharging por—Aah!

FX: Lourna stumbles and falls, another cadet—Lalutin—running straight toward her.

LALUTIN:
Watch out.

LOURNA:
Sorry!

FX: Lalutin charges on.

LALUTIN: (RUNNING OFF MIC)
Stupid rookie. Look where you're going.

FX: The rest of the cadets continue. The instructor droid trundles over on treads.

INSTRUCTOR DROID:
Cadet Inun. On your feet.

FX: Lourna slips as she tries to stand.

LOURNA:
Yes, sir.

FX: Footsteps again as she starts to run, unsteady at first, but then faster as the scene proceeds.

INSTRUCTOR DROID:
The rest of your squad are proceeding up the hill.

LOURNA:
(WITH GRIT) I know.

INSTRUCTOR DROID:
You should be, too.

LOURNA:
I know!

FX: All the time we hear her feet pounding the mud under the following. The droid keeps pace with her, its treads rumbling.

INSTRUCTOR DROID:
That's it. That's it.

LOURNA:
Yes, Instructor.

INSTRUCTOR DROID:
Faster.

LOURNA:
Yes, Instructor!

INSTRUCTOR DROID:
Not fast enough. Increase weight of gravity pack by twenty percent.

LOURNA:
What? No!

FX: There's an electronic whine ending in a thud. Lourna drops to her knees in the mud.

LOURNA: (CONT)
(CRIES OUT)

INSTRUCTOR DROID:
On your feet, cadet.

LOURNA:
(PANTING)

INSTRUCTOR DROID:
Unless you want to give up.

LOURNA:
No. (MORE FORCIBLY)

FX: Again she forces herself on, picking up speed, the droid hovering next to her.

LOURNA: (CONT)
(PANTING AS SHE RUNS, BUT WITH PURPOSE. SHE IS NOT GOING TO LET THIS BEAT HER)

INSTRUCTOR DROID:
Good. Good.

FX: We hear the feet of the cadets up ahead.

LOURNA:
(PANTING) No.

INSTRUCTOR DROID:
Well?

LOURNA:
(SHOUTING) Out of the way!

FX: Pounding footsteps as she powers past the other cadets.

LOURNA: (CONT)
Coming through!

LALUTIN:
Hey!

FX: Footsteps as Lourna runs ahead.

LOURNA:
(CALLING BACK) What's the matter, cadet? Never been beaten by a stupid rookie?

CUT TO:

SCENE 91. INT. THE *RESTITUTION*. MEDBAY—THE PRESENT.

Atmos: As before, but this time there is an eerie singing in the next room. The same spooky nursery rhyme sung over and over and over, muffled by the wall.

FEMALE PRISONER:
(SINGING, REPEATED)

Shrii ka rai ka rai

We're coming to take you away

They'll do what they can,

and they'll do what they must,

When they find you, all there'll be is dust.

LOURNA:
Shut up!

PRISONER:
(CONTINUES SINGING NURSERY RHYME)

LOURNA:
Shut up. Shut up. Shut up!

FX: Doors open.

SESTIN:
Sal?

LOURNA:
Sestin. What are you doing here?

SESTIN:
Got myself on the roster for sick bay. Nothing too exciting but it beats lugging equipment in the workrooms. How are you doing?

LOURNA:
I'd be doing a lot better if she'd (SHOUTS) keep it down!

SESTIN:
Ah yes. That'll be Leela from Block D. Mad as a bag of monkey-lizards, that one, but harmless enough.

LOURNA:
I'll take your word for it. The same song, Sestin . . . for two days straight. The exact same song.

SESTIN:
Ready to come back to the block?

LOURNA:
So ready.

SESTIN:
Then I have good news. I heard Wittick talking to the doc. You're heading back today.

LOURNA:
Great. (BEAT) Really. That's great.

SESTIN:
You sure about that?

LOURNA:
Wittick's made me promise that the business with Muglan is done.

SESTIN:
That's good. Because it needs to be. I hear he's been dropping by a lot.

LOURNA:
I guess I'm a person of interest.

SESTIN:
Hmm.

LOURNA:
And what does that mean?

SESTIN:
Just be careful.

LOURNA:
Of Wittick. I think he's one of the good ones. Well, as good as they get.

SESTIN:
I was thinking more of when you're back on the block. If Hest thinks that you're in bed with one of the guards, especially one who isn't in her pocket.

LOURNA:
We're not—

SESTIN:
I know. I'm just looking out for you. Us wormheads have to stick together, huh?

LOURNA:
I get it, Sestin. I know how things work. In here. Out there. Whatever the Republic says. There's always someone being stepped on and someone doing the stepping.

SESTIN:
And which were you? Out there?

LOURNA:
You'd be surprised.

CUT TO:

SCENE 92. INT. CARIDA MILITARY ACADEMY. LOURNA'S QUARTERS—NIGHT.

Atmos: A small room.

FX: A comm unit bleeps and is answered.

OPPO RANCISIS: (COMMS, BADLY DISTORTED)
Cadet.

LOURNA (TEENAGE):
Master Rancisis. It's been a while since you called.

OPPO RANCISIS: (COMMS, BADLY DISTORTED)
I'm overseeing the construction of a new Temple Outpost on Falaston. The farthest from Coruscant so far! Communications are going to be—

FX: His words are lost in static for a moment.

OPPO RANCISIS: (CONT, COMMS, BADLY DISTORTED)
—going to be more difficult.

LOURNA:
They sound pretty bad already.

OPPO RANCISIS: (COMMS, BADLY DISTORTED)
We're already on our way. The relay network . . .

FX: More static continuing until his next line.

LOURNA:
(FRUSTRATED) Great. (BEAT) Master Rancisis?

OPPO RANCISIS: (COMMS, BADLY DISTORTED)
—and your studies are going well?

LOURNA:
I guess.

OPPO RANCISIS: (COMMS, BADLY DISTORTED)
There's no need for guesswork. Captain Reese has been sending me your reports. You're excelling in just about every aspect of your training. Physical. Technical. He says you have a natural affinity for flight.

LOURNA:
Yes, but—

OPPO RANCISIS: (COMMS, BADLY DISTORTED, THE WORDS IN BRACKETS LOST IN THE STATIC)
There is only one area [that needs work, as] far as I can see. Captain Reese says there have been moments where you struggle with [how did he put it, with the] chain of command.

LOURNA:
(SIMMERING) I'm trying my best, but it's difficult.

OPPO RANCISIS: (COMMS, BADLY DISTORTED)
Life is always difficult, cadet. But you must persevere (STATIC) you must strive.

LOURNA:
Why? I'm not like you or Dal. I should never have agreed to this. I barely had a chance.

OPPO RANCISIS: (COMMS, BADLY DISTORTED, PATCHES OF STATIC AS BEFORE)
It will be difficult to communicate once I arrive [at the outpost, but know that] I will be thinking of you, willing [you to succeed as you have already succeeded].

LOURNA:
Hello?

OPPO RANCISIS: (COMMS, NOW BARELY DECIPHERABLE)
[The] Force will [be with you, cadet. Now and for always.]

FX: The line dissolves into nothing but static.

LOURNA:
Master Rancisis. Can you hear me?

FX: Lourna bangs the comm terminal, but it doesn't change the white noise. The Jedi is gone.

LOURNA: (CONT)
Hello?

Lourna loses her temper.

LOURNA: (CONT)
(ROARING IN FRUSTRATION)

FX: Lourna tries to rip the comm terminal from the wall.

LOURNA: (CONT)
What if I don't want to persevere, you slithering hairball? What if I don't want to strive? (ANOTHER PRIMAL ROAR OF ANGER)

FX: She rips the terminal from the wall and it crashes to the floor.

CAPTAIN REESE:
Cadet Inun.

LOURNA:
(SHOCKED, SPINNING AROUND) Captain Reese. I didn't see you there.

CAPTAIN REESE:
Evidently. That is academy property.

LOURNA:
I know.

CAPTAIN REESE:
Academy property that you have just destroyed.

LOURNA:
Yes, but—

CAPTAIN REESE:
Did I give you permission to speak, cadet?

LOURNA:
No, sir, but I'm trying to explain.

CAPTAIN REESE:
Fifty laps.

LOURNA:
What?

CAPTAIN REESE:
Fifty laps of the Academy Square wearing a gravity pack. And then you will rebuild that communications equipment by hand. Do I make myself clear?

LOURNA:
(NOT HAPPY) Sir.

CAPTAIN REESE:
I said, do I make myself clear?

LOURNA:
(FORCING HERSELF TO PLAY THE GAME) Sir. Yes sir.

MUSICAL SEGUE:

SCENE 93. INT. THE *RESTITUTION*. K BLOCK. COMMON AREA.

Atmos: As before.

FX: Doors open.

FRY:
In you come.

LOURNA:
Thank you, Counselor Fry.

FRY:
We'll be watching.

LOURNA:
I'm sure of it.

FX: Doors close.

LOURNA: (CONT)
Well, here we are. Back in K Block.

SESTIN:
Home sweet home, eh?

LOURNA:
Sestin. Hi.

SESTIN:
Glad to be back?

LOURNA:
Actually, it almost makes me miss Leela and her "Shrii ka rai ka rai." I'd forgotten how everyone looks at you all the time.

SESTIN:
Don't worry. We'll be making a planet drop soon. Your first work stop.

LOURNA:
Where?

SESTIN:
They never tell you. Safety precautions. We never even know what system we're in, just shuttled down and put to it.

LOURNA:
Sounds great.

SESTIN:
There's extra credits to be had. Goes up to five a day when we're planetside.

LOURNA:
Extra protein mash for me then.

SESTIN:
(LAUGHS) Wanna play pocket nuna-ball?

LOURNA:
Not really.

SESTIN:
Thank void for that. I can't stand the game.

LOURNA:
Think I'm just going to hole up in my cell. Stay out of trouble.

FX: We move with Lourna as she crosses the common room, her footsteps sounding on the deck plates.

SESTIN: (OFF MIC)
(CALLING AFTER HER) She's learning! Stars alive! A reekcat *can* change its spots.

LOURNA:
(CALLING BACK) Don't bet on it. (IMMEDIATELY RE-GRETS IT, MUTTERING TO HERSELF) Gambling problem, remember. Not the best choice of words.

FX: Footsteps as she continues walking.

SESTIN: (OFF MIC)
(CALLING AFTER HER) Remember what I said. Watch yourself.

PRISONER 1:
(MUTTERED) Look who's back.

LOURNA:
(BREATHING THROUGH HER NOSE, TRYING TO KEEP CALM)

PRISONER 2:
(MUTTERED) Heard she was one of Dee's. You ever saw her at the Great Hall?

PRISONER 1:
Nah. Not me. Stuck-up schutta.

LOURNA:
(TO HERSELF) Ignore them. Just ignore them.

FX: Muglan lurches in front of her, the sound of the slime on her massive bulk disgusting to hear.

MUGLAN:
Talking to yourself, Twi'lek?

LOURNA:
I don't want any trouble, Muglan.

MUGLAN:
Should've thought about that before you messed with Ola's stuff.

OLA HEST:
Now, now, Muglan. That's all forgiven and forgotten. Sal's learned her lesson, haven't you, little wormhead.

LOURNA:
Don't call me that.

MUGLAN:
What did you say?

OLA HEST:
No. She's right. It was disrespectful of me, and I *hate* being disrespectful. Good to have you back, honey. I hope we can be pals.

LOURNA:
Sure, Hest. Whatever you say.

CUT TO:

SCENE 94. INT. THE *RESTITUTION*. LOURNA'S CELL—CONTINUOUS.

FX: Cards snap down onto a table.

TASIA:
And that, my friends, is a Dead Man's Hand. Again.

QUIN:
I don't believe it. You're cheating, Tasia.

FX: The insectoid they're playing chitters in annoyance.

TASIA:
(MOCK INSULT) Quin. How could you say that. I never cheat.

FX: A deck plate creaks at the door.

LOURNA:
That so?

TASIA:
Sal. You're back.

LOURNA:
Looks like it. Didn't want to interrupt your game.

TASIA:
Reckon Quin and Rekanaktric are pleased of it. Aren't you, girls?

FX: More sullen chirping from the insectoid.

TASIA: (CONT)
I have not got cards hidden up my sleeves! The very thought!

FX: Angry chirping. The insectoid throws down her hand and storms out of the room.

TASIA: (CONT)
Yes, that's it, Rek. Scuttle off. (TO QUIN) Sore loser, eh, Quin?

QUIN:
I don't blame her.

TASIA:
It's not like we're playing with real credits.

FX: Tasia starts gathering the cards.

TASIA: (CONT)
Deal you in, Sal?

LOURNA:
No thanks. I just want to talk.

TASIA:
And I want to play.

FX: She starts dealing the cards out again, continuing under the following conversation.

LOURNA:
Not smart. The two of you being here. With me.

TASIA:
Don't know what you mean.

LOURNA:
Your little insurance policy. I could kill you both now.

TASIA:
(SCOFFS) The state you're in? I doubt it.

LOURNA:
Just tell me one thing. Did you take it?

TASIA:
Did I take what?

LOURNA:
The comlink. From Hest's cell.

TASIA:
Not me.

LOURNA:
Then why did she think it was you?

TASIA:
You know how it is, Lourna. People make mistakes.

LOURNA:
Sal. The name is Sal.

TASIA:
See. I rest my case.

FX: She flips down a card.

TASIA: (CONT)
Look, you did your job. Hest believes you, and I think she actually respects you for standing up against that Gloovan. You did us all a favor. I would've come to see you in sick bay, but couldn't get a pass.

LOURNA:
You're telling me your new friend Hest couldn't help.

QUIN:
You can talk.

LOURNA:
What does that mean?

TASIA:
You think no one's heard. How handsome Counselor Wittick kept popping in to see you while you recovered. I wondered how long it would be before someone got their teeth into him. Never thought it would've been you.

FX: There's banging outside: Counselor Fry banging her (inactive) stun baton against the cell doors.

FRY:
Everyone out of their cells. Counselor Wittick wants you in the common area now.

TASIA:
Speak of the Sith. Did you hear that, Quin? Counselor Wittick wants us in the common area.

QUIN:
Wants Sal more like.

LOURNA:
You're pathetic. Both of you.

TASIA:
Yep, you run along, Sal. (CALLS AFTER HER) Mustn't keep lover boy waiting!

Quin and Tasia laugh.

CUT TO:

SCENE 95. INT. THE *RESTITUTION*. COMMON AREA—CONTINUOUS.

Atmos: The hubbub of the collected prisoners gathered together.

WITTICK:
Okay. Everyone settle down. (RAISING HIS VOICE SLIGHTLY) Settle down.

FX: The babble subsides.

WITTICK: (CONT)
Thank you. Now, the *Restitution* is about to make its next stop. Many of you are new here and so won't know the procedure. Counselor Fry?

FX: A hologram activates.

FRY:
This is our destination, a small planet largely covered in woodland. The main settlement recently became the target of a pirate raid, most of the buildings burned to the ground.

TASIA:
(SOTTO) Sounds like our kind of people.

QUIN:
(SNIGGERS)

FRY:

Teams will be sent to the surface to help with the relief efforts. The Republic has provided several prefabricated shelters. Three parties will construct the buildings while the rest will help clear what remains of the town and local logging station.

TASIA:

Why not send in droids?

WITTICK:

Droids are expensive, Tasia, and often break down. Whereas a workforce dedicated to repaying their debt to society will get the job done in half the time.

QUIN:

(SOTTO) That told you.

FRY:

The rules are simple. You will listen to staff. You will do the work. There will be no interaction with the local population other than those individuals already cleared by the *Restitution*.

TASIA:

What about the equipment?

WITTICK:

All power rigs and tools are already loaded in the shuttles. Everyone should've received the appropriate training on how to use them by now.

QUIN:

Not everyone, Counselor Wittick.

WITTICK:

I'm sorry?

TASIA:

Our friend Sal has been in the sick bay. Unless she's not coming down to the surface with us.

WITTICK:

Work parties have yet to be assigned.

TASIA:
And you'll be seeing to her personally? Making sure she's up to speed.

PRISONERS:
(GENERAL SNIGGERING)

WITTICK:
That is enough for now. Teams will be announced first thing tomorrow. Everyone back to their cells.

OLA HEST:
But lockdown isn't for another hour?

WITTICK:
I mean everyone.

FX: General groaning from the crowd.

LOURNA:
Nice work, Tasia.

TASIA:
Nothing to do with me.

OLA HEST:
You need to get your man under control, hon.

LOURNA:
He's not—

MUGLAN:
I'd keep walking if I were you.

FX: Footsteps as Ola Hest and her goons stalk off.

SESTIN:
I told you to be careful.

LOURNA:
He's not my anything.

TASIA:
Why don't you tell him that?

WITTICK:
A word please, Krost.

LOURNA:
(SIGH) Yes, Counselor Wittick.

FX: They move to the side.

WITTICK:
(SOTTO) I don't know what you've been saying.

LOURNA:
Nothing. There's nothing to say.

WITTICK:
Exactly. And we need to make sure we keep it that way. I want to help you, Sal, but rumors have a way of turning nasty around here. For everyone.

LOURNA:
But, Wittick—

WITTICK:
But nothing. Do you understand?

FX: He strides off.

LOURNA:
They're all the same. Every last one of them. Put them in a uniform and they think they can do what they want . . .

CUT TO:

SCENE 96. INT. CARIDA MILITARY ACADEMY. SHIP HANGAR—DAY.

Atmos: A busy hangar, the cadets learning how to maintain ships. Tools clanging. Droids chirping. We can hear someone using a servodriver, a form of wrench, in the foreground.

FX: Clipped footsteps as Captain Reese walks among his cadets.

CAPTAIN REESE:
That's it, cadets. You're doing well. Remember, a good officer knows every millimeter of their vessels. Every nut and every bolt. That is why exercises like this are so important. You must be able to repair and maintain your ships.

WILSON:
(WHISPERED) I thought that's what mechanics are for?

LALUTIN:
(WHISPERED) Tell me about it. We shouldn't be doing this crud. Not like that Twi'lek. There's a gearhead if I ever saw one.

They both snigger, stifling their merriment as Reese suddenly stops near them.

CAPTAIN REESE:
Cadet Lalutin. Is there something you wish to share with the rest of the squad?

LALUTIN:
No, sir.

CAPTAIN REESE:
I'm glad to hear it. What about you, Wilson?

WILSON:
Nothing, sir. We were just . . .

CAPTAIN REESE:
You were just what?

LALUTIN:
Discussing the starfighter's . . . um . . .

WILSON:
(QUICKLY) Field stabilizers.

LALUTIN:
Yeah. That's it. The field stabilizers.

CAPTAIN REESE:
Well, maybe if you concentrated on the matter at hand . . .

LALUTIN:
Yes, sir.

WILSON:
Of course, sir.

FX: Reese continues walking. We stay with him.

CAPTAIN REESE:
Listen to your training droid. I want these ships ready to fly within the hour. Within the hour.

LOURNA (TEENAGE):
(TO HERSELF) Why? It's not like we're going anywhere.

TRAINING DROID:
Cadet Inun. Warning. Bolts are still loose.

LOURNA:
Yes, I know. Keep it down, will you?

FX: A squeak as she tightens the bolt, which continues beneath the following.

LOURNA: (CONT)
(WITH EFFORT AS SHE TIGHTENS THE BOLT) The last
thing I need is anyone else on my back.

TRAINING DROID:
My only purpose is to facilitate learning.

LOURNA:
Yeah, yeah.

FX: We hear the clank of tools being rifled through across the bay.

LALUTIN: (OFF MIC)
Hey, Wilson. You got a servodriver?

LOURNA:
(SOTTO) Why don't you look in your mouth? It's big enough.

WILSON: (OFF MIC)
Not me. What about Inun?

LOURNA:
(SOTTO) Please don't come over. Please don't come over.

FX: Lalutin approaches.

LALUTIN: (COMING UP ON MIC)
Cadet Inun.

LOURNA:
(SOTTO, TRYING TO IGNORE HIM) He came over.

LALUTIN:
What's that?

LOURNA:
(STILL WITH EFFORT AS SHE CONTINUES TO
TIGHTEN THE BOLT) Nothing. What do you want, Lalu-
tin?

LALUTIN:
Your servodriver.

LOURNA:
I'm *using* my servodriver.

LALUTIN:
Yeah, and now I need it.

LOURNA:
Tough.

LALUTIN:
Cadet. Give me the driver.

FX: Lourna jumps up, her anger getting the best of her.

LOURNA:
How much?

LALUTIN:
What?

LOURNA:
How much do you want it?

LALUTIN:
Are you threatening me?

LOURNA:
What if I am?

WILSON:
(WALKING UP) Then you're in serious trouble.

LOURNA:
Stay out of this, Wilson.

WILSON:
I'm afraid I can't do that. You're a first-year cadet. When a first-year like you is asked for something by a senior like Lalutin, your response is, "Yes, sir. Here you are, sir. Is there anything else I can do for you, sir?"

LOURNA:
You can't pull rank. Neither of you. You're no better than me.

LALUTIN:
And that's where you're wrong.

LOURNA:
Really? Looked at the assessment scores lately? Because I have.

LALUTIN:
Hand it over.

WILSON:
Or we report you to Captain Reese.

LALUTIN:
For insubordination.

LOURNA:
(LAUGHS) Can you hear yourselves? Playing soldiers.

WILSON:
No one's playing, cadet. Carida is—

LOURNA:
Carida is a sham. And so are you. You flounce around, pretending that you're going to change the galaxy, when the truth is that you're going to end up in a pointless administrator's office pushing pointless files around a pointless computer.

And that's if you're lucky.

WILSON:
And what happens if we're not lucky?

LOURNA:
Oh, that's the killer. If you're not lucky you'll be back here, squeezed into a uniform that never used to be so tight and teaching the next generation of deluded, self-important gasbags who are fool enough to walk through those doors.

LALUTIN:
(SEETHING) Give me the servodriver, Inun.

LOURNA:
Fine. Do you know what? Take it. I don't care anymore.

FX: The rustle of a uniform as she holds it out.

LOURNA: (CONT)
Go on then. What are you waiting for?

LALUTIN:
It's covered in engine juice.

LOURNA:
You surprise me.

LALUTIN:
Clean it.

LOURNA:
What?

LALUTIN:
On your uniform.

LOURNA:
You have got to be kidding me.

FX: Footsteps of them taking a step closer to each other.

LALUTIN:
Clean it. Now.

LOURNA:
(TAKES A BREATH, THEN TO HERSELF) To hell with this.

*FX: Thwack. Lourna brains Lalutin with the servodriver. The Selkath
goes down.*

LALUTIN:
(GRUNT)

WILSON:
Lalutin!

LOURNA:
Whoops! It's got more than grease on it now.

WILSON:
(CALLING OUT) Someone get a medic over here! Lal? Lalutin? Stars! He's not breathing.

LOURNA:
Sounds like my cue to leave. Here, Lal. Don't forget your servodriver.

FX: It clatters to the ground.

WILSON:
You little—

FX: He throws himself at Lourna and they fight.

FX: Footsteps as Captain Reese comes running back up.

CAPTAIN REESE:
(RUNNING) What in the Core's name is going on here. Wilson! Inun! Stand down!

LOURNA:
(WITH EFFORT AS THEY FIGHT) That's not my name.

FX: She smacks Wilson hard.

WILSON:
(GRUNTS)

LOURNA:
It was *never* my name. He was better than me. And would never have done this!

FX: Lourna climbs up the starfighter ladder. We stay with her.

CAPTAIN REESE:
Inun! Get down from that fighter.

LOURNA:
With all due respect, Captain . . . you can get spaced.

FX: She swings herself into the cockpit, the seat squeaking.

WILSON: (OFF MIC)
(BREATHLESS) Captain. Lalutin needs help. She . . . she's killed him.

FX: Beeps as Lourna primes the engines. The whir of the starfighter coming online.

LOURNA:
(SHOUTING) You'll all need help if you don't stand back. Those thrusters are about to get really hot.

CAPTAIN REESE:
(SHOUTING UP AT HER) Get out of that cockpit.

LOURNA:
Sorry, can't hear you. The canopy's coming down. Look how smoothly it's going. I did well there. Master Rancisis would be over the moons.

FX: The whine of the canopy coming down, followed by a hiss. The atmosphere changes to the enclosed space of a cockpit.

LOURNA: (CONT)
And sealed. Now let's turn up the heat, shall we?

FX: More beeps from the controls. The engines fire.

FX: A comlink opens.

CAPTAIN REESE: (COMMS)
Cadet Inun. You will power down that fighter and surrender yourself for disciplinary action immediately.

LOURNA:
Maybe Cadet Inun would do that.

FX: Sudden roar of the engines.

LOURNA: (CONT)
But Lourna Dee definitely wouldn't. (WHOOPS AS SHE TAKES OFF)

FX: Wheels against the deck. The thunder of the engine roaring.

CUT TO:

SCENE 97. INT. CARIDA MILITARY ACADEMY. SHIP HANGAR—CONTINUOUS.

FX: We cut to the same sound outside the fighter, the noise unbelievably loud.

CAPTAIN REESE:
(YELLING INTO COMLINK) Inun!

FX: The fighter takes off.

CAPTAIN REESE: (CONT)
All cadets to their ships!

WILSON:
Why?

CAPTAIN REESE:
What do you think? We need to get after her.

WILSON:
But what about Lal?

CAPTAIN REESE:
The medical droids will look after him.

FX: Reese climbs up a ladder.

CAPTAIN REESE: (CONT)
Just tell me you finished priming my fighter.

WILSON:
(SHOUTING UP AT HIM) Sir, wait—

CAPTAIN REESE:
She won't get far. Not without a hyperdrive.

FX: The whine of the canopy coming down as before, followed by the hiss and the shift in atmos to the enclosed cockpit.

WILSON: (MUFFLED, OUTSIDE)
Captain Reese. You don't understand.

CAPTAIN REESE:
Let's go!

FX: Captain Reese fires the engine as we heard Lourna doing earlier, but this time the engine splutters.

CAPTAIN REESE: (CONT)
What's happening?

FX: Comlink opens.

LOURNA (TEENAGE): (COMMS)
Having problems, Captain?

CAPTAIN REESE:
Cadet?

LOURNA: (COMMS)
If I was skilled in starfighter maintenance—and of course, I am—I'd say that the safety protocols have prevented your launch.

CAPTAIN REESE:
Safety protocols can be overridden.

LOURNA: (COMMS)
Not when your fuel injectors are loose. I'd recommend the use of a servodriver if you can find one.

CAPTAIN REESE:
(CRYING OUT IN FRUSTRATION) *INUN!*

CUT TO:

SCENE 98. EXT. SPACE.

Atmos: A starfighter flies by.

CUT TO:

SCENE 99. INT. LOURNA'S STARFIGHTER.

Atmos: Inside the cockpit, the engine muffled. Lourna is pressing buttons in a flurry.

LOURNA (TEENAGE):
Oh, I enjoyed that.

FX: The comm activates.

OFFICER: (COMMS)
This is Carida Control. Your vessel has been taken without authorization.

LOURNA:
You don't say.

OFFICER: (COMMS)
As per academy regulations, the engine will now shut down and a recovery beacon be activated.

LOURNA:
No it won't.

FX: She presses one final button. We get a small electronic sound of a system shutting down.

LOURNA: (CONT)
That's your override overridden. Please send my compliments to your training staff, Carida. I couldn't have done any of this without you.

OFFICER: (COMMS)
Return that fighter immed—

FX: A beep as Lourna kills the channel.

LOURNA:
Bye. (BLOWS OUT, HER ADRENALINE STILL SURGING)

We stay with Lourna for a moment as she continues to fly.

LOURNA: (CONT)
Looks like it's just you and me now, fighter. The question is, where do we go? Home? What's the point. And there's no point chasing after Master Rancisis. He'd only send me to another Carida on another planet. (IMPERSONATING THE JEDI MASTER) "You must continue to strive, cadet." And you, Curlylocks, can go stick your tail in a sarlacc.

FX: More beeps from the computer as she lays in a new course.

LOURNA: (CONT)
Guess I'm just going to have to make it up as I go along. (SHOUTING) Do you hear that, universe? No one is ever going to tell me what to do again! No one!

MUSICAL SEGUE:

SCENE 100. EXT. ARBRA—DAY—THE PRESENT.

Atmos: A pleasant forest world. We would be able to hear the birds singing (and the indigenous mammals making a yi-yi sound) if it weren't for the sound of a shuttle landing.

FX: The ramp lowers.

SECURITY DROID:
Prisoners will disembark.

FX: The prisoners' boots clang on the metal as they walk down the ramp. The engines finally cut off and we hear the sounds of the forest.

SESTIN:
(BREATHING IN) Will you just smell that air?

LOURNA:
(NOT HAPPY) Yeah. It's great, Sestin.

SESTIN:
Now sound like you mean it, Sal. I live for these moments.

TASIA:
Being forced to work?

SESTIN:
Getting off the *Restitution*. Hearing birds in the trees—

FX: More yi-yis in the undergrowth.

SESTIN: (CONT)
And whatever those things are. You'll learn to appreciate the drop points, too.

LOURNA:
And the hard labor? Will I learn to love that, too?

FX: Footsteps as Ola Hest walks down behind them.

OLA HEST:
Sestin's right. You've got to take what you can get in this life.

LOURNA:
And you'd know all about that, wouldn't you, Hest?

SESTIN:
She's joking. Aren't you, Sal?

LOURNA:
Yeah. I'm laughing it right up.

FX: They're off the ramp now, onto a forest pathway.

OLA HEST:
Ah sweet Sestin. Our resident peacekeeper. What are you gonna do, hon?

SESTIN:
Hmm?

OLA HEST:
When you're released? When you're back out there in the stars without a security droid looking over your shoulder?

SESTIN:
Breathe a sigh of relief . . . that I don't have to look after this one anymore.

LOURNA:
Nice.

OLA HEST:
(LAUGHS) I sure am going to miss you, Sest. Come on, girls.

FX: Footsteps as they barge by, knocking into Lourna.

PARR:
(GRUNTS)

LOURNA:
No please. Don't mind me.

FX: Footsteps as they continue on, carrying on beneath the following.

LOURNA: (CONT)
Why are *they* in such a hurry?

SESTIN:
Best not to ask.

LOURNA:
She had a point, though. Hest. What *are* you gonna do?

SESTIN:
When I get out? See my kids. If they want to see me.

LOURNA:
You have children?

SESTIN:
Two boys. Here.

FX: She pulls a small holoprojector out of her pocket, the fabric rustling. There's an electronic beep, and a small holo projects.

SESTIN: (CONT)
That's them. Silus and Ita.

LOURNA:
Cute holo.

SESTIN:
They'll be all grown up now, of course, but . . . oh, the hug I'm going to give them. They'll need a tractor beam to break free.

FX: Another beep and the holo cuts off.

SECURITY DROIDS:
Prisoners will form three lines.

FX: Footsteps as they follow the order.

SESTIN:
Yeah, yeah. We know the drill.

TASIA:
There you are, Sal. What kept you?

LOURNA:
The thought of seeing your face when I got here, Tasia.

SESTIN:
See. You can crack a joke.

LOURNA:
I prefer to crack heads.

SESTIN:
You're never going to change, are you?

LOURNA:
Not if I can help it.

WITTICK:
Okay, listen up, Work Party Three. We are scheduled to be here for five days. Nights will be spent back on the *Restitution;* the rest of the time you'll be here, rebuilding the damage done in the raids.

TASIA:
(WHISPERED) Not just any raid. See those?

LOURNA:
(WHISPERED) They're hard to miss.

SESTIN:
(WHISPERED) What're you looking at?

TASIA:
(WHISPERED) The slashes on that trunk over there.

SESTIN:
(WHISPERED) Claw marks?

TASIA:
(WHISPERED) Lightning bolts.

LOURNA:
(WHISPERED) This was the Nihil.

TASIA:
(WHISPERED) Ride the storm.

LOURNA:
(SHUSHES HER)

FRY:
Your arm rings will register your location, and if you even think about running . . . anyone want to fill in the rest? Tasia?

TASIA:
They'll zap us so hard we won't be able to run anywhere for weeks.

WITTICK:
(SOUNDING WEARY) You'll be *temporarily* incapacitated. But I hope we won't need to use them. We've had seven stops without an incident. Let's keep the streak going. Work hard and there will be bonuses for all. Extra credits for the commissary.

LOURNA:
(SOTTO, SARCASTIC) All hail the Republic.

TASIA:
(SOTTO, SARCASTIC) The wise and generous Republic.

WITTICK:
We will now hand you over to the local Republic emissary for your full briefing.

FX: Footsteps approach.

LOURNA:
(SOTTO) Oh no.

SESTIN:
(SOTTO) What is it?

WITTICK:
Administrator Lalutin.

LALUTIN:
Welcome, Counselor Winnick.

WITTICK:
It's Wittick actually.

LALUTIN:
(DISMISSIVE) Yes, yes, of course.

LOURNA:
(WHISPERED) Someone somewhere *really* doesn't like me.

LALUTIN:
Prisoners. I don't have to tell you that your work here is of vital importance. The settlers on this world have had their lives turned upside down by scum. By degenerates. The very dregs of the Outer Rim.

TASIA:
(SOTTO) What do you reckon he'd say if he knew some of those "dregs" were standing right in front of him?

LOURNA:
(SOTTO) Oh, he knows. He's enjoying this.

LALUTIN:
Do I like having to rely on you people to put things right?

WITTICK:
Administrator, I'm not sure that is helpful.

LALUTIN:
(IGNORING HIM) No. No I don't.

OLA HEST:
(SOTTO) The feeling's mutual, honey.

LALUTIN:
But Chancellor Soh insists that the prisoner rehabilitation program is the first in a long list of reforms to the Republic's carceral system. That it demonstrates beyond doubt that we are all one Republic.

WITTICK:
Administrator—

LALUTIN:
I am talking, Counselor Winnick. I need our friends here to know that I will be watching all of them closely. The settlers of Arbra have suffered enough. They neither desire nor deserve any more heartache. Do I make myself clear?

WITTICK:
I can guarantee there will be no trouble. Our people know what they're doing.

LALUTIN:
Hmm. (TO THE GROUP) This way, all of you.

FX: Footsteps as he walks off.

WITTICK:
(NOT HAPPY) You heard the administrator. Let's go.

FX: Footsteps as they traipse after him.

TASIA:
(SOTTO) He's fun.

OLA HEST:
(SOTTO) Not to mention stupid. So, we're on Arbra. Anyone know where that is?

SESTIN:
(SOTTO) Don't get any ideas, Hest.

OLA HEST:
(SOTTO) Wouldn't dream of it, Sestin.

LOURNA:
(SOTTO) Knew I should've hit him harder.

SESTIN:
(SOTTO) Who? The Selkath. You know him?

LOURNA:
(SOTTO) Knew him. Long time ago, back at the . . . (CATCH-ING HERSELF) Well, let's just say I thought he was long gone.

TASIA:
(SOTTO) More unfinished business, Sal? It's getting to be a habit with you, isn't it?

LOURNA:
(SOTTO) Tasia?

TASIA:
Yeah?

LOURNA:
Go run into a tree.

MUSICAL SEGUE:

SCENE 101. EXT. ARBRA. OLD LOGGING STATION—LATER.

Atmos: Similar to before. Gentle breeze in the trees. Birdsong. The yi-yi of the alien mammals.

Lourna is clearing debris using a load lifter. We hear metal creaking as she tries to shift it.

LOURNA:
(EFFORT. SNARLING THROUGH GRITTED TEETH)

SESTIN:
You good, Sal?

LOURNA:
(STILL WITH EFFORT) No. This damn lifter. Clear the old logging station, they say. Bonuses for all, they say. And with what? Is this really the best equipment they can—[provide?]

FX: There's a crash as the metal structure slips from her lifter's arms.

LOURNA: (CONT)
For void's sake.

SESTIN:
Hey. Easy now. Easy.

LOURNA:
Don't tell me to take it easy!

SESTIN:
(STERN) I'm trying to help.

LOURNA:
(FORCING HERSELF TO BREATHE) I know. I . . . I know.

SESTIN:
You need to be careful. You're going to hurt yourself if you carry on like that, load lifter or no.

FX: The hiss of the powerlifter's arms, accompanied by a worrying metallic creak.

LOURNA:
You call this a load lifter? Piece of druk.

FX: Another whine as she swings an arm around.

SESTIN:
We work with the tools we're given.

LOURNA:
Yeah, well some of us are given better tools. Did you see the power rigs Hest and her cronies were handed?

SESTIN:
Hest is a special case.

LOURNA:
Why? What *makes* her so damn special?

FX: They continue working throughout the following, Lourna in her load lifter, Sestin on foot. We hear clangs and shifting metal beneath the dialogue, the characters displaying effort from time to time as if they're lifting heavy weights.

SESTIN:
Do you know what Hest did? Why she's here?

LOURNA:
No. Should I?

SESTIN:
Ola Hest has killed more people than most of us have even met.

LOURNA:
Am I supposed to be impressed?

SESTIN:
No, you're supposed to stay out of her way. She's dangerous.

LOURNA:
Well, maybe I am, too.

SESTIN:
Come on. I admit, I don't get you, Sal. Perhaps I never will. But you're no murderer.

LOURNA:
Ha! Shows what you know.

SESTIN:
Maybe. Maybe not. But I do know that Ola Hest spent the best part of thirty years working as an enforcer for the Hutts. Do you know how they finally got her? The Reps?

LOURNA:
No.

SESTIN:
The Hutts sent her to collect protection money from a children's medcenter on Novor. The Sisters of the Ninth Plane, who were running the place, well, they wouldn't pay up. Told her to leave. She left all right, but not before she turned her frigate's thrusters on the sanctuary. Brought the walls down on them. The Sisters. The young ones. No one survived.

She claims it was an accident, but she knew what she was doing. She wanted everyone to know. They say a Jedi tracked her down, dragged her kicking and screaming from the halls of Gardulla's Palace. The Blade of Bardotta. You heard of him?

LOURNA:
Yeah. Yeah, I have, as it happens.

SESTIN:
That's why you treat Ola Hest with kid gloves. Why you don't antagonize her.

LOURNA:
Because she might drop a building on you? People have tried worse.

SESTIN:
Like that guy back there?

LOURNA:
Lalutin? In his dreams.

SESTIN:
So what did he do to you?

LOURNA:
It doesn't matter.

SESTIN:
What did you do to him then?

LOURNA:
Doesn't matter.

FX: Sestin throws a lump of metal down on the ground in frustration.

SESTIN:
For pity's sake, it's like trying to get blood from a Vintian with you. Why won't you talk to me?

LOURNA:
Why do you care?

SESTIN:
Because I'm not stupid. I can see when someone's hurting. When they're throwing up walls.

FX: Lourna is doing her best to ignore Sestin, using the lifter to shift wreckage, metal beams creaking as she tries to move them.

She continues working underneath the following dialogue, becoming more and more angry and frustrated.

LOURNA:
(WITH EFFORT AS SHE WORKS) The only reason I'm hurting is because this damn lifter isn't working.

SESTIN:
Yeah, that's bantha crap. Like most of what comes out of your mouth.

LOURNA:
Then why do you talk to me?

SESTIN:
Because if I don't, who else will? Or is that the point? Is that what you're doing? Alienating anyone who comes close. Anyone who can help.

LOURNA:
(ANGRY) I don't want anyone's help!

FX: Sudden screech of metal as the wreckage she's trying to move collapses.

LOURNA: (CONT)
Kriff!

SESTIN:
Sal!

FX: It crashes down on her, pinning her to the ground.

LOURNA:
(CRIES OUT)

SESTIN:
Stars' end!

LOURNA:
Get it off me. Get it off.

SESTIN:
Don't panic.

LOURNA:
Don't panic?

SESTIN:
I'll get help.

FX: Sestin opens a comlink.

SESTIN: (CONT)
Counselor Wittick? Administrator Lalutin?

LOURNA:
Not him.

SESTIN:
Beggars can't be choosers. (TO COMM) Counselor Wittick. Come in please?

FX: The metal creaks as Lourna tries to move it.

LOURNA:
It won't budge.

SESTIN:
Sal, don't. You'll—

FX: The wreckage collapses even more.

LOURNA:
(THROUGH GRITTED TEETH) Get myself in even worse trouble! Too late!

SESTIN:
Hello? Hello? Somebody please respond. There's been an accident at the old logging station. Sal is trapped. We need help.

FX: More static.

SESTIN: (CONT)
Why don't they answer?

LOURNA:
Maybe they can't hear . . . interference from the forest? Metal deposits in the trees?

SESTIN:
Is that even a thing?

LOURNA:
I don't know. Just help me.

SESTIN:
Yes. Okay. Um . . .

FX: She grabs hold of some of the metal.

LOURNA:
What are you doing?

SESTIN:
What you asked! (BRACING HERSELF) Push when I push, yeah?

LOURNA:
Yeah.

SESTIN:
On three.

LOURNA:
No time for that! Push now!

FX: Lourna's powerlifter arms creak, as does the metal trapping her, but the wreckage won't budge.

BOTH:
(EXTREME EFFORT)

LOURNA:
Keep going.

SESTIN:
I can't . . . it's too . . . heavy.

FX: They stop, the metal settling again.

LOURNA:
We need to try again.

SESTIN:
It's not stable enough. The entire thing will slide if we're not careful.

LOURNA:
I don't care.

SESTIN:
Well, I have no urge to see you decapitated, no matter how much of a pain in the ass you are.

LOURNA:
Only because I'd come back and haunt you.

SESTIN:
I believe you. Stay there.

FX: She scrabbles away.

LOURNA:
Is that supposed to be funny? (CALLING AFTER HER) Where are you going?

SESTIN:
(CALLING BACK) To fetch the others.

LOURNA:
Hurry!

Sestin is already gone.

LOURNA: (CONT)
(TO HERSELF) Please.

FX: Footsteps from behind. Slow. Determined.

LOURNA: (CONT)
Sestin? That was quick. Did you find anyone?

LALUTIN:
Yes. I found *you.* Which was a surprise, I can tell you.

LOURNA:
Lalutin.

LALUTIN:
I never thought I'd see you again.

LOURNA:
You need to help me get out of here.

LALUTIN:
Thought about it, though. Thought about little else for years.

LOURNA:
It's crushing me.

FX: Footsteps as Lalutin walks calmly around her.

LALUTIN:

Yes. It does look painful. Do you know what else is painful? Having your skull fractured. Spending four months in the infirmary. Watching everyone else graduate. Did you hear what happened to Wilson? No, I guess you didn't. Why would you? He got a cozy little job on Coruscant. Training diplomats. Can you believe it?

LOURNA:

Lalutin, please.

LALUTIN:

But me . . . I ended up here. Working in places like this, with criminals like you.

FX: He stops pacing.

LALUTIN: (CONT)

The funny thing is, I talked to that idiot guard and he called you Sal. Had never even heard of someone called Inun. Made me wonder which was your real name. What is it? Inun? Sal? Maybe . . . Lourna.

LOURNA:

How do you know that name?

LALUTIN:

Did you think I would forget you? Or I wouldn't recognize you, even under a mask?

FX: He activates a holoprojector.

LALUTIN: (CONT)

This was all over the HoloNet for months. Lourna Dee. A reward for information that would lead to her capture. Five thousand credits.

LOURNA:

That's not me.

LALUTIN:

Of course it is. Look at the head-tails. Oh, I remember those head-tails. But it was no good before. I didn't know where you were. If you were even still alive. But now . . . now you're here.

That reward, that was before they thought you'd died. Imagine what you'll be worth now. And I don't mean the credits. I don't care about the money.

I won't be wasting my time on planets like this once they know I've found you. Won't have to sully myself with prisoners and jumped-up guards. I'll have the pick of any job I want.

All it takes is one call to Starlight Beacon. Let's make it now, shall we?

FX: A beep as he tries to open a channel.

LALUTIN: (CONT)
Hello? Hello, can you hear me? This is Administrator Lalutin with important information about the fugitive known as Lourna Dee.

LOURNA:
You won't be able to get through.

LALUTIN:
Hello?

LOURNA:
There's no reception here. But maybe we can cut a deal, Lalutin. Maybe there's some other way I can help you.

FX: There's a burst of static and . . .

VELKO JAHEN: (COMMS, DISTORTED)
This is Starlight. Please can you repeat your message.

LALUTIN:
Ah, of course.

LOURNA:
Lalutin. Don't do this.

LALUTIN:
This is Administrator—

FX: A single bolt shoots in, slamming into Lalutin.

LALUTIN: (CONT)
(SCREAMS, DIES)

FX: His body crashes down, the comlink clattering to the ground seconds later.

VELKO JAHEN: (COMMS)
Hello? This is Starlight. Please respond.

LOURNA:
Lalutin?

VELKO JAHEN: (COMMS)
Repeat: Please respond.

LOURNA:
What the hell is happening? Who's there?

FX: Tasia rushes from the trees.

TASIA:
You really know how to make enemies, don't you? Is there anyone else?

LOURNA:
(RELIEVED) Tasia. Where did you get a blaster? Actually, who cares. You need to get me out of this.

VELKO JAHEN: (COMMS)
This is Starlight Beacon. Do you require—[assistance?]

TASIA:
That's enough of that.

FX: She crunches the comlink beneath her foot.

LOURNA:
Listen. Sestin's gone to get help, but I can barely breathe.

PAN: (OFF MIC, MASKED)
That makes two of us.

LOURNA:
(RECOGNIZING THE VOICE) What?

FX: Heavy footsteps as Pan pushes his way through the trees, lurching forward, his portable ventilator hissing. The wheeze of a ventilator.

PAN: (MASKED)
Look at you. Trapped like a scrap rat.

LOURNA:
Pan? Pan Eyta?

PAN: (MASKED)
Hello, Lourna. I've been looking forward to seeing you again.

END OF PART FOUR

PART FIVE

REVENGE

SCENE 102. EXT. ARBRA. OLD LOGGING STATION—CONTINUOUS.

Atmos: As before. Pan wheezing.

TASIA:
What did I tell you, Pan? Told you I'd lead you to her.

PAN: (MASKED)
And you kept your word, Tasia. I won't forget that.

LOURNA:
How can you be here?

PAN: (MASKED)
I ask myself the same every day.

LOURNA:
You're supposed to be dead.

PAN: (MASKED)
Same goes for you. And yet here we are. Two corpses.

LOURNA:
It won't get you anywhere. The others will be here soon.

TASIA:
No they won't.

LOURNA:
Sestin went to fetch Wittick.

TASIA:
She never made it.

LOURNA:
What did you do?

TASIA:
Like you care about her.

LOURNA:
She is a good person.

TASIA:
Is that why she ended up here?

LOURNA:
How long have you been working with him?

TASIA:
With Pan? Not long. Few weeks.

LOURNA:
Since we've been on board the *Restitution*? That doesn't make sense.

TASIA:
You sure about that?

LOURNA:
What have you got there? (REALIZING) Ola's comlink. It *was* you.

TASIA:
I'm insulted you even doubted that.

LOURNA:
Then what? You called him? How did you even know he was out there?

PAN: (MASKED)
She didn't. I picked her up bleating away on an old Nihil frequency. Calling Ro, of all people.

LOURNA:
Like he'd help.

PAN: (MASKED)
My thoughts precisely. But it couldn't have come at a better time . . .

CUT TO:

SCENE 103. INT. PAN'S SHIP. FLIGHT DECK— FLASHBACK.

Atmos: The deep rumble of Pan's heavy cruiser, Pan's ventilator chugging away, the Dowutin wheezing.

TRILOK:
There's no sign of a ship, Pan. Prison or otherwise.

PAN:
The *Restitution* has to be here. (BREAKS INTO A COUGH) Just has to be.

TRILOK:
I've told you; this is a wild goota chase. If there was anyone in this sector, we would've found it by now.

PAN:
My contact on Starlight—

TRILOK:
Said the survivors of the *Lourna Dee* had been transferred to prison ships, I know, but we've hit three hulks now and there's still no sign of her. What if she didn't make it off her ship? What if the Er'Kit you met on Sran was lying? What if she really *is* dead?

PAN:
(SHOUTING) He wasn't lying, and she isn't dead. Is that clear?

FX: The click of a blaster.

PAN: (CONT)
Or should I find myself a new pilot?

TRILOK:
It's clear. It's clear. You can put the blaster down.

FX: The blaster drops to the arm of Pan's chair.

PAN:
(BREATHING HEAVILY) Sweep the comm channels.

TRILOK:
Again?

PAN:
Again.

FX: The equivalent of a radio tuning. Lots of different static and signals.

TRILOK:
There's nothing. Not even a deep-space probe.

A distorted voice cuts through the static.

TASIA: (COMMS, DISTORTED)
Cyclone alert. Nine. Seven. Eight. Zero. Five.

PAN:
Wait. What's that?

TRILOK:
Just interplanetary chatter.

FX: Trilok pushes buttons.

TASIA: (COMMS, DISTORTED)
Cyclone alert. Nine. Seven. Eight. Zero. Five.

TRILOK:
Some kind of weather warning.

PAN:
No, it's not.

FX: Pan punches buttons now.

PAN: (CONT)
Cyclone alert. We read you.

TASIA: (COMMS, DISTORTED)
Cyclone alert. Nine. Seven. Eight. Zero. Five.

PAN:
She can't hear me. Boost the signal.

TRILOK:
Why? I thought we were looking for a prison ship?

PAN:
Do it!

CUT TO:

SCENE 104. EXT. ARBRA. OLD LOGGING STATION.

Atmos: As before.

TASIA:
Got through in the end.

LOURNA:
Happy for you.

TASIA:
Couldn't believe who it was.

LOURNA:
Let me guess. Pan said he would bust you out if you told him where to find me?

And you believed him?

PAN: (MASKED)
Tasia. I need you to check on the others . . . Make sure we're not . . . interrupted.

TASIA:
I told you. The old woman's been dealt with.

PAN: (MASKED)
And I'm telling you . . . to check on the others!

TASIA:

Fine. Fine. Just don't kill her before I get back, yeah? I want to see that for myself.

PAN: (MASKED)

(GROWLS IN THE BACK OF HIS THROAT)

FX: Tasia pushes through the trees.

LOURNA:

Good luck with that one. You two deserve each other.

PAN: (MASKED)

You don't trust her?

LOURNA:

Haven't you heard . . . I don't trust anyone. (GRUNTS IN PAIN) Look, if you're going to gloat . . . at least can you do it where I can see you.

FX: Pan trudges around her.

LOURNA: (CONT)

There you are.

PAN: (MASKED)

Happy now?

LOURNA:

Happier than your tailor. What happened to all your fine clothes, Pan? All the gold? Did the ventilator ruin the line of your suit?

PAN: (MASKED)

Still the same old Lourna.

LOURNA:

Haven't you heard? I'm Sal now.

PAN: (MASKED)

Not for much longer.

FX: He removes his mask.

PAN: (CONT)

(SIGHS IN RELIEF) That's better.

LOURNA:
Look at the state of you.

PAN:
Am I supposed to believe you care?

LOURNA:
In all honesty I'm surprised to see you on your feet. You look like death.

PAN:
Feel it, too. With every breath. Thanks to you and Ro.

LOURNA:
That wasn't me. I didn't know what he was planning. The syringe. The poison. None of it.

PAN:
And yet, you gave me the antidote.

LOURNA:
I gave you an anti-toxin. I had no idea if it would work.

PAN:
Here's a news flash. It didn't.

LOURNA:
Just too stubborn to die, eh?

PAN:
Found a medic on Port Yonder. Someone who made Doc Uttersond look hygienic. But he fixed me up as best he could. Fitting this . . .

FX: A clank as he shifts the ventilator unit on his back.

PAN: (CONT)
You don't want to know how many drugs I have to take every day just to think straight. How my own blood burns in my veins.

LOURNA:
Anything to survive, huh?

PAN:
This isn't surviving. This is existing. Existing for two reasons.
I vowed that before I died, I'd . . . (COUGHS WETLY) . . . I'd
kill you . . . and I'd kill Ro . . . Not necessarily in that order . . .

LOURNA:
Well?

PAN:
Well, what?

LOURNA:
Is Ro dead?

PAN:
I don't know. I can't find him. He's gone . . . to ground . . .

LOURNA:
Figures.

PAN:
No one even knows he exists . . . outside of the Nihil . . .

LOURNA:
Outside what's left of the Nihil . . .

PAN:
Same thing . . . But when I find him . . . (BREATHING HEAV-
ILY IN ANTICIPATION) I'll crush his head . . . like I crushed
that damn helmet of his . . .

LOURNA:
Because that *really* worked for you last time.

PAN:
Hmmm. Still insufferable . . . even at the end.

LOURNA:
You know me, Pan. You should . . . you were there at the beginning . . .

FADE TO:

SCENE 105. INT. NURASENTI. BAR—THE PAST.

FX: A crash. Someone is thrown into a shelf full of bottles, most of which smash on impact.

BAR OWNER:
Hey! No fighting! No fighting!

CUSTOMER:
Don't try to stop 'em, Karter. I've got five ingots on the Holwuff.

CUSTOMER 2:
Are you nuts? The Mando is gonna win.

CUSTOMER:
(LAUGHS) You really think that's a Mando under that armor? How many bucketheads have head-tails peeking out of their helmet?

CUSTOMER 2:
Dunno! Never seen one!

FX: A punch. A hard one.

CUSTOMER 2: (CONT)
Like the Holwuff never saw that punch coming. (LAUGHS) That *had* to hurt.

FX: A comlink burbles. The fight continues in the background. The comlink burbles again.

CUSTOMER 2: (CONT)
You not going to get that?

CUSTOMER:
(NOT HAPPY) Don't believe this.

FX: A beep as he answers this.

CUSTOMER: (CONT)
Whoever this is, it better be good. I'm watching a fight here.

FX: More bottles smash.

CUSTOMER: (CONT)
Korval, you old warthead. Can I call you back? No. I'm on Nurasenti. Some bar near the spaceport.

FX: Another punch.

CUSTOMER: (CONT)
You'd love it. There's this joker in busted-up Mandalorian iron getting their butt handed to them by a Holwuff berserker.

CUSTOMER 2:
The Mando's gonna win, I tell you.

CUSTOMER:
You wish. (BEAT) No, not you, Korv. That's Sneef. Dumb Arcona bet me five big ones that the tin-head is going to come up roses . . . against a Holwuff, right! Like anyone can win against one of those—

FX: There are three sudden blaster shots, going into a body at point-blank range, followed by a beat, and then another shot.

CUSTOMER 2:
You were saying?

FX: A body drops to the ground.

CUSTOMER:
For void's sake.

CUSTOMER 2:
That's five ingots you owe me. Or you could just stump up for a bottle of Mind Eraser.

CUSTOMER:
(SIGH) You heard the man, Karter.

BAR OWNER:
You're lucky it's still in one piece.

FX: A bottle is slammed down in front of them.

CUSTOMER 2:
Pleasure doing business with you.

FX: A clank of Lourna's armor as she walks up.

LOURNA: (HELMETED)
Heard you were betting on me.

CUSTOMER 2:
What? Who, me?

LOURNA: (HELMETED)
How did you do?

CUSTOMER 2:
(LAUGHING) Better than the Holwuff.

LOURNA: (HELMETED)
That your winnings?

CUSTOMER 2:
Y-yeah.

LOURNA: (HELMETED)
Don't mind if I do.

FX: Scrape of the bottle as she picks it up.

CUSTOMER 2:
Hey, that's mine.

LOURNA: (HELMETED)
You wanna take it off me? (TO THE BAR) Any of you want to take it off me?

CUSTOMER 2:
Tell you what . . . you keep it. I was just leaving.

CUSTOMER:
You and me both. I need to take this outside.

FX: They rush off.

CUSTOMER: (CONT, GOING OFF MIC)
Sheesh. That was intense. Korval, you should see what she did to that 'serker.

FX: Door swings shut. The bar is quiet now, the customers having fled.

BAR OWNER:
Gee. Thanks. Smash my stock. Chase my customers away. Wonderful.

LOURNA: (HELMETED)
You gonna throw me out?

BAR OWNER:
Could I?

FX: The clank of Lourna's armor as she stalks to a corner of the bar.

LOURNA: (HELMETED)
I'll be in the booth.

BAR OWNER:
That's what I thought. (CALLING AFTER HER) And hey, if you wanna keep up that disguise, you might wanna pull up the hood. Your lekku are showing.

LOURNA: (HELMETED)
Thanks.

BAR OWNER:
(UNDER BREATH) Kriffin' Twi'leks.

CUT TO:

SCENE 106. EXT. ARBRA. OLD LOGGING STATION— PRESENT DAY.

Atmos: As before. The trees. The birds. The wheeze of Pan's ventilators.

PAN:
Seems to me . . . you've always been running from the past . . . wearing one disguise or another . . .

LOURNA:
Yeah. Trouble is that the past has a habit of catching up with me.

PAN:
Like now.

LOURNA:
Like now. Like then. Like always . . .

CUT TO:

SCENE 107. INT. NURASENTI. BAR—THE PAST.

Atmos: The bar is empty of everyone but Lourna. At least, that's what she thinks.

FX: Footsteps approach her booth.

BALA:
This seat taken?

LOURNA: (HELMETED)
That depends if you're . . . (REALIZES WHO IT IS) paying.

BALA:
You okay there? Had a little too much eraser?

FX: She pushes the bottle away.

LOURNA: (HELMETED)
Not me. What can I do for you?

BALA:
My name is Bala Waleen. I'm the Keeper of Aaloth.

LOURNA: (HELMETED)
Keeper.

BALA:
I don't suppose you've heard of it. It's a small Twi'lek colony in the Gaulus sector.

LOURNA: (HELMETED)
I've heard of it.

BALA:
You have. Well, good. (AN AWKWARD BEAT) May I sit?

LOURNA: (HELMETED)
Nothing stopping you.

BALA:
Thank you.

FX: He sits.

BALA: (CONT)
Your voice. It's familiar.

LOURNA: (HELMETED)
No reason why it should be.

BALA:
You don't come from around here?

LOURNA: (HELMETED)
No.

BALA:
But you've made quite an impression.

LOURNA: (HELMETED)
(WANTING TO GET BACK TO BUSINESS) You were telling me about Aaloth.

BALA:
I was. Our supply lines have been . . . disrupted recently.

LOURNA: (HELMETED)
What kind of supply?

BALA:
Does it matter if our credits are good?

LOURNA: (HELMETED)
No.

BALA:
I'm glad to hear it. Our ships are being targeted by a group who call themselves the Nihil. Little more than cutthroats, really . . .

LOURNA: (HELMETED)
But more than you can handle.

BALA:
Our customers are getting jumpy. Consignments haven't been reaching their destination . . .

LOURNA: (HELMETED)
Consignments where your customers have paid in advance?

BALA:
More or less. We understand each other then?

LOURNA: (HELMETED)
Absolutely.

BALA:
How much will it cost?

LOURNA: (HELMETED)
Three hundred ingots.

BALA:
(SPLUTTERING) Three hundred?

LOURNA: (HELMETED)
That's my price. Seems to me if you're here, you've already exhausted every other option.

BALA:
Two hundred.

LOURNA: (HELMETED)
Three hundred.

BALA:
Two fifty.

LOURNA: (HELMETED)
Three. Hundred.

(BEAT)

BALA: (ANNOYED)
Anything else?

LOURNA: (HELMETED)
Yes. I'll need a ship.

BALA:
You don't have one of your own?

LOURNA: (HELMETED)
I didn't say I needed a fighter . . .

CUT TO:

SCENE 108. INT. NIHIL STORMSHIP. FLIGHT DECK.

Atmos: The rumble of engines. Wreckpunk playing over the speakers. Lots of feedback.

FX: Heavy doors open. Jinnix, a large Colicoid, rolls in before unfurling, its four insectoid legs clattering down.

When the Colicoid speaks, there is an insectlike buzz to its voice.

JINNIX:
Strike. Turn that noise off.

There is no response.

FX: A blaster shot destroys the main speaker.

JINNIX: (CONT)
I said, turn it off.

TOWL:
Apologies, my Storm. I didn't hear you arrive.

JINNIX:
Is that an excuse? The Nihil don't make excuses.

TOWL:
It wasn't an excuse.

JINNIX:
One of my drone-mates once gave me an excuse, listing the reasons they couldn't protect the queen when our nest was attacked by hueches. Do you know what I did?

TOWL:
No, my Storm.

JINNIX:
I ripped off their head and feasted on their ganglia.

TOWL:
The hueches?

JINNIX:
No. My drone-mate. They were . . . delicious. I wonder how you would taste, Towl. I've never eaten Nikto.

PAN: (COMMS)
I find that hard to believe, Jinnix.

FX: This younger Pan sounds healthier. No ventilator. No death rattle in his throat.

JINNIX:
(UNPLEASANTLY SURPRISED) Tempest Runner Eyta. I didn't realize you were on the comm.

PAN: (COMMS)
Neither did most of your bridge crew.

JINNIX:
I shall punish them immediately.

PAN: (COMMS)
You always did like playing with your food. But maybe you should wait until you've completed your next job.

JINNIX:
Job?

PAN: (COMMS)
My informer in the Hutt Cartel advises me that another shipment of glitterstim is being transported along the Roon way.

JINNIX:
Another? Already?

PAN: (COMMS)
I could send a different Storm if you think that's unlikely.

JINNIX:
(EAGER) No. We will intercept. Navigator. Plot course for the Abrion sector.

H7-09:
At once, my Storm.

PAN: (COMMS)
I'll have a Path transmitted. Rendezvous with the *Elegencia* once you have the stim.

JINNIX:
We ride the storm, Tempest Runner.

PAN: (COMMS)
Just get it done. Eyta out.

CUT TO:

SCENE 109. INT. CARGO SHIP. THE *TYCOON TRADER*. COCKPIT.

Atmos: The ship is traveling through hyperspace, an RL droid (a precursor of the RX line and therefore sounding a lot like DJ RX) at the controls.

RL-18:
I'm not sure this is a good idea.

LOURNA: (HELMETED)
I'm not sure I asked for your opinion, droid.

RL-18:
Actually, my name is Ar-El Eighteen.

LOURNA: (HELMETED)
Actually, I don't care.

RL-18:
I was only saying.

LOURNA: (HELMETED)
Although if Bala is using pilot droids, he deserves to be losing cargo.

RL-18:
I'll pretend I didn't hear that.

LOURNA: (HELMETED)
And I'll pretend you don't exist. (BEAT, THEN A SIGH) Why am I doing this?

RL-18:
I assume it is because you are being paid an obscene number of credits.

LOURNA: (HELMETED)
It was a rhetorical question.

RL-18:
An obvious question if you ask me. You are a mercenary. Mercenaries go where they get paid. They have no personal code or—

LOURNA: (HELMETED)
Tolerance for overly chatty rust buckets. (SIGHS) It seemed like such a good idea. Setting up in this sector of all places. Making a name for myself. Is it any wonder that Bala and I would run into each other? And what exactly did I think would happen? What did I think I'd feel?

(BEAT)

RL-18:
Sorry. Was all that rhetorical as well, or . . .

FX: The click of a blaster.

LOURNA:
Yeah, I'm gonna shoot you.

RL-18:
(EEP!)

FX: The comm unit chirps.

LOURNA:
Saved by the comms, droid. That'll be our illustrious employer.

RL-18:
Allow me.

FX: The droid activates the comm.

RL-18: (CONT)
This is the *Tycoon Trader,* pilot Ar-El Eighteen at the controls. Please identify yourself.

BALA: (COMMS)
Yes, yes. I know who you are.

LOURNA: (HELMETED)
He wants to talk to me.

RL-18:
Why is everyone so rude today?

LOURNA: (HELMETED)
Can I remove his vocalizer, Bala?

BALA: (COMMS)
Be my guest. Any sign of trouble?

LOURNA: (HELMETED)
No. Have you identified the leak?

BALA: (COMMS)
Not yet, but we're working on it.

LOURNA: (HELMETED)
Whoever they are, they mustn't know where the spice is coming from—

BALA: (COMMS)
Or our mines would be crawling with Nihil by now. We'd like to keep it that way.

LOURNA: (HELMETED)
Roger that. Will report in when we have news. I suggest keeping communication to a minimum. You never know who's liste—

FX: There's suddenly a "krump," an alarm immediately going off as they are pulled out of hyperspace.

Both Lourna and the droid react to the sudden stop.

LOURNA: (CONT, HELMETED)
What happened?

FX: The droid frantically hits controls.

RL-18:
We've been pulled out of hyperspace.

LOURNA: (HELMETED)
I can see that. Felt it, too.

RL-18:
I'm not surprised. Acceleration compensators are offline. Comms are offline.

LOURNA: (HELMETED)
Maneuvering thrusters?

FX: A computer gives a very unfriendly boop.

RL-18:
Care to hazard a guess?

LOURNA: (HELMETED)
Good.

RL-18:
Good? Are you malfunctioning? How is any of this good?

LOURNA: (HELMETED)
No need to blow a processor. We have them exactly where they want us.

CUT TO:

SCENE 110. INT. NIHIL. STORMSHIP. FLIGHT DECK.

Atmos: The stormship is flying a Path through hyperspace. This is the first time we've heard this, so it would be great if we could get a new sound effect for the process, perhaps a twisted version of traveling through hyperspace, more tempestuous somehow (pun intended).

PAN: (COMMS)
Well, Jinnix?

JINNIX:
We are coming to the end of the Path, Pan.

H7-09:
Reentering realspace in five, four, three, two—

FX: The whump of reentering realspace, again slightly more violent than a usual jump out of hyperspace.

TOWL:
There it is.

PAN: (COMMS)
Well?

JINNIX:
Standard cargo vessel.

H7-09:
Bigger than expected.

PAN: (COMMS)
Let's hope the spoils are just as impressive. Eyta out.

FX: The comlink shuts off.

JINNIX:
Maybe now we will be able to get on with our jobs. Any movement?

H7-09:
None. The cruiser seems dormant. Propulsion and defenses offline.

TOWL:
In other words, the gravity mine did its job. They're dead in the stars.

JINNIX:
Gas torpedoes?

TOWL:
Locked and loaded.

JINNIX:
Fire.

CUT TO:

SCENE 111. INT. THE *TYCOON TRADER*. COCKPIT.

Atmos: As before.

FX: There are thuds deep in the vessel, the sound of torpedoes piercing the hull.

RL-18:
What's that?

LOURNA: (HELMETED)
You've not been raided before?

RL-18:
Several times.

LOURNA: (HELMETED)
Then you should know.

RL-18:
They wipe our memories every time. Means we don't panic in a crisis, paralyzed with fear and trepidation.

LOURNA: (HELMETED)
And what are you doing now?

RL-18:
Panicking!

LOURNA: (HELMETED)
Zariin give me strength.

FX: Beeps as she presses controls.

RL-18:
Now what are you doing?

LOURNA: (HELMETED)
Activating internal cameras.

FX: The sounds of a screen flicking on.

LOURNA: (CONT, HELMETED)
There.

RL-18:
What are they?

LOURNA: (HELMETED)
Torpedoes.

RL-18:
I can see that. But there was no explosion.

LOURNA: (HELMETED)
These tubes don't detonate. They puncture.

RL-18:
Why?

FX: The hiss of gas through speakers.

LOURNA: (HELMETED)
Because their payload is unique.

RL-18:
Gas!

LOURNA: (HELMETED)
They call it a war-cloud. Murder on your lungs and almost as rough on ship's sensors.

FX: The picture flickers accompanied with audible interference. RL-18 flips controls.

RL-18:
You're not kidding. What few systems we had are shutting down. What do we do?

LOURNA: (HELMETED)
We wait.

RL–18:
Okay. Now I *know* you're joking.

LOURNA: (HELMETED)
There's nothing to worry about, Ar-El. I've studied these guys.
Everything is going to plan.

CUT TO:

SCENE 112. INT. NIHIL STORMSHIP. CORRIDOR—CONTINUOUS.

FX: We hear the rumble of a boarding tube being deployed, muffled behind an air lock, but vibrating through the hull.

LOURNA: (HELMETED, V.O.)
The Nihil will be extending a boarding tube.

FX: A muffled clang.

LOURNA: (CONT, HELMETED, V.O.)
Locking onto our hull. Burning through the durasteel.

FX: The air lock opens, heavy and industrial. We can hear the sound of metal being cut ahead, almost imagine the sparks flying.

TOWL:
All right. Masks on.

FX: They pull on their masks and perhaps we go into Towl's mask, hearing him breathing close to the mic. The rest of the scene is from his POV.

TOWL: (CONT, MASKED)
Let's go.

FX: Heavy footsteps as the Nihil stomp forward and the cutting continues. There's no need to hurry. They've done this before.

LOURNA: (HELMETED, V.O.)
It'll leave a gaping hole in the side of our ship when the tube disengages, but the Nihil don't care. There won't be any survivors by the time they're finished.

FX: The cutting stops.

TOWL: (MASKED)
Well?

H7-09: (MUFFLED SLIGHTLY THROUGH TOWL'S MASK)
The hull is breached.

TOWL: (MASKED)
Then kick the door open, for void's sake.

FX: The droid kicks the hull, the cut section crashing down into the corridor on the other side.

LOURNA: (HELMETED, V.O.)
Then they'll be in, protected from the war-cloud by their masks.

FX: We hear footsteps running on deck plates, muffled by Towl's mask.

LOURNA: (CONT, HELMETED, V.O.)
They'll split, a couple of Strikes heading for the hold while the rest sweep through the ship, taking our crewmembers, checking for loot.

That's when they'll get their first surprise.

FX: Repeated laser blasts from ahead.

NIHIL:
(WILHELM SCREAM)

TOWL: (MASKED)
What the— Take them down!

FX: The Nihil return fire with extreme prejudice.

LOURNA: (HELMETED, V.O.)
Nihil weapons are crude but powerful—some little more than clubs and bludgeons—and the Nihil themselves are so jacked up on stims that even if they're hit, they'll barely feel the pain.

TOWL: (MASKED)
(ROARS AS HE ATTACKS)

FX: Towl smashes an automatic gun turret with his club. There's a small explosion.

TOWL: (CONT, MASKED)
What the hell?

H7-09: (MUFFLED)
Automated defenses.

TOWL: (MASKED)
So where's the crew?

FX: They carry on running.

LOURNA: (HELMETED, V.O.)
They'll carve their way through the ship until they find the cockpit.

FX: Cockpit doors open ahead of them.

LOURNA: (CONT, HELMETED, V.O.)
And that's when you come in.

TOWL: (MASKED)
Light 'em up.

LOURNA: (HELMETED, V.O.)
Sorry 'bout that.

RL-18:
No, wait. Don't—

FX: Blasterfire.

RL-18: (CONT)
(SCREAMS)

FX: RL-18 is destroyed. His parts tinkle to the floor.

H7-09: (MUFFLED)
More automation.

FX: H7-09 kicks RL-18's wreckage.

H7-09: (CONT, MUFFLED)
The pilot was a droid.

TOWL: (MASKED)
Is no one alive on this ship?

LOURNA: (HELMETED, BEHIND HIM)
Unfortunately, yes.

TOWL: (MASKED)
Huh?

LOURNA: (HELMETED)
Unfortunately for you, that is.

FX: She fires a blaster.

TOWL: (MASKED)
(SCREAMS)

CUT TO:

SCENE 113. INT. NIHIL STORMSHIP. FLIGHT DECK.

Atmos: As before.

JINNIX:
Jinnix to boarding party, come in.

FX: The comlink opens, only for Jinnix to be greeted by the sounds of mayhem. Blasterfire. A fight.

TOWL: (COMMS)
(SCREAMS)

JINNIX:
Boarding party? TOWL?

H7-09: (COMMS)
We are under attack, my Storm.

FX: More blasterfire over the comm.

H7-09: (CONT, COMMS)
Single crewmember. Wearing—

FX: An explosion sounds over the comm.

JINNIX:
Aychseven?

There's no response even though the battle continues.

JINNIX: (CONT)
Aychseven! (STILL NO RESPONSE) I'm coming over.

FX: Jinnix rolls himself into a ball and trundles off.

CUT TO:

SCENE 114. INT. THE *TYCOON TRADER.* COCKPIT.

**PAN: (COMMS, COMING UP ON MIC AS JINNIX AP-
PROACHES)**
Jinnix. Jinnix, come in. Is the raid a success?

FX: Jinnix trundles forward into the cockpit.

PAN: (CONT, COMMS)
Jinnix, report!

FX: Jinnix unfurls, legs clattering down.

JINNIX: (MASKED)
I am on the ship, Tempest Runner.

PAN: (COMMS)
And?

FX: Jinnix scampers over to Towl's body.

JINNIX: (MASKED)
And Towl is dead.

PAN: (COMMS)
Dead?

JINNIX: (MASKED)
Stand by.

PAN: (COMMS)
I will not. You will tell me what is happening.

FX: Jinnix picks up H7-09's broken body.

JINNIX: (MASKED)
Aychseven. Are you still operational?

FX: The whir of H7's inner workings struggling to obey.

When it speaks, the droid's voice is distorted.

H7-09:
They were wa-wa-wa-waiting for us. Us.

JINNIX: (MASKED)
Who were?

PAN: (COMMS)
Jinnix, what's happening?

JINNIX: (MASKED)
Oh. Go to hell!

PAN: (COMMS)
Jinnix. Don't you da—

FX: Jinnix kills the comm with a click.

JINNIX: (MASKED)
How many of them were there, Aychseven?

(NO RESPONSE)

FX: Jinnix shakes the droid.

JINNIX: (CONT, MASKED)
Aychseven. How many?

FX: Another comlink opens.

NIHIL 2: (COMMS)
Storm. This is Blackwing. There's—

FX: The sound of a head being cut off. Slllck!

JINNIX: (MASKED)
Blackwing? Blackwing, report.

LOURNA: (COMMS, HELMETED)
Blackwing can't get to the comm right now . . .

H7-09:
My Storm . . .

LOURNA: (COMMS, HELMETED)
Or ever again.

H7-09:
(WINDING DOWN) There was only one of theeeeeemm-mmm . . .

JINNIX: (MASKED)
(A BELLOW OF FRUSTRATION)

FX: Jinnix throws H7-09's body down.

JINNIX: (CONT, MASKED)
Whoever you are, I'm coming for you. Do you hear? I'm coming for you!

FX: Jinnix rolls into a ball and rumbles off.

CUT TO:

SCENE 115. EXT. ARBRA. OLD LOGGING STATION.

Atmos: As before.

PAN:
I should've known . . . the first time our paths crossed . . .

LOURNA:
That I'd be the death of you?

PAN:
That you'd be trouble. Seems like yesterday. Jinnix cutting me off, my crew flying the *Elegencia* along the very same path I'd given him, finding his Stormship and the damn cruiser side by side . . .

I should've opened the *Elegencia*'s cannons there and then. Reduced you to atoms when I had the chance.

LOURNA:
And sacrifice a hold full of glitterstim? I don't think so.

PAN:
But there was no glitterstim, was there? The holds were empty.

LOURNA:
Not quite . . .

CUT TO:

SCENE 116. INT. THE *TYCOON TRADER.* HOLD.

FX: Jinnix rolls toward us.

JINNIX: (MASKED)
Where are you? Where?

FX: A massive explosion.

JINNIX: (CONT, MASKED)
(SCREAMS)

CUT TO:

SCENE 117. EXT. ARBRA. OLD LOGGING STATION.

Atmos: As before.

PAN:
What kind of lunatic mines their own hold with thermal detonators?

LOURNA:
The kind that is setting a trap.

PAN:
Did you know Jinnix was a Colicoid before he attacked?

LOURNA:
No way to. Soon found out, though.

PAN:
I wish I'd been there to see it. Did you really think you could cut through his chitin?

LOURNA:
I had to try.

PAN:
How did you do it?

LOURNA:
Do what?

PAN:
Kill him. I never asked.

LOURNA:
You really want to know?

PAN:
Neither of us are going anywhere.

LOURNA:
It was simple enough. I let him win.

CUT TO:

SCENE 118. INT. THE *TYCOON TRADER*. HOLD.

FX: We head into the fight. Lourna is slammed down onto the deck, her armor clanking against the plates.

LOURNA: (V.O.)
He had the upper hand. I was on my back, pinned down, looking up at those jaws. Those teeth. Do you know what he did?

LOURNA: (HELMETED)
(GRUNT OF PAIN)

FX: The sound of a long tongue lapping metal.

LOURNA: (V.O.)
He licked the helmet I was wearing. Actually licked it. To this day, I don't know why. Maybe it was an alpha thing. Maybe he just liked the taste of *beskar*. Either way, it gave me the moment I needed.

FX: A hand closes around one of Jinnix's teeth.

JINNIX:
(HUH?)

LOURNA: (V.O.)
I grabbed one of those fangs and pulled, pulled as hard as I could.

FX: The tooth is ripped free.

LOURNA: (CONT, V.O.)
Guess it must have come loose in the blast.

FX: The sound of a tooth punching armor plating.

JINNIX:
(WAIL OF PAIN)

PAN: (V.O.)
You stabbed him with his own tusk.

LOURNA: (V.O.)
As if you wouldn't have done the same.

LOURNA: (HELMETED)
(GRUNT OF EFFORT)

LOURNA: (V.O.)
Talk about a dead weight.

FX: Lourna pushes Jinnix off her, his body crashing to the floor.

LOURNA: (HELMETED)
(CATCHING HER BREATH)

We stay with Lourna's breathing under the following.

LOURNA: (V.O.)
I thought that was it. That's one. (BEAT) Jinnix even provided me with the means to get back on my feet, a bandolier of stims around his thorax.

LOURNA: (HELMETED)
(STILL BREATHLESS) Aren't you the gift that keeps on giving.

FX: She pulls an injector free from Jinnix's body and slams it into her leg, injecting the stim with a hiss.

LOURNA: (CONT, HELMETED)
(A RAGGED SIGH AS THE DRUG TAKES EFFECT)

LOURNA: (V.O.)
The fight hadn't gone as well as I'd wanted, but the result was the same.

FX: Lourna pushes herself up, dropping the empty injector to the floor.

It clatters on the deck.

LOURNA: (CONT, V.O.)
The Nihil were dead, the war-cloud was lifting, and I'd earned my fee. Now I could move on to the second stage of my plan . . . Until you showed up, of course . . .

FX: The sudden click of a blaster behind her.

LOURNA: (HELMETED)
How long have you been standing there?

PAN: (MASKED)
Long enough. Hands up and turn around. Slowly.

LOURNA: (HELMETED)
I'm turning. I'm turning. No weapons. See?

FX: Shuffle of feet against deck plates as Lourna does what she is told . . . for once.

PAN: (MASKED)
I find that hard to believe. Nihil—take her.

FX: Footsteps as Nihil rush in and grab her. She lets them.

LOURNA: (HELMETED)
Hey! I surrendered!

PAN: (MASKED)
Get that helmet off.

FX: The helmet is yanked off roughly.

LOURNA:
Watch it!

PAN: (MASKED)
A Twi'lek.

LOURNA:
And I guess you're a Dowutin, but it's hard to be sure through that mask. Hardly fair, is it? You can see me, but I can't see you.

PAN: (MASKED)
(CHUCKLES)

FX: Creak of Pan's leather as he goes to pull his mask off.

NIHIL 3: (MASKED)
(SHOCKED) Tempest?

PAN: (MASKED)
Shut it.

FX: He pulls the mask clear.

LOURNA:
There you are. Never seen a Dow like you.

PAN:
Is that a compliment?

LOURNA:
If you want it to be. Why didn't you shoot me?

PAN:
Because I wanted to see who it was that could take down a Colicoid. That could wipe out an entire Storm.

LOURNA:
And what do you see? (BEAT) Well? (ANOTHER AGONIZING BEAT)

PAN:
Someone punching above their weight.

LOURNA:
Maybe. But I'm also someone who can give you *exactly* what you want . . .

MUSICAL SEGUE:

SCENE 119. EXT. AALOTH PALACE.

Atmos: A pleasant day on Aaloth. A skycar flies above, its engines buzzing.

FX: Bala is striding across the square, his footsteps ringing out on the flagstones.

BALA: (COMING UP ON MIC)
Hello, Assessor? It's Bala. No, I'm back on Aaloth. I need to talk to you about the quotas. What Ryloth is demanding is completely impossible? (BEAT) Hello? Hello, Assessor—are you there?

FX: More footsteps approach: one of the protestors from part 2, now working for Bala.

TWI'LEK PROTESTOR 3:
(HURRYING UP) Keeper Waleen! Bala!

FX: Crunch underfoot as Bala stops and turns.

BALA:
Ah, Delan. Do you know what's happening with offworld communications? I was talking to Ryloth and got cut off.

TWI'LEK PROTESTOR 3:
Well, someone's getting through. We've just received word from Nal Hutta. Renza is wondering when she can expect further shipments.

BALA:
When we can be sure they'll get through the pass. One moment.

FX: He activates a comlink.

BALA: (CONT)
Boona. Come in please.

TWI'LEK PROTESTOR 1: (COMMS)
I'm here, Keeper.

BALA:
Ah, at least internal comms are working. Any word from our freelance friend?

TWI'LEK PROTESTOR 1: (COMMS)
Who?

BALA:
The mercenary.

TWI'LEK PROTESTOR 1: (COMMS)
Nothing yet, sir. I—

FX: The rest of the sentence is lost in static, the signal jammed.

BALA:
Boona? Boona, are you there?

There are screams in the distance.

BALA: (CONT)
What in Zar's name?

FX: A large ship is roaring in, low over the settlement. A very large ship. The Elegencia, *opening its laser banks on the streets below. Cue more screams, more panic, increasing in volume below the following . . .*

TWI'LEK PROTESTOR 3:
Keeper. That ship. It's the Nihil.

BALA:
Here? On Aaloth?

TWI'LEK PROTESTOR 3:
Bala. Run!

FX: Running footsteps as Twi'lek Protestor 3 takes her own advice.

BALA:
(STILL FROZEN TO THE SPOT) She must have failed.

FX: The ship gets nearer, as do the laser blasts.

BALA: (CONT)
(COMING TO HIS SENSES) This can't be happening!

FX: Bala runs, but it's too late. The cacophony of sounds overtakes him, a shot from up above.

BALA: (CONT)
(SCREAMS)

FX: An explosion blossoms, overwhelming the soundspace.

MUSICAL SEGUE:

SCENE 120. EXT. THE RUINS OF AALOTH PALACE—SOON AFTER.

Atmos: Fires are burning as weeping sounds in the distance.

A shuttle's ramp lowers in the shadow of the Elegencia, *which hovers above.*

FX: Heavy, confident footsteps as Pan stomps down the ramp.

More footsteps as a Twi'lek runs up to intercept him.

TWI'LEK PROTESTOR 2:
Death to the raiders.

PAN:
Not today, thank you.

FX: He shoots her.

TWI'LEK PROTESTOR 2:
(SCREAMS AND DIES)

FX: Pan stops at the foot of the ramp.

PAN:
(BREATHES IN) Ahh. The sweet tang of victory.

FX: A scuffle as Bala is dragged in front of him.

BALA: (COMING UP ON MIC)
(STRUGGLING)

NIHIL 3: (COMING UP ON MIC)
Tempest Runner. We found the Keeper . . . trying to crawl to his ship.

PAN:
Running at the first sign of trouble. A true man of the people.

BALA:
(SPITS AT PAN)

PAN:
(AMUSED) If you think I've never been spat upon, you're mistaken.

BALA:
Why are you doing this?

PAN:
I thought that would be obvious. Why put all the effort into stealing shipments when we can have the entire planet?

BALA:
Who was it who told you about us? Who betrayed us?

PAN:
Does it matter?

BALA:
It was that Mandalorian, wasn't it? The mercenary.

PAN:
(AMUSED) You still think she was Mandalorian?

FX: Footsteps behind Pan, descending the ramp.

LOURNA:
Hello, Bala.

BALA:
Who? (REALIZATION DAWNS) No.

LOURNA:
Yes.

BALA:
It can't be. I thought you were . . .

LOURNA:
Dead? Not yet. (TO PAN) Well, what do you think, Pan?

PAN:
It's everything you said it was.

LOURNA:
And more.

BALA:
How could you? Your own planet. Your home.

LOURNA:
My planet? My home? This rock stopped being my home the moment you butchered my family, the moment you turned me over to a Zygerrian.

PAN:
(CHUCKLING) I knew I was going to like you.

LOURNA:
So what happens now? I've given you Aaloth.

PAN:
And I've given you your revenge. What happens next depends on you.

LOURNA:
I want in.

PAN:
Good.

LOURNA:
I'll mine this place for you. For the Nihil. Strip it to the core if need be.

PAN:
(AMUSED) Anything else?

LOURNA:
(SHRUGS) I wouldn't mind the Colicoid's ship.

PAN:
The *Toothspike*.

LOURNA:
Is *that* its name? (SCOFFS) That'll have to change.

PAN:
Is that so? Anything spring to mind?

LOURNA:
Funny you should ask. Can I borrow your blaster, my Tempest?

PAN:
If you think you can handle it.

FX: A clunk as he hands it over. It sounds heavy.

LOURNA:
There is one name I could use for the ship. A name that means a lot to me.

FX: Footsteps as she turns slowly toward Bala.

BALA:
(SCARED) Please. Please don't.

FX: The click of her blaster.

LOURNA:
A name that was forsaken. That was denied.

BALA:
(WHIMPERING NOW) I'm sorry.

LOURNA:
Tell me the name, Bala.

BALA:
(SOBS)

LOURNA:
Tell me the name!

BALA:
(SHRIEKING) Lourna! Lourna Dee!

LOURNA:
(SMILES, THEN TAKES A BEAT) And don't you forget it.

FX: She shoots Bala in the head.

FADE TO:

SCENE 121. EXT. ARBRA. OLD LOGGING STATION— THE PRESENT.

Atmos: As before. The wheeze of Pan's ventilator reminding us how much has changed.

PAN:
You always liked the sound of your own name. Shame you're not using it anymore. (NO RESPONSE) Lourna? (STILL NO RESPONSE) No.

FX: He stomps forward.

PAN: (CONT)
Don't you dare. Don't you dare rob me of my vengeance.

FX: Creaks of metal as he starts to lift the wreckage. Crashes as he flings it aside.

PAN: (CONT)
You're not to die yet. Not until I allow it.

FX: Footsteps as Tasia runs up.

TASIA:
Pan? What the void is going on here? Do you want everyone to hear?

PAN:
She's not breathing.

TASIA:
Isn't that kind of the point?

PAN:
Help me!

TASIA:
Why? You got what you wanted. Now get me out of here.

PAN:
You really think I care about you?

FX: He turns on Tasia, pinning her against the old wall of the logging station.

TASIA:
(STRANGLED) Let go.

PAN:
Have you any idea how many times I thought about dying? What I endured to get here. Lugging this ventilator on my back wherever I go, a constant reminder of how I had been bettered, first by Ro, and then by *her*.

TASIA:
(BARELY ABLE TO BREATHE) You're . . . choking . . . me.

PAN:
And here you are, bleating about your freedom? (SHOUT-ING) What freedom do I have?

FX: He slams her against the wall again.

TASIA:
(WEAK, BARELY AUDIBLE) Pan.

FX: Tasia gives one tiny last breath.

PAN:
(HIS ANGER GONE. NUMB) To hell with you all.

FX: Pan flings Tasia's body aside.

We pause on him breathing for an intense moment.

PAN: (CONT)
(SOFTER) I shall have my revenge.

FX: He tramps back over the wreckage, grabbing the last of the metal.

PAN: (CONT)
(STRAINING) Just as I gave you yours on Aaloth.

FX: He tosses the wreckage aside with a crash.

PAN: (CONT)
I shall take your broken, twisted body to Ro. Throw you at his feet. See the fear in those soulless eyes before I slit his throat. (COUGHS WETLY) The Jedi will probably thank me. Pan Eyta, Nihil slayer, that's what they'll call me. (LAUGHS, THE LAUGHTER BECOMING ANOTHER COUGH)

FX: His comlink chimes.

PAN: (CONT)
(KEEPS COUGHING)

FX: The bleep continues. Pan grabs it and accepts the call.

PAN: (CONT)
What?

TRILOK: (COMMS)
Boss. Have you found her? We should go.

PAN:
I've found her.

TRILOK: (COMMS)
Then it's done.

PAN:
I'm bringing her in.

TRILOK: (COMMS)
Alive?

PAN:
No.

TRILOK: (COMMS)
I don't understand.

PAN:
(LOST IN HIS THOUGHTS AS HE BENDS DOWN TO PICK HER UP, ALMOST TENDERLY) There was a time when I thought we'd rule the galaxy together, side by side. Before the upstart. Before Ro.

TRILOK: (COMMS)
Did she hurt you? Do you need me to come find you?

FX: Rustle of clothes as Pan picks Lourna up.

PAN:
You're so light now, Lourna. Like a scrap of wind. How could someone so strong weigh so little?

TRILOK: (COMMS)
Is it the pain? Do you need more stims?

PAN:
(SNAPPING) No, it is not the pain. And it's not Dee. She's dead. Gone. It's over.

LOURNA:
Not yet.

PAN:
(TAKES A SHARP INTAKE OF BREATH, A SECOND TOO LATE)

LOURNA:
(GRUNT OF EFFORT)

FX: She stabs him in the neck with shrapnel.

TRILOK: (COMMS)
Boss!

LOURNA:
Colicoid. Dowutin. You're all the same. Big, ugly . . .

FX: Thud as Pan goes down on his knees.

LOURNA: (CONT)
. . . and too quick to write me off. And you were so impressed when you heard how I killed Jinnix, and yet you fell for the same trick. Idiot.

FX: The blade thuds to the ground.

PAN:
(WEAK) Lourna . . .

FX: Pan collapses in a heap.

TRILOK: (COMMS)
Boss! We're coming to get you. Stay where you are.

LOURNA:
I don't think so.

FX: She crushes the comlink beneath her foot.

LOURNA: (CONT)
Whoops. Broken.

PAN:
(WEAK) Smashing the comlink won't help . . . They'll . . . burn this forest down.

LOURNA:
You always did enjoy a good cremation.

PAN:
You're not getting out of this one.

LOURNA:
Shows how much you know. With all your tubes and wires keeping you alive.

FX: She pulls the first tube out of the ventilator with a pop.

LOURNA: (CONT)
Let's see how you'll do without them.

PAN:
I don't need my ventilator . . . I've survived this long hating you . . . I'll survive longer . . .

LOURNA:
Somehow, I doubt that . . .

FX: She pulls another tube free.

PAN:
Nowhere . . . to . . . run, Lourna.

FX: She pulls the last one out with a pop.

PAN: (CONT)
(UNABLE TO BREATHE)

LOURNA:
It always rankled me that I never saw you die over Cyclor. Finally I get to put that right.

FX: There are blaster shots in the distance. They continue throughout the rest of the scene, getting nearer, accompanied by shouts and screams.

LOURNA: (CONT)
That'll be your friends.

PAN:
What did I tell you? Too . . . late . . .

LOURNA:
Not when there's a ship to steal.

FX: She tries to run, but crashes forward to the ground.

LOURNA: (CONT)
(CRIES OUT)

PAN:
Not today.

LOURNA:
(PAINED) Let go of my leg. Let go.

PAN:
Forget Ro. Dying with you . . . seems right somehow. Side by side (GIVES A WET LAUGH) Maybe we'll . . . haunt him together.

FX: A load lifter comes crashing through the trees, a cacophony of splintering wood and hydraulics.

SESTIN:
(SHOUTING) Sal!

LOURNA:
Sestin?

SESTIN:
Sorry it took so long. Got knocked over the head. Couldn't find Wittick. Not exactly seeing straight. But found this load lifter. (BEAT) Is that a Dowutin?

LOURNA:
Push him into the logging pit.

SESTIN:
What?

LOURNA:
Just do it!

PAN:
No.

LOURNA:
Cremation. Burial. It's all the same to me.

SESTIN:
(MAKING A DECISION) It'll be a miracle if I'm ever released, hanging around with you.

FX: The load lifter surges forward. Lots of hydraulics and stomping.

SESTIN: (CONT)
(SHOUTING OUT) Yaaaaaaaaa!

PAN:
(WEAK) No!

CUT TO:

SCENE 122. INT. THE *RESTITUTION*. MEDBAY.

Atmos: As before. We focus on the beep, beep, beep on the monitoring device for a moment before Wittick speaks.

WITTICK:
Sal? Sal.

LOURNA:
(STARTS, JOLTED BACK TO THE PRESENT)

WITTICK:
Lost you there for a moment.

LOURNA:
I'm sorry. I'm finding it hard to concentrate.

WITTICK:
Do I need to call the medics?

LOURNA:
No. No. I'm good.

WITTICK:
We're okay to continue?

LOURNA:
Yeah.

WITTICK:
Recommence recording.

FX: The whir of a recording device.

WITTICK: (CONT)
So what happened when Sestin arrived in the powerlifter?

LOURNA:
Sestin. She saved me.

WITTICK:
By shoving the Dowutin into the logging pit.

LOURNA:
Yes.

FX: We hear an echo of Sestin shouting. The powerlifter charging forward. The crash of metal.

WITTICK:
And the Republic administrator?

LOURNA:
The Dowutin killed him.

WITTICK:
Shot him in the back.

LOURNA:
Yes.

WITTICK:
While you were trapped beneath the wreckage.

LOURNA:
I think Administrator . . . sorry, I've forgotten his name.

WITTICK:
Lalutin.

LOURNA:
Administrator Lalutin, yes. I think he was going to find help, just like Sestin.

WITTICK:
And Prisoner One-Three-Five?

LOURNA:
Tas . . . (COUGHS) Tasia tried to stop the Dowutin from killing me. Is she—?

WITTICK:
Still in a coma. The doc said she might not make it. There's talk of her being transferred to a medical facility. Maybe even Starlight.

LOURNA:
Good.

WITTICK:
Good?

LOURNA:
That she's going to be looked after. What about the Dowutin?

WITTICK:
Missing.

LOURNA:
What?

WITTICK:
The cleanup report came in this morning. His body's gone.

LOURNA:
(LOSING HER COOL A FRACTION) But it can't be. He died. I saw him die.

FX: Another flashback echo. The metal being pushed into the pit.

WITTICK:
Sal. Calm down. I only know what I've read. Most of the raiders got away. We lost eleven prisoners in total. Eight dead and three escaped.

LOURNA:
So he could still be out there . . .

WITTICK:
Who?

LOURNA:
The Dowutin . . . I can't remember. I can't even remember being brought back to the ship.

WITTICK:
With that much shrapnel in you, I'm not surprised.

LOURNA:
I fell . . . trying to get away from him. Landed on the wreckage.

FX: An echo of the moment when Pan and Lourna fell.

PAN: (ECHO)
What did I tell you? Too . . . late . . .

LOURNA: (ECHO)
Not when there's a ship to steal.

FX: She tries to run, but crashes forward.

LOURNA: (CONT, ECHO)
(CRIES OUT)

WITTICK:
You're lucky that Sestin found you when she did.

LOURNA:
Yeah. Lucky. (PULLING HERSELF TOGETHER) What happens now?

WITTICK:
Now? Now you go back to K Block. Doc reckons the synthskin will hold.

LOURNA:
No, I mean for us. For the work crew.

WITTICK:
We're on our way to the next stop.

LOURNA:
We've already left?

WITTICK:
What happened on Arbra was no one's fault. Governor Arman knows that and the Republic does, too.

LOURNA:
And the prisoners that escaped?

WITTICK:
They'll be found.

LOURNA:
Who were they?

WITTICK:
We should probably move on.

LOURNA:
No, I mean . . . was it anyone from our block?

WITTICK:
You mean was it Ola Hest and her friends?

LOURNA:
I guess.

WITTICK:
No. They tried to get away, but were stopped by the security droids. Fry even thinks they orchestrated the entire thing.

LOURNA:
To escape?

WITTICK:
Maybe. There's no evidence they were in league with the raiders. You didn't recognize any of them?

LOURNA:
The raiders? No. They weren't Nihil.

WITTICK:
And you can't think of any reason the Dowutin singled you out.

LOURNA:
He didn't. I was trapped. He blundered through, saw the administrator, thought there was something worth stealing. He was talking to someone, on a comlink.

WITTICK:
Looks like that was their leader. A Gormak.

LOURNA:
Are you sure?

WITTICK:
They matched the description. Reptilian. Frills along the side of their head. The Republic found a name in the records.

LOURNA:
Trilok. That's what he said. (WINCES)

WITTICK:
That graft giving you trouble?

LOURNA:
I'll live. It's what I do.

WITTICK:
Recording off.

FX: The recording device stops.

LOURNA:
Are we done?

WITTICK:
I don't know.

LOURNA:
What do you mean?

WITTICK:
Something's not right.

LOURNA:
I told you what happened.

WITTICK:
Not with the raid. With you. I've lost track of the people I've seen on this ship. Women coming and going. Sometimes coming back far too long. I've also seen that look before.

LOURNA:
What look?

WITTICK:
The look in your eyes, Sal. You're hiding something.

LOURNA:
Is that a surprise? This is a prison. People have secrets.

WITTICK:
Yes. People do. And sometimes those secrets are what keeps people locked up. Not the ship. Not the blocks. Not the cells. The bars here . . .

FX: He taps his temple.

WITTICK: (CONT)
. . . in our heads.

LOURNA:
(TAKES A BREATH, WAITING A MOMENT BEFORE SPEAKING, UNSURE) I thought I was going to die. I mean, I've thought that before, too many times, but back there, under all that metal, looking up at him . . . I really thought it was the end . . . and for the first time . . . (HER VOICE CRACKS) . . . for the first time I welcomed it.

WITTICK:
Hey. If you're thinking this way, we can help. I can help. There are people. An entire wing of therapists.

LOURNA:
(INTERRUPTING) No. (BEAT) No. You're a good man, Wittick. I can see that. I recognize it in other people, at least. In the past I used it. Saw it as a weakness I could exploit. I don't deserve people being nice to me. Trying to help. If I did, I wouldn't have ended up here. And there's no way out. Not now. I'm still trapped. Can still feel that wreckage weighing down on me. And there's nothing I can do.

WITTICK:
You can trust me.

LOURNA:
I can't.

WITTICK:
You can tell the truth.

LOURNA:
(LAUGHS BITTERLY BUT GENTLY)

WITTICK:
The recorder's off. No one's listening. It's just you and me.

LOURNA:
But why? Why would you help? You don't know me. You don't know what I've done, not really.

WITTICK:
No. And that goes both ways. I told you . . . I've seen so many people pass through this ship and facilities like it. For so many years. Sometimes I wonder what good we do. Yes, we rebuild and we put right, but then things like Arbra happen, more often than you think.

I honestly believed that things were getting better. That the *galaxy* was getting better. I believed what the chancellor said, and not just about the reforms to the prison services. Starlight Beacon. The Republic Fair. I was going, you know. To Valo. Was going to meet up with my sister and her kids. My nephew was so excited about seeing the *Innovator*.

And that's gone. All of it.

LOURNA:
Because of people like me.

WITTICK:
No.

LOURNA:
Yes. Because of the Nihil.

WITTICK:
No. I have to believe it's worth it. All of this. I have to believe that there is going to be a way out.

LOURNA:
(ANOTHER SAD SNORT) For light and life . . .

WITTICK:
I want it to be true.

LOURNA:
And I don't know why you're telling me all this.

WITTICK:
Because I see something else in you.

LOURNA:
Not you as well.

WITTICK:
What do you mean?

LOURNA:
First there was that Mon Calamari on Starlight Beacon. Then Sestin. And now you. You all want to see something in people. You want hope. But believe me, I'm not the person to give it. I'm not the person to put your trust in.

WITTICK:
But you could be. That's the thing. I saw it the first time you were in sick bay. When you were recovering. When you took the blame for something you didn't do, to save Sestin. Because you did save her, Sal, long before she saved you.

LOURNA:
Sestin's worth it. She's one of the few people . . .

WITTICK:
That you can trust?

LOURNA:
I wouldn't go that far. I never trust anyone. It never ends well.

WITTICK:
Is that why you never really look anyone in the eye?

LOURNA:
I'm used to wearing a mask.

WITTICK:
I know. And you're still wearing one, right now. Sal, or whatever you're called.

LOURNA:
I'm called Sal.

WITTICK:

And I'm not stupid. I know that's not your name. Other people know it, too. Or suspect it. I see them looking at you. Hear the whispers.

LOURNA:

What did I tell you? Nothing's changed. And it won't.

WITTICK:

Not if you don't let it. Not unless *you* change.

PAN: (ECHO)

Seems to me . . . you've always been running from the past . . . wearing one disguise or another . . .

WITTICK:

Not unless you trust someone.

LOURNA:

You won't like it. If you knew who I was.

WITTICK:

You can't be sure of that.

LOURNA:

You'll lock me up.

WITTICK:

You're already locked up.

LOURNA:

Or you'd send me away.

WITTICK:

Or I'll help you. If you let me. First step . . .

LOURNA: (ECHO)

Tell me.

WITTICK:

Tell me who you are.

LOURNA: (ECHO)

Tell me the name!

WITTICK:

Tell me who you are. Really.

LOURNA:
(SOUNDING VULNERABLE FOR THE FIRST TIME) Who am I?

OPPO RANCISIS: (COMMS)
Cadet?

LOURNA: (ECHO)
My name is Sal.

MEDICAL DROID: (ECHO)
Unit 4978/7179.

INSTRUCTOR DROID: (ECHO)
Cadet Inun. On your feet.

TWI'LEK PROTESTOR 2: (ECHO)
Aww. Is the little princess hurt?

LOURNA:
My name . . .

LOURNA: (ECHO)
Tell me the name!

LOURNA:
My name's Lourna Dee . . . (SUDDENLY FULL OF EMOTION) and I really need your help.

END OF PART FIVE

PART SIX

RENEWAL

SCENE 123. INT. THE *RESTITUTION*. WORKROOM—DAY.

Atmos: A workroom on the prison ship. Lourna is fixing equipment, using a plasma torch.

FX: The bong of an announcement about to be made.

PRISON ANNOUNCEMENT: (LOUDSPEAKER)
All prisoners. Ten minutes to end of current work cycle. Repeat: Ten minutes to end of cycle.

FX: Footsteps as Wittick walks through the workroom.

WITTICK:
You heard that, people. Ten minutes and then you get to enjoy the delights of the commissary. Let's start winding up. Finish your work on the repairs and stow your tools.

FX: Lourna's plasma torch flickers.

LOURNA:
Dammit.

FX: Footsteps as Wittick walks up to her.

WITTICK:
Sal? How are you getting on?

LOURNA:
Fine.

WITTICK:
You don't sound like it.

LOURNA:
I said I'm doing fine.

WITTICK:
Seriously. It's good work. That loader is going to be as good as new when you're finished.

FX: Lourna slams her tool down on the worktable, the flame cutting out.

LOURNA:
I'm not a gearhead.

WITTICK:
I never said you were.

FX: Lourna picks up the tool.

LOURNA:
Just leave me be, will you, Wittick? I can't concentrate with you hovering at my shoulder like a damn droid.

FX: She tries to light the torch, the flame spluttering.

LOURNA: (CONT)
Kriffing plasma torch. The filament's blown.

WITTICK:
Easily replaced.

LOURNA:
Why are you so obsessed with fixing everything?

WITTICK:
Let's have a chat in the office, shall we.

LOURNA:
There's no need.

WITTICK:
I think there is. Come with me.

LOURNA:
(SIGHS)

FX: Scrape of Lourna's chair. Two sets of footsteps as they walk to the office connected to the workroom, passing a hovering droid, the hum of its repulsors coming up and down on mic as they pass.

WITTICK:
Keep an eye on everyone, droid.

SECURITY DROID:
Yes, Counselor Wittick.

WITTICK:
After you.

CUT TO:

SCENE 124. INT. THE *RESTITUTION.* WORKROOM OFFICE—CONTINUOUS.

Atmos: A small office at the end of the workroom. We can still hear the work being continued through the open door, although it's slightly off mic.

FX: Footsteps as they enter.

LOURNA:
Okay, we're here. You want to close the door?

WITTICK:
You know I can't do that.

LOURNA:
Of course. Rules are rules.

WITTICK:
What is going on with you?

LOURNA:
I'm working. Isn't that what I'm supposed to be doing? Maintaining equipment for the next drop.

WITTICK:
You know what I mean.

FX: Footsteps as he moves closer.

WITTICK: (CONT)
(DROPPING VOICE) You said you wanted my help.

LOURNA:
(ALSO DROPPING HER VOICE) I know. And I did.

WITTICK:
And that's changed?

LOURNA:
No. I . . . It's difficult for me to trust people.

WITTICK:
But you've been working on that with your therapist.

LOURNA:
My therapist. Have you spent time with one of those people?

WITTICK:
Yes. We have mandatory sessions three times a week.

LOURNA:
Of course you do.

WITTICK:
But what *about* me. You trusted me. You told me who you really are. And what's happened?

LOURNA:
How do you mean?

WITTICK:
Did I betray that trust?

LOURNA:
I've not been marched off the ship by Jedi if that's what you mean?

WITTICK:
That's exactly what I mean, Sal. You took me into your confidence and I have respected that. Put my neck on the line. And still you're acting up. Still you're being difficult.

LOURNA:
Perhaps I'm still struggling to understand why.

WITTICK:
Why what?

LOURNA:
Why you would put your neck on the line? Why you would care? Perhaps the others are right.

WITTICK:
What others?

LOURNA:
Is this all so I have to do what you say? So you have power over me?

WITTICK:
No.

LOURNA:
And where is that power going, huh? Will there be a locked door? An office with no windows. No cameras. Just you and me where I have to repay the favor by any means possible.

WITTICK:
No! That is absolutely not what this is about.

LOURNA:
Then what is it?

WITTICK:
Sal. I know that most people are out for what they can get, even in here, but this . . . this is about giving you a new start. You're right. When you told me who you were, I could have handed you over . . . but what would that solve? You tell me the Nihil are finished.

LOURNA:
Looked that way to me.

WITTICK:
Then what good would it do if I told anyone who you are? You'll be transferred out of here for interrogation, everyone would want a piece of you. Governments. Individuals.

LOURNA:
And shouldn't they get it? What about Valo? What about your nephew missing the *Innovator*?

WITTICK:
I can't see how giving you up would change that. But seeing you serve your time gladly. Rebuilding what you destroyed. That's worth more to me . . .

LOURNA:
Than justice?

WITTICK:
Than anything. After all these years . . . you're my last chance.

LOURNA:
For what?

WITTICK:
To do something good. To see someone change. Really change. What I want, more than anything, is to see you walk out of here with a new life, untainted by who you used to be. A life to believe in.

LOURNA:
And what if you don't?

FX: A security droid hovers outside the room.

SECURITY DROID: (OUTSIDE)
Counselor Wittick. The work cycle is at an end. Do you require assistance?

WITTICK:
No, we're good. I'll be out in a minute. Check that the prisoners' tools are all locked up.

SECURITY DROID: (OUTSIDE)
Yes, Counselor Wittick.

FX: The security droid whirs away.

LOURNA:
I should go, too. Clear up my workstation.

WITTICK:
Sal, wait. You do believe me, don't you?

LOURNA:
I want to. I really do. I've lived so many lives, Wittick. More than you know. Reinvented myself over and over and it's never been my choice. Not really. It's always been about someone else. Always been about surviving, or about being the person other people think I am. That I should be.

WITTICK:
You should be free to live your own life. A good life.

LOURNA:
Now, wouldn't that be fantastic? Because void knows, it's never been that way before . . .

CUT TO:

**SCENE 125. INT. THE *LOURNA DEE.* FLIGHT DECK—
THE PAST.**

Atmos: On board the ship formerly known as the Toothspike. *Lourna
Dee is on the flight deck, sitting in her command chair.*

H7-09:
Are you sure you want to do this, my Storm?

LOURNA:
Did you used to question your former Storm, Aychseven?

H7-09:
No, Lourna.

LOURNA:
I'm glad to hear it. I would hate to regret rebuilding you.

H7-09:
It's just once—

LOURNA:
Once we do this there's no going back.

H7-09:
And it will hurt.

LOURNA:
And I will hurt you if you don't shut that vocabulator and get
on with it. You should be honored. You're the only one in my
storm that I would trust to do this.

H7-09:
And the only one who will suffer if it goes wrong.

LOURNA:
Then make sure it doesn't.

H7-09:
Yes, Lourna.

LOURNA:
That's better.

FX: A creak as she leans back in the chair.

LOURNA: (CONT)
Proceed.

FX: We hear the sudden buzz of a dental instrument, a file that will sharpen Lourna's teeth.

H7-09:
Open wide.

FX: The sound puts all of us on edge as the file makes contact with Lourna's teeth, a painful, excruciating sound that we hold for a few beats before we hear footsteps as one of Lourna's crew hurries in.

NIHIL:
My Storm.

FX: The filing continues.

LOURNA:
(HOLDING HER MOUTH OPEN SO WE CAN'T MAKE OUT THE WORDS) Not now.

NIHIL:
But it is important.

LOURNA:
(AS BEFORE) Not now!

H7-09:
I think she means it, Strike.

NIHIL:
But it's a message from No-Space. A summons.

FX: Lourna pushes the droid's hand away, the sound of the file going back to the earlier buzz, which continues beneath the following.

LOURNA:
Wait. What kind of summons?

NIHIL:
From the Tempest Runner. All Nihil are to gather at the Great Hall for a Meet.

LOURNA:
A what?

H7-09:
Revels, my Storm.

LOURNA:
(SNORTS) A party? Will there be streamers?

H7-09:
It's more than that . . . a chance to be seen. By the Runners. By the Eye.

LOURNA:
To be seen, eh? Then you better continue with my teeth. (TO THE NIHIL) You. Strike. Send a response. The *Lourna Dee* will be there, but first . . .

FX: She punches him.

NIHIL:
(GRUNTS)

LOURNA:
That's for interrupting me. Aychseven, get back to work.

H7-09:
Yes, my Storm.

FX: The horrible scraping, filing noise continues.

FADE TO:

SCENE 126. EXT. THE GREAT HALL. NO-SPACE— LATER.

Atmos: We are on a vast platform in an area of the galaxy known as No-Space, accessible only by the Nihil's Paths. The Great Hall is a vast platform protected from the vacuum by energy fields that contain breathable air.

A party is in full swing, the Nihil gathering together for revels and debauchery. Wreckpunk blares. There are shouts, cheers, Nihil of all different species celebrating together. Think of it as a cross between a rave and every scene you've ever seen in Viking movies of hairy brutes enjoying too many flagons of mead in packed taverns.

Here, anything goes . . .

LOURNA:
Definitely no streamers.

H7-09:
Is this your first time in the Great Hall, my Storm?

LOURNA:
Does it show?

H7-09:
Not at all. You look absolutely intimidating.

LOURNA:
The teeth are working then.

H7-09:
Is that why you've done it?

LOURNA:
What did we say about questions, Aychseven?

H7-09:
Of course. My apologies.

LOURNA:
It's impressive, though. The Hall.

H7-09:
If you like that kind of thing.

LOURNA:
What's not to like? A repulsor disk hanging in . . . in whatever No-Space is.

H7-09:
Cosmic dust mainly.

LOURNA:
Assessible only by Asgar Ro's paths. Did he build it? Asgar? Did he build the Hall?

H7-09:
I have no idea. (NOTICING SOMETHING) Watch out.

FX: A Nihil barges into her.

LOURNA:
(GRUNTS) Hey!

NIHIL 2:
(DRUNK) Ride the storm!

LOURNA:
Walk into me again and the only thing you'll be riding is a stretcher.

NIHIL 2:
Yeah! Yeah!

FX: Sloppy footsteps as the Nihil blunders on.

LOURNA:
He did realize that was a threat, right?

H7-09:
The amount he's consumed, I doubt he even realizes where he is.

FX: Pan approaches.

PAN: (COMING UP ON MIC)
Or what a lucky escape he's just had.

LOURNA:
Pan. (CORRECTING HERSELF) I mean, Tempest Runner.

PAN:
(LAUGHS) No need to stand on ceremony here, Lourna. All are equal at a revel. (DROPPING TO A WHISPER) Although if anyone barged into me like that I'd break their legs.

LOURNA:
(LAUGHS)

PAN:
Paths' end! That's some smile you've given yourself.

LOURNA:
You like it?

PAN:
Teeth that sharp would give Asgar Ro a run for his money. Like a mouth full of daggers.

LOURNA:
He's here. The Eye?

PAN:
Doing the rounds. You wanna meet him?

LOURNA:
Should I?

PAN:
Why not? He should meet my finest Storm. Ditch the droid.

LOURNA:
Have fun, Aychseven. Try not to get into trouble.

FX: They walk away, leaving H7-09 behind.

H7-09:
Hmm. And where is the fun in that?

FADE TO:

SCENE 127. EXT. THE GREAT HALL. NO-SPACE—CONTINUOUS.

Atmos: As before, elsewhere in the revels.

KASSAV: (OFF MIC)
You should have heard them, Asgar. On their knees, the lot of them, begging me. "Don't destroy the Reliquary. Please don't destroy the Reliquary. This is holy ground."

ASGAR:
And what did you do, Kassav?

KASSAV: (OFF MIC)
What else could I? As the steward said, the Reliquary was holy . . .

ASGAR:
You destroyed it, didn't you?

KASSAV: (OFF MIC)
A proton bomb right in the middle of the Chamber of the Unknown Spirits. There's sure a lot of *holes* in it now.

FX: Both laugh.

LOURNA:
Is that him?

PAN:
That's Asgar Ro, our illustrious Eye.

LOURNA:
And the Weequay?

PAN:
(WITH DISGUST) *That* is Kassav.

LOURNA:
Your counterpart. Another Tempest Runner.

PAN:
Don't remind me. Lousy smash-head. Watch yourself around him.

LOURNA:
He's dangerous?

PAN:
(SNORTS) He wishes. But his hands have a habit of wandering when he's on spice. Reckon you could snap them off with those new fangs of yours?

LOURNA:
I can certainly try.

PAN:
Don't hold back on my account. (CALLS AHEAD) Asgar!

ASGAR:
Pan! There you are. And this must be the newest star in your Tempest.

LOURNA:
Lourna Dee.

ASGAR:
It's a pleasure to finally meet. We've heard a lot about you, haven't we, Kassav?

KASSAV:
You run the mines on Aaloth.

PAN:
Among other things. Lourna's storm has been on fire.

ASGAR:
So I hear. And what do you think of the Great Hall, Lourna?

LOURNA:
It's impressive.

FX: Marchion Ro approaches. Younger. Less confident. With a chip on his shoulder the size of Alderaan.

MARCHION RO: (COMING UP ON MIC)
If defenseless.

ASGAR:
Ah, so my son has decided to join us.

MARCHION RO:
Father.

ASGAR:
You'll have to excuse Marchion. He worries. About everything.

MARCHION RO:
We are standing on a durasteel platform protected only by vacuum shields. If we were attacked . . .

ASGAR:
By whom? No one knows this place exists, and even if they did, look out there in the dust clouds . . . What do you see, boy?

MARCHION RO:
Ships.

ASGAR:
Nihil ships. Every Strike, Cloud, and Storm gathered together.

MARCHION RO:
Which, again, weakens us.

KASSAV:
Ha! Let them come.

ASGAR:
Whoever "they" are. But now that Pan has arrived, we can bring the revels to order. Kassav? If you would do the honors?

KASSAV:
Huh?

MARCHION RO:
He wishes to speak.

KASSAV:
Then why didn't you say so? Cover your ears.

FX: Kassav fires into the air, the bolts loud and numerous.

MARCHION RO:
Careful! If he pierces the energy fields . . .

PAN:
He won't.

KASSAV:
(SHOUTING) Silence for the Eye! Silence!

The noise of the crowd subsides to a low rumble. Kassav stops firing.

ASGAR:
Thank you, Tempest Runner. (RAISING HIS VOICE) Welcome one and all to the Great Hall. It is too long since we have been gathered here as one. The great storm!

Wild track: The crowd cheers, the noise going on a little too long.

FX: Kassav fires again.

KASSAV:
Shut your faces and let the man speak!

ASGAR:
Yes. Thank you, Kassav. Although I understand the exuberance. Understand the high spirits! The Tempests have raged far and wide and the rewards have been great. The Nihil are feared!

Wild track: The crowd cheers.

ASGAR: (CONT)
The Nihil are unstoppable!

Wild track: Even more cheers.

ASGAR: (CONT)
(SHOUTING OVER THE CHEERS) And yet . . .

KASSAV:
Silence!

Wild track: The crowd quiets again, a little unsure. What is the Eye saying?

ASGAR:
And yet . . . not everyone has been paying their part. Not everyone has been paying their dues.

LOURNA:
(WHISPERED) What's he talking about?

PAN:
You'll see.

ASGAR:
When I brought you together . . . When I forged a new storm . . . we made a pledge to each other, to the Nihil. The spoils of our raids are split three ways. A third goes to those Storms, Clouds, and Strikes who performed the raid as is right and proper; a third goes to your Tempest Runner; and if you made use of the Paths, a third goes to your Eye. To me.

It is a good system. A simple system. A system that makes us stronger every day . . . but it only works if everyone plays their part. From the Storms, to the Clouds, to the Strikes . . . (BEAT) and to the Runners!

KASSAV:
Bring him out!

LOURNA:
Pan?

FX: There is argy-bargy at the back of the crowd, a struggle as a Frong is dragged forward in chains. He isn't coming quietly.

Wild track: The crowd becomes agitated at the spectacle.

XANAVEN:
Let go of me! You cannot do this! You will release me this instant!

LOURNA:
Is that—?

PAN:
Xanaven.

LOURNA:
But I thought he was a Tempest Runner, too.

PAN:
He is.

LOURNA:
Then why is he in shackles?

ASGAR:
(TO THE CROWD) There he is! The traitor! The Runner who thought he was above the Nihil!

XANAVEN:
Why are you doing this? Asgar! I will be free!

ASGAR:
Hold him. Hold him.

FX: The Tempest Runner is pulled in front of the Eye, still struggling.

XANAVEN:
(CRYING OUT IN FRUSTRATION)

ASGAR:
This is why I summoned you all. To see what happens when one of our own turns against us. When they ignore the Rule of Three.

Xanaven, whom I counted as the greatest of us. Xanaven, who rebelled against his own nature, a Frong who broke free of the cowardice and servitude of his people to rise through our ranks, becoming Tempest Runner at my invitation and the invitation of his peers.

Xanaven who has been keeping raids secret, not declaring the spoils. Xanaven who stole Paths from other Tempests, from Pan and Kassav . . . from you!

Wild track: The crowd becomes livid.

KASSAV:
What have you got to say for yourself, Xana?

XANAVEN:
I say it's not true. I say I paid my dues.

ASGAR:
I say you're a liar!

XANAVEN:
Of course I'm a liar! I'm Nihil, aren't I? But I never kept anything for myself. I lived by the Rule of Three. It's you that's the leech, Asgar. You that's the bloodsucker.

PAN:
Silence!

FX: Pan hits Xanaven hard.

ASGAR:
Thank you, Pan. (TO THE CROWD) We have gathered here to witness the passing of one Tempest and the creation of another, but before a new Runner can rise, another must fall. Marchion, give me my blade.

MARCHION RO:
Father.

ASGAR:
(HISSING) Quicker, boy. What are you doing?

FX: A blade sings as it is drawn from a scabbard.

FX: Xanaven struggles all the more furiously.

XANAVEN:
No!

ASGAR:
For the storm!

ALL:
For the storm!

ASGAR:
For the Nihil!

FX: Chains are dragged from the hands that have been gripping them.

LOURNA:
Asgar! Look out! He's breaking free!

XANAVEN:
I'll kill you! (GIVES BATTLE CRY)

FX: Xanaven is free, chains clanking as he attacks.

ASGAR:
(A SUDDEN CRY OF FEAR)

LOURNA:
No! Protect the Eye!

PAN:
Lourna!

FX: Lourna jumps on Xanaven.

XANAVEN:
(CRY OF FRUSTRATION) Get off me, Twi'lek! Get her off.
(CRIES OUT)

KASSAV:
Am-Shak's teeth!

PAN:
No. Lourna Dee's!

KASSAV:
Have you ever seen anything like it?

FX: The Frong's body crashes to the floor.

PAN:
Xanaven will never see anything again, that's for sure.

KASSAV:
Is he dead?

LOURNA:
(SPITS) You are safe, my Eye.

MARCHION RO:
Father?

ASGAR:
(HISSING TO HIS SON) Away from me, boy. (TO THE THRONG, BREATHLESS BUT TRYING TO REGAIN CONTROL) There! You saw it with your own eyes. The treachery of Xanaven . . . and also the bravery of this member of Pan's mighty Tempest who risked her own life to save that of her Eye. A true Nihil.

PAN:
Lourna. Get back here.

ASGAR:
No, Pan. She is yours to command no more.

PAN:
What?

ASGAR:
(SHOWBOATING) I promised you a new Runner, and here she is.

KASSAV:
(HISSING TO ASGAR) No. This is not what we agreed.

LOURNA:
What is happening?

PAN:
(NOT HAPPY) You've just made a name for yourself.

ASGAR:
Behold Tempest Runner of the Nihil—Lourna Dee!

LOURNA:
What?

ASGAR:
Say her name! (CHANTING) Lourna Dee! Lourna Dee!

Wild track: The crowd pick up the chant. Lourna Dee! Lourna Dee!

KASSAV:
(HISSED) Pan . . .

PAN:

(HISSED BACK) There's nothing we can do. (JOINING IN) Lourna Dee. Lourna Dee. (REPEAT)

KASSAV:

(GROWLING, BUT EVENTUALLY JOINING IN, IF RELUCTANTLY) Lourna Dee. Lourna Dee. (REPEAT)

ALL:

Lourna Dee. Lourna Dee.

LOURNA:

(LAUGHING TO HERSELF OVER THE CHANT) A girl could get used to this. (LAUGHING TO THE END OF THE SCENE)

ALL:

Lourna Dee. Lourna Dee. Lourna Dee.

SOUNDSCAPE FADES AWAY TO:

SCENE 128. INT. THE *RESTITUTION*. K BLOCK. COMMON AREA.

Atmos: As before.

FX: Doors open. Hum as the security droid leads Lourna and other prisoners in.

SECURITY DROID:
Enter.

FX: Footsteps as the prisoners file in.

SECURITY DROID: (CONT)
Prisoners have one hour of free time before lockdown.

LOURNA:
Yeah, yeah. We know the drill.

SESTIN: (COMING UP ON MIC BEHIND LOURNA)
See, I told you you'd get used to it after a while, Sal.

LOURNA:
Sestin. Good day?

SESTIN:
Long day.

LOURNA:
You wanna swap? If I spend another hour patching up load lifters . . .

SESTIN:
Trust me, the sick bay isn't much better. At least the load lifters don't complain as much as sick prisoners. I don't know how the doc puts up with it. I'm just there to mop the floors and I've had enough by the end of the shift.

LOURNA:
Has Tasia been moved yet?

SESTIN:
To Starlight? No. It's weird. They keep saying she's going to be transferred and yet every day she's there, on her ventilator.

LOURNA:
Still out of it.

SESTIN:
Dead to the world. (BEAT) That's the point where you usually say "good."

LOURNA:
Maybe I'm trying harder these days.

SESTIN:
Glad to hear it. Wanna grab a holoflick before lockdown? I've got credits.

LOURNA:
No. I'm good. I'm gonna head back to my cell. Got some thinking I need to do.

SESTIN:
Sounds ominous. Anything I can help with?

LOURNA:
No. It's just something that Wittick said. It's nothing. Honestly.

SESTIN:
If you're sure . . .

FX: Footsteps as Sestin moves off.

SESTIN: (CONT, MOVING OFF MIC)
You know where I'll be if you change your mind.

LOURNA:
Yeah. I do.

FX: Footsteps as Lourna continues walking. A chair scrapes just ahead of her.

OLA HEST:
Sal. Where are you headed, honey?

FX: Footsteps as Lourna keeps walking.

LOURNA:
Just want to get my head down, Hest.

FX: Scrape of Lourna's feet as Ola Hest stops her.

OLA HEST:
Maybe you should take Sestin up on that offer, hon. A little holodrama might help you relax.

LOURNA:
(GETTING SUSPICIOUS) No. I don't think so.

OLA HEST:
(WITH MORE THREAT) Think about it.

LOURNA:
Why don't you want me to go to the cells?

OLA HEST:
Don't know what you mean.

LOURNA:
Where're Muglan and Parr?

OLA HEST:
It's none of your concern.

LOURNA:
Like hell it's not.

FX: She pushes past her. Footsteps as she carries on.

OLA HEST:
Sal. Sal, you just stop there.

CUT TO:

SCENE 129. INT. THE *RESTITUTION*. QUIN'S CELL.

FX: The sound of a body being slammed against a wall.

QUIN:
(CRIES OUT)

MUGLAN:
What was that, Quin? Did we say you could scream?

QUIN:
(WHIMPERING) No.

MUGLAN:
But I definitely heard a scream. You heard a scream, didn't you, Parr?

PARR:
(AGREES IN AQUALISH)

QUIN:
(SOB) Why are you doing this? I've done nothing to you.

MUGLAN:
But how do we know that, eh? Your little friend stole from Hest and then buddied up to us. *You* buddied up to us.

QUIN:
I don't know what you're talking about. Please.

FX: Footsteps as Lourna runs in.

LOURNA:
Quin? What's going on here?

MUGLAN:
This has nothing to do with you, wormhead.

LOURNA:
I told you not to call me that.

MUGLAN:
You think I care? Get out. This has nothing to do with you.

QUIN:
Sal. Help me. They just barged in.

MUGLAN:
She's not going to do anything, Quin. She's leaving.

LOURNA:
No. I'm not going anywhere.

MUGLAN:
(GROWLS) Get her out of here, Parr.

PARR:
[AQUALISH—Gladly.]

FX: The sound of Parr grabbing Lourna.

LOURNA:
Get your hands off me, Parr.

FX: The scuffle continues.

PARR:
[AQUALISH—Don't tell me what to do.]

LOURNA:
And there you go, honking away. Don't you get it, Parr? No one can understand you, and even if they could, they wouldn't care what you have to say.

FX: Parr hits Lourna.

LOURNA: (CONT)
(GRUNTS, TAKING IT) Thank you.

PARR:
[AQUALISH—For what?]

LOURNA:
For making this easier.

FX: Lourna hits Parr back.

CUT TO:

SCENE 130. INT. THE *RESTITUTION*. WITTICK'S OFFICE.

Atmos: As before.

WITTICK:
That wasn't clever, was it, Sal?

LOURNA:
I don't know what you mean, Counselor Wittick.

FX: Wittick slams his hand on the desk.

WITTICK:
Dammit, Sal. You know exactly what I mean. Punching Parr. Breaking her cheekbone. And as for Muglan.

LOURNA:
Muglan came at me. I stopped her.

WITTICK:
By sending her to sick bay.

LOURNA:
I did what the Jedi would do.

WITTICK:
The Jedi?

LOURNA:

They never attack, only respond. They never kill, only disable. In that way, I'm better than them. Both Muglan and Parr can still walk.

WITTICK:

The governor wants you in isolation.

LOURNA:

What have Muglan and Parr said? Have they made a complaint?

WITTICK:

No. They say you were all fooling around. That it got out of hand.

LOURNA:

What about Hest?

WITTICK:

I'm trying to help you here, Sal.

LOURNA:

And I'm trying to help you.

WITTICK:

How do you work that out?

LOURNA:

Did you see her? Hest? When Parr and Muglan were led off. Did you see everyone else looking at her? Hest set her dogs on Quin and Quin is safe. I am safe. No one is speaking out against me. Even Muglan and Parr are keeping quiet, because they realize that Hest's power, Hest's influence isn't what it was. Because of what happened this afternoon, Wittick. She's alone right now, in her cell, sitting there like a Karkarodon that's lost its teeth.

WITTICK:

Karkarodon teeth grow back.

LOURNA:

(SIGHING) You're not listening.

WITTICK:
I am, I'm just—(HE COUGHS)

LOURNA:
Wittick? (GENUINELY WORRIED) Jon?

WITTICK:
I'm just worried, that's all.

LOURNA:
You're as white as a Gigoran.

WITTICK:
Can you blame me? Keeping you on a leash is a full-time job. The governor—

LOURNA:
The governor wants me in a cube, you said. But you're looking out for me.

WITTICK:
He won't be so easy to convince next time.

LOURNA:
But that's just it. There won't be a next time. Not now. You see that, don't you? You wanted to give me a second chance. Well, that goes both ways. You've never looked so tired. Worrying about me. Worrying about the *Restitution*. You want to make a difference and this is how we can do it. Me on the ground and you—

WITTICK:
Keeping you out of a cube.

LOURNA:
We could make this place *really* work. The way it should. The way you want it to, without having to wait for the chancellor's reforms or for the Senate to pass new legislation. We could start here. Now. At the grass roots.

WITTICK:
It's not that easy. There are always . . . consequences.

LOURNA:
Of course there are. I know that. More than most. But I also know what I'm doing. I'm not going into this blindly.

I've made that mistake before.

WITTICK:
What do you mean?

LOURNA:
I've never told you. Never told anyone, what it was like to be a Tempest Runner. Maybe it's time . . .

CUT TO:

SCENE 131. INT. THE *NEW ELITE* —THE PAST.

Atmos: Wreckpunk plays. A crowd is gathered around a table.

WET BUB:
Mesa gonna win. Yousa know dat, right, Kassav?

KASSAV:
You must be scared . . . if you're trying to put me off with all that Gungan nonsense. Yousa no talken like dat, Bub!

WET BUB:
I talk how I damn well want. (GIVES GRUNT OF EFFORT)

DELLEX:
Come on, Kassav. Finish him off. I've got ten credits resting on it.

KASSAV:
Just ten?

DELLEX:
Everyone knows you're not gonna lose, boss. It's the same every time Bub challenges you to an arm wrestle. You break his scrawny wrist.

WET BUB:
Who you calling scrawny, Dellex? I'll take you on next. I'll take you *all* on.

KASSAV:
Ha! That's what I like about you, Bub. You never give up, even when you don't (EFFORT) stand . . . a . . . chance!

FX: Kassav wins, slamming Wet Bub's hand down in time with "chance."

WET BUB:
(CRIES OUT IN ANGER)

Wild track: The crowd cheers.

KASSAV:
(VICTORIOUS) What did I tell you? Huh?

DELLEX:
Pay up, Grav. Ten credits, fair and square.

WET BUB:
(BREATHING HEAVILY) Again.

KASSAV:
Your arm won't take it. I don't wanna break you.

FX: Footsteps as Lourna pushes her way through the crowd.

LOURNA:
Maybe I should try?

KASSAV:
Lourna! You made it! Welcome to the *New Elite.* How do you like it?

LOURNA:
Do you *really* want me to answer that?

KASSAV:
Yes.

LOURNA:
(DRIPPING WITH SARCASM) It's *exactly* the kind of ship I imagined you'd have, Kassav.

KASSAV:
(TO THE CROWD) I think she likes it!

FX: The crowd cheers.

DELLEX:
Yeah, she didn't say that.

KASSAV:
But you did say you wanted to challenge Wet Bub . . .

WET BUB:
Anytime. Pull up a stool, Dee. I'm ready for you.

LOURNA:
I don't want to wrestle Wet Bub.

WET BUB:
(SHOWBOATING) Ha! She's scared.

LOURNA:
No she isn't. She wants to wrestle Kassav.

Wild track: The crowd responds with ooooohs.

KASSAV:
(LAUGHS) Is that so?

LOURNA:
Why waste energy on a Storm when I can take the Tempest Runner. No offense, Bub.

WET BUB:
None taken. This I want to see.

LOURNA:
Give me your spot.

WET BUB:
Gladly.

FX: Lourna sits.

LOURNA:
Ready, Kassav?

KASSAV:
To wipe that smile off your chops? Always, Lourna.

DELLEX:
Fifty credits she wins.

WET BUB:
You don't want the boss to hear that, Dellex.

KASSAV:
Doesn't bother me, Bub. Take the bet. It's easy money.

LOURNA:
You're confident.

KASSAV:
Are you ready?

LOURNA:
I'm not the one showboating.

FX: Their hands slap together.

KASSAV:
(AMUSED) I'm going to enjoy this. One. Two. (WITH EFFORT) Three.

BOTH:
(GRUNT AS THEY TAKE THE STRAIN)

Wild track: The crowd cheers them on.

WET BUB:
Go on, boss. Go on!

DELLEX:
She's strong.

WET BUB:
But he's stronger.

KASSAV:
(WITH *EXTREME* EFFORT) Damn right I am.

LOURNA:
(WITH EFFORT, BUT NOT AS MUCH) Doesn't look like it from where I am.

KASSAV:
(GRUNT OF FRUSTRATION)

WET BUB:
Finish her, Kass. She's laughing at you.

KASSAV:
(GRUNTS THROUGH GRITTED TEETH)

LOURNA:
(STRAINED) Must be all that smash. It's got to you, Kassav.
Not as strong as you were.

KASSAV:
(MORE EFFORT)

LOURNA:
(STRAINED) You . . . could always . . . yield.

KASSAV:
Never!

WET BUB:
That's it, boss. You show her. (STARTING CHANT) Kas-sav.
Kas-sav. (REPEATS)

Wild track: Kas-sav. Kas-sav. Kas-sav.

DELLEX:
You shouldn't have taken that bet, Bub.

WET BUB:
He never loses. Kas-sav. Kas-sav. Kas-sav. (REPEAT)

LOURNA:
(GRUNT OF EFFORT, BUT SHE'S STILL IN CONTROL)

KASSAV:
nnnaaaAAAAAAA—Enough!

*FX: A scrape of his stool as he stands, breaking the arm wrestle. The
wild track breaks off, too.*

WET BUB:
Hey! What are you doing, boss?

LOURNA:
We done already?

KASSAV:
(QUICKLY, TO THE CROWD, TO SAVE FACE, PANTING AS HE SPEAKS) This is why the Nihil are strong. Because the Tempest Runners are strong. Equal in every way.

DELLEX:
(SOTTO) I'd like to see him wrestle Pan.

KASSAV:
What's that?

DELLEX:
Nothing.

KASSAV:
(SUDDENLY NOT FINDING THINGS SO FUNNY) What did you say?

WET BUB:
She said nothing, boss. Did you, Dellex?

DELLEX:
No. You're right, boss. The Nihil is strong. We ride the storm . . . (TO THE CROWD) Isn't that right?

Wild track: The crowd respond with cheers. Whoops. A few "Yeah, ride the storm."

KASSAV:
(STILL BREATHING HEAVILY, ANGRY) Everyone back to your stations. The party's over. Go!

FX: The crowd disperses, eager to be away from Kassav when he's angry. A comlink beeps.

LOURNA:
Good timing.

KASSAV:
(STILL ANNOYED) Is that him?

LOURNA:
Looks like it.

KASSAV:
We'll take it in my cabin.

FX: Footsteps as he stalks off, spitting on the deck plates.

LOURNA:
Lucky me.

CUT TO:

SCENE 132. INT. THE *NEW ELITE*. KASSAV'S CABIN— CONTINUOUS.

Atmos: Wreckpunk still plays in the background, but it's muffled through the walls.

FX: A door opens, the music louder for a moment, and Kassav stomps in, followed by Lourna.

KASSAV:
Shut the door behind you.

LOURNA:
Kassav. If you're embarrassed . . . it was just a game . . .

KASSAV:
Shut the door!

LOURNA:
(SIGHS)

FX: She shuts the door, the atmosphere outside muffling again. Kassav hits a control. A holo of Pan activates.

PAN: (HOLO)
You took your time.

LOURNA:
Pan.

PAN: (HOLO)
What's wrong with Kass? He's got a face like a sloppet's backside.

KASSAV:
Nothing.

PAN: (HOLO)
You been running, Kassav? You sound out of breath.

KASSAV:
Let's just get on with it. We know why we're meeting.

PAN: (HOLO)
Asgar.

LOURNA:
I still don't see the problem.

KASSAV:
Because you're his favorite.

LOURNA:
That's crap and you know it is.

KASSAV:
Do we? You shouldn't even be here. It should be Xanaven. But you killed him, didn't you?

LOURNA:
I *thought* Xanaven was a traitor.

PAN: (HOLO)
That's what you were supposed to think. What *everyone* was supposed to think.

LOURNA:
Then your plan worked, didn't it?

KASSAV:
No, it didn't. Xanaven was supposed to kill that bastard in front of everyone. Until you stepped in. (MOCKING) "Protect the Eye. Protect the Eye."

LOURNA:
(ANGRILY) How was I supposed to know it was a setup?

PAN: (HOLO)
Well, you know now. And here we are, still in the same position. Asgar taking his cut.

KASSAV:
A cut which should be ours.

LOURNA:
Yeah, but we need the Paths. Without them . . . what are we?

KASSAV:
We're the storm. We were the storm long before Asgar.

LOURNA:
I thought he united the Nihil.

PAN: (HOLO)
You shouldn't believe everything he says.

KASSAV:
Asgar neutered us and continues to neuter us, like a spayed targon. Sure, we need his Paths—and Am-Shak knows that sticks in my gullet—but what we don't need is Asgar Ro telling us not just what to do, but when to do it. That wasn't the deal. That was *never* the deal.

LOURNA:
So we reinforce what was agreed. When he formed the pact.

PAN: (HOLO)
He won't listen. It's gone too far for that. He's tasted power and likes it. I can understand that. We all do.

KASSAV:
Which is why he needs to be dealt with.

LOURNA:
Dealt with?

KASSAV:
Permanently.

LOURNA:
But what about the Paths?

KASSAV:
We'll still have them.

LOURNA:
How?

PAN: (HOLO)
The boy.

LOURNA:
Marchion?

KASSAV:
Runt of the litter. Have you seen him? Cowering in his father's shadow.

PAN: (HOLO)
Asgar will never listen to us, Lourna. Never hand over the Paths.

KASSAV:
But Marchion . . . Marchion we can control. Marchion will do what we say.

PAN: (HOLO)
He'll still get a cut. But it will be reduced.

LOURNA:
And what happens to the rest?

KASSAV:
What do you think? It stays with us. Where it belongs.

PAN: (HOLO)
Asgar may have initiated the pact, but we alone have made the storm strong.

KASSAV:
At least some of us have.

LOURNA:
And what if I don't agree?

KASSAV:
You don't agree to a bigger cut? You don't agree to more control?
More independence? We never signed up for a leader.

PAN: (HOLO)
We *are* the leaders.

KASSAV:
The Rule of Three. Not four. And definitely not one.

LOURNA:
It's a lot to take in.

KASSAV:
Not really. You have a choice.

PAN: (HOLO)
You're either with us . . .

KASSAV:
Or you're dead.

CUT TO:

SCENE 133. INT. THE *LOURNA DEE.* LOURNA'S PRIVATE QUARTERS.

ASGAR: (HOLO)
And what was your answer, Lourna?

LOURNA:
What do you think, Asgar? I told them what they wanted to hear.

ASGAR: (HOLO)
Before running straight to me.

LOURNA:
I owe you a lot.

ASGAR: (HOLO)
More than you owe them? More than you owe Pan?

LOURNA:
The galaxy is full of Pans. But there's only one you.

ASGAR: (HOLO)
(CHUCKLES, IMPRESSED BY HER GALL) You are infinitely fascinating. Where are you now?

LOURNA:
Back on my ship.

ASGAR: (HOLO)
And the others?

LOURNA:
Following the plan.

ASGAR: (HOLO)
Ah yes. The plan. Tell me, where am I to meet my premature demise?

LOURNA:
You're to be invited to the *Elegencia.* Pan will say it's because he's worried about Kassav, that Kass's more . . . unsavory habits are beginning to take their toll.

ASGAR: (HOLO)
And then he'll what? Slit my throat?

LOURNA:
It won't be him. We drew lots.

ASGAR: (HOLO)
And who was the lucky winner?

LOURNA:
Kass. He's going to be waiting for you on the *Elegencia.*

ASGAR: (HOLO)
Where I'd least expect him. And what about you?

LOURNA:
What about me?

ASGAR: (HOLO)
Where will you be when I meet my doom?

LOURNA:
Gathering the Nihil.

ASGAR: (HOLO)
To inform them of my death.

LOURNA:
And to comfort your son.

ASGAR: (HOLO)
Ah, yes. Poor orphaned Marchion.

LOURNA:
But it's not going to work. You know what they're planning. You can prepare.

ASGAR: (HOLO)
Prepare? Prepare for what, Lourna?

LOURNA:
Isn't it obvious? They'll both be on the *Elegencia.* Pan *and* Kassav. All it would take is one thermite bomb near the *Elegencia*'s core . . .

ASGAR: (HOLO)
And you'd be in charge.

LOURNA:
Not just me. Both of us.

ASGAR: (HOLO)
Is that right?

LOURNA:
We could start again.

ASGAR: (HOLO)
Restructure the Nihil?

LOURNA:
Why not?

ASGAR: (HOLO)
You need to be careful, Lourna.

LOURNA:
What do you mean?

ASGAR: (HOLO)
I like the way you think, Lourna. Really I do. You thought that if you brought me this information we could form an alliance, you and I.

LOURNA:
Yes.

ASGAR: (HOLO)
Rebuild the Nihil from scratch. In our image. Using our Paths.

LOURNA:
Exactly. I've been thinking—

ASGAR: (HOLO)
(CUTTING HER OFF) The trouble is, Lourna, they aren't *our* Paths. They're mine. They have been a part of my family for generations, and will eventually pass to Marchion. Do you understand me?

LOURNA:
(QUIETER) Yes . . . my Eye.

ASGAR: (HOLO)
You are ambitious. I like that. And your loyalty will be rewarded. Is this connection secure?

LOURNA:
Of course.

ASGAR: (HOLO)
Then this is what we will do. I will suggest a raid. Maybe . . . Shili.

LOURNA:
You'll move against the Togrutas?

ASGAR: (HOLO)
It has to be large enough to warrant sending the combined forces of Pan's and Kassav's Tempests.

LOURNA:
Won't they wonder why I'm not involved?

ASGAR: (HOLO)
They won't care. They'd prefer it, to be honest. More spoils for themselves, not to mention the prestige . . . until . . .

LOURNA:
They hit trouble.

ASGAR: (HOLO)
The Togrutas will receive an anonymous tip that they are coming. A warning. From you.

LOURNA:
You want me to sell them out?

ASGAR: (HOLO)
You've already done that.

LOURNA:
They'll kill me.

ASGAR: (HOLO)
They'll never know.

LOURNA:
Why? Because the Togrutas will finish them?

ASGAR: (HOLO)
No, no, no. The Togrutas are impressive, but Kassav and Pan
are hard to kill. They'll escape, but their Tempests will be
decimated, their positions within the storm in jeopardy. If
they want to survive, they'll have to win back the trust of
their people. They'll need quick wins. Easy targets. They'll
need Paths.

LOURNA:
From you.

ASGAR: (HOLO)
Precisely. Pan and Kassav are treacherous, but they're no fools.
They won't bite the hand that can save them.

LOURNA:
You've got it all worked out, haven't you?

ASGAR: (HOLO)
Always.

LOURNA:
And if I tell them?

ASGAR: (HOLO)
What I have planned? That is a risk, of course. Just as it was a
risk to tell *me* about their little coup. The question is, Lourna . . .
who do you trust more? Think about it. *Gaze Electric* . . . out.

FX: A beep as the communication is cut.

LOURNA:
Oh, I can trust you, all right, Asgar. I can trust you to stab me in the back at the first opportunity. (LETS OUT A PRIMAL CRY OF FRUSTRATION, AS WE'VE SEEN BEFORE)

FX: Lourna kicks equipment over in her quarters in anger.

LOURNA: (CONT)
What was I thinking? How could I have been so naïve?

FX: The door chimes.

LOURNA: (CONT)
(SNAPS) Yes.

FX: The door opens.

H7-09:
Tempest Runner?

LOURNA:
Aychseven.

H7-09:
Is everything as it should be? I heard a commotion.

LOURNA:
Do we have any Paths that will take us back to No-Space?

H7-09:
To the Great Hall? Is the Eye expecting us?

LOURNA:
No. Which is precisely the point.

H7-09:
I don't understand.

LOURNA:
(KEEPING HER TEMPER) Do we have a Path?

H7-09:
Yes. Yes, of course.

LOURNA:
Excellent. Have it transferred to our smallest Strikeship. But tell no one. Do you understand? Not a soul.

H7-09:
Consider it done. (BEAT) Of course, I do have one question.

LOURNA:
Which is?

H7-09:
What's it worth?

LOURNA:
(LAUGHS) Spoken like a true Nihil. And you're right, of course. Information is power. I should have remembered that.

FX: There is an electronic beep, followed by a shrill electronic whine.

H7-09:
(ELECTRONIC GARGLE)

LOURNA:
Luckily, I did remember to have a few safeguards installed when you were rebuilt, Aychseven. Remote memory wipe. Behaviorial overrides.

H7-09:
(ELECTRONIC GARGLE CONTINUES)

LOURNA:
I'll just have to transfer the Path myself. That's better anyway. Neater. Fewer loose ends.

FX: The whine comes to a sudden stop.

H7-09:
(GASPS, CONFUSED) Tempest Runner?

LOURNA:
Aychseven.

H7-09:
Is everything as it should be? I heard a commotion.

LOURNA:
Yes, thank you. Everything is exactly as it should be.

MUSICAL SEGUE:

SCENE 134. INT. THE *RESTITUTION*. K BLOCK. COMMON AREA—THE PRESENT.

Atmos: As before, the prisoners relaxing in the block. Chatter and general hubbub.

FX: The bong of an announcement.

PRISON ANNOUNCEMENT: (LOUDSPEAKER)
All prisoners. The *Restitution* is entering a communication relay post. Communication with family members is now permitted. Repeat: communication with family members now permitted. Please make your way to comm booths.

FX: Footsteps as Lourna walks through the common area. Quin comes up on mic, but Lourna keeps walking.

QUIN:
Hey, Sal.

LOURNA:
Hey, Quin.

QUIN:
I just wanted to say—

LOURNA:
Not now, eh? I'm tired.

OLA HEST: (COMING UP ON MIC)
I'm not surprised. You've had a busy day. Cozying up to that hunky guard of yours.

LOURNA:
Don't know what you're talking about, Hest.

OLA HEST:
Of course you don't. But don't worry, your pal will be back from the sick bay, too, the little do-gooder.

FX: Lourna continues.

OLA HEST: (CONT, OFF MIC)
(CALLING AFTER HER) If you don't want to cuddle up to Wittick, I'm sure Sestin will be more than happy to oblige. Remember what I said, Sal. She knows how it works. What's got to be done to survive. So no one gets hurt.

LOURNA:
(SOTTO) Still with the threats. Why don't you do us all a favor, Hest . . .

FX: Lourna walks into her open cell, the atmosphere changing, the sounds of the common area becoming quieter.

LOURNA: (CONT)
(SOTTO) . . . and introduce your head to a blaster.

FX: She sits, her bed creaking.

LOURNA: (CONT)
(SIGH) Wouldn't that be nice?

QUIN:
(FROM DOOR) Sal? Can I come in?

LOURNA:
(WEARY) Quin, I said I'm tired. I just want to be alone. You've got your cell. I've got mine.

FX: Quin enters the room.

QUIN:
I know, and I'll be out of your ... well, I'll be out of here before you know it.

LOURNA:
That would be good.

QUIN:
I just wanted to say ... thank you.

LOURNA:
Don't mention it.

QUIN:
But I think I need to. We ... we didn't get off to the best of starts. I went along with Tasia. I thought it was smart ... with the Nihil gone. Being here. In this place.

LOURNA:
You wanted protection.

QUIN:
I was scared. That's not easy to admit to your ... (WHISPERED) to your Tempest Runner ...

LOURNA:
There's nothing wrong with being scared. And I'm not your Tempest Runner anymore.

QUIN:
She didn't tell me, you know. That she had contacted Pan. I don't think she was going to take me with her.

LOURNA:
No, I doubt she was. Do the others know ... the ones from his Tempest? Do they know that was Pan down there?

QUIN:
They think Pan's dead. I checked with them—even Deng. You know the Swokes with all the horns. They think the Jedi killed him, on the *Elegencia*.

LOURNA:
Thanks ... for finding out. I appreciate it.

QUIN:
One of them was talking about you. From back in the day. Not Deng. A Siniteen. They were there when you were made Tempest Runner. They said it was incredible. They said that if you were still alive . . .

LOURNA:
What? They'd kill me.

QUIN:
No. That the storm would never have burned out. That we would still be something. That we wouldn't be here.

LOURNA:
Shows how much they know, doesn't it? (BEAT) I need to sleep, Quin.

QUIN:
Sure. I'll be going.

LOURNA:
Yeah. Good.

FX: Quin turns but stops, kicking a small device accidentally. It skitters over the floor.

QUIN:
Hey. What's this?

LOURNA:
I thought you were going.

QUIN:
This yours?

LOURNA:
What?

QUIN:
An old holoprojector.

LOURNA:
(WITH URGENCY) What? Give me that.

FX: She gets up quickly, taking the projector.

QUIN:
Sure.

LOURNA:
Where did you find it?

QUIN:
Over there. By the door.

FX: An electronic beep and then a hum as the hologram activates.

QUIN: (CONT)
Cute kids. They yours? I didn't know.

LOURNA:
They're not mine. They're Sestin's. Silus and Ita. She never lets this out of her sight. That's what Hest meant.

QUIN:
Hest?

LOURNA:
She knows what must be done . . . so no one gets hurt. Dammit, Sestin.

FX: Footsteps as Lourna suddenly rushes out of the cell.

QUIN:
Sal?

CUT TO:

SCENE 135. INT. THE *RESTITUTION.* K BLOCK. COMMON AREA—CONTINUOUS.

Atmos: As before, the bustle noisier now.

FX: Lourna marches up to one of the guards.

LOURNA:
Counselor Fry. I need to get to sick bay.

FRY:
Are you sick?

LOURNA:
No. But it's important.

FRY:
I don't think so.

LOURNA:
You don't understand.

FRY:
Back to your cell, Krost.

LOURNA:
Okay. Then call Wittick.

FRY:
(SNORTS) Right.

LOURNA:
I mean it. He'll listen, even if you won't.

FRY:
This is your last warning, Krost. The governor is just looking for an excuse to make an example of you (GETS UP IN HER FACE) and so am I.

FX: Footsteps as Quin rushes up to intervene.

QUIN: (COMING UP ON MIC)
Sal. Sal. What about a game of Klikklak, eh? We can deal you in.

FRY:
Sounds like a good idea. Find something constructive to do with your time.

LOURNA:
(STILL STARING THE GUARD DOWN) Yeah. Why not? But we use my cards, okay. I don't trust Remou's pack.

FX: Footsteps as they turn and head back through the common area, Quin having to rush to keep pace.

QUIN:
What was *that* all about?

LOURNA:
Is Fry still looking at us?

QUIN:
Yeah.

LOURNA:
Then keep walking. This way.

FX: A beat and then they stop.

LOURNA: (CONT)
(CONSPIRATORIALLY) Okay, Quin. You need to give me two minutes.

QUIN:
For what?

LOURNA:
I'm going back to my cell for my sabacc deck, remember? Two minutes and then you come looking for me. Got it?

QUIN:
I come to your cell.

LOURNA:
Yeah.

QUIN:
Okay, but—

LOURNA:
Just do it. Okay?

QUIN:
(STILL NOT SURE)

FX: Footsteps as Lourna continues. We stay with her.

LOURNA:
(SOTTO) How did she ever make Cloud?

FX: She enters her cell, closing the door behind her.

LOURNA: (CONT)
Okay. Need to make sure the cameras can't see . . . (BEAT) The bed frame will have to do.

FX: She rattles the frame.

LOURNA: (CONT)
Should be hard enough. (BLOWS OUT) Will only hurt for a minute, Lourna. Only a minute.

FX: Lourna headbutts the bed frame.

LOURNA: (CONT)
(GRUNTS WITH THE IMPACT)

FX: And she does it again, the impact sounding more painful.

LOURNA: (CONT)
(MORE OF A GASP THIS TIME)

FX: She slumps down to the floor.

LOURNA: (CONT)
(BREATHING HEAVILY) Ow.

FX: Quin hurries in.

QUIN:
(PLAY-ACTING) Sal . . . what's taking you so—(SEES THE STATE OF LOURNA) Stars' end. What have you done to yourself?

LOURNA:
(BREATHING HEAVILY) Go fetch help. Say I slipped, hit my head. Tell them there's a lot of blood.

QUIN:
There *is* a lot of blood.

LOURNA:
Then you won't be lying. Go.

QUIN:
I'm going. I'm going.

FX: Footsteps as Quin rushes out. We stay with Lourna.

QUIN: (CONT, GOING OFF MIC)
Counselor Fry! Counselor Fry! There's been an accident. We need to get Sal to sick bay.

LOURNA:
(RAGGED BREATH FOR A COUPLE OF BEATS) I hope I'm wrong about this, Sestin. I really hope I'm wrong.

MUSICAL SEGUE:

SCENE 136. INT. THE *RESTITUTION*. MEDBAY.

Atmos: Quiet. The beep of a life-support system and the wheeze of a ventilator. A medical droid is working over a bed, servos whirring.

FX: There's the creak of a deck plate behind it. The droid spins around.

MEDICAL DROID:
Hm? What are you doing in here? This room is restricted. You are not—

FX: There's a click and the droid deactivates.

MEDICAL DROID: (CONT)
(AS IF RUNNING DOWN) permitted to enter . . .

FX: A final click as the droid goes silent.

SESTIN:
Sorry 'bout that. They really should make droids like you trickier to deactivate.

FX: She moves to the bed. We hear the ventilator wheezing for a couple of beats.

SESTIN: (CONT)
Hi, Tasia. It's Sestin. Can you hear me? (BEAT) No. Good. That's good.

FX: The hum of a vibroscalpel.

SESTIN: (CONT)
I'm sorry. Really, I am.

FX: Another creak of the deck plate.

LOURNA:
(QUIET, COMMANDING) Sestin.

FX: Sestin spins around.

SESTIN:
Sal?

LOURNA:
Put the scalpel down, Sestin.

SESTIN:
I can't. Hest said . . .

LOURNA:
We can deal with Hest.

SESTIN:
She has my kids, Sal. She has my boys. She has an entire network out there, ready to do whatever she wants. Bounty hunters. Assassins. Why do you think she had a comlink for Tasia to steal?

LOURNA:
We can get help.

SESTIN:
No.

LOURNA:
Wittick will listen.

SESTIN:
No, Sal. She said she will hurt them if I talk to anyone. I shouldn't even be talking to you.

LOURNA:
Sestin, you're weeks from getting out. Weeks from seeing Silus and Ita.

SESTIN:
Not if they're dead. I need to be quick, Sal. They'll check on the droid soon.

LOURNA:
We can find another way. You don't want this blood on your hands.

SESTIN:
(BARELY AUDIBLE) I have to. I'm sorry.

FX: Scrape of boots on the floor as she turns to stab Tasia.

LOURNA:
Sestin. No. I mean it.

FX: She lunges at Sestin, grabbing her hand.

SESTIN:
Get off me!

LOURNA:
You can't fight me, Sestin.

SESTIN:
I've got to do this.

LOURNA:
No.

FX: She elbows Sestin.

SESTIN:
(GASPS)

LOURNA:
No, you don't.

FX: Sestin goes down. The scalpel clatters on the floor, the vibration kicking off.

SESTIN:
The scalpel.

LOURNA:
(STRUGGLING WITH HER) Leave it.

SESTIN:
Give it to me.

FX: Lourna scrabbles for it, kicking back hard.

LOURNA:
I said leave it.

FX: A beat of them both breathing heavily.

SESTIN:
You didn't have to kick me so hard.

FX: Scrape as Lourna picks up the scalpel, getting to her feet.

LOURNA:
I have the scalpel. You're not getting it back. At least you had the sense to wear gloves. No fingerprints. That's good.

SESTIN:
But the boys . . . Hest meant it, Sal. If Tasia lives, the boys die. I can't let that happen.

LOURNA:
No. (BEAT) And neither can I.

FX: The hum of the vibration starts again. Scrape of boots as Lourna turns abruptly, stabbing Tasia with the scalpel, the hum muffled by the bedsheets.

FX: An alarm sounds on the life-support machine. Outside, footsteps come running.

LOURNA: (CONT)
Sorry, Tasia. But you would've done the same to me given half the chance.

SESTIN:
Lourna. What have you done?

LOURNA:
What you couldn't. (SHOUTING AS SESTIN GOES TO MOVE) No. Stay on the floor. Stay on the floor. They're coming.

FX: Footsteps as medical staff burst in.

MEDIC:
Void's teeth! Guards!

MEDIC 2:
Put the scalpel down.

LOURNA:
I am. Do you see? I'm putting the scalpel down of my own volition.

FX: It clinks on the floor.

SESTIN:
(SOBBING) Sal.

LOURNA:
There. Now I'm backing up. There's nothing in my hands. I am unarmed.

FX: Security droids hover in.

SECURITY DROID:
Report.

MEDIC:
The Twi'lek stabbed the patient. Secure her.

FX: The droids hover forward, slamming Lourna into the wall. All the time the alarm is still wailing.

LOURNA:
(GRUNTS) Not so hard, boys.

SECURITY DROIDS:
The prisoner will not struggle.

LOURNA:
(PAINED) The prisoner isn't! The prisoner is cooperating!

FX: Wittick runs in.

WITTICK:
What's happening—(SEES THE SCENE IN FRONT OF HIM) Lourna?

LOURNA:
Jon!

SESTIN:
I don't understand . . . who's Lourna?

MEDIC:
The patient's blood pressure's dropping.

WITTICK:
What have you done?

SESTIN:
Who is Lourna?

LOURNA:
(WITH EFFORT, BEING RESTRAINED) Counselor Wittick. Ola Hest coerced me into killing Tasia. She was threatening the family of my friend, Sestin Blin, taking her revenge on me by (GRUNTS) threatening those (GRUNTS AGAIN) closest to me. Hest has an entire network spreading out from the *Restitution* like a glitterstim web.

MEDIC:
We're losing her!

LOURNA:
Sestin found me beside Tasia's bed and tried to stop me. She tried to stop me from doing what Hest wanted.

FX: The life-support machine gives a flatline. Beeeeeeeeeep.

MEDIC:
She's gone.

WITTICK:
Why didn't you come to me? I could've helped.

LOURNA:
No. This is the only way. This is who I am, Jon. That's just the way of it. It's who I've always been . . .

CUT TO:

SCENE 137. INT. THE GREAT HALL. NO-SPACE—THE PAST.

Atmos: A throng of Nihil assembled together. Wood logs are being piled up nearby, thunking together.

FX: Footsteps as Kassav walks up.

KASSAV:
Pan.

PAN:
Kassav.

KASSAV:
And here we are then. Back in the Great Hall.

PAN:
A little sooner than we expected. Are you sure this is a good idea? Building a funeral pyre here of all places.

KASSAV:
It's the Nihil way. At least that's what the little pretender said.

PAN:
As if he knows. (WITH DISTASTE) Marchion Ro.

KASSAV:
Let him mourn his father, Pan. We owe him that much.

FX: Footsteps as Lourna approaches.

LOURNA:
Careful, Kass. It almost sounds like you care.

KASSAV:
(NOT HAPPY TO SEE HER) Lourna. I wondered when you'd show your face.

LOURNA:
Wanted a rematch, did you?

KASSAV:
I wanted a word. (CLOSER) It was you, wasn't it? Who finished him off?

PAN:
(WARNING) Keep your voice down.

KASSAV:
No one's listening, and even if they were, they won't remember, not with the amount of spice we've circulated in the last hour.

PAN:
(SARCASTIC) Wonderful.

KASSAV:
(TO LOURNA) Well? What have you to say for yourself, Dee?

LOURNA:
It doesn't matter who killed him, only that he's dead.

KASSAV:
Of course it matters! We had a plan.

LOURNA:
The plan changed. I don't see the problem.

KASSAV:
The problem is that we can't trust you.

LOURNA:
Why not?

FX: She steps in closer.

LOURNA: (CONT)
(CONSPIRATORIALLY) We're in this together now, Kassav.
The three of us. In it up to our necks. If one of us goes down
for Asgar's death . . .

KASSAV:
We all go down. Is that what you're saying?

PAN:
No one is going down. We proceed as we planned. We let Marchion have his ceremony and then tell him how it's going to be.

MARCHION RO: (MASKED)
How what's going to be?

FX: Booted footsteps approach, a cloak swishing.

*When Marchion speaks he's more confident than we heard before, more
like the Marchion Ro we know from the future.*

PAN:
Marchion. I came as soon as I could. I am so sorry for your loss.

MARCHION RO: (MASKED)
You are?

PAN:
Your father gave us so much.

MARCHION RO: (MASKED)
It wasn't him. It was my family. My father was a link in the
chain, nothing more. A chain that leads to me.

KASSAV:
Is that his helmet?

MARCHION RO: (MASKED)
It's been in the family for generations. I think it suits me. Oh,
and one more thing, Pan.

PAN:
What's that?

*FX: Marchion Ro takes a step toward Pan, more confident than the
Tempest Runners have ever seen.*

MARCHION RO: (MASKED)
(QUIET, SINISTER) Call me Marchion one more time and I will feed you your tusks. Do you understand?

PAN:
What?

MARCHION RO: (MASKED)
Now if you'll excuse me . . . I have deadwood to dispose of.

FX: Confident booted footsteps as he strides away from a dumbstruck Pan.

KASSAV:
What just happened?

PAN:
No one talks to me like that.

MARCHION RO: (MASKED)
(ADDRESSING THE THRONG) My fellow Nihil. You honor me with your presence. You honor my father. This is a day of sorrow, but it is also a day of renewal. Rebirth.

FX: He lifts a blaster in his gloved hand, the leather of his jacket creaking.

MARCHION RO: (CONT, MASKED)
This blaster belonged to my father and now it will send him along the Great Path as I light his ceremonial pyre. We ride the storm.

Wild track: We ride the storm.

MARCHION RO: (CONT, MASKED)
(LOUDER) We ride the storm!

Wild track: (Louder) We ride the storm!

FX: Marchion Ro fires into the funeral pyre, the wood igniting to roar beneath the following.

MARCHION RO: (CONT, MASKED)
(SPEAKING OVER THE FLAMES) When I found my father, in those last moments, he knew his time had come. He knew

he was at the end of his journey. But he also knew that *our* journey together was only beginning. My father knew the storm would continue for all time and that, even as his own name was forgotten, the Nihil would endure. I stand before you, proud to claim my birthright. Proud to be the Eye of the Storm.

KASSAV:
(NOT HAPPY) Pan . . .

MARCHION RO: (MASKED)
(STILL TALKING TO THE CROWD) Together we will ride the storm. You. Me. Your Tempest Runners. *My* Tempest Runners.

PAN:
What did he say?

MARCHION RO: (MASKED)
And no one will be able to stand in our way!

FX: The crowd begins to chant: Ro! Ro! Ro! Ro! Ro! The chant rises in volume and fervor below the following.

KASSAV:
This can't be happening.

PAN:
Well, it is. It is!

LOURNA:
There is a slight possibility we may have miscalculated.

PAN:
You think?

Wild track: The chant of Ro's name continues, echoing as we mix into the next scene.

FADE TO:

SCENE 138. INT. THE *RESTITUTION*. AN ISOLATION CUBE—THE PRESENT.

Atmos: A small room, the thrum of the Restitution *in the background.*

LOURNA:
"We may have miscalculated." The story of your life, Lourna.
The story of your life.

FX: There's a bang on the wall behind Lourna.

OLA HEST: (MUFFLED THROUGH THE WALL)
Are you in there, Lourna? Can you hear me?

LOURNA:
Shut up, Ola.

OLA HEST: (MUFFLED)
I know you can hear me.

LOURNA:
(LOUDER) Shut up!

OLA HEST: (MUFFLED)
Everyone knows your secret now, don't they? They know who
you are.

LOURNA:
I don't care.

OLA HEST: (MUFFLED)
They know where you are, too. Locked in an isolation cube. No way out.

LOURNA:
Yeah, and you're locked in the cell right next to me.

OLA HEST: (MUFFLED)
I hear Governor Arman is putting the call through to the defense coalition. It won't take the Jedi long to arrive. And I bet they'll be furious.

LOURNA:
I don't think the Jedi do furious.

OLA HEST: (MUFFLED)
And Wittick . . . he won't be able to protect you this time. He's been removed from his duties, poor little lover boy. What do you think about that, "Tempest Runner"?

FX: Lourna stands, angry.

LOURNA:
(SHOUTING) You got what you wanted, didn't you? Tasia is dead. And Sestin had nothing to do with it. Nothing! (TRIES TO GET HER TEMPER UNDER CONTROL) They've got her kids, Ola. The Republic. You can't touch them. Not anymore. You can't touch any of them. You're finished.

OLA HEST: (MUFFLED)
I don't think so. Haven't you heard, honey? I'm the one who's *untouchable.*

FX: Boom! There is an explosion. The ship shakes. A klaxon sounds.

LOURNA:
What is that?

PRISON ANNOUNCEMENT: (LOUDSPEAKER)
All prisoners to their cells. This is not a drill. All prisoners to their cells.

FX: The sound of lasers against the hull. More explosions.

LOURNA:
That's laserfire. The *Restitution* is under attack. Is this you, Ola?

FX: When she gets no response, she bangs her fist against the wall.

LOURNA: (CONT)
I said, is this you?

OLA HEST: (MUFFLED)
No. No, of course it's not. (SHOUTING OUT) Droid! Droid, what's happening? Tell me what is happening!

FX: More sounds of attack. The ship shakes again.

LOURNA:
(REACTS TO SUDDEN MOVEMENT) It can't be the Jedi. They'd have no need to attack.

OLA HEST: (MUFFLED)
Then who could it be?

LOURNA:
(REALIZATION DAWNING) They didn't find him. They didn't find his body.

FX: Lourna starts to pace.

LOURNA: (CONT)
He's come for me. Unfinished business.

OLA HEST: (MUFFLED)
What business? Who are you talking about, Lourna?

LOURNA:
Pan. Pan Eyta. I escaped him once . . . but I won't again. Not when he's on the hunt.

END OF PART SIX

PART SEVEN

RECKONING

SCENE 139. INT. THE *RESTITUTION*. COMMON AREA—THE RECENT PAST.

Atmos: As before.

QUIN:
Sestin.

SESTIN:
(LOOKING UP, REALIZING QUIN IS THERE) Quin.

QUIN:
May I sit?

SESTIN:
I . . . I think I'd rather be alone.

QUIN:
I understand. I'm sorry.

FX: She turns to leave.

SESTIN:
Actually, Quin. Maybe it would be good to speak.

QUIN:
Sure.

FX: She sits.

QUIN: (CONT)
How are you doing?

SESTIN:
I've been better. It's all a lot to take in, you know. What Sal did . . . who she is . . . I guess I shouldn't even call her that anymore . . .

Lourna Dee. That's who they're saying she is . . . she *was* . . . I don't know. I can't get my head around it.

QUIN:
All I know is this place feels like it's on a knife-edge. With Hest in iso. Muglan and Parr still in the sick bay . . . no one knows who's in charge.

SESTIN:
Don't let Counselor Fry hear you say that. She looks like the tooka that's got the canakal.

QUIN:
See? Wittick's gone, too. Everything's changed, and no one knows what's going to happen.

SESTIN:
We know exactly what'll happen. We'll be locked in our cells for the night, let out to prepare for the next stop tomorrow. We'll eat slop in the mess . . .

QUIN:
Hey!

SESTIN:
. . . and be sent on janitor duty. Then it'll be back here to count the minutes until we're back in our cells. Nothing's changed, Quin. And it'll continue the next day and the one after that.

QUIN:
Not for you. At least you'll be out of here soon.

SESTIN:
Maybe. I don't know what the governor is going to do with me.

QUIN:
You're here, aren't you? Not in a cube. Because you didn't do anything wrong. Lourna killed Tasia.

SESTIN:
Had they known each other long?

QUIN:
Long enough.

SESTIN:
(SIGHS) I knew she was Nihil, but . . . but I thought she was a grunt, you know?

QUIN:
A grunt?

SESTIN:
(QUICKLY) I'm sorry. I didn't mean . . . (SIGHS) you know what I mean.

QUIN:
Yeah, I do.

SESTIN:
What was it you called her? Her rank?

QUIN:
She was a Tempest Runner.

SESTIN:
That means she was in charge, yeah?

QUIN:
One of the big three, yeah.

SESTIN:
Was she bad? I mean, did she do bad things?

QUIN:
I don't think you can say any of us were good.

SESTIN:
But . . . the Republic Fair. The Hyperspace Disaster. She was a part of all that?

QUIN:
Yeah. A lot of us were.

SESTIN:
But she was behind it. Her and the others. They planned the attacks.

QUIN:
I honestly don't know. That stuff was . . . it was above my grade. I'm a Cloud. *Was* a Cloud. I didn't even take part in many raids. I was just a slicer. Hacking into whatever my storm needed me to break.

SESTIN:
Your storm. (BEAT) I honestly believe I was beginning to understand who she was . . . even if she didn't know herself. And now . . .

FX: Boom. It's the same explosion we heard in the last part. The first attack. The klaxon sounds.

PRISON ANNOUNCEMENT: (LOUDSPEAKER)
All prisoners to their cells. This is not a drill. All prisoners to their cells.

Wild track: The prisoners in the common area react with shock.

QUIN:
What was that?

SESTIN:
I don't know.

FRY: (OFF MIC)
(SHOUTING) You heard them. Back to your cells. Move!

QUIN:
What should we do?

SESTIN:
I don't think we have any choice.

FX: Laserfire echoes through the hull from outside.

CUT TO:

SCENE 140. INT. THE *RESTITUTION*. SECURE CELL.

Atmos: As before. The klaxon is still wailing and continues throughout the scene to keep the tension up, accompanied by the sounds of laserfire. Lots of urgency.

FX: Lourna is slamming on the wall, trying to get someone's attention.

LOURNA:
Hey! Droid! Anyone!

FX: Outside, a security droid whirs up.

SECURITY DROID:
The prisoner will stand back from the door.

LOURNA:
The prisoner will not.

OLA HEST: (MUFFLED)
For once I'm with Lourna. What's going on out there?

SECURITY DROID:
That is privileged information.

FX: Another explosion rocks the ship.

OLA HEST: (MUFFLED)
Well, here's some information, privileged or otherwise. If you don't tell us what's happening, I'll have you smelted in the power core, and don't think I couldn't.

LOURNA:
Not helping, Hest.

SECURITY DROID:
The prisoners will be silent.

LOURNA:
Listen to me, droid. If I'm right, and I know I am, the person who is attacking this ship won't stop until he's found me.

FX: There is another explosion. The ship shakes.

LOURNA: (CONT)
He will kill everyone in his way.

FX: The droid hovers away slightly.

SECURITY DROID:
Please stand by.

LOURNA:
I will not stand by.

FX: Lourna slams the wall again in frustration as she speaks.

LOURNA: (CONT)
I will not die in this cube.

FX: Through the door we hear a screen being switched on and an inter-face arm like R2-D2's being connected to a computer.

SECURITY DROID:
Activating exterior cameras.

FX: The interface arm whirs in the connector.

LOURNA:
Well?

OLA HEST: (MUFFLED)
Can you at least tell us what you're seeing, honey?

SECURITY DROID:
That is privileged information.

OLA HEST: (MUFFLED)
Remember the power core.

FX: *Another explosion. Another shake.*

SECURITY DROID:
(GIVES A SQUEAL OF ALARM)

LOURNA:
Just tell me this, droid. Do you see a ship clamping onto the hull?

SECURITY DROID:
I am not permitted to disclose.

LOURNA:
Tell me!

ORA HEST: (MUFFLED)
I can see the screen.

LOURNA:
And?

ORA HEST: (MUFFLED)
It's a ship, all right. The ugliest ship I've ever seen.

FX: *A whine reverberates through the* Restitution, *the sound of the attacking ship cutting through the hull.*

LOURNA:
Do you hear that, droid? They're cutting through the hull. They're preparing to come on board.

SECURITY DROID:
The prisoner will be silent.

LOURNA:
If you won't let us out, at least warn Governor Arman. Tell him what I said. Tell him that it's Pan Eyta, former Tempest Runner of the Nihil. Tell him to broadcast a distress signal.

SECURITY DROID:
I will contact the governor.

LOURNA:
Good.

FX: There's a troublesome bloop, followed by a beat as the droid tries again, and then another bloop.

LOURNA: (CONT)
What's wrong?

SECURITY DROID:
Internal communications are overloaded. Multiple messages.

LOURNA:
It's only a matter of time before they're jammed and then we're *really* on our own. You need to go to the governor yourself. Tell him.

SECURITY DROID:
Agreed. Prisoners will remain in their cells.

LOURNA:
Like we have an option.

FX: The droid hovers off.

OLA HEST: (MUFFLED)
That wasn't smart, sweetie.

LOURNA:
We have to get word out somehow.

OLA HEST: (MUFFLED)
But if this Eyta character is looking for you . . . ?

LOURNA:
He'll come here. If you're lucky he'll ignore you. It's me he wants.

OLA HEST: (MUFFLED)
And if I'm not lucky?

LOURNA:
(BEAT) Then I wish I could say it was pleasant knowing you.

MUSICAL SEGUE:

SCENE 141. INT. THE *RESTITUTION*. COMMON AREA.

Atmos: As before, the whine of the cutting louder still both in the common room and over the comm.

FX: Prisoners are banging on the doors of their cells.

Wild track: Prisoners shouting. Some scared. Some riled by the danger.

FRY:
Settle down, the lot of you!

QUIN: (SHOUTING, MUFFLED THROUGH DOOR)
Settle down? What's happening, Counselor Fry?

FRY:
I'm trying to find out, Quin!

FX: The beep of a comlink being opened.

FRY: (CONT)
This is Counselor Fry on K Block. Please respond. Are you reading me?

GUARD 2: (COMMS)
Fry?

FRY:
Who's that?

GUARD 2: (COMMS)
Counselor Hazeltow, L Block. The governor's dispatched us to check deck seven. (BEAT) Oh stars.

FX: We hear the cutting nearer, harsher through the comms.

FRY:
What is it?

GUARD 2: (COMMS)
They're almost through the hull. (TO HIS CREW) Take defensive positions. Droids, form a wall.

SECURITY DROIDS: (COMMS)
Understood.

FRY:
Hazeltow.

GUARD 2: (COMMS)
Stand by, Fry. (TO CREW) Stand by, everyone.

FX: The cutting ceases. The sudden absence over the comm is eerie, although the noise from the cells continues.

FRY:
Has it stopped? Hazeltow?

FX: More noise from the cell.

FRY: (CONT)
(TO THE PRISONERS) Shut up, the lot of you. I can't hear.

FX: We hear a clang of metal over the comm.

FRY: (CONT)
(TO THE COMMS) Hello? Hazeltow, report.

GUARD 2: (COMMS)
They're through.

FX: We hear gas being expelled over the comm.

FRY:
What's that?

GUARD 2: (COMMS)
(COUGHING)

FRY:
What's going on?

GUARD 2: (COMMS)
(CHOKING) Gas! Stars, it stings.

FX: Blasterfire comes over the comm.

GUARD 2: (CONT, COMMS)
(SCREAMS)

FRY:
Hazeltow!

FX: More gas. More blasters. Then, abruptly, the comms go dead.

FRY: (CONT)
What?

FX: Fry hits a button, just once at first and then repeatedly as it has no effect.

FRY: (CONT)
Hello? Report. Someone report.

FX: She switches channels.

FRY: (CONT)
Control. This is Counselor Fry. K Block. Please respond. (NO ANSWER) I said respond!

FX: She hits the comm in frustration.

FRY: (CONT)
Respond!

SESTIN: (MUFFLED)
Counselor Fry? Are comms down?

FRY:
I'm not telling you again, Blin.

SESTIN: (MUFFLED)
But maybe we can help? Quin was a slicer. She may be able to get through to someone.

FRY:
No one is getting out of their cell. Not until this is over.

FX: There are suddenly numerous clunks of doors unlocking.

COMPUTER:
Cell doors: Unlocked.

FRY:
What?

FX: Every door slides open.

COMPUTER:
Cell doors: Open.

FX: The prisoners all start exiting their cells.

Wild track: A mixture of excitement and fear from the prisoners.

FRY:
No, no, no, no.

FX: Fry's stun baton buzzes.

FRY: (CONT)
Everyone. Back in your cells. Back in your cells.

PRISONER 1:
Don't think so, Fry!

FX: The prisoner rushes Fry.

PRISONER 1: (CONT)
(BATTLE CRY)

FRY:
Get back!

FX: She shocks them.

PRISONER 1:
(CRIES OUT)

PRISONER 2:
Get them!

SESTIN:
No, wait!

FX: The prisoners surge forward.

Wild track: A bloodthirsty mob.

FRY:
(YELLING) Security droids! We have a code two-eight-five in progress! (MORE PANICKED) Security droids!

CUT TO:

SCENE 142. INT. THE *RESTITUTION*. SECURE CELL.

Atmos: As before. Sounds of laserfire deep in the ship.

FX: The clunk of Lourna's cell unlocking.

COMPUTER:
Cell doors: Unlocked.

LOURNA:
What the—

FX: The door opens, as does Ola's cell next to her.

COMPUTER:
Cell doors: Open.

OLA HEST:
Will you look at that? Someone's looking out for us.

LOURNA:
No they're not.

FX: Lourna hurries over to a computer terminal and flicks switches. More uncooperative bloops.

LOURNA: (CONT)
Comms are down. The computer isn't responding.

OLA HEST:
So?

LOURNA:

So it is exactly what I would have done in a raid. Cause as much chaos as possible. Open the cells on a prison ship.

OLA HEST:

(REALIZING) And you'll have a riot on your hands.

LOURNA:

Prisoners against guards. Confusion. Fear. The perfect recipe for a raid.

OLA HEST:

(COUGHS, FINDING IT HARD TO BREATHE) Ugh. What's that smell?

LOURNA:

A war-cloud. It's being circulated by the atmosphere regulator.

OLA HEST:

Isn't there some kind of filter?

LOURNA:

Nothing's working, Ola. The system's been hacked. (TO HER-SELF) Need to get away. Find an escape pod. Hope they don't notice.

OLA HEST:

Leave the rest of us to hang, eh?

LOURNA:

What?

OLA HEST:

I mean . . . I get it. You and me, we're hardly bosom buddies, but you and Sestin? I can't believe you'd turn your back on her.

LOURNA:

I have to. He's going to kill me.

OLA HEST:

We'll see.

FX: Ola Hest launches herself at Lourna, pinning her against the wall.

LOURNA:
Get off me!

OLA HEST:
Can't do that, honey. If he wants you that bad, then he can have you.

FX: Wham! Ola Hest slams her against the wall.

LOURNA:
(CRIES OUT)

OLA HEST:
Whether you're conscious or not makes no difference to me.

FX: Wham! She slams Lourna against the wall again, even harder.

LOURNA:
(CRIES OUT)

CUT TO:

SCENE 143. INT. THE *RESTITUTION.* K BLOCK. COMMON AREA.

Atmos: There's a full-blown riot in process.

Wild track: Shouts, snarls, grunts, and calls. And beneath it all, the sound of people choking. The war-cloud is spreading.

SECURITY DROID:
Prisoners will surrender.

FX: The zap of the security droid's stun batons discharging. The fight continues in the background beneath the following action.

PRISONER 1:
(SCREAMS)

SECURITY DROID:
Prisoners will return to their cells!

SESTIN:
(CHOKING ON THE FUMES)

QUIN:
Sestin!

SESTIN:
I'm here. I'm here. (COUGHING) This kriffing smoke.

QUIN:
(COUGHING) It was a lot better when I used to wear a mask.

SESTIN:
Where's the door? I can't see.

QUIN:
Over here. This way.

SESTIN:
I'm right behind you.

FX: Footsteps as they stumble forward.

FRY:
No you don't.

FX: The sound of a stun baton striking, a body hitting the deck.

QUIN:
Sestin!

FRY:
No one's escaping on my watch.

FX: Her stun baton discharges.

CUT TO:

SCENE 144. INT. THE *RESTITUTION*. SECURE BLOCK.

Atmos: As before.

Lourna is pinned against the wall.

LOURNA:
(CHOKING) Can't breathe.

OLA HEST:
That's the general idea, hon.

LOURNA:
(BARELY ABLE TO SPEAK) Ola. He'll. Kill. Us.

OLA HEST:
No. He'll kill you. Me? I'll get a ride out of here. And if he won't play ball, then maybe I'll just take his ship.

LOURNA:
(CHOKING) You. Don't. Know him. And—

FX: Suddenly she knees Ola Hest in the stomach.

LOURNA: (CONT)
(WHEEZING BUT ABLE TO BREATHE AGAIN)—you never will.

OLA HEST:
(WINDED) Damn wormhead. I'll kill you. Rip your head off.

LOURNA:
You can try.

FX: Lourna bites Ola Hest hard, as if biting through raw meat.

OLA HEST:
(GIVES A BLOODCURDLING YELL)

FX: A masked guard appears at the door.

WITTICK: (MASKED)
Drop her.

OLA HEST:
Get her off me! She's got a bite like a swamp shark! Get her—

FX: There's a stun shot. A body hits the deck.

LOURNA:
What the hell? You could've stunned me!

WITTICK: (MASKED)
Better that than you killing her.

LOURNA:
That's a matter of opinion.

FX: He removes his mask.

WITTICK:
Put this on. (COUGHS)

LOURNA:
Jon! I thought you were suspended.

WITTICK:
I decided to reinstate myself.

LOURNA:
Any idea where they are?

WITTICK:
The last report put them on deck seven heading straight for K Block.

LOURNA:
Sestin. Dammit.

WITTICK:
(COUGHING) There's no guarantee she's even there. The cell doors have all been opened.

LOURNA:
I noticed. She won't survive. Not in a riot. And not against Pan.

WITTICK:
Pan?

LOURNA:
I'll explain on the way.

FX: She rushes off, Wittick going after her.

WITTICK:
Wait. Lourna. Take the rebreather. The gas is everywhere.

CUT TO:

SCENE 145. INT. THE *RESTITUTION*. K BLOCK. COMMON AREA.

Atmos: As before. The riot still in full force.

FX: The stun baton is discharging.

FRY:
(SHOUTING) Stay down! Do you hear? (COUGHING) Stay down!

QUIN:
(CRIES OUT)

FX: Footsteps run in. A gun comes up.

WITTICK: (MASKED)
Fry! Drop it!

FRY:
Wittick?

WITTICK: (MASKED)
Drop the baton.

LOURNA:
She's not going to. (SUDDEN EFFORT)

FX: She kicks Fry.

FRY:
(CRIES OUT)

FX: Fry hits the deck, the stun baton clattering to the ground.

LOURNA:
Now she has. Quin?

FX: The stun baton scrapes as it's picked up.

QUIN:
I've got it. I've got the stun baton.

LOURNA:
Where's Sestin?

SESTIN:
(COUGHING NEARBY) I'm here. (COUGHING) I'm here.

LOURNA:
What did she do to you?

SESTIN:
It's nothing.

LOURNA:
It doesn't look like nothing. Quin?

QUIN:
Yes, Runner.

FX: The stun baton discharges.

FRY:
(CRIES OUT)

WITTICK:
That is enough!

LOURNA:
We've only just started. Quin, give me that stick.

QUIN:
Here.

WITTICK:
Lourna, I'm not going to tell you again.

LOURNA:
Someone needs to get through to them.

FX: Lourna slams the baton against a door.

LOURNA: (CONT)
(SHOUTING) Hey! Hey! Listen up!

FX: When there's no response Lourna strikes the door again.

LOURNA: (CONT)
Listen up! All of you!

FX: The fighting starts to stop, although there's no silence, thanks to the wailing klaxon and the sounds of distant blasters.

PRISONER 1:
You! You're Lourna Dee.

LOURNA:
Yes. Yes, I am, and if you want to get out of this alive, you'll listen to me. Listen!

FX: The fighting stops for now.

LOURNA: (CONT)
Better. The crew that's working its way through this ship, they won't stop until everyone is dead, both guard and prisoner.

PRISONER 1:
Sounds to me like they're Nihil.

LOURNA:
We can't be sure of that. And if you think they'll stop to ask if you're a Strike or a Cloud, then you're a fool. You'll just be another obstacle in their way.

SESTIN:
So what do you want us to do?

LOURNA:
Wittick. Can we get hold of any weapons?

FRY:
No way.

WITTICK:
You can't expect me to do that.

FX: There's an explosion elsewhere in the ship.

LOURNA:
Can't I? This ship is now a battleground, Jon. If we want to survive, we need to be armed.

FRY:
(PAINED) And what happens when it's all over? You just hand the blasters back?

LOURNA:
One step at a time.

FRY:
That's not good enough.

LOURNA:
It's as good as you're going to get, unless you want to face them on your own.

WITTICK:
I can show you to an armory.

FRY:
Wittick!

WITTICK:
It'll be on my head. Not yours.

FRY:
Damn right it will be.

FX: Blasterfire is getting closer.

FRY: (CONT)
But I guess I don't have much choice. Do I at least get my baton?

LOURNA:
No. Quin—here.

FX: She throws it, Quin catching it in midair.

QUIN:
Got it.

LOURNA:
But only use it on the enemy, do you hear? (TO THE CROWD)
Do you all hear? This is a case of us and them now. Are you
with me? I said, are you with me?

PRISONER 1:
Do we have a choice?

LOURNA:
Not if you want to live.

MUSICAL SEGUE:

LOURNA:

LOURNA II:

LOURNA:
Sestin? (VOICE STRAINED BY

SCENE 146. INT. THE *RESTITUTION.* CORRIDOR.

FX: Multiple footsteps hurry down a corridor.

WITTICK: (MASKED)
This way.

SESTIN:
(COUGHING)

LOURNA:
Sestin?

SESTIN:
(VOICE STRAINED, AS IF HER THROAT HAS BEEN
BURNED) I'm good. (COUGH) It's fine.

LOURNA:
Will there be respirators at the armory, Wittick?

WITTICK: (MASKED)
Not enough for everyone.

FX: Starts unbuckling mask.

WITTICK: (CONT, MASKED)
Here. Give her this.

SESTIN:
(COUGHING) No, you keep the mask. (COUGHS) You're
the one with the blaster. You need to be able to breathe.

FRY:
Glad one of us is a realist. (FRUSTRATED) Where are we?
We've taken a wrong turn.

WITTICK: (MASKED)
No we haven't. It's just up here.

*FX: They approach a corner. There are clanking, mechanical chittering
noises ahead.*

FRY:
What's that?

PRISONER 2:
You don't want to know.

QUIN:
She does if she wants to survive.

LOURNA:
Quin's right. Hold up. Everyone.

FX: They all stop.

WITTICK: (MASKED)
Let me look.

*FX: Wittick looks around the corner, the clanks, whirs, and chittering
continuing. Ahead, scav droids are moving weapons.*

WITTICK: (CONT, MASKED)
What are they?

LOURNA:
Scav droids. Engineered to dismantle, salvage, and steal.

FRY:
They're taking the weapons. What are you waiting for, Wittick? Shoot them.

WITTICK: (MASKED)
There're too many.

QUIN:
They're old models.

LOURNA:
Pan's fallen on hard times, like the rest of us.

QUIN:
Still dangerous, though.

WITTICK: (MASKED)
Quiet. There's someone coming.

FX: Footsteps ahead.

REEMAN: (MASKED)
The droids have cleared the armory, boss. I'm bringing them back in.

FRY:
What *is* that thing?

LOURNA:
A Reeman. From Katarr. I worked with one a long time ago.

PRISONER 2:
Looks like a way outta here to me.

SESTIN:
Hey, where are you going?

FX: Footsteps as Prisoner 2 breaks ranks, stepping around the corner.
Clunk: The Reeman's blaster comes up.

REEMAN: (MASKED)
Stop where you are.

PRISONER 2:
No need to shoot, my friend. I ride the storm, like you.

REEMAN: (MASKED)
Like hell you do.

FX: The Reeman shoots Prisoner 2.

PRISONER 2:
(CRIES OUT, DIES)

LOURNA:
What did I tell them?

WITTICK: (MASKED)
I've got him.

LOURNA:
No, Wittick. Wait.

FX: Blaster bolt as Wittick shoots.

REEMAN: (MASKED)
(CRIES OUT, DIES)

WITTICK: (MASKED)
He's down.

FX: The scav droids surge forward, chittering angrily, their legs clattering on the floor.

LOURNA:
And the droids know where we are.

WITTICK: (MASKED)
You all fall back.

FX: He fires another couple of shots, hitting the nearest scuttling droid, which explodes.

LOURNA:
No. We need you with us. You'll never take them all out on your own. Let's go.

FX: The droids continue toward them.

FRY:
Go? Go where?

LOURNA:
Back this way.

FRY:
Back toward the block?

LOURNA:
No. Down a level. To the workshops.

SESTIN:
(REALIZING) To the load lifters.

LOURNA:
Exactly!

FX: The droids surge around the corner, chasing them, Wittick firing bolts at them.

CUT TO:

SCENE 147. INT. THE *RESTITUTION.* STAIRWELL.

FX: A door opens onto an echoing stairway.

QUIN:
In here.

FRY:
Stairs? In this smoke? We'll break our necks.

QUIN:
It's either that or play slice 'n' dice with the scav droids.

LOURNA:
Stop arguing and move. Wittick?

FX: A couple more shots from Wittick's blaster. A droid explodes.

WITTICK: (MASKED)
I'm here, but we've lost half our people.

LOURNA:
You can mourn them later if you want to. Go.

FX: Footsteps as they start running down.

All the characters are coughing except for Wittick, who is still wearing his rebreather.

FRY:
We're going. We're going.

FX: The droids burst into the stairway above them.

WITTICK: (MASKED)
They're following us.

LOURNA:
What did you expect?

FX: Wittick fires again. Another droid explodes.

FRY:
How much charge does that thing have left?

LOURNA:
Not enough.

FX: A stumble as Sestin misses a step.

SESTIN:
(CRIES OUT)

QUIN:
Sestin. Are you okay?

SESTIN:
(VOICE STILL HOARSE) Don't worry about me. Keep going.

FX: Footsteps as Fry reaches a landing.

FRY:
(CALLING BACK) Here's the door. (EFFORT) It's jammed.

FX: She presses buttons.

FRY: (CONT)
It won't open.

QUIN:
Let me.

PRISONER 1: (OFF MIC)
(SCREAM) It's got me. It's—

FX: Saws whir.

PRISONER 1: (CONT, OFF MIC)
(DEATH CRY)

FX: More shots from Wittick. The scav droid explodes.

WITTICK:
It's a bloodbath!

FX: He shoots again.

WITTICK: (CONT)
We're losing too many people!

FX: He keeps firing.

LOURNA:
Quin. Can you get the door open?

QUIN:
If I can get past the access plate.

SESTIN:
(WHEEZING) Use the baton.

FRY:
No. We'll need that against the droids.

WITTICK: (MASKED, OFF MIC)
Whatever you're going to do—hurry!

QUIN:
Stand back!

FX: Quin shocks the controls, opening up a panel.

SESTIN:
That got it open.

QUIN:
Okay. I can work with this. Fry, you want the baton? Here . . .

FX: A whoosh as she throws it.

QUIN: (CONT)
Catch.

FRY:
No, wait. I can't see.

FX: Fry fumbles it, and it clatters on the floor.

FRY: (CONT)
You idiot. I've dropped it now.

FX: Fry starts searching the floor blindly.

QUIN:
Keep it down, will you? Some of us are trying to work.

LOURNA:
Can you open it?

QUIN:
These fingers were made for slicing!

FRY:
I can't find it!

FX: A scav droid scuttles out of the smoke, attacking Fry.

FRY: (CONT)
(SCREAMS)

SESTIN:
It's got Counselor Fry.

FRY:
(SCREAMS)

LOURNA:
Jon?

FX: Wittick's blaster clicks but doesn't fire.

WITTICK: (MASKED)
Blaster's out of charge.

LOURNA:
Great.

SESTIN:
Lourna. I found it. The baton. Coming over.

FX: She skitters it over the floor.

LOURNA:
Got it. (TO THE DROID) Scavenge this!

FX: Lourna activates the baton and slams it into the scav droid. It squeals, legs writhing, tools whirring.

LOURNA: (CONT)
(WITH EFFORT) Any time now, Quin.

QUIN:
Almost there.

LOURNA:
I can't keep this—

FX: A bladed limb grazes Lourna's arm.

LOURNA: (CONT)
(CRIES OUT)—down for long!

FX: More arching electricity from the stun baton.

WITTICK: (MASKED)
Here come the rest.

FX: A beep and the door slides open.

QUIN:
Done it.

LOURNA:
All of you. Get through.

SESTIN:
What about you?

LOURNA:
Go!

WITTICK: (MASKED)
Lourna. Behind you.

FX: Another scav droid rears up.

FX: Wittick whacks it away with the blaster rifle.

LOURNA:
Strong hit.

WITTICK: (MASKED)
Batted for the phaseball team back in the academy.

LOURNA:
With a blaster rifle?

WITTICK: (MASKED)
First time for everything. How are you doing?

FX: A last squeal as Lourna pushes the stun baton through the droid's processor.

LOURNA:
It's dead. Help me with Fry.

FX: They grab Fry, dragging her to the door.

FRY:
(CRIES OUT AS SHE'S MOVED)

LOURNA:
Void, she's heavy. Even when she's missing an arm.

WITTICK: (MASKED)
What?

LOURNA:
Just keep moving.

FX: The droids skitter nearer.

QUIN:
(FROM THE DOOR) Hurry!

FX: They cross the threshold.

LOURNA:
We're through.

WITTICK:
Is that everyone?

LOURNA:
Anyone who's still alive. Close the door.

FX: A beep and it closes, droids immediately banging on the other side.

QUIN:
Done.

WITTICK: (MASKED)
It won't last for long.

SESTIN:
I can't believe we're all that's left.

FX: The droids start to slice through the door, continuing to the end of the scene.

FRY:
(PAINED) Where's the baton?

LOURNA:
On the other side of the door. In the droid.

FRY:
So we've no way to defend ourselves?

WITTICK: (MASKED)
We will soon enough. This way.

FX: They continue on, the droids almost through the door behind them.

CUT TO:

SCENE 148. INT. THE *RESTITUTION*. CORRIDOR.

Atmos: Scav droids scurrying along the corridor behind our group.

QUIN: (MASKED)
There it is. The workshop.

LOURNA:
Please let this door work.

FX: The door slides open.

QUIN:
Yes!

OLA HEST:
You!

LOURNA:
I don't believe it. Ola. What are you doing here?

OLA HEST:
Thinking I should kill you where you stand.

MUGLAN:
I'd be happy to.

LOURNA:
Good to see you, too, Muglan.

FX: The scav droids skitter closer still.

WITTICK: (MASKED)
No time to argue. In! In!

FX: They bundle in, the door sliding shut. There's the squeal of a scav droid that pushes a leg through the door.

QUIN:
It's got a leg through.

SESTIN:
Can't get the door closed.

FX: The droid squeals like a wild animal, its other legs scraping against the door.

OLA HEST:
Sestin. Hammer. Catch.

FX: She throws it and Sestin catches it.

SESTIN:
Got it!

FX: Clang, clang, clang. She strikes the leg with the hammer until it breaks.

SESTIN: (CONT)
(BREATHLESS) I did it. It's broken. (DESCENDS INTO A COUGHING FIT)

FX: The door slides shut.

LOURNA:
Quin. Lock the door.

OLA HEST:
It was *supposed* to already be locked.

PARR:
(APOLOGIZES IN AQUALISH)

FX: Beeps as Quin locks the door.

QUIN:
It's locked.

FX: The sound of cutting begins.

FRY:
(GROGGY) And we're trapped.

LOURNA:
Haven't you passed out yet?

FRY:
Not . . . getting rid . . . of me that . . . (GROANS)

FX: Wittick removes his mask.

WITTICK:
Fry? Fry. Stay with me? I'm not losing you, too.

QUIN:
She's best out of it.

SESTIN:
Quin!

QUIN:
Look at this place. So much for weapons.

LOURNA:
Ransacked.

FX: She kicks a component that scoots across the floor.

LOURNA: (CONT)
The droids got here first.

QUIN:
You sure it was them?

OLA HEST:
Yes. Because obviously we'd sabotage our own chance of survival.

LOURNA:
What happened?

OLA HEST:
After you left me for dead, you mean? I dragged myself to the sick bay, found these two lugheads, and came here . . .

LOURNA:
Great minds . . .

FX: She starts rifling through parts.

MUGLAN:
It's no good. We've already checked. They didn't leave any of the good stuff.

FX: Lourna selects a tool.

WITTICK:
Is there a plasma torch?

OLA HEST:
You want to use a torch against those things?

WITTICK:
No, I want to cauterize Fry's wound.

FRY:
What?

QUIN:
Maybe we should let her bleed out.

LOURNA:
No. Jon's right. We need everyone on their feet if we're going to get out of here.

FX: A scrape of metal as she finds a tool.

LOURNA: (CONT)
Jon. Catch.

FX: She throws it. Wittick catches it.

WITTICK:
Thanks.

FRY:
I'm not sure about this.

WITTICK:
Here. Bite on this rubber tubing.

FRY:
Wittick.

WITTICK:
Just do it.

FX: The torch fires (although we don't hear it burning the flesh).

LOURNA:
We need to block this door. Muglan. Can you help me with these shelves?

OLA HEST:
That won't stop them.

LOURNA:
No. (GRUNT OF EFFORT)

FX: The metal shelves squeal against the floor. They're heavy.

LOURNA: (CONT)
(WITH EFFORT) But it might slow them down.

MUGLAN:
Ola?

OLA HEST:
(BEGRUDGINGLY) Help her.

FX: Squeal of metal as Muglan and Lourna move the shelves.

SESTIN:
(WHEEZING) Wait. What's that?

QUIN:
Where?

SESTIN:
There. Behind the shelves.

OLA HEST:
An access hatch.

QUIN:
To a maintenance shaft?

LOURNA:
There's only one way to find out. Parr. That pry bar. By your feet.

PARR:
[AQUALISH—This one?]

FX: Parr kicks it over to her.

LOURNA:
Yeah. That's the one.

FX: Lourna puts the crowbar to work. The access hatch drops down.

QUIN:
It's a shaft all right.

OLA HEST:
A very cramped shaft.

LOURNA:
It's either that way or back through the doors.

OLA HEST:
When you put it like that. Parr, you go first.

PARR:
[AQUALISH—Why me?]

OLA HEST:
Because I told you to. Get in there.

PARR:
[AQUALISH—I don't think I wanna work with you anymore.]

FX: Parr crawls into the tunnel.

LOURNA:
Everyone, get in after her. Wittick. How's Fry doing?

WITTICK:
She's still with us.

FRY:
I won't be able to make it through there.

OLA HEST:
(WITH EFFORT) Then stay behind.

FX: The sounds of Hest squeezing through the hatch.

SESTIN:
Sal . . . I mean, Lourna. How do we know where it leads?

LOURNA:
We have to take our chances.

SESTIN:
But what if it leads into more of those droids?

LOURNA:
Then we're dead either way.

MUSICAL SEGUE:

SCENE 149. INT. THE *RESTITUTION.* MAINTENANCE SHAFT.

Atmos: Close and claustrophobic. The group are squeezing their way along, shuffling along on their elbows, clangs of metal accompanying their movements, their breath loud and urgent.

We stick with this for a couple of beats and then . . .

OLA HEST:
Can't you go quicker?

PARR:
(FROM AHEAD) [AQUALISH—I'm going as fast as I can.]

OLA HEST:
Well, it's not fast enough.

SESTIN:
(COUGHS)

LOURNA:
You're not telling me that cough is normal.

SESTIN:
Of course it's not normal. But I'll live.

LOURNA:
It's the war-cloud. It's scarred your lungs. We need to get you help.

SESTIN:
Before or after we escape the homicidal droids?

PARR:
(CALLING BACK) [AQUALISH—I see a hatch.]

OLA HEST:
(CALLING BACK) Parr's found a way out.

FX: Behind them, scav droids push themselves into the shaft.

WITTICK:
(FROM BEHIND) And just in time. They're coming.

LOURNA:
Move!

FX: Lourna and the others crawl by. We stop with Fry and Wittick.

FRY:
(WEAK) Wittick. I can't.

WITTICK:
I'm not leaving you behind, Fry.

FRY:
You have to. I'm not being a hero. That's the last thing I want to be, but I'm done. Look. Does this look like someone who's about to get away? (LETS OUT A GRUNT OF PAIN AS SHE PULLS UP HER JACKET.)

WITTICK:
Stars. Your stomach.

FRY:
Yeah. It's as bad as it looks. I haven't the strength . . . to carry on . . .

WITTICK:
Fry.

FRY:
I'll try to slow them down. But promise me, Wittick. Don't let any of that scum escape, do you hear? It's on you.

WITTICK:
Seriously?

FRY:
Promise me.

WITTICK:
(RELUCTANTLY) Good luck.

FRY:
Yeah. 'Cos that will help.

FX: We stay with Wittick as he carries on, the sounds of the droids behind him.

FRY: (CONT)
Come on then, you metal bastards!

FX: Fry kicks at them.

FRY: (CONT)
(YELLING) Come on!

FX: The scav droids get louder.

FRY: (CONT)
(SCREAMS)

CUT TO:

**SCENE 150. INT. THE *RESTITUTION*. MESS HALL—
CONTINUOUS.**

*Atmos: Outside the shaft now, Fry's scream echoing from within the
tunnel.*

Lourna is helping Sestin out.

WITTICK:
(STILL INSIDE THE SHAFT) Hurry! Hurry!

FX: The scream suddenly cuts off but the chitter of the droids doesn't.

FX: Scramble as Lourna helps Sestin out.

LOURNA:
That's it, Sestin. You're out.

SESTIN:
(WHEEZING) Thanks.

LOURNA:
Jon? (BEAT) Jon!

FX: Wittick makes it to the door.

WITTICK: (IN SHAFT)
(PANTING) I'm here.

LOURNA:
What about Fry?

WITTICK:
Didn't you hear?

LOURNA:
Wish I could say I'm sorry. Let me help.

WITTICK:
Thanks.

FX: Wittick clambers out.

WITTICK: (CONT)
The commissary?

LOURNA:
Let's shut this first before we worry about where we are.

FX: A scav droid makes it to the hatch, skittering out.

SESTIN:
Lourna! Look out! One's getting through.

LOURNA:
Help me shut it!

FX: They push on the hatch. It clangs down on the writhing droid.

SESTIN:
(EFFORT) It won't close.

WITTICK:
(EFFORT) Not with that thing in the way.

FX: More droids are behind the one trying to get through.

LOURNA:
There're more of them!

OLA HEST:
Muglan. Chair.

FX: She shoves it across to the Gloovan, the legs squealing on deck plates.

OLA HEST: (CONT)
Go smash!

MUGLAN:
Finally! (ROAR OF FURY AND EFFORT)

FX: She slams the chair onto the droid over and over and over, screaming all the time. The droid shatters, parts tinkling on the floor.

SESTIN:
She did it!

LOURNA:
It doesn't matter unless we get this closed! (ONE LAST GRUNT OF EFFORT)

FX: The hatch slams down, shutting the droids on the other side. They immediately start trying to cut through.

SESTIN:
There.

LOURNA:
It won't hold for long.

QUIN:
Maybe it won't have to.

FX: Shifting metal as Quin starts rooting around the broken droid.

OLA HEST:
What are you doing?

QUIN:
The droid's comm unit. It still looks attached.

WITTICK:
So?

QUIN:
So, once a slicer . . .

FX: A few electronic beeps as she works the machine. A saw bursts through the hatch.

SESTIN:
They're through.

FX: Another beep . . . and the saw stops. In fact all the droid sounds stop.

QUIN:
. . . always a slicer.

WITTICK:
What did you do?

QUIN:
Sent them back to their ship.

LOURNA:
How much more control could you establish through that thing?

QUIN:
I don't know. It's pretty beaten up.

MUGLAN:
I was told to smash it.

WITTICK:
She's bought us time. That's what's important. The question is what we do with it.

SESTIN:
What about the galley?

PARR:
[AQUALISH—Are you hungry?]

SESTIN:
No, Parr, I'm not hungry. But as much as I hate it, we need to defend ourselves. Kitchens have knives.

OLA HEST:
And so did this droid.

FX: The shiiiing of her picking up a knife from the wreckage.

OLA HEST: (CONT)
Will you look at this blade?

LOURNA:
It's a start. The galley's through here, right?

FX: She presses the door control. It beeps but doesn't open.

LOURNA: (CONT)
It's locked.

QUIN:
Two-six-eight. That's the code. Two-six-eight.

LOURNA:
Thanks. You keep working on that droid.

QUIN:
You've got it.

FX: She enters the code. Each number in the following dialogue is punctuated by a beep of the keypad.

LOURNA:
Two. Six. Eight.

FX: The door opens and gas rushes out (maybe using a wind sound to give an idea of it billowing out).

ALL:
(COUGHS)

OLA HEST:
More of that damn gas.

SESTIN:
(COUGHING) Thicker than ever.

LOURNA:
Wittick. Give me that mask. I'll see what I can find.

OLA HEST:
Why you?

LOURNA:
You've already got a knife.

WITTICK:
Here. But I'm coming in with you.

FX: Lourna pulls the mask on.

LOURNA: (MASKED)
You won't be able to breathe. Don't worry, it's not like I can go anywhere.

FX: A bong of an announcement.

MUGLAN:
Who the hell is making announcements?

LOURNA: (MASKED)
It doesn't matter.

GOVERNOR: (LOUDSPEAKER)
(SOUNDING NERVOUS, READING) "Lourna Dee."

OLA HEST:
Are you sure about that?

WITTICK:
That's the governor.

GOVERNOR: (LOUDSPEAKER)
"This . . . this is a message for . . . for Lourna Dee. Surrender now and no one else will get hurt."

LOURNA: (MASKED)
They've got to be kidding.

GOVERNOR: (LOUDSPEAKER)
"Keep running and . . . and . . ." (BREAKING FROM THE SCRIPT, SPEAKING QUICKLY) If anyone can hear this, call for help, send for the Jedi—

FX: A blaster shot sounds over the loudspeaker.

GOVERNOR: (LOUDSPEAKER)
(SHORT CRY)

PAN: (LOUDSPEAKER, SOUNDING WORSE THAN EVER)
That was stupid.

QUIN:
Is that . . . ?

PAN: (LOUDSPEAKER)
But I hope the same won't be said of you, Lourna, if you're still out there.

LOURNA: (MASKED)
(WITH DISTASTE) Pan.

PAN: (LOUDSPEAKER)
We've primed the ship to explode. Thirty minutes, that's all you have.

WITTICK:
He's joking.

LOURNA: (MASKED)
I wouldn't bet on it.

PAN: (LOUDSPEAKER)
And just in case you're thinking of running, here's an offer for everyone else. Bring me Lourna Dee and you'll be spared. I'll even take you with us. Think of it as early release for good behavior, your ticket to freedom. All I need is Lourna Dee, in thirty minutes, on deck seven. Tick. Tick. Tick.

FX: The loudspeaker clicks off.

SESTIN:
What are we going to do now?

OLA HEST:
Do you even have to ask?

FX: A scuffle as she grabs Lourna.

QUIN:
Lourna!

WITTICK:
Let her go, Hest. Put down the knife.

OLA HEST:
You heard what the Dowutin said. She's our ticket out of here. My ticket out of here.

QUIN:
You can't trust him, Hest.

OLA HEST:
I don't trust anyone. Sorry, ladies.

MUGLAN:
To be fair, it's hardly a surprise.

WITTICK:
We're not going to let you take her.

LOURNA: (MASKED)
No. She's right. This is the only way.

SESTIN:
Lourna, you can't mean that.

LOURNA: (MASKED)
I do. If Hest takes me in, you all still have a chance. If she doesn't, everyone dies.

OLA HEST:
So what's it to be?

MUSICAL SEGUE:

SCENE 151. INT. THE *RESTITUTION*. HOLD.

Atmos: A large echoey storage area. Scav droids skitter in the background, waiting to be given orders. We focus on the soundscape for a few moments before footsteps approach. It's Ola Hest with Lourna, who's wearing the rebreather, her breath heavy through the mask.

OLA HEST:
Hello? Is anyone there?

HEAVY:
Trilok. Trilok, we've got company.

FX: Footsteps as Trilok approaches.

TRILOK:
So I see. Can we help you?

OLA HEST:
I have something you want.

LOURNA: (MASKED)
(GASPS)

TRILOK:
Is that her? Under the mask? Is that Lourna Dee?

OLA HEST:
It is unless my knife slips. Which it could at any minute.

FX: One of the heavies steps forward.

OLA HEST: (CONT)
If *any* of you move.

FX: The scav droids skitter.

OLA HEST: (CONT)
And that goes double for those damn scav droids. We've had enough trouble with them as it is.

HEAVY:
I could take her, boss.

PAN:
Don't you dare.

TRILOK:
Pan. Pan. You need to stay on the ship.

FX: Pan's heavy and sluggish footsteps as he hauls himself forward, leaning heavily on a staff.

PAN: (BARELY ABLE TO BREATHE)
Don't tell me . . . what to do, Trilok.

OLA HEST:
I mean it. One more step.

PAN:
I need to see . . . under that mask . . . I need to make sure . . .

FX: Pan's shuffling footsteps continue.

OLA HEST:
Stop where you are, you lumbering—

FX: A sudden blaster bolt. Ola Hest drops, the knife clattering.

OLA HEST: (CONT)
(DIES)

PAN:
I'm not so blind . . . Ottegan . . . that I can't fire . . . a blaster.

TRILOK:
Pan. Remember what we agreed. (BEAT) Pan.

FX: Pan limps to a stop.

PAN:
You. Twi'lek. Take off the mask.

TRILOK:
Pan. We had an agreement.

PAN:
(BELLOWING) I need to see who it is. (CALMING, GASP-
ING FOR BREATH) She's used decoys before.

LOURNA: (MASKED)
No more decoys, Pan.

FX: Lourna pulls off the mask.

LOURNA: (CONT)
Not anymore.

PAN:
(ALMOST TENDERLY) Lourna.

LOURNA:
You didn't have to kill her.

PAN:
She had a knife to your throat.

LOURNA:
I know. That was the plan.

PAN:
Plan?

TRILOK:
Boss. Boss, if that's her, if that's Dee, we should go. Like we
agreed.

PAN:
What? No. We're going nowhere. I need to know what she
meant.

TRILOK:
But, Pan . . .

LOURNA:
What did he promise you, Trilok? That you were going to hand me over to the Republic? Claim the reward . . . or maybe amnesty. A pardon for your crimes.

PAN:
Tell me what you meant, Lourna.

LOURNA:
That was it, wasn't it? That's how he got you to attack a Republic ship?

TRILOK:
Pan?

LOURNA:
You know he's going to kill me, don't you? Look at him, Trilok. Do you really think he cares about the future?

PAN:
I have no future. And neither do you unless you tell me what you meant.

FX: A click of Trilok raising a blaster.

TRILOK:
Put the blaster down, Pan.

FX: Another clunk of another blaster.

HEAVY:
You need to listen to Trilok, boss.

TRILOK:
Step away from her. Now.

PAN:
(SHOUTING) What. Was. The. Plan?

LOURNA:
To give everyone time to get here.

FX: Footsteps as Muglan, Parr, Sestin, Quin, and Wittick step up behind Lourna.

WITTICK:
By the authority granted to me by the Republic Correctional Alliance, I order you all to drop your weapons.

PAN:
What is this?

HEAVY:
Trilok? What should we do?

SESTIN:
You have everything under control, Lourna?

LOURNA:
For the first time in a long time, Sestin.

QUIN:
You sure about that? Looks to me like they're the ones with all the guns.

MUGLAN:
Yes, but they're all pointing at him.

PARR:
(HONKS IN AQUALISH)

MUGLAN:
Yeah, Parr. The one who just killed our boss.

TRILOK:
Stay back. All of you.

WITTICK:
Or what? You can't shoot us while you're aiming at him.

TRILOK:
Who said anything about shooting. Droids . . .

FX: *The scav droids chitter.*

TRILOK: (CONT)
Attack.

LOURNA:
Now, Quin!

QUIN:
On it.

FX: There's a beep like we heard from the comm unit in the last scene followed by a sudden electronic squeal. The scav droids become agitated.

HEAVY:
Trilok. The droids. Something's happening to them.

LOURNA:
Not something. Someone. The best hacker I ever had on my Tempest. Once a slicer . . .

FX: The scav droids turn on the bad guys.

LOURNA: (CONT)
. . . always a slicer.

FX: The droids attack Trilok and the heavy, blades whirring, drills buzzing.

PAN:
No.

HEAVY:
(SCREAMS)

TRILOK:
Stay back.

FX: Trilok blasts the nearest droid, but the rest continue.

TRILOK: (CONT)
Stay bac—(SCREAMS)

WITTICK:
Quin! We were only supposed to incapacitate them!

LOURNA:
They look pretty incapacitated to me. What about you, Pan?

FX: She strikes out, kicking Pan. Thud.

PAN:
(GRUNTS)

LOURNA:
How do you think they look?

FX: Another kick. The blaster drops from his grip.

PAN:
The blaster.

LOURNA:
I'll take that.

FX: Scrape of metal as she swipes it up.

LOURNA: (CONT)
On your knees.

WITTICK:
Lourna!

LOURNA:
Do it, Pan.

PAN:
(GROWLS DEEP IN HIS THROAT)

FX: A heavy thud as he drops to his knees.

PAN: (CONT)
There. Is that better?

LOURNA:
Much.

PAN:
Then it's your turn. You've won. Finish it.

WITTICK:
No.

FX: Footsteps as Wittick rushes up to her.

WITTICK: (CONT)
Not like this.

PAN:
Finish it, Lourna.

WITTICK:
Remember what we talked about. A new life. A new life . . .

LOURNA:
To believe in.

But that's impossible now, isn't it? Not now. There's no walking away from this. Everyone will know who I am.

FX: More footsteps as Sestin steps forward.

SESTIN:
I already know who you are. You're my friend. The woman who gave up your freedom so I could see my sons. You're Sal.

LOURNA:
(LAUGHS WRYLY) Sal.

PAN:
What are you talking about? You're Lourna Dee. Do you hear me? Finish this. Finish it.

LOURNA:
It's already finished. Quin?

QUIN:
Yes?

LOURNA:
Stand down the droids.

QUIN:
Are you sure?

LOURNA:
Yes. Wittick? Take the blaster. He's all yours.

PAN:
Lourna. No.

FX: Footsteps as Lourna starts to walk away.

PAN: (CONT)
Don't walk away. Don't you dare walk away from me!

END OF PART SEVEN

PART EIGHT

REBIRTH

SCENE 152. INT. THE *RESTITUTION*. FLIGHT DECK.

Atmos: Computers burble in the background.

WITTICK:
To anyone who can hear my voice. This is Counselor Wittick (WINCES) of the correctional vessel *Restitution*. Come in, please. Please come in.

LOURNA:
Still nothing?

WITTICK:
No. Any luck with those transmitters, Quin?

FX: A few electronic beeps as Quin works the controls.

QUIN:
The scav droids are working on it. I don't think they're used to putting things back together.

PAN:
They're not going to thank you, Lourna. You know that, don't you?

LOURNA:
Can't we put him in a cube.

WITTICK:
As soon as the droids have got the cell controls back online.

QUIN:
Next on the list.

WITTICK:
Until then he stays where he is, up here on the flight deck with us (WINCES) where we can see him.

LOURNA:
Jon? Jon, what's wrong?

FX: A door opens. Footsteps as Sestin walks in.

SESTIN:
(COUGHING) You mean he hasn't told you yet?

LOURNA:
Told me what?

FX: Sestin throws a bottle of pills down in front of Wittick.

SESTIN:
(WHEEZING) There. I got those from sick bay. (COUGHS PAINFULLY) Or what's left of it.

LOURNA:
What are those?

WITTICK:
Nothing.

FX: Lourna snatches up the bottle and we hear pills shaking inside.

LOURNA:
Heart stims? Are you sick? Was it the gas?

WITTICK:
No.

SESTIN:
Why do you think he was always in the infirmary? He wasn't coming just to see you . . .

LOURNA:
Wittick?

WITTICK:
The stims control it, more or less. The last few hours have been . . . well, they've been tough.

SESTIN:
Ain't that the truth.

LOURNA:
Is it serious? (NO ANSWER) Is it?

FX: A beep from a computer.

QUIN:
Looks that way to me.

LOURNA:
Quin?

QUIN:
Sorry. I can't help myself. I see a computer system and I have to break it. Ship logs. Personnel records.

WITTICK:
Shut that down.

LOURNA:
This says . . . this says you were due to be medically discharged at the end of your next tour of duty. And you never said anything.

WITTICK:
I didn't think it was important.

LOURNA:
All that talk about the future and you never said a word except . . . (REALIZING) except about how I was your last chance to do something good.

(BEAT)

It was never about me, was it?

WITTICK:
Lourna, listen.

PAN:
(CHUCKLES)

LOURNA:
It never is, is it? All those . . . noble words and aspirations. A life to believe in. You're just like the others. Just like Bala. Rancisis. Just like Asgar.

WITTICK:
I don't know what you're talking about.

PAN:
(LAUGHING) I do.

LOURNA:
Do you know what he called me? Asgar? "His greatest work." His. And I fell for it. I keep on falling for it. Putting on new masks when they tell me. Filing my teeth. Even trying to do the right thing for once in my life. And it's never about me. Always about what I can do for them.

PAN:
(LAUGHING HEARTILY)

LOURNA:
Shut up, Pan.

PAN:
Why should I? Isn't this all part of the plan, Lourna? New allies. New friends. (THE SMILE IN HIS VOICE DROPS AWAY) You're pathetic.

FX: Static suddenly crackles from the flight deck speakers.

QUIN:
They've done it. The droids have fixed the comm array.

WITTICK:
Internal or external?

QUIN:
Both. We're being signaled from the main exercise hall.

WITTICK:
Can you put it through?

QUIN:
Let me see.

FX: Quin presses a button. There's a burst of static and then . . .

PARR: (COMMS)
[AQUALISH—Can anyone hear me?]

MUGLAN: (COMMS, DISTORTED)
Of course they can hear you, web-breath.

WITTICK:
Muglan? Muglan, this is Counselor Wittick.

MUGLAN: (COMMS)
We've done what you said. Gathered everyone together.

WITTICK:
Can we see?

QUIN:
I think I can get the cameras working.

FX: She activates a screen.

QUIN: (CONT)
There.

WITTICK:
Good stars. Is that all there is?

LOURNA:
(HER VOICE JUST A LITTLE HARSHER) What about guards? How many guards?

MUGLAN:
None. We couldn't find any. Not alive anyway.

WITTICK:
None at all?

LOURNA:
Security droids?

QUIN:
Most are offline.

WITTICK:
But you said we have external comms.

QUIN:
Yes. Just stabilizing the receivers. We should be able to access the nearest relay network . . . now.

FX: We hear static over the speakers, a voice, barely understandable, beneath it all.

ZEETAR: (COMMS, HEAVILY DISTORTED)
Cyclone alert. Nine. Seven. Eight. One. Five.

SESTIN:
What is that? Is it the RDC?

QUIN:
Working on it.

FX: The static starts to clear, the words distorted but not as badly as before.

ZEETAR: (COMMS, DISTORTED)
Cyclone alert. Nine. Seven. Eight. One. Five.

PAN:
Well, will you listen to that . . .

QUIN:
(KNOWS EXACTLY WHAT IT IS) Lourna?

WITTICK:
I don't understand. What is that?

LOURNA:
Fate. No. Not fate. An opportunity. Quin. Can they hear me down there?

QUIN:
They can do more than that.

FX: Beeps as she presses buttons.

QUIN: (CONT)
They can see you as well.

FX: Footsteps as Wittick walks up to Lourna.

WITTICK:
Lourna. What are you doing?

LOURNA:
I'm sorry, Jon.

WITTICK:
For what?

LOURNA:
For giving this to you in the first place.

FX: We hear Lourna grabbing the blaster.

SESTIN:
Lourna.

WITTICK:
Lourna. Give me the blaster.

PAN:
That's my girl.

LOURNA:
(PITCHING UP VOICE) Prisoners of the *Restitution.* Some of you will know the Dowutin tied to the chair behind me. You may have even been loyal to him once. But he was not loyal to you. He attacked this ship, killing just about everyone on board because he wanted to kill me before he died. In that he failed.

PAN:
I'm not dead yet.

LOURNA:
Yes. Yes, you are.

FX: She shoots, killing Pan with a single blaster bolt. He crashes back.

SESTIN:
Lourna! You killed him!

WITTICK:
You need to stop this.

FX: Lourna spins, bringing her blaster around to aim at Wittick.

LOURNA:
Don't tell me what to do. No one is ever allowed to tell me what to do. Never again.

SESTIN:
Lourna, please. Listen to me. This isn't you.

LOURNA:
No. No, no, no, no, no! Why would you do that? Why would you, of all people, tell me who I am? I decide who I am, Sestin. Not you. Not anyone. Do you understand?

SESTIN:
(SCARED) Yes.

LOURNA:
(GENUINELY SAD) I so wanted you to see Silus and Ita.

SESTIN:
(CRYING) Lourna. No. Don't say that.

FX: A click of the blaster.

WITTICK:
There's only enough charge in that blaster for one more shot.

LOURNA:
You don't know that.

WITTICK:
I'm pretty sure I do.

LOURNA:
(PITCHING HER VOICE UP) Listen up, everyone. I once heard a man speak at his father's funeral. He said it was a day of sorrow, but also one of rebirth. Of renewal. Today is the same. Today you can go free. There are escape pods all over this ship. Shuttles in the bays, some of them even still operational. You can run right now. Or you can come with me. You can make sure you are never imprisoned again. Are you with me?

QUIN:
Yes. I'm with you, Lourna.

LOURNA:
That's one. How many others?

MUGLAN: (COMMS)
I'm with you.

Wild tracks: Prisoners shout "I'm with you. I'm with you" over the comms.

WITTICK:
They'll hunt you down if you do this, Lourna. They'll find you.

LOURNA:
Not this time. Is the emergency signal still broadcasting, Quin?

FX: Quin presses a control.

ZEETAR: (COMMS, DISTORTED)
Cyclone alert. Nine. Seven. Eight. One. Five.

QUIN:
Sounds like it.

LOURNA:
Then it's time to make a decision.

SESTIN:
(SOBBING) Lourna.

WITTICK:
Lourna, please.

LOURNA:
One. More. Shot.

FX: She fires.

CUT TO:

SCENE 153. EXT. SPACE.

Atmos: The deep rumble of deep space. We hold on that for a few beats and then we hear a distant beep. Beep. Beep.

FX: A space cruiser flies toward us.

PILOT: (COMMS)
This is RDC patrol vessel *Moonseeker*. We have located the distress beacon. Single escape pod floating in the Darkknell system.

VELKO JAHEN: (COMMS)
Moonseeker, this is Starlight. Do you read any life signs?

PILOT: (COMMS)
Inconclusive, Starlight. Will bring pod on board.

VELKO JAHEN: (COMMS)
Understood, *Moonseeker.* Keep us informed.

PILOT: (COMMS)
Roger that.

FX: Maneuvering thrusters fire.

CUT TO:

SCENE 154. INT. PATROL VESSEL HOLD.

FX: The hum of engines. Beeps of a computer.

PILOT:
That's it, Tee-Four.

FX: An astromech bleeps.

PILOT: (CONT)
Gently does it. Gently.

FX: The thud of the escape pod coming to rest on the deck.

PILOT: (CONT)
Moonseeker to Starlight. The escape pod is safely on board. We'll have the droids open it now.

FX: An astromech bloops and whirs across to the pod, extending a manipulator arm. We hear it connect and spin in the socket.

VELKO JAHEN: (COMMS)
Acknowledged. Any idea where it's from?

FX: The pilot presses buttons.

PILOT:
It's registered to the *Restitution.*

VELKO JAHEN: (COMMS)
The correctional vessel?

PILOT:
You know it?

VELKO JAHEN: (COMMS)
We transferred a number of prisoners to there a month or two ago.

FX: The hatch opens.

PILOT:
We've got the hatch open.

FX: He runs over.

VELKO JAHEN: (COMMS)
Any survivors?

FX: The astromech bleeps excitedly.

PILOT:
One. (TO SURVIVOR) Hello?

FX: He clambers into the pod.

PILOT: (CONT)
Hello. Can you hear me? You're safe.

SESTIN:
(WEAK) Safe?

PILOT:
This is a defense coalition vessel. What's your name?

SESTIN:
Sestin. Sestin Blin.

PILOT:
Can you tell me what happened, Sestin?

SESTIN:
(COUGHING) We were attacked. It was a Nihil. A Dowutin.

VELKO JAHEN: (COMMS)
Did she say Nihil?

SESTIN:
I need to see my children. Can you help me find my children?

PILOT:
You said your ship was attacked. The *Restitution,* yes? Where is the *Restitution* now?

SESTIN:
I . . . (COUGH) I . . . don't know. My friend . . . My friend got me into an escape pod. Launched me into space.

PILOT:
Your friend.

SESTIN:
Sal. (COUGHS) I knew her as Sal.

PILOT:
And do you know if Sal survived as well?

SESTIN:
(BEAT) No. (COUGH) No. I think she's gone.

CUT TO:

SCENE 155. INT. A NIHIL CRUISER—LATER.

Atmos: The deep rumble of engines.

FX: A Talpini in a heavy powersuit clumps in.

ZEETAR:
Report. Has anyone responded to the emergency message?

NIHIL STRIKE:
No one, Tempest Runner.

ZEETAR:
(DISBELIEVING) No one at all?

FX: A comm unit starts beeping.

ZEETAR: (CONT)
Is that—?

NIHIL STRIKE 2:
An incoming holo.

ZEETAR:
Let me see.

FX: A hologram crackles into view.

MARCHION RO: (HOLO)
Zeetar.

ZEETAR:
Ro. You live.

MARCHION RO: (HOLO)
As do you.

ZEETAR:
I thought you were dead. I thought the Nihil . . .

MARCHION RO: (HOLO)
The storm never dies, Zeetar.

ZEETAR:
The storm is not what it was.

MARCHION RO: (HOLO)
How many ships do you have in your Tempest, Zeetar?

ZEETAR:
(NOT WANTING TO SAY) Nine.

MARCHION RO: (HOLO)
Nine?

ZEETAR:
Including this one.

MARCHION RO: (HOLO)
What of your own Dreadnought?

ZEETAR:
The *Technocrat* was lost to the Jedi. I barely escaped with my life.

MARCHION RO: (HOLO)
Can you get to the hall?

ZEETAR:
If we can have Paths. You still have Paths, don't you, Ro?

MARCHION RO: (HOLO)
I will send you what I have. We will rendezvous there and make our plans.

ZEETAR:
What of Lourna? I heard—

MARCHION RO: (HOLO)
Lourna is dead.

ZEETAR:
And her Tempest?

MARCHION RO: (HOLO)
We do not need her Tempest. I have something far more effective.

LOURNA: (COMMS)
Now, this I must hear?

Music swells.

ZEETAR:
Lourna? I don't understand.

LOURNA: (COMMS)
Why am I not surprised? Hello, Marchion. Missed me?

NIHIL STRIKE:
Tempest Runner. A ship is coming in.

FX: The thump of a ship coming out of hyperspace next to them.

ZEETAR:
Is that her?

NIHIL STRIKE:
The registry says it's a Republic prison ship. The *Restitution.*

CUT TO:

SCENE 156. INT. THE *RESTITUTION.* FLIGHT DECK—CONTINUOUS.

MUGLAN:
Tempest Runner. Should we power the weapons?

LOURNA:
Of course not, Cloud Muglan. We are the Nihil. We do not fire on each other.

MARCHION RO: (COMMS)
I am glad to hear it. Republic records said . . .

LOURNA:
Republic records said I was lost, but the Republic was wrong. I was merely . . . biding my time.

MARCHION RO: (COMMS)
Biding your time for what?

FX: A door slides open behind her. Footsteps as Quin enters.

QUIN:
My Tempest, it is ready.

LOURNA:
Ah, let me see, Storm Quin.

FX: A clank of metal as Quin passes a certain something to Lourna.

QUIN:
I hope it's to your satisfaction.

LOURNA:
It's perfect. Identical to the original in every way. You were wasted in the galley. They should have had you in the repair shop.

MARCHION RO: (COMMS)
Lourna, I asked you a question.

LOURNA:
And I will answer you, when I'm properly dressed.

FX: She puts on her mask. We hear the hiss of the hydraulics. The breathing apparatus activating.

LOURNA: (CONT, MASKED)
There. That's better. What is a Tempest Runner without her mask?

ZEETAR: (COMMS)
You can hardly be a Tempest Runner without a Tempest, Lourna.

LOURNA: (MASKED)
Oh, but I have a Tempest, Zeetar. A new Tempest. A strong Tempest. A Tempest who will follow me to the ends of the galaxy. While it seems to me that you have nothing. Neither of you. We should discuss that. On my terms. And on my ship.

MARCHION RO: (COMMS)
Your ship . . . This *Restitution.*

LOURNA: (MASKED)
Oh, that's not her name. Storm Quin. Will you tell Marchion Ro the name of this vessel.

QUIN:
The *Lourna Dee,* Tempest Runner.

LOURNA: (MASKED)
That's right. The *Lourna Dee.*

And don't you forget it.

THE END

Acknowledgments

FX: A slurp of coffee. A mug is placed on a desk.

AUTHOR:
Hello? Starlight Beacon? Do you read me? I wish to transmit my thanks. Is this getting through?

FX: There is no response.

AUTHOR:
Hmmm. Well, I'll try anyway. First of all I need to thank Elizabeth Schaefer at Port Del Rey as well as Lucasfilm Publishing's very own high council, Masters Heddle, Hidalgo, Martin, and Stein, for their guidance and support. Thanks also must be made to Nick Martorelli at relay point PRHA and our wonderful cast and crew for bringing the drama so vividly to life.

FX: Author takes another sip of coffee, followed by the crunch of a biscuit.

AUTHOR:
Then there are my fellow Luminati: Claudia Gray, Justina Ireland, Daniel José Older, and Charles Soule, plus George Mann, who helped me navigate plot points and problems alike. And we can never forget Grandmaster Siglain who keeps this ship on course come what may.

There are a galaxy of other names to mention, from my agent Charlotte to our amazing cover artist Katerina Balikova, plus Kristin Baver and Krystina Arielle for spreading the High Republic love far and wide.

And, of course, there is my co-pilot Clare. Where would I be without you? Lost in hyperspace, that's where!

FX: The coffee cup is drained.

AUTHOR:
There, that's it. If I've forgotten anyone I apologize. We are all the Republic, after all. Transmitting now.

FX: A clack of a keyboard followed by a beep.

AUTHOR:
Do you have it? Starlight Beacon? Are you there? (BEAT) What am I talking about? Of course Starlight is there. What in void's name could happen to it, anyway?

FX: Swallows nervously.

About the Author

CAVAN SCOTT is a *New York Times* bestselling author and screenwriter who has written for such popular worlds as *Star Wars, Doctor Who, Star Trek,* Assassin's Creed, *Transformers, Pacific Rim,* and Sherlock Holmes. A story architect for *Star Wars: The High Republic,* Cavan is the writer of *Star Wars: The High Republic: The Rising Storm, Star Wars: Dooku: Jedi Lost, The Patchwork Devil, Sleep Terrors,* and *Shadow Service,* and has written comics for Marvel, DC, IDW, Dark Horse, *2000 AD,* and *The Beano.* A former magazine editor, Cavan Scott lives in the United Kingdom with his wife and daughters. His passions include learning the concertina, folklore, the music of David Bowie, and scary movies. He owns far too much LEGO.

cavanscott.com

Read on for an excerpt from

THE FALLEN STAR

By Claudia Gray

The tragic events of the Republic Fair have galvanized the galaxy. The Jedi and the Republic have gone on the offensive to stop the marauding NIHIL. With these vicious raiders all but defeated, Jedi Master AVAR KRISS has set her sights on LOURNA DEE, the supposed Eye of the Nihil, and has undertaken a mission to capture her once and for all.

But unbeknownst to the Jedi, the true leader of the Nihil, the insidious MARCHION RO, is about to launch an attack on the Jedi and the Republic, on a scale not seen in centuries. If he succeeds, the Nihil will be triumphant, and the light of the Jedi will go dark.

Only the brave Jedi Knights of STARLIGHT BEACON stand in his way, but even they may not be enough against Ro and the ancient enemy that's about to be unleashed. . . .

Prologue

The Longbeam cruiser slipped into the Nefitifi system as smoothly and silently as a sharp needle piercing black cloth. Only a few million years before, a star in this previously binary system had exploded, leaving behind a nebula of extraordinary scale. Trails of deep-purple and dark-blue gases laced between the planets, radioactive and opaque, hiding the entire system within swirls of mist.

Many smugglers had, in the past, taken advantage of that mist.

The Jedi now believed the Nihil were using it, too. It was their last place to hide.

"Any signals?" Master Indeera Stokes asked her Padawan.

Bell Zettifar, next to her, shook his head. "Nothing on any frequencies. It's completely quiet out there."

"It shouldn't be." Master Nib Assek shook her head, her gray hair painted silver by the shadows in which they stood. (When a Longbeam ran on half power to avoid attention—as this one now did—lighting dimmed accordingly.) "Gun runners have used this part of space for a long time. You'd expect beacons, tagged cargo in asteroids, something of that sort. Instead . . . nothing."

Bell glanced over at a fellow Padawan, the Wookiee Burry-aga, who stood by Master Assek's side. Their shared look confirmed that they understood what was implied: The Nefitifi system was *too* quiet. Finding no activity here was like landing on Coruscant and finding it deserted: proof positive that something was very wrong.

Here it could only mean that the Nihil were near.

"They must be using silencers," Bell said to Master Indeera. "Satellites or shipboard?"

"Shipboard, I suspect. We'll soon find out." His Master squared her shoulders; her Tholothian tendrils rippled down her back. Bell felt the shiver of anticipation that went through the Jedi cohort aboard; the Force was warning them of what was about to come. Master Indeera put her hand on her lightsaber hilt. "The other Longbeams report similar readings—or lack thereof. The Nihil must be very near."

Finally, action. A chance to move on the Nihil. Bell had wanted this—*needed* it—ever since the loss of his former Master, Loden Greatstorm. Not for vengeance. Greatstorm would never have wanted that. For the knowledge that Bell had done something, *anything,* to counteract the evil that had robbed his Master of his life. The Nihil were already beaten, it seemed—Master Avar Kriss seemed on the verge of capturing their leader, the Eye, at any moment—but neither Bell nor the rest of the galaxy would be at peace until the threat had been laid to rest forever.

The debacle at the Republic Fair months ago could've damaged confidence in the Republic—and in the Jedi—past repair. Instead the Nihil were now on the run. The corner had been turned. This entire part of the galaxy would soon be wholly safe once more.

Once everyone else had regained their confidence and security, maybe Bell would, too.

As the Longbeam passed through another thick golden cloud of gases, Master Indeera was the first to say, "They're above us. Almost directly overhead." Burryaga growled in assent.

Ship sensors almost immediately began to flash, but the true warning came to them through the Force. Bell's senses heightened; his muscles tensed. Readiness galvanized him on every level.

Here it comes, he thought as he looked out the cockpit. The dark, swirling nebula gases became translucent as the Longbeam rose, revealing the underbelly of the Nihil ship. Bell imagined the warning alarms on that ship's bridge, the frantic rush of activity as they prepared to fight—for by this point, surely, the Nihil had realized that the Jedi had come to fight.

But the Jedi had been ready from the instant they left Starlight Beacon, and their moment had finally come.

For Master Loden, Bell thought, *and that no one else may ever suffer at the Nihil's hands as he suffered.*

The initial boarding attack had been designed for precisely this moment: The mother ship of the Jedi group seized the Nihil craft in its tractor beam, holding it fast, as the Longbeam on which Bell and his compatriots stood angled itself to attach to one air lock and block several others. Docking— rough, uneven, forced—shook the entire vessel, but the team remained steady and alert, recognizing as one the moment when the vibration signaled their penetration of the hull.

"For light and life!" Master Assek cried as they dashed into the Nihil ship.

Bell had rarely felt the Force with him so powerfully as he did at the moment he rushed forward into a blazing array of blasterfire, slashing through the air that surrounded him so closely he could feel the heat. The scent of ozone filled Bell's breath. Yet his lightsaber blade deflected every blaster bolt so smoothly that it seemed to be moving itself, aiming without any conscious work from Bell other than fierce concentration. All around him, he saw a sea of faceless, soulless masks—Nihil shooting, scattering, scrambling—and, advancing upon them, the Jedi swift and sure.

"Now!" Master Indeera called over the fray, acknowledgment of the warning from the Force they all felt. Bell ducked behind a metal girder to shield him for the seconds it took to strap on his breather. No sooner had he done so than the telltale hiss from the air vents revealed that the Nihil's poison gases had been deployed.

Too late, Bell thought with satisfaction. *It's your turn to be too late.*

Master Indeera led the charge toward engineering, or what passed for it on the cobbled together, jury rigged Nihil vessel. Bell and Burryaga fell in directly behind. It would be up to Master Assek to hold off the Nihil near the air lock; Bell's job was to paralyze this ship.

Even running at top speed, Bell could tell that this ship was ramshackle to the point of hazardousness; the interior was dismal, dull, and strictly utilitarian. What made someone want to live like this? To join the Nihil, visit infinite pain and destruction upon innocents throughout several systems, and for what? Life on a dark, dank ship creeping along the edges of space, with only the dim spark of potential future riches to provide any light—something that was no life at all.

Bell's wonderings only took up one small part of his consciousness, musings he'd examine later. The present moment was for completing his mission.

Green gas filled the corridors with toxic haze, to which the Jedi remained impervious thanks to their breathers. However, the gases meant that Bell *felt* the door ahead of them before he saw it. Master Indeera and Burryaga must have as well, because they all skidded to a halt at the same moment.

"Should we knock?" Bell asked. Burryaga groaned at the terrible joke.

Master Indeera simply plunged her lightsaber into the door's locking mechanism. The heated glow of melting metal illuminated all their faces in pale-orange light for the instants it took for the door to give way. It stuttered open to reveal only a skeleton crew, most of them young and unarmed, and all too willing to surrender.

It helped Bell, knowing that he wouldn't have to take additional lives. What had to be done, had to be done—but the pain he felt over the tragedy of Loden Greatstorm remained sharp. It could've pushed him in dangerous directions. Instead he was satisfied with their capture, no more.

You taught me well, Master, Bell thought to the memory of the man that he carried within his mind.

Once they'd finished rounding up the prisoners, Burryaga whined curiously.

"Yeah, seems like a low crew contingent to me, too," Bell said. "Do you think Marshal Kriss's pursuit of the Eye of the Nihil has shaken them up? They might have deserters by the hundreds, even thousands." He didn't like the idea of Nihil escaping any justice for the atrocities they had already committed, but the most important thing was making those atrocities stop. If the price of saving so many lives was a few Nihil deserters getting off scot-free, so be it.

We've gone on the offensive, Bell told himself. *We've outplayed the Nihil at their own game. We did it for you, Master Loden, and for every other person who suffered as you—*

Bell couldn't even think about it.

Burryaga didn't seem to notice Bell's distraction, for which

Bell was grateful. Instead the great Wookiee shook his head and growled.

"Sure, it was easy," Bell agreed. "I don't know if it was *too* easy, though. No point in worrying about it if the Nihil are finally collapsing."

In that, at least, Burryaga completely concurred.

Regald Coll had more of a sense of humor than most Jedi. At least, that was what non-Jedi told him. Most of the other members of the Order didn't agree.

Or, as Regald would argue, they just didn't have enough of a sense of humor to appreciate his own.

"So what is it with the storm terminology?" he asked his newest prisoners, a fierce-eyed adult named Chancey Yarrow and a young woman who had identified herself only as Nan. "You're all supposed to be one big storm, but each group breaks down into Tempests and Strikes and Clouds. How far does it go? Is one Nihil on their own, I don't know, Slightly Overcast?"

The prisoners had been caught near a Nihil fleet in the Ocktai system, just one of the many raids on the Nihil occurring simultaneously. However, their ship wasn't definitively a part of that group, and at first he'd thought they'd probably just question the women before letting them go. But Nan had pulled a blaster on the first Jedi she saw, which prompted an identity check, which then revealed her true affiliation.

Nan looked furious at having been caught. On the other hand, Chancey Yarrow's face remained utterly unmoved as she said, "You're not as funny as you think you are."

"Probably not," Regald agreed. "Because I think I'm hilarious, and really, nobody's that funny." Enjoying his own jokes was enough for him.

"I'm not Nihil any longer," Nan said. The words sounded

strange—as though she had to force herself to say them. "We work for—" She cut off as she caught sight of her companion. Chancey Yarrow's icy glare could've frozen lava. Regald thought about making a "blizzard" joke to go with the whole storm theme, decided against it. Nan finally finished, "We work for ourselves. I haven't been with the Nihil for months now."

"Convenient timing," Regald said. "And who knows? Maybe you're telling the truth. But you'll have to prove it before we can let you go."

Meanwhile, the *Gaze Electric* rested in quiet space between systems far away from the Jedi battle. No one on board even bothered monitoring the current Jedi activity, much less worrying about coming to the defense of their comrades. Instead it seemed as though nothing much was happening other than some random, ordinary housekeeping. Certainly nobody paid any attention as Thaya Ferr—a mere assistant, not a fighter—made her way through the long corridors.

Thaya was a human woman of middle years and nondescript appearance: flat brown hair pulled back into a practical tail, basic standard coverall, no telltale streaks, no mask, no weapon. She held nothing more interesting than a simple datapad.

This 'pad led her to the first door, the crew quarters for an Ithorian woman. Thaya sounded the chime and arranged a blank, uninterested smile on her face before the door slid open.

"Good morning," Thaya said with all the meaningless cheer of a droid. "You'll be happy to know that the Eye of the Nihil has found a new place for you, one ideally suited to your talents. Details are here." She handed over a small datacard never pausing, lest the Ithorian say something. "Please report to the main docking bay for a transport at thirteen hundred hours today. Thank you!"

At that Thaya walked away, still smiling, leaving no opportunity for argument, gratitude, or any response at all. The Ithorian's reaction was irrelevant. She would obey, which meant she would depart the ship days before the Ithorian male she was partnered with. That Ithorian's departure needed to go unnoticed—and getting rid of the main person who would notice helped with that.

It served other purposes, too. But Thaya would turn to those when she'd finished delivering this first set of transfer orders.

As soon as she was done, she hurried back to the bridge of the *Gaze Electric*. To the Eye. To Marchion Ro himself.

He sat in the captain's chair, studying reports. Thaya could tell they had details about attacks on other Nihil ships—ships loyal to Lourna Dee, and therefore hardly Nihil at all anymore, in her opinion—and she gave them all the attention she knew Ro would wish her to give them, which was none. Instead she stood nearby, patiently waiting to be noticed.

Some on the bridge smirked at Thaya Ferr, and she knew why. She wasn't a power player; she was only someone who ran errands for Marchion Ro.

Many people underestimated how much could be learned from such errands, or how much a leader might come to rely on someone who took care of such mundane, trivial concerns.

Thaya Ferr saw things more clearly.

Finally, Ro spoke to her. "You've put through the transfers?"

"Yes, my lord. I'll prepare the next orders for delivery later in the day."

A few ears had pricked up at the mention of "transfers"—evidence, perhaps, that some had lost the confidence and favor of Marchion Ro? There would be an appetite for names, details, the better to sneer over the fallen. As of yet, none of those on the bridge suspected that a transfer order might be coming to *them*—which was precisely how Ro wanted it, and precisely how Thaya intended to deliver.

Marchion Ro moved on to a different subject—one, Thaya noted, guaranteed to draw attention away from any talk of transfers. "It appears Lourna Dee's capture is imminent."

"Do the Jedi still believe she is the Eye of the Nihil?" She said this in precisely the tone of disbelief she calculated would be most flattering to Ro.

He smiled just as she had foreseen. "They'll know the truth very soon, Ferr. For the moment, let them have their fun. Let them enjoy believing they have defeated the Nihil.

"They will never have the luxury of that belief again."

Chapter 1

Stellan Gios was among those Jedi who perceived the Force as the entire firmament of stars in the sky. Points of brilliant heat and energy, seemingly distanced from one another by infinite absence and cold—but actually profoundly connected. Families, friends, tribes, organizations: Each formed a different constellation, carving shape and meaning from the sky. (Were not he, Avar Kriss, and Elzar Mann such a constellation? Stellan had always thought so, even in childhood.) The Force shone forth from them all, illuminating the vast dark; if Stellan but had the ability to perceive every living being, it would have the same effect as being able to see every star in the universe at once: total, pure, all-encompassing light.

Rarely had he felt so close to that ideal moment as he did on this day.

Colorful banners streamed in the sunshine, fluttering over a throng of thousands who were laughing, eating food from tents and carts, and enjoying the beautiful day and—at last— a sense of true safety and belonging. Or so Stellan liked to think.

Finally, he thought, *we've regained the joy the Nihil stole from us for so long. At last we can celebrate our unity the way we should've been able to from the beginning.*

Stellan stood at the head of the Starlight delegation upon a dais that overlooked the celebration. In the eyes of most of the galaxy, Eiram was an insignificant place, a tiny dot on a star chart too obscure to bother with. But this had been one of the worlds that had led the campaign for this part of space to finally join the Republic, which made their recent mission here all the more symbolic.

Eiram had recently suffered a storm—the kind of vicious cyclone only a handful of planets could muster, one that had at its apex covered almost an entire hemisphere. Terrible winds had badly damaged the desalination structures that supplied the planet's only fresh water. This was a crisis that would devastate an independent planet, leading to a mass exodus or even starvation.

But planets in the Republic had a reason to hope.

"And so, instead of returning to its place in the heavens, Starlight Beacon was transported here, to Eiram!" The storyteller gestured at the holo that showed Starlight being towed through outer space, for only the second time ever, following a lifesaving mission to the planet Dalna. Ringed around the storyteller, dozens of children oohed and aahed in wonder. The shimmer of the holo was reflected in their bright eyes. "The Republic and the Jedi came to save us all, by bringing us water, supplies, and most of all . . . hope."

Stellan felt a faint twinge of regret that he hadn't been here to personally oversee the station's moving and the beginning of the repairs. He'd still been on Coruscant then, so he'd tasked Master Estala Maru with supervising every step—not because he doubted the specialists, but because it was so important for this to be absolutely right. Nobody in the galaxy paid more attention to detail than Maru.

Upon Stellan's return two days prior, the repairs for the desalination plant weren't entirely complete. All they had to do now, however, was attach the sluice gates—something that would be accomplished as soon as the tow craft were available, a week or two at most. The people of Eiram might still have water rationing in place, but the rations were generous, and after several weeks of hardship the planet was ready to celebrate.

Stellan said as much to Maru, who replied, "Right. It's the perfect time for everybody. But it doesn't hurt that this is when the chancellor happened to be free."

"Such is the state of politics," Stellan said.

In truth, it was good of Chancellor Soh to have made the time to attend, even holographically. The flickering images next to him on the dais saw her sitting comfortably in an informal chair, her enormous targons lying on either side of her, dozing in the contentment of beasts. Stellan's eyes met Lina Soh's, briefly—each sharply conscious of the memories of the Republic Fair. The image of Stellan lifting her unconscious body from the rubble had already become iconic: both of the evil of the Nihil, and of the resilience of the Republic. Thus the two of them were in a strange way bound together in the public eye; in the same way, Stellan had become *the* Jedi, the symbol of the Order.

"*If we're a constellation,*" Elzar Mann had said, before leaving for his retreat, "*the Council has made you the polestar.*" Stellan would've liked to disagree, but he couldn't.

Stellan wasn't sure how he felt about that. So he was guiltily relieved that the chancellor hadn't attended in person. Otherwise there would've been pressure to come up with some new iconic image, somehow.

From the Jedi Council, his fellow members Masters Adampo and Poof watched via their own holograms as well. Cam droids hovered amid the streamers and balloons, capturing the event for people from Kennerla to Coruscant. No matter how distant this part of the frontier might be from the Galactic Core, the people of Eiram could know themselves to be truly as much a part of the Republic as any other world.

"They've needed this," Stellan murmured as he looked out at the revelry of the crowd.

Maru surprised him by answering, "*We've* needed this."

And that was the truth of it. Stellan's keen gaze picked out white-and-gold-clad figures among the festival-goers: Bell Zettifar and Indeera Stokes, sipping bright-orange ram'bucha from their cups; Nib Assek helping OrbaLin to make his way toward the dancers, the better to watch their performance; and Burryaga, playing with some of the tinier children. Being a Jedi was a sacred duty—but the light demanded more than obedience and sacrifice. Sometimes a Jedi had to be open to the simple, pure experience of joy. Today they all had that chance.

"A fine thing to see, isn't it?" Regasa Elarec Yovet of the Togruta was there in person, standing near the flickering image of Chancellor Soh.

It was the chancellor who answered, though Stellan entirely agreed: "It is, Your Majesty. And it's about time."

"It is almost time, my lord," said Thaya Ferr.

Marchion Ro gave his underling the slightest nod as he stared into the depths of the holographic star chart. His preselected targets glowed red among the whiter stars, and he studied each one in turn.

These were ordinary worlds. Large and prosperous enough to be of note at least to neighboring systems, not so large as to have strong planetary defenses or to draw undue attention. He walked through the holographic chart, imagining the suns and planets pushing apart to let him pass.

The worlds he had chosen had two things in common: First, they all had good communications systems that would allow them to reach officials on Coruscant within minutes.

Second, they were all very, very far from Starlight Beacon.

He smiled his bloodless smile. "Begin."

Aleen: a planet neither particularly obscure nor noteworthy. Although Aleen had been racked by wars in its distant past, it was now a place where nothing of significance had happened in a very long time—even by its own inhabitants' reckoning— and nothing of significance was anticipated for perhaps an even longer time to come. The legends of the wars were enough to make every soul on Aleen satisfied with an uneventful life.

Yeksom: one of the longest-standing Republic member worlds on the Outer Rim, one that had suffered terrible ground-quakes in recent years. The Republic was helping the planet rebuild, but it was a protracted, painstaking process. Its people remained guarded, uncertain, sad-eyed; everyone had lost someone in the quakes, and grief veiled the world's gray sky.

Japeal: a planet on the frontier, newly bustling, with no fewer than three small space stations in various stages of construction. Its temperate climate and plentiful water practically invited settlers to find a place they might call their own. Dozens of species set up storefronts and eateries; engineers mapped bridges and roads; families put finishing touches on brand-new, prefab homes.

Tais Brabbo: Anyone on Tais Brabbo who wasn't up to no good had taken a wrong turn somewhere. Rumor had it the Hutts had considered moving some operations onto Tais Brabbo but decided against it—the place was too corrupt even for them. It was a good place to get lost, and on any given day it housed millions of souls who wanted nothing more than to remain out of sight of any authorities more powerful than the ineffectual local marshals.

On each of these very different planets, under four different shades of sky, millions of very different individuals were going about tasks as divergent as spinning muunyak wool or taking bounty pucks when they each heard the exact same sound: the thudding hum of spacecraft engines descending.

All those millions of people looked up. They all saw Nihil ships streaking down out of the sky—numerous as raindrops— the beginning of the Storm.

Explosives dropped. Plasma weapons fired. The assault slammed into homes, factories, bridges, cantinas, medcenters, hangars. There was no specific target, because everything was a target. It seemed the Nihil wanted to cause mayhem for mayhem's sake, which nobody who had heard of them found difficult to believe.

One passenger ship leaving Japeal at that very moment got lucky. It took damage—a devastating hit to its port side—but was able to limp out of orbit and even get into hyperspace. Its crew and surviving passengers thought it was a miracle they were still alive and might even remain so, if they could get to help in time.

The so-called "miracle" was, in fact, no more than a standing order Marchion Ro had given before the Nihil attack began. Some people *needed* to escape—because the Nihil needed them to run straight to Starlight Beacon, where they would be given comfort, medical treatment, and the full attention of the Jedi.

No sooner had Stellan Gios returned to Starlight Beacon from Eiram than the news of the Nihil attacks arrived. Estala Maru, normally not given to bad language, used phrases considered obscene on most planets when word came in of the Aleen assault. "Still more Nihil, still attacking, and for what? Nothing, so far as I can tell. They're not even bothering to plunder ships or planets any longer." He shook his head grimly. "The Nihil mean to cause us more trouble so long as there's even one Cloud remaining."

"This isn't close to the scale of destruction we saw from the Nihil at first," Stellan said, reminding himself as much as Maru. "We've made real progress. We ought to have expected to see the Nihil thrash around in the group's death throes. For now, our attention should remain on helping those affected. It looks like some damaged ships are heading our way, no doubt with some injuries aboard—"

"Already on it," Maru said. The man's fanatical attention to detail only sharpened in times of crisis, and Stellan had rarely been gladder of this. "I've sent a couple of the Padawans to ready the medical tower for a few extra patients."

"Excellent." Stellan put one hand on Maru's shoulder, a gesture of gratitude. "Maru, sometimes I think you're the one holding this place together."

"And don't forget it," Maru sniffed. His grumpy demeanor was only a thin shield, however; Stellan saw the glimmer of satisfaction in Maru's gray eyes.

Stellan hurried away, leaving the situation that was being taken care of to deal with the many that had yet to be resolved. A few damaged ships had already signaled their need of a place to land, and more would be coming.

In truth, he was somewhat more disquieted by the Nihil assaults than he'd let on to Maru. Stellan had had misgivings about Avar Kriss's search for the Eye of the Nihil from the very beginning; it felt too much like a personal vendetta. Avar had walked away from Starlight Beacon—her assignment from the

Council, the very symbol of the Republic in this part of space—all in the hope of making a capture others could have made equally well. Was it possible that her search had antagonized the Nihil, driven them to lash out instead of skulking off into oblivion?

Or maybe these scattered attacks are a sign that Avar's plan is working, Stellan allowed. *The Eye is fleeing from her, possibly losing contact with the Nihil at large. Perhaps what we're seeing is the Nihil newly decentralized, lashing out wildly before falling apart.*

If so, Stellan would be the first to apologize to Avar for doubting her. Until they knew more, however . . . he would keep his own counsel.

An electronic voice chirped: "Master Stellan Gios?"

Stellan half turned to see a logistics droid rolling toward him, coppery and bright, with a vaguely humanoid body above a rolling base. "Yes—are you delivering a message?"

"The message is that you are my new master. I am Jayjay-Five One Four Five and I stand ready to label, prioritize, sort, file, collate, and otherwise organize every aspect of your existence." The droid practically vibrated with readiness to begin.

"There must be a mistake, Forfive," Stellan said. "I haven't ordered any droid, and the Council would've mentioned—"

"I am a gift," JJ-5145 declared with apparent pride. "I come compliments of Elzar Mann, who sends word that as he can no longer be your right hand, he wished for me to serve in that capacity."

There was almost nothing Stellan would've wanted less than a droid following him around to organize everything.

Which, of course, Elzar knew perfectly well.

Stellan had previously been concerned about sending Elzar off to work through his current crisis without accompanying him—as he had first planned, and in fact promised. In the end, Stellan's many tasks had not allowed him any opportunity to

STAR WARS: THE FALLEN STAR   593

step away, and he'd found an excellent replacement to guide Elzar through this difficult passage. But he'd worried that Elzar might on some level resent it . . . and in Elzar's current state of mind, that resentment could too easily have turned to darkness.

It now appeared that Elzar wasn't resentful in the slightest—and only irked enough to play a practical joke.

JJ-5145 said, "You have remained silent for three point one seconds. Do you lack clarity on how to prioritize your thoughts? Voice them and I can help you order them most efficiently."

"That's quite all right, Forfive," Stellan hurriedly replied. "How about you help the Padawans get the medical tower organized? That would be of great assistance." He guided the droid on its way, relieved to have something else for it to do. Later he would ask it to schedule some other tasks for a few days in the future.

One of those tasks would be, "Think up the ideal revenge for a practical joke."

The first ship to arrive at Starlight Beacon after the Nihil attacks was neither damaged nor carrying the injured; it was the Longbeam tasked with bringing some of the Jedi back from their raids on the Ocktai system, with a handful of prisoners in tow.

Bell Zettifar, fresh from checking supply stores in the medical tower, prepared to assist in the prisoner unloading—but his Master, Indeera Stokes, waved him off. "There are only a handful of captives, and if help is needed, I can supply it," she said. "Take some time to yourself."

No doubt she'd noticed how dark his mood remained, months after Loden Greatstorm's death. Bell didn't want his new Master to think he didn't appreciate her—to let his admiration and grief for his old Master cloud his new apprenticeship. (And it was clear he needed more time as an apprentice. Bell's conviction that he was ready to become a Knight had turned to dust with Master Loden.)

That was something he should consider later. For now, there was little to do besides say, "Thanks, Master Indeera."

She nodded as she began to walk away. "We'll all have plenty to do soon enough. Best to take free time where it can be had."

Burryaga, who was also at liberty, asked with an inquisitive growl whether Bell might want to meditate together. Dual meditation techniques sometimes succeeded where solo efforts failed; it was often easier to calm another person, or to be calmed by them. It wasn't a bad idea, but a shadowy form at the far end of the corridor reminded Bell that there was something much more important to do first—someone he hadn't been able to visit since returning to Starlight from Eiram that morning.

"Hang on just a second," he said to Burryaga before dropping to his knees and opening his arms wide for the shape hurtling toward him. "C'mon, Ember!"

The charhound bounded from the shadows and leapt onto Bell, welcoming him back with all the enthusiasm she could muster, which was a lot. Bell allowed a couple seconds of frantic licking before he put his hand out to calm his pet. Her fur blazed warm against his palm. "Steady, Ember, steady. I'm back now."

Ember wriggled with delight, and Bell couldn't help grinning. There was nothing like a pet to remind you to release your worries and live in the moment.

Burryaga made a low, huffing sound. Bell glanced up to see his Wookiee friend watching Jedi Knight Regald Coll lead the two Nihil prisoners away. One was a tall, fierce woman with long braids and cheekbones sharp enough to cut. The other was a girl not even his own age, her hair pulled back in a tail, her garments slightly too large for her body—creating the illusion she was even younger than her true years.

Bell knew the young woman's face, not from personal experience, but from security briefings.

"*I thought of Nan as almost still a kid*," Reath had warned them, soon after word had come of her capture. "*She's not. She's as capable as any Padawan—arguably more than me, because she fooled me completely. Don't take Nan for granted.*"

Bell figured that speech was mostly about making Reath Silas feel a little better for having been so skillfully deceived. But as he watched Nan walk away, head unbowed despite her cuffed wrists, Bell found himself hoping Regald Coll had heard that warning, too.

"I suggest waiting before you question them," Regald told Stellan Gios. "Our transport was small. The Nihil prisoners might've heard about their comrades' successful attacks, and if so, that'll make them—"

"Overconfident," Stellan finished for him. "Exultant, even. Convinced help will come quickly. When it doesn't, then, perhaps, they'll be ready to talk."

"They claim they're not Nihil any longer," Regald said, "but the girl called Nan was absolutely with the organization just a few months ago, and it's a really convenient time for her to have left it, don't you think?"

"But not impossible." Stellan looked thoughtful. "If she did leave the Nihil, and we can figure out why—it could provide some valuable information about how to psychologically disarm the group."

"It would save a lot of time. Still? I kinda doubt it." Regald missed the old days when he had worked in the Jedi crèche, where when you saw a problem (three-year-old fascinated by fire), the solution was obvious (remove three-year-old from vicinity of fire). "Will you handle the interrogation yourself, or will Elzar Mann take point? I'm happy to assist, but I've got to warn you, my jokes make me a little less than intimidating. Though there's always the chance the captives will reveal all, just to get me to shut up."

Amusement played on Stellan's features. "I'll call on you if I become truly desperate. Elzar, I fear, is unavailable. He's off doing something even more important."

"And what in the worlds would that be?"

"Elzar is taking some time to strengthen his ties to the Force," Stellan said. "Connecting with the greater Jedi he may yet become."

Chapter 2

The oceanic planet Ledalau possessed only a few thousand square meters of land, all within one tiny archipelago. Long ago, this world had possessed mighty continents, but it had been more than a millennium since the waters had swallowed them whole. Few relics of the ancient civilizations remained; the planet currently possessed few resources and less infrastructure. Thus Ledalau was left almost entirely alone. That was what made it the perfect meditative retreat.

It also turned out to be the perfect place to get your pride handed to you on a platter.

Elzar had been skeptical upon his arrival several weeks before. The islands were at an upper latitude, which made the weather disappointingly cool and foggy. He was of the opinion that it was easier to concentrate when you weren't cold. It had then been pointed out to him that nobody needed to practice what came easy, and if he only wanted to do what he could already do, he might as well have stayed on Starlight.

So he'd abandoned his early, halcyon notions of a tropical retreat and set himself to his task. His temporary home was a small stone structure, no more than a room and a privy. Elzar had no comm devices, no forms of entertainment, no droids—only the few items he would need to be totally self-sufficient, and a guide who cut him no slack whatsoever.

Once the mental noise of upheaval had died down, he began grappling with the truths that had brought him here:

I have begun drawing upon the dark side for my strength in the Force.

Elzar had not turned; nor did he feel he was close to turning. This was not a way of life for him—he still believed all the good and true lessons he had learned from Yoda as a youngling, then as a Padawan from his wise Master Roland Quarry. But anger was unavoidable. Fear was unavoidable. Extreme circumstances created extreme emotions. Denying them served no purpose. Why not use them?

Many weeks of meditation later, Elzar still felt those questions were valid. However, he'd also come to realize that every Sith Lord in history had probably asked the exact same questions until the darkness held them completely in its grip.

Where do you draw the line? Elzar asked himself. *You don't know. You can't know. And that's why you can't travel down that path at all.*

It had also become clear to him that part of the reason he was so deeply opposed to denying emotion was because negative feelings weren't the only ones he was trying to deny.

Even here, it had been hard for him to face that truth. But the truth within him demanded to be known. At night, when he looked up at Ledalau's three broad, shining moons, he imagined them as pinpoints of light in Avar Kriss's sky.

They'd never meant to become attached. Padawans often fooled around together on the sly; adolescence, a phase in virtually every sentient species, demanded its due. Instructors and Masters pretended not to notice as long as nobody went too far. When relationships formed, reprimands were rare. Instead a Master would promptly take her apprentice away on a long-term mission far from any Jedi temple. By the time a reunion could take place, both younger people had generally grown up, gained perspective, and moved on.

Elzar and Avar hadn't had to be torn apart. They'd been reasonable. Responsible. They'd known what they were doing and what the limitations had to be.

So Elzar had believed. But even though he had grown up and gained perspective, it appeared he couldn't move on.

How much of my confusion and anger is rooted in my feelings for Avar? So he had asked himself as he meditated on his knees, sometimes for hours at a stretch. *How much energy do I waste, trying to reconcile that which can never be reconciled?*

There, at least, the barriers stood strong. While Elzar felt—no, *knew*—that Avar still had feelings for him as well, he also knew that she would never break her vow. So why did this trouble him so?

Finally, he realized: It wasn't the lack of answers that weighed on him. It was the refusal to even ask the questions.

Once he knew that, the rest began to fall into place. Elzar fell into a rhythm: morning meditation and exercise, a light meal, deeper meditative practices, more exercise, a dinner substantive enough to allow for a good night's sleep. He allowed himself to feel moments of anger and frustration without drawing upon them as fuel. He gave himself permission to think of Avar when he gazed up at the night sky.

And he submitted to the tasks given to him—even his current very wet, cold, and irritating one—out of respect for his guide, a Jedi Knight only a few years his senior, one who made her path as a Wayseeker.

"Concentrate." Orla Jareni always sounded faintly amused, even at moments like this. "Be in this moment. In this very breath."

Elzar inhaled deeply and resumed his handstand in the instant before the next wave crashed.

When Orla had first suggested that he work on meditating in the water, Elzar had been only too happy (even, truth be told, a little bit smug) to reply that he often did precisely this. As he described his meditation method, he'd expected her to be impressed.

But Orla Jareni didn't impress that easily.

"Right," she said. "You go with the flow. You move where the water takes you. Then you're surprised when you wind up someplace you never meant to be. I want you to practice standing firm against the water. Not to reject its power—to coexist with it. To accept it, and yet hold fast."

"Which means . . . ?"

She'd gestured at the rocky shoreline. "Walk out about four or five meters, give me a handstand, and hold it despite the tide." And that was what Elzar had been practicing every day since.

The water—only wrist-deep between waves—went up almost to his waist when the waves rolled in, heavy and shockingly cold. Elzar dug his fingers into the sand and called upon the Force to steady him. Within a few seconds, the wave rolled out again, leaving him wet and gasping, but still in place.

"Excellent," said Orla, safe and dry on the shore.

"I'm not a great meditator," Elzar called back. "But I really enjoy not drowning."

"Luckily you're good at *that*."

Another wave roared toward him, and Elzar closed his eyes. This time it was easier to forget that Orla was there and to accept the gift the ocean had to give him.

He let his awareness flow from his body through the water, until he could sense all the other life-forms teeming around him: fishes, shell-dwellers, plants that sprouted from the depths to sway in the tides. It was a communion he'd relished in the past, but that connection was different now, somehow stronger for his refusal to completely surrender to it. His body remained still, a cliff against the waves: vulnerable to time, but strong in this moment. It took Elzar a while to realize that each individual wave hardly registered with him now; his breathing had naturally taken on the water's rhythm, and his sense of oneness with the life around him felt more vital, more real, than even the sand beneath his palms.

Equilibrium, he thought, and he remained in that place, mentally and physically, for the hour it took for the tide to start going out.

Elzar flipped back onto his feet and landed ankle-deep in seaweed and silt, an interesting sensation. On the shore, Orla Jareni was drawing her snow-white cloak around her. "You've come a long way. The first time you tried this, I couldn't decide whether you swallowed more seawater or sand."

He grinned. "Praise? From you? I must be doing something right."

"My praise is difficult to earn," she agreed. "That's why it's worth something to you, I hope."

"It is. You can hardly imagine how much." Elzar paused. "I'm going to refrain from 'tinkering' with the Force for a while after this. A long while, I expect."

Orla cocked her head. The cool sunlight made her skin almost glitter, like fresh snow. "When I advised you to stop doing that, I never meant for you to refrain forever. You're an intuitive Force-user, Elzar. It's a strength, not a weakness, once you've figured out your boundaries."

"I haven't yet, though. And I feel strong enough now to keep going as I am."

"You do realize you're still limiting yourself?" Orla raised one sharply angled eyebrow. "Not just in how you use the Force, but in using the Force itself?"

"I know," Elzar admitted. "It feels like . . . like an injured leg.

I know I'll be able to put weight on it again, but not yet. Or am I getting that wrong, too?"

"Nope. Sounds reasonable to me. We Jedi spend so much time honing our Force abilities that sometimes other abilities get pushed aside. Maybe it's good for you to spend a while discovering your strengths beyond the Force, too."

Elzar toweled his damp hair, which had grown a bit long and shaggy during his time on Ledalau. "Tell me, though—how will I know when it's time to . . . open back up again?"

When she wished, Orla Jareni had a wicked smile. "Trust yourself, stupid. Now finish drying yourself off and pack up."

"Today?" He knew she had planned for them to depart soon, but she had withheld the specific date, so he would experience time more fluidly.

"Within the hour, if you can hustle."

Elzar hustled. This was the benefit of bringing so little; he was both dry and ready to go within the hour.

Working with Orla Jareni had surprised Elzar from first to last. His friend Stellan Gios had connected the two of them, which—given Stellan's general doubt of Wayseekers—had been odd enough to start with. Then Orla herself turned out to be flinty, funny, and even more of an iconoclast than Elzar himself. Her unflinching tutelage had focused him more profoundly, more swiftly, than he would've thought possible.

(Elzar had been inwardly embarrassed when he realized that, subconsciously, he'd been assuming he'd be able to bring Orla around to doing things his way. He hadn't understood how much he'd been flirting with women lately until he'd met one who had no use for that whatsoever.)

If Orla thinks I'm ready, I must be, he reminded himself as he finished packing up. *Because there's no way she'd ever cut me any slack.*

Elzar was grateful she'd been his teacher, so much so that he almost felt guilty about sending Stellan that logistics droid.

But not quite. He grinned as he fastened his bag, ready to go.

He stepped out of his small stone structure to see that the fog had rolled in, thick and wet. Gathering his cloak around him, he called out, "Orla? Where are you?"

"This way!" Her voice came from the distance, and he set out to follow.

They'd spent nearly all their time on the shore, meaning that the interior of this small island remained almost unknown to him. Once sand no longer mingled with soil, the ground grew foggier, bumpier, almost rolling. Elzar hurried on, aware of Orla some measure ahead of him, and only vaguely curious as to how they planned to leave.

Then, amid the mists, he caught sight of the plinth.

It was not especially tall—perhaps the same height as Elzar himself—nor did it retain any of the ceremonial carvings or paint it must have worn in millennia past. Time had worn away everything but the smooth, brownish surface of the stone. Had this once stood over a sacrificial altar? In this moment, surrounded by silence and the swirling fog, Elzar could not help feeling the sacredness of this place, this moment.

Was it his imagination, or was the Force stronger here? Elzar was pretty sure he hadn't dreamed it up.

I bet our ride isn't even here yet, he mused as he studied the plinth. *Orla wanted me to find this ancient relic, to understand it the best I can. If I can.* Should he kneel? Close his eyes? How best could he pay respect to a culture he neither knew nor could scarcely guess at?

"Elzar?" Orla's voice was closer, and he glimpsed her outline taking shape amid the fog as she strode toward him.

"I'm right here," Elzar confirmed, waiting for her next instructions. The plinth loomed before his eyes, its sense of presence intensely real, almost as though it were looking back at him.

"Oh, good," said Orla, grinning as she finally came within clear view. "You've met our navigator."

Elzar stared at her, nonplussed. Then he turned his head back toward the plinth. It wasn't his imagination; it *was* looking back at him.

"This rock—" he began.

"Is not a rock," Orla finished. She gave the plinth a friendly sort of nudge. It didn't move. "This is our Vintian navigator for the trip back to Starlight. He's known by his nickname, which happens to be Geode. Geode, this is Elzar Mann, Jedi Knight."

"Um," Elzar said. "Pleased to meet you." Geode said nothing, what with *being a rock* and all, and was Orla testing him, maybe?

Orla didn't seem overly concerned with his reaction, though. Instead she continued on toward their ship. Elzar followed, glancing over his shoulder every few seconds. Geode didn't move to follow them. Yes, Elzar decided, definitely just a test.

Their destination proved to be a small cargo ship, blue-tiled with a bulbous cockpit that almost looked comical. On the ramp, a young human girl with tan skin and long, dark hair checked pressure gauges at the air lock. Without turning around, she called out, "Welcome back, Orla!"

"Thanks, Affie." Orla gestured toward the girl. "Elzar Mann, Affie Hollow—and vice versa." Affie acknowledged him with only a nod. "And let me introduce you to the captain of the *Vessel,* Leox Gyasi."

"Greetings, fellow traveler of the void," said a tall, rangy man who'd appeared at the top of the ramp. He had dark-gold hair, richly wavy; a loose shirt that hung open to the middle of his chest; and around his neck, a collection of strands of beads in many colors from many worlds. "A pleasure to make your acquaintance."

"The *Vessel*," Elzar said, comprehending now. "Of course. I heard about your trip to the Amaxine station."

"That was a hell of a thing." Leox's stare was distant, as though he were more focused on that past adventure than on the here and now. If in fact he was focused on anything. Given the distinct whiff of spice in the air, Elzar suspected that was a big *if.* "Geode, buddy, looks like it's time to fly. Let's get prepped."

Elzar startled to realize that the plinth now stood only about a meter from his shoulder. *So it wasn't a test,* he realized. *Our navigator really is a . . . a rock.*

Okay, a Vintian. But Vintians look a whole lot *like rocks.*

The young woman, Affie, cocked her head as her expression darkened; Elzar realized she wore a small comm piece in one ear and was now alarmed by something she was hearing. "What's wrong?" he asked.

"The Nihil," Affie said. Elzar swore to himself; Orla swore out loud. Affie continued, "We have a few reports of attacks from—from all over, basically. Just a handful of worlds, but they're scattered. They don't have anything in common. And the Nihil aren't even taking anything. Just causing damage and running off."

"No good can come of that." Captain Gyasi either had sobered up in a hurry or wasn't as spice-soaked as Elzar had first guessed, because he was already checking data on a small terminal panel within the boarding bay, his long fingers swiftly bringing up page after page of new data. "They haven't hit anyplace especially close to here, though."

"At least we have a safe path back," Orla said, somewhat relieved.

Elzar couldn't take the same comfort. After the Republic Fair, and given the seemingly imminent capture of the Eye, he'd hoped they wouldn't have to deal with the Nihil again for a long, long time. Instead they were back—just for some low-level harassment, it appeared, but any Nihil activity was enough to set him on edge.

Still, this wasn't anywhere near the scale of the earlier Nihil attacks. *It might mean Avar's given them enough hell that they've learned some respect,* Elzar thought. She seemed capable of that.

Surely Avar Kriss was capable of anything.

Far away, aboard the *Gaze Electric,* Marchion Ro stood before his chosen few.

Werrera was an Ithorian, silent and wary; Leyel was a human, stout and short, with thick graying hair tied in a braid almost to her waist; Cale was a Pau'an with even longer fangs than most but no other distinguishing features. The three of them were all highly competent technicians, but they had not distinguished themselves within the Nihil in any of the usual ways: neither especially ruthless nor merciful, neither brilliant nor weakminded.

But they *believed.*

The promise of the Nihil—the golden future Ro had spoken of to them all—for most, it was a hope, a dream. Within these three, it *lived.* They had such faith in that future that, in a sense, they had reached it already. This was their gift to their families and friends, a promised land to which they already held title, one they were helping to give to countless others throughout this part of the galaxy.

Only that level of belief could fuel the task Marchion Ro needed them to accomplish.

As for these individuals' family members and friends—or what, within the Nihil, passed for friends—every single one of them had been reassigned to other ships, far from the *Gaze*

Electric, and had departed Ro's ship at thirteen hundred hours. They would have no chance to protest. To change their loved ones' minds about taking on this vital assignment. They'd never even realize these people were missing, not until it was far too late.

"You should wipe all data banks clean upon disembarking, and leave only the false logs and permissions," Ro said to the three loyalists who stood before him. Those false logs identified their ship as a run-of-the-mill independent hauler, notable only for its license to transport wildlife, in this case supposedly a shipment of rathtars. (Nobody would be in a hurry to confirm that information by personally inspecting the cargo.) "Let the Jedi believe in those. You will reveal the truth soon enough."

"Yes, our Eye." Cale—who tended to speak for the group—gazed at Ro with such reverence that it was almost more unnerving than gratifying. But Marchion Ro was not easily unnerved. "We are ready."

"I know that you are. I believe in you all." Ro put hands on both Werrera's and Leyel's shoulders. Cale didn't need it. "You will not disappoint me. You will deliver unto us the greatest victory the Nihil have ever known."

The thrill that swept through them was palpable. Ro knew they would do his bidding. They would never turn back.